A TERRIBLE DUTY

Tarrah Adler knew that this would be the end of it. The Special Prosecutor, she looked up at the cameras now, and around at the Representatives, and finally to the Speaker of the House.

Either they'd be able to force the vote now, get the impeachment today, or they'd wasted their chance. By showing their hand—by being here at all—the pro-impeachers had revealed themselves. Before, there had been hope safe under a veil of secrecy. But if they lost now there would be no more hope, and there was no time left for it anyhow.

For those protecting the President, they'd burned their bridges behind them as well. So now it would now be total war. And the technology it would be waged with was the Constitution…a centuries-old set of rules that could never have foreseen any of this.

For anyone else, it might have been too much. Too terrible a duty, to wreak more havoc on a nation already so traumatized. But Tarrah had always known that, sometimes, the medicine was *supposed* to taste bad. As the cameras zoomed in, the world held its' breath as she started to speak.

Also by Turner Tomlinson:

The Shooter Act

Cancer Was

SHOOTER
ACT II
WINSPEAR'S REVENGE

By Turner Tomlinson

Dark Scan Publishing

ISBN: 978-0-9975724-4-5

Published by Dark Scan Publishing, LLC.

Cover design by Obed Gonzalez.

Printed in the United States of America

http://turnertomlinson.com

Contents

To a whole host of people who have allowed me to focus that something like this takes.

We live in a strange time.

Extraordinary events keep happening that undermine the stability of our world. Suicide bombs. Waves of refugees. Donald Trump. Vladimir Putin. Even BREXIT.

Yet those in control seem unable to deal with it. And no one has any vision of a different or a better kind of future.

—Adam Curtis, Introduction to the 2016
BBC Documentary HyperNormalisation

Prologue—The Story So Far

"We're in trouble," Jack said to Kay Luo. Their eyes met across the backseat of a hacked autocar.

Kay might have made some comment about stating the obvious, but instead, she swallowed hard, looking again out the window at the passing city. Trying again to use the handle that should open the door. Still locked.

Still trapped.

It had started with Jack pulling a gun in LAX, unveiling a conspiracy surrounding the controversial Shooter Act. A grand experiment in fighting fire with fire: Any mass shooter was condemned to be removed from history entirely, deleted from every database, their families silenced, every picture destroyed. Jack knew best what to expect when he walked into LAX that day. After all, he'd helped get the Shooter Act passed in the first place.

Why'd he do it? Because the Shooter Act was being abused. Used by the psychotic ex-soldier Duncan McAvoy to not just remove shooters from the history books, but to remove people in the *way* too. Of himself... and of whomever he was working for.

It was when Jack found out about one of McAvoy's victims, Katelyn Patterson, that he knew he had to do something. She'd been silenced and removed to prevent a massive scandal at the behemoth corporation, NEXT Automotive, a conglomerate set up by President J. Woolston Winspear and a host of other investors just after his election.

They tried to get rid of Jack too, but while he was holed up in LAX, a brilliant scheme unfolded. An investigation was conducted at light speed as a group of strangers, unwitting recruits in Jack's plan, used every trick they could to find the truth.

One of these strangers, Kay Luo, became a target, and she and Jack somehow escaped death at the hands of Duncan McAvoy. And in the process, they got the final, crushing bit of information that the investigation needed: McAvoy named his handler as Clayton Scarly, the long-time business associate of President Winspear. The arbiter of Winspear's blind trust.

His partner in crime.

Unsurprisingly, Winspear denied any connection. While NEXT Auto's stock plummeted to new lows, sending ripples through first US, and then global stock markets, and while a country divided called for the impeachment of the president, Jack recovered from a gunshot wound received from the bloodthirsty McAvoy.

In the hospital bed, he and Kay discussed the obvious conclusion: J. Woolston Winspear was using his power to not just grow richer, but to make his enemies disappear. He was not just a crook, but a dictator dressed in democratic clothing.

And he had to be stopped.

But what they realized too late was that someone like Winspear—someone with that much to lose—would play as dirty as he could to win.

When they left the hospital a few hours ago, hopping into a NEXT Autocar they'd called up, they realized their mistake only after the doors were locked. In a single instant, all the confidence and revolutionary excitement of the moment gave way to the drain-swirl pull of terror. As the car moved along, Jack couldn't help but wonder where it had all gone wrong. It wasn't with the Shooter Act. It wasn't at LAX. It wasn't even when his fiancé was killed all those years ago.

Somehow, he knew the root of it was in electing a madman in the first place.

Part 1—Tangled Webs

I'll say what we all know: that the way this thing works is to find an edge, any edge at all, and to do that you have to be thinking outside the box. That's how you get an edge in business: by being the first one to swing at a ball nobody else even knows is there, and to hit it out of the park. But to operate outside the main stream of things, you have to be willing to do what nobody else is doing. And not doing what everyone else is doing often means not following the rules everybody else is following.

—Excerpt from *The First Trillion's the Hardest*,
by J. Woolston Winspear

1

3 Years Earlier: The Election of J. Woolston Winspear

S oon, things would be different.

The room was all movement and yelling. You could smell the alcohol in the air, the fumes rising with the heat of a long night, updrafts swirling around silver flecks of confetti that searched their way down, the room erupting with another round of cheering at the screens.

Ronald J. Bowers, co-founder of Bowers & Associates, had more to cheer for than most, but he gave only a half-smile and sipped his drink at the announcement.

The final votes were in. It was nearly midnight, and Florida had been the linchpin once again. A majority of the elector-ate votes had just now been confirmed, and James Woolston Winspear would be the next president of the United States.

Despite everything, they'd done it.

Bowers looked around at a room crowded with suits and dresses, the elegance of some of the latter drawing a stark contrast to the news anchor, who towered on the projector screen in an opposition-colored pantsuit.

Throughout the room they were smiling and hugging each other, but on screen the anchor was lost. She looked confused, reading someone's lips off camera, admitting again that the last thing anyone expected had actually happened. Her brow furrowed, she started saying something into her mic with a subtle shake of the head, but Bowers didn't hear it. They turned down the volume of the news, the music coming up, finally time for celebration.

Silver balloons decorated the corners of the white-walled banquet hall, and some were tied down here and there, floating above table centerpieces, vibrating with the thrum of energy that flowed through the room. Now people were untying them, letting them drift up toward the high ceilings. It was one of those moments. One that Bowers knew he'd never forget, as scorching whiskey stained his taste buds, adrenaline surging at the thrill of it all, the very air seeming to sparkle as the light caught thousands of pieces of confetti that swirled down.

A piece of it grazed Bowers' eyebrow and he brushed it away, looking around the room, thinking.

What would they say when they reflected on this night? What word would future historians land on as they tried to capture the whole thing, crazy as it had been?

"Fractious"?

"Unprecedented"?

"Monumental"?

Nothing seemed powerful enough. Bowers wondered how the settlers who first came upon the Grand Canyon felt. How adventurers to the New World might have described their first sighting of a grizzly bear charging at them from the depths of eerily still woods, a beast rumored only in deep imagination, too fully real to escape from.

"Earth shattering"?

"Terrifying"?

But even those didn't capture the sheer topsy-turvy, stranger-than-fiction feel of the thing, which even now had not ended but only changed course slightly. The Titanic zagging toward the iceberg, not away from it.

"Unbelievable"?

On the campaign trail, when Winspear's detractors took a look at his platform and accused him of wanting to dismantle the very system that was trying to elect him, he hadn't blinked.

"What good is a Constitution that collapses when you blow on it from a new direction?"

"Unreal"?

But now Bowers thought about the final run up to election night, and he knew exactly what word they'd use:

"Tragic."

He downed the drink, savoring the last of his Bulleit and Coke before handing the glass off to the bar. A moment of reflection, rare in this line of work. He'd heard someone at the firm once describe what they did as "retrofitting an aircraft in flight," and he had to admit that's what it felt like most of the time.

Strategic Forecasting. Business Consulting. Management Guidance. Any one of these euphemisms would do to cover the broad scope of Bowers & Associates' deliverables. They were the doctors of business. The priests of Nasdaq pulpits. They were the real deal, I-don't-get-the-joke suits that you called in when a business was far too valuable for the people formally in control to be making any decisions.

And for Winspear, they were going to be the people running the country.

Bowers started working his way around the room, eyes sharp for the Man Himself: J. Woolston Winspear, *president-elect.*

"Fantastic job," said a man reaching through the crowd, tall, his high cheekbones slicing down so that even as he smiled he looked bird-of-prey serious.

Bowers took the outstretched hand in both of his, shaking, nodding a thanks to the soon-to-be vice-president, Wilson Applegate.

"We didn't do it alone," Bowers chimed back, sliding easily into the extroverted patois he'd picked up like a foreign language over the decades.

He hated this part of the job, but like executing a rigorous downsizing, this was just another module of work. *Play the crowd. Make sure things flow.*

And on that front, his night wouldn't really be over until the acceptance speech was delivered.

"Seen our boy around anywhere?" he asked Applegate.

"Not for a bit, no. He'll turn up though."

Then Applegate took a half step toward him, swooping down closer to Bowers, keeping hold of his hand and gripping it tighter as he said in a hushed tone, "How's he doing?"

Bowers raised an eyebrow, nodded his head, and broke eye contact.

"He's—" The muscles in his cheeks worked as he bit down, thinking of what to say. "—still going."

Applegate nodded approvingly. "I suppose that's all we can ask for. I don't know how he'd've gotten through this without you."

"Well, there's still plenty to do," Bowers said. "Four years of work at least." He smiled again, and Applegate let his hand fall.

"Maybe even eight?"

Bowers laughed and they both melted back into the crowd.

He continued to move through the room, finally getting annoyed and pulling a chair out to stand on.

There were two, maybe three hundred people here, but Bowers shook his head. No sign of Winspear. He glanced at the projector screen and caught the words "acceptance speech" in the closed captioning. Now he looked to the stage that was on the other end of the ballroom. The one where

Winspear would stand and give one of the two speeches they'd prepared. A sound-check crew was testing the connections, and the news cameras were looking around for the same thing Bowers was.

He stepped off the chair and didn't bother replacing it under the table as he headed for a set of double doors at the side of the room. Outside, a few guests raised their glasses to him and he smiled, not stopping to exchange pleasantries. Everyone else might be celebrating, but the business of the night wasn't finished until Winspear gave that speech.

Bowers moved past them, toward the elevators, and while he waited for the doors to open, he looked down the dimly lit hallway. Echoes of the celebration made their way down. The background hum of laughter and music were finally silenced by the elevator doors, and then Bowers was alone. As the elevator started to move, he swallowed hard. He heard himself breathing, a controlled, deep exhale. On his arm, goosebumps, and it wasn't cold at all.

Something was wrong.

Earlier, Winspear had wanted to retreat to his room. Bowers wanted him on hand for PR purposes, but the man had never been one to take stage directions. Before he'd left, though, Bowers had told him to be back down for the final announcement, and Winspear had agreed.

As the elevator moved, Bowers wished it would go faster, feeling a tightness in his neck, checking his watch out of habit. The watch which had been a gift, after all, from the soon-to-be president. A relic from a former era of their partnership, the light catching it differently ever since the glass had cracked.

It reminded him of Winspear when he was younger. When they'd met. He was a rascal of a businessman then, with a few crazy ideas and a hundred-million-dollar shipping company to his name. Today, Bowers had checked the basket of stocks he watched daily and calculated the overall market capitalization of Winspear Shipping. That scrappy shipping company he'd helped Winspear with over the years now had a value of just over two trillion dollars. The biggest company in the world. Arguably the biggest *thing* in the world, measured by either value or mass. Or ambition.

Bowers had been along for that ride, and for his impeccable service, he could count the richest man in the world—possibly in all of human history—as a close friend. He'd been there for all the highs and, recently, the cracked-glass lows. So, when he stepped off the elevator and looked at the door to Winspear's room, seeing that there were four Secret Service agents standing outside, he was perhaps better equipped than anyone to guess what had happened.

"I told you two in the hall and two inside at *all times*," he said, jogging down the hall. "He's not to be left alone."

"Sorry sir, he told us to—"

"James!" Bowers shouted through the door, not waiting for a response before raising a fist and banging on it. "James, are you in there? We need you for the speech."

He paused for a moment. No response. Only the news playing full blast from a TV somewhere on the other side of the door.

Bowers looked at the Service agents.

"I told you not to leave him alone," he said again, his mind starting to race as they muttered excuses and Bowers fished his phone out of his pocket. He dialed Winspear and brought it up to his ear. One of the agents started to say something but Bowers held a hand up and listened to the phone ring once, twice, no answer.

He shook his head.

"Break it down. *Now!*"

The agents looked confused but for only a heartbeat. One of them stepped into place and squared himself up with the doorframe, then he gave it a hard kick just next to the handle that sent it slamming open, crashing against the wall inside and shattering something, maybe a mirror. The TV blared at max volume, the news anchor filling time before the acceptance speech with the type of banter you might expect.

"... in what will surely be remembered as one of the most polarizing and extreme elections of modern history..."

The living room area was down a short hall from the kicked-open door, and Bowers could see the crumpled figure there, a dark mass cast in the harsh light of the huge TV screen.

Bowers rushed forward.

"Get the medical team up here! *Now!*"

He had to shout over the TV, which blared away, unaware of the drama unfolding on the hotel room's plush carpet.

"... what many agree will be a grand experiment of a new way to run the country, with a truly legendary man to lead it..."

All at once Bowers was on his knees next to Winspear, rolling him onto his back. There was an empty lowball glass on the floor next to him, and near that an empty pill bottle. On the glass coffee table, various minibar liquors were lined up neatly in a row, equally spaced, all of them empty but their caps carefully replaced.

"Jesus, James," Bowers breathed, opening one of Winspear's eyes with one hand and trying to feel for a pulse at his wrist with the other.

One of the Service agents started to say something, but Bowers didn't hear it.

"Turn the lights on!" he shouted back, trying to focus, feeling the ghost of what might be a heartbeat at his fingertips. Still, the news blared.

"... there was almost no chance of a Winspear presidency just six short months ago, but advance polls have proved vastly inaccurate..."

They were crowding in, and Bowers could feel sweat dripping down his back, down his face, pooling at the tip of his nose. Time seemed to slow—or speed, he couldn't tell which—as adrenaline surged. This was not one of the things Harvard Business School covered. Not even in the advanced classes.

"Is he breathing?" someone asked.

"No," Bowers said. "One of you get down here, get ready to breathe for him."

He shifted, placing his hands on Winspear's chest in a V. If he wasn't breathing that's what you were supposed to do, right? Bowers started to pump, cursing under his breath, trying to tamp down any emotions and to act. To just act. Methodically. Reliably. Keep going. Advice he'd given Winspear as the election had ramped up and as he'd struggled to deal with it all. With more than any man should be asked to deal with.

He was furious that it had come to this, but he wasn't surprised. Winspear had won the election, but in the process of achieving what he thought he wanted, he'd lost the only thing that really mattered to him.

"… and then, of course, there was the tragic death of Sierra Winspear just one month ago."

Bowers pumped.

"A hit-and-run collision at a campaign stop, which enthralled the world and seemed to open the voters' hearts to Winspear in an outpouring of sympathy…"

"What's the count supposed to be," he asked, not stopping. "How many times am I supposed to do this?"

"30," one of the agents said, kneeling down next to him.

"C'mon, dammit," Bowers growled down as he pumped away. *"Come on!"*

"Others credit the dramatic change to Winspear's policies since the accident, such as the promise to roll back any red tape and regulation slowing the autonomous driving industry, which he claims could prevent once and for all the type of accident that led to his wife's tragic death…"

"Tell me when—"

"—okay, go," Bowers said, leaning back on his haunches as the Secret Service agent delivered a series of breaths.

"… has put his money where his mouth his, setting aside a chunk of his substantial fortune for a new public-private enterprise rumored to be called NEXT Automotive…"

Bowers leaned in again, restarting the compressions, and there was yelling in the corridor behind them. He pumped again and again, looking at Winspear's face for anything. Any motion. Any sign of life.

"*Come* on, dammit."

"*... not to mention the controversial gun control bill, the so-called Shooter Act, which Winspear and Vice-President-elect Applegate have promised to pass in their first hundred days. The only thing anyone can seem to agree on is that, no matter what, we're in for a very interesting four years.*"

Bowers kept pumping. Then all at once the medical crew was there, and they were pushing him out of the way, taking charge. He got up and took a step back, looking at Winspear's lifeless body on the floor. They were tearing his shirt open. All around Bowers the world seemed to be fading away. He backed up until he ran into something—one of the chairs in the room, and he started to lower himself slowly. Halfway down, his legs gave out. He collapsed into the chair, his ears ringing, as he watched the medical team try to revive him.

Then he glanced up at the TV. They were showing the podium downstairs, where the acceptance speech was expected.

"Christ," he said, feeling a new wind pick him up out of the chair. "Stay *with* him this time," he shouted, pushing past the Secret Service agents and out into the hall.

They watched him leave, whispering updates into unseen microphones.

A moment later, one of the medical team was saying, "*Clear,*" and preparing to give the body in front of him a shock from a portable defibrillator. Winspear's torso jerked up against the pulse, and all of them waited for a second, and then the paramedic monitoring for a pulse said, "Again," and up on the TV screen someone stepped behind the podium. It was Bowers, red-faced but otherwise in a successfully applied mask of control.

"I hope you all don't mind," he started, "but the president-elect is busy taking a call from his opponent right now," he smiled wide, practiced, the telltale quiver in his lower lip not giving away anything, he hoped. The room erupted in laughter and more cheers, and Bowers waved them away, preparing to deliver Winspear's speech for him. A few words on behalf of the president-elect, whom he hoped would still be alive by the end of his own victory speech.

2

3 Years Later: Camp David

The fire crackled, sending small wisps of ember-edged paper flying up and out with the smoke. And sparks, some of them nearly reaching the carpet a few feet out from the fireplace as someone stabbed at the hot mix with a fire iron. The flames licked greedily at a new stack of thick card stock and colored envelopes that had been tipped into the raw heat of the fire's core.

Winspear stabbed the iron poker into the mix once more then replaced the poker in the holder. He stared into the fire, watching the papers curl.

R. J. Bowers was sitting across from the fireplace, and he turned to the wooden double doors at the opposite end of the small room. They were at the edge of the Camp David complex, but the fire kept the chill on the other side of the door well enough.

As if cued by Bower's glance, one of the Secret Service agents reached up to his ear, listening. His Adam's apple bobbed with a subvocal response. Then he said, "Sir, they're coming in to land."

President Winspear reached into the burlap bag that he'd dragged to the edge of the fireplace. He pulled out another handful of envelopes.

Christmas cards.

Each addressed to the president of the United States.

"About time," he said, tossing them in, staring as the flames turned the pastel colored greetings into carbonized ash.

There was a sharp wind outside, and it howled now, covering the sound of the approaching helicopter. Winspear joined Bowers at the other chair across from the fire.

"I'll say it one more time," Bowers offered. "I don't approve of any of this."

"I know," Winspear said, "and I appreciate your concern."

Bowers didn't bother to reiterate what he'd already tried unsuccessfully to convince Winspear of: that what he'd done to Jack Paulson and Kay Luo was, at its heart, kidnaping. And that, considering the circumstances, it would look very, *very* bad.

But Winspear didn't care. He'd changed in the last few weeks. Though that wasn't right. He'd *changed* more than three years ago, Bowers knew. And it had slowly gotten worse since then, the years that had come to be known as the "hermit presidency."

But in the last few weeks, since Jack Paulson had pulled out a gun in LAX and told the world about the massive Shooter Act conspiracy, Winspear had withdrawn even more. It reminded Bowers of a hyperbolic curve going right off the chart, but for the man in front of him, that wasn't quite how you'd describe it. Not off the chart, more like *over the edge.*

"There's still time—" Bowers started, but Winspear looked at him, face stubbled, eyes sunk deep into dark-rimmed sockets, and Bowers didn't finish his sentence.

They both sat there for a moment, the smell of the fire rich with scents of cedar but edged by something acrid and foul.

"We both know that's not true," Winspear said.

"Applegate's right about the timeline," Bowers said, trying to focus Winspear on the silver lining, if there was one. "Only a few days left before the Senate breaks for Christmas. There are enough supporters still in the House to prevent impeachment. At least for now."

"Maybe," Winspear agreed, "but then what? The inevitable pushed off until when, next quarter? Bowers, I..." he trailed off, shaking his head, and not for the first time Bowers wished that the Secret Service men weren't here, that he might have a moment alone with Winspear. Not as his advisor and supposed coconspirator, but as his old friend.

What was he about to say? That he'd tried? That he did the best he could? That he regretted what had happened with Katelyn Patterson and Jack Paulson and the whole bloody Shooter Act ordeal?

Or maybe, Bowers thought, maybe he was about to say that he wished he'd finished the job properly on election night. That what he'd lived through since Sierra's death had been a sort of waking hell in which everything continued to get worse until whatever final ultimate crash hit.

And right on cue—such a crash was only a few votes away in the Senate.

Bowers had watched that emotion growing in Winspear over the years, accelerated by the events at LAX, and he knew the danger of that. The danger of the self-fulfilling prophecy, that Winspear expected the worst at every turn and seemed to somehow conjure it up.

Case in point: When Jack Paulson and Kay Luo had participated in what would probably be remembered as the biggest and most public whistleblowing event in US history, instead of turning the situation to his advantage as Bowers had suggested, the president had played a classically reckless wild card. He'd had them kidnaped off the street like some third-world dictator.

The helicopter was touching down outside, and a moment later there was the familiar sound of the engine whine dulling to a stop behind the howl of wind.

"Sir," one of the Secret Service agents said, "they're bringing them in."

"Fine," Winspear said, clearing his throat as he stood.

A moment later the door opened, and past the rush of cold air two dark-suited agents jerked Jack Paulson and Kay Luo inside.

Jack saw the president immediately and stopped short, just as the agent guiding Kay Luo by the forearm practically threw her forward. She ran halfway into Jack and stumbled to a stop before she saw who was standing in front of them, and as the door slammed shut behind them, they both stared up at the president who was cast in the glow of firelight.

They'd seen him on TV. In countless videos. They'd heard him speak and watched the documentaries, the news reports. The richest, most powerful man in the world: J. Woolston Winspear.

Not one of them had done him justice.

Winspear looked from Jack to Kay and back, hands in the pockets of his long, wool coat. After a moment, he smiled.

"Welcome to Camp David," he said.

And as they stared up at him, the smile cracked and Winspear laughed.

The hair on the back of Kay's neck stood up.

"You can't do this," Jack said, and despite himself there was a tremble in his voice.

"Oh?" Winspear said in mock surprise, raising his eyebrows. He made a point of looking around the room, to the fire, to the door opposite the one Jack and Kay had come in, and then he leaned in slightly and said, "It appears as though I *can*, Mr. Paulson."

"You won't get—"

"*What?* Get away with this?" Winspear said, cutting him off. He laughed again as he said, "Away with what exactly? You think I'm some comic-book villain with a master plan?"

Jack furrowed his brow.

He and Kay looked at each other, and Kay said "This... what you're doing is kidnaping. Suppression," she shook her head, mouth open in disbelief.

"That's certainly one perspective," Winspear said. "What about rendition? Are you familiar with the term?"

Kay and Jack looked at each other again with some alarm. Bowers stood up and took a position near Winspear.

He reached out as if he might somehow control the situation by physically forcing it into place as he spoke, saying "I think what the president is trying to communicate, is that the man who tried to kill you both—Duncan McAvoy—is still at large."

"Your henchman, you mean," Jack said.

Winspear's face darkened.

"*That's* why you two are here, dammit. Because you think you know what's going on, but you're too—"

"James," Bowers said, cutting him off.

And to Jack's amazement, it worked. Winspear looked over at this man—whomever he was—and stopped. He closed his mouth and took a deep breath. Jack wondered who in the world had enough sway to interrupt this mad-king president.

"Duncan McAvoy is still at large," Bowers explained, "and we thought—"

He looked from Jack to Winspear, nodding his head slowly as he took a step forward.

This was Bowers on damage control, bridging Winspear and his de facto prisoners, and he'd already come up with a way to try to manage this particular crisis.

"The president thought it would be wise, since you are participants in what is an ongoing investigation, to take you into *protective custody* in case Duncan McAvoy or someone else tries to come after you again."

Kay and Jack looked at each other.

"That's right," Winspear said as he watched them. "Have your silent conversation about how that's just another lie. That's all they say about me now, isn't that right? Lies, lies, lies, all the way down?"

Jack said nothing, not sure if this was some kind of trap or just more needling.

"Tell me," Winspear said. "Tell us all, why don't you? What exactly it is you think I've done?"

He turned from them, as if disinterested, and stalked back to the fire, reaching again for the burlap mailbag.

"You..." Kay started, her voice shaky, "... you set up Katelyn's Patterson's murder. She was going to blow the whistle on NEXT Auto and you—"

Winspear tossed a handful of cards into the fire, and as he watched them burn said, "You're half right, she *was* going to ruin NEXT Auto's quarter with her little discovery. But I didn't set up her murder, and the fault in the NEXT Auto code that led to those crashes, the cover-up—" he shrugged as he used the fire poker to stoke the flames. "I found out about it the same time that you did, when it was broadcast live during Jack's little stunt." He turned and pointed at them with the fire poker as he added, "You're welcome for the *pardon* by the way."

Jack said nothing, but he watched the tip of the poker sway through the air, steaming from the heat.

"Let me guess, in your story, that's part of the cover up, right? Pardon you as window dressing? To make it look like I didn't know what was going on, that I thought you really deserved to be let off for taking a gun into an *international airport?*" Winspear shook his head. "You're lucky to be alive, Jack."

"I didn't—" Jack couldn't find the words for a moment. "The pardon *was* just a trick. A PR stunt. Part of the cover-up."

"Oh yes," Winspear said, rolling his eyes. "It's all hoaxes and crisis actors out there."

His voice trailed off as he turned back to the fire, shaking his head. Whatever he said next was lost under his breath, though Jack was almost sure he heard the word *"delusional."*

Bowers stepped in, calmly taking the fire poker from Winspear and replacing it in its holder.

"The pardon was what was best for everyone," he said. "Ms. Luo, if you'll continue?"

"Katelyn was murdered by Duncan McAvoy." She sighed, lowering her voice as she added, "Or rather, he blackmailed her into killing *herself.*"

"And the reporter," Winspear said, "Kelley Oakley. She was streaming it all when he tried to kill *you*. I was watching that, you know? Everybody was watching and listening when the bastard said he was working with Scarly."

"That's right. Clayton Scarly," Jack said, "the arbiter of your blind trust. The one who had the most to lose if anything happened to NEXT Auto's share price."

"Wrong again, Jack. As *arbiter* of the trust, he had *nothing* to lose. The one who had the *most* to lose was me. Which no doubt leads you to your final erroneous conclusion, that I was working with Scarly and McAvoy to do my dirty work like some kind of off-brand Nixon." He paused, smiling at them. "How close am I?"

Kay and Jack looked at each other again. Had he just admitted it all?

Winspear laughed. "That close, eh? The only problem is, after Bowers here," he nodded to him, "Clayton Scarly is one of the most trustworthy business partners I've ever had the pleasure of working with. I left him in charge of my blind trust for a rather obvious reason: I *trusted* him. And I still do. He would never have done this, or anything like it."

Jack shook his head. "Then why would McAvoy name him?"

"Because he was told to," Winspear said.

And Bowers added, "That's the best we can figure, anyhow."

Kay asked: "Told by who?"

Winspear took a deep breath before answering.

"By whoever's trying to frame me."

3

"Alright then," Bowers said, as they entered the next room over.

After a long pause, Winspear had settled into one of the chairs near the fireplace, and Bowers had quietly motioned them out of the room.

"Sorry about that," he said when the door between them and Winspear shut. "He's not in good spirits today."

"If that was him not in good spirits I'd hate to see him when he's *really* down," Kay said, "and I hope you won't mind me asking just who the hell you are?"

"And why we're *still here*?" Jack said.

Both of them staring pointedly at Bowers, who frowned, turning quickly over his shoulder to the two agents in the room with them.

"We're fine in here."

They nodded and turned to leave.

"Oh wait," he turned to Jack and Kay, raising a hand, "Coffee, water?"

"I'm sorry," Kay said. "I didn't realize this was a social visit."

Bowers nodded, turning back to the agents. "Send in a pot with three cups and a few water bottles, please."

They nodded, and Bowers jerked his head toward the middle of the room where a sunken couch ringed a low, dark oak table.

Jack followed him by instinct, realizing only now that he was holding Kay's hand.

"Wow," Kay said, turning to take in the room as they crossed it.

It was, she thought, as if a 1500-square-foot flat had been passed through a cabin-themed filter.

Bowers sat at the plush, leather couch, and as she and Jack followed, Kay looked from the wood table to the stone fireplace that reached up impressively high, all the way to the ceiling, which she guessed was 14 feet high. On either side, the walls gave way to huge picture windows that let blizzard-grey light in. Up in the corner, a black blister hung off the ceiling, a camera.

Jack took a seat next to her and Bowers saw them both looking around.

"Nice isn't it? I always wonder just how many types of wood are in just this one room. Watch out for that guy," he said, gesturing over their shoulder.

They turned to see that on the other side of the door they'd entered through, a stuffed bear stood in the corner aimed inward and frozen in a permanent attack.

"Your question from earlier, Ms. Luo," he said, scratching his head. "My name is Ronald Bowers, R. J. Bowers and Associates."

"And you work for Winspear?"

"I work for the president, yes, in an advisory capacity. I've worked with him for decades, in his other businesses, as has much of my firm."

"So, what are you, chief of staff or something?" Jack asked.

"Oh no. We like to keep it vague. *Advisor* is all I ever tell people on the outside."

"And on the inside?" Kay asked. "What does the president think of you as?"

Bowers thought for a moment, then smiled. "You know, the chief of staff position was originally created by McKinsey and Associates when *they* were hired to come in and retool the executive branch?"

"Really?" Despite the situation, Kay was truly intrigued. "I didn't realize they ever had a formal management review."

"Well," Bowers said, opening his hands out as if that explained it, "here I am. Here we both are, Winspear and I, retooling again."

The door opened, and a staff member, carrying a tray with a coffeepot, cups and water bottles, came over and set it on the low table between them.

"Go ahead," Bowers said, gesturing toward it and filling his own cup, the steam rising against the slight chill of the room.

"Alright then, *Mr. Bowers*," Jack said, refusing the invitation on principle. "Maybe you can start by telling us why we've been kidnaped and continue to be held against our will?"

"*Protected* against your will," Bowers corrected, taking a sip of his coffee and holding Jack's stare. "The truth is, there are ways you can help us."

"Jesus," Jack said. "You think after everything—" but Bowers waved him off.

"Please, Mr. Paulson, hear me out." Their eyes met. "Can I have your permission to explain?"

Something about that, about actually stopping to ask permission, disarmed Jack. He'd been expecting a lot of things here, but politeness wasn't one of them. He blinked.

"Fine."

"Everything Winspear just told you is top secret, and it is also the full truth as we understand it. We believe the president is being framed. We don't know who's behind it, but we know whoever it is planned it far, far in advance. They've been running Duncan McAvoy as a double agent—someone on the inside—who they could use to subvert the Shooter Act from within. And our working theory is that when Duncan was found out, we believe he was *told* to name Scarly."

"What proof do you have?" Kay asked, taking a cup and filling it from the silver pot.

"That's where you two come in." He Said.

Jack's arms were still crossed, but he could smell the brew when Kay leaned back with it. She looked at him, sipping from her cup, crossing one leg over the other so that her body was turned toward his. Their eyes met, and she raised her eyebrows. Jack sighed, relaxing his arms and uncrossing them to reach for coffee as they both turned to Bowers.

Despite everything else, they were intrigued.

"My firm," Bowers went on, "along with some of the more advanced intelligence units this country has to offer, has been investigating this as much as they can in the last few weeks, and one of the more interesting parts has been a sophisticated fraud that is somehow being executed on NEXT Auto's share price."

"Fraud?" Jack asked. "In what way?"

"It's all very technically sophisticated, very quant, if that word means anything to you," Bowers said, and he smiled in Kay's direction as he added, "but as I understand it that sort of jargon is just up your alley, Ms. Luo."

"You've done some research on us," Kay said, "though I can't say I didn't expect that."

For years Kay had owned and operated her own hedge fund—Nine Muses Capital. It was a good fund, routinely outperforming the market, even surviving the oil crash, though only just. She'd followed the fall of NEXT Auto's share price almost reflexively over the last few weeks, since LAX, and one thing she'd noticed was that it didn't seem to be going down far enough.

"You're talking about a short squeeze?"

Bowers nodded. "Precisely."

"I'm sorry," Jack said, holding his cup in both hands and feeling the warmth in his fingers. "You'll have to decode that for me."

"Since everything that happened, NEXT Auto has lost only about 20% of its share price," Kay explained, "and that doesn't jive with the number of sellers shorting it. You understand shorting a stock, right?"

"More or less," he said. "Shorting it is like selling a share with the hopes of buying it back at a lower price. It's what you do if you want to bet *against* a company. That its stock will go down."

"Very good," Bowers said, "and although the negative PR and fundamental issue—the massive error in NEXT Auto Version 1 code that led to both wrongful deaths, and by way of a corporate-level cover-up, wrongful imprisonment of dozens of innocent people—although those things should lead to a massive public disownment of the company, it is somehow staying afloat. Losing roughly 20%, in this case— it's just not bad enough. Especially when you consider that the rest of the market is struggling even worse."

"The short squeeze," Kay went on, "is what happens when people shorting the stock are squeezed by buyers keeping the price up. Every day more and more people short the stock expecting it to start going down further, but someone is squeezing them—continuing to buy shares and, for lack of a better term, *pumping money in* to keep the share price up."

"That sounds illegal," Jack said.

"Actually, it isn't," Bowers explained, "at least not in principle. *However*, my analysts have been tracing the squeezers as best we can, and they're not individual investors. It's actually a handful of shell companies. We've identified seventeen of them so far, though they appear to be logging on and off at random in an attempt to hide the flow of funds."

"Shell companies?" Jack asked. "Like offshore accounts?"

"Something like that," Kay said, turning to him. "Have you ever seen that game where someone hides a ball under a cup and then mixes it up with other cups, then you try to guess which one the ball is under?"

"Sure," Jack shrugged.

"Well, originally, that game was played by hiding something under big seashells and moving them around, hence the term, 'shell company.'"

"And in this case," Bowers said, "the *ball* is money. The shell companies are used as a sort of sleight of hand to hide the flow of cash from A to B."

"That's a pretty common tactic then?" Jack asked.

"Oh yes," Kay said. "So common that there are organizations overseas that churn out companies with fake boards of directors and P. O. boxes that don't exist, selling them off the shelf specifically to be used as shells."

"And all the companies involved in this short squeeze you're talking about, we know those are all shells?"

"As best we can tell," Bowers said. "They're young. All created within the last decade, and all of them were acquired at some point by an umbrella corporation that, one way or another, falls under either Winspear Shipping or Winspear Robotics."

"Aha!" Kay said. "Taking capital from one company and using it to keep another failing company afloat is commingling investor funds. Without their consent, that *is* illegal."

"Very good," Bowers said.

"I'm sorry," Jack said, "but I thought you were explaining some proof you had that Winspear *isn't* behind all of this."

"Correct," he said, "and since the president turned all of his assets over to Clayton Scarly when he signed over the blind trust, he has had no say whatsoever in what his companies have been doing."

"So Scarly..."

"Yes, it would appear so," Bowers said, refilling his cup as he continued. "But as you heard, Winspear believes that Scarly being involved in this is categorically out of the question."

"And you?" Kay asked. "What do you think?"

"I never worked with Scarly, but I think Winspear is a good judge of character. They worked together in his early days, from what I've heard. Scarly was already managing his own limited empire by the time I began working as a partner with Mr. Winspear."

"You didn't answer the question," Kay said.

Bowers smiled. "I think…" he paused, his eyes going up and over as he searched for the right words, "that anyone will backstab you for a price. Maybe with all that power and control Scarly thought he could get away with it." He shrugged. "That said, we can't find any direct connection between Clayton Scarly and Duncan McAvoy."

"All *that* proves is he covered his tracks well." Jack said.

"Perhaps."

"And," Jack went on, "call me crazy, but has anyone *asked* Clayton Scarly what the hell is going on here?"

"That brings me to my second point," Bowers said, "unfortunately, the way a blind trust works is very, *very* strict. President Winspear has not had any direct contact with Scarly since they signed the papers shortly after the election." Bowers took another drink while Jack and Kay waited for him to go on. "And unfortunately, Scarly has been missing for the last year and a half."

Kay scoffed. "He's the arbiter of one of the largest business empires in the world. What do you mean he's *missing?*"

Bowers shrugged. "We've been in touch with his family, other business partners—none of them know anything. All of his communication channels are encrypted and shielded from US intelligence investigations as part of the blind trust—there had to be no way for the president to abuse his power and somehow reach a hand in to guide things."

"That's ridiculous," Jack said. "People don't just drop off the grid like that."

"I'm afraid this one has," Bowers said. "All we know is that the last time he took a public autocar he used it to drop himself off at the Winspear Camplex."

Jack pictured the wild sprawl where the heart of Winspear's companies were built. The massive industrial area where the NEXT Auto factory, the main Winspear Shipping facility, and the HQ for Winspear Robotics all commingled in a campus so big it had earned a new word.

"The Camplex," he repeated.

"It makes a certain amount of sense," Bowers explained. "His office would have been in Winspear Shipping, of which he was made temporary president and CEO as part of the blind trust. And there are actually dorms—including private executive suites—on site from before they went full automated."

"So you think he's, what, hiding out?" Jack asked.

"It's the best we can figure. He's dark on all comms, all credit cards, everything. We think, *I* think, he's holed up in there."

"Pulling all the strings from afar." Kay said. "It's a little too convenient, don't you think? If he was going to disappear somewhere, why there? Why the Camplex? Surely you don't think he's been *living* there."

"Why not?" Bowers countered. "It's the perfect cover. Rooms to sleep in. Any food you can store at room temperature and ship is on a shelf somewhere." He shrugged. "There's really no reason to leave, especially if he's *trying* to hide. And even if he's not doing something nefarious, we still need to get in touch with him to find out what's going on with the manipulation of NEXT Auto's share price. Not to mention he's probably the only person that can sort out this situation with Duncan McAvoy once and for all."

"You need to find him to clear the president's name," Jack said.

"That's the sum of it, yes." Bowers nodded. "Winspear leaves tomorrow for the Camplex. He wants to ask him in person what this has all been about. He'd have gone sooner but, ironically, he's had to wait for the okay from the legal department to even attempt contact—the blind trust being a very strict situation."

"And where do we come in?" Kay said.

"I'm glad you asked," Bowers put his cup down. "My analysts think that the short squeeze on NEXT Auto's price is being controlled algorithmically, and they think they've found a flaw. But before I say anything else about it I'll need you to sign an NDA. The long and short of it is that we need help from a massive amount of outside funds to test our theory, and we thought that with your—*particular interest* in the situation, you might be willing to help."

"And me?" Jack said. "I suppose you want to use me as bait for McAvoy?"

"Quite the opposite," Bowers said. "As much as you seem to think that the president is operating at the apex of a conspiracy that would like to have you killed, we actually recognize the great service you did for the nation. Actually, should it come to public hearings and, God forbid, an impeachment trial, your perspective on things will be instrumental in clearing up this whole incident." Jack's lips parted. "We would like you to stay here, under the protection of the Secret Service. You would not tell anyone, and you would not be bait… Duncan McAvoy is a serious, mentally unstable psychopath, and he's still out there."

He held Jack's gaze for a beat, for the first time not smiling or trying to convey any kind of comfort or comradery. Jack realized he was deadly serious.

"Now," Bowers said, standing, "there are certain matters that require my attention for most of the rest of the day, I'm afraid, so you'll have the evening and night to think about it. You are both free to go of course, and if that's your decision you'll be flown to the location of your choice, care of Uncle Sam. Someone will be through in a few minutes to explain where your bedrooms are and take dinner orders. I hope to have answers from both of you at breakfast."

He stood, buttoning his suit jacket, and reached out to shake Kay's hand, then Jack's.

"I meant what I said about you doing a service to your country, and that goes for both of you," Bowers said as he turned to leave. "And I hope you'll choose to do it again now."

4

"Jack?" He heard Kay's voice from the hallway.

"In here," he said over his shoulder. "Check this out."

She stepped into the room. "What is this, a church?"

"A chapel," Jack said, not taking his eyes off the wall to the right of the pews. The chapel was built into one side of the Camp David complex. Almost the entire wall Jack was facing was glass.

"It's beautiful," Kay said, taking it in with him. There were panels of stained glass, the largest of which hung in the center, the familiar image of a bald eagle clutching olive branches and arrows, all done in the jagged edges of colored glass. Light from outside gave the image a gentle glow, and enough of it trickled through the clearer portions of glass to catch on pieces of dust drifting in the quiet space. It peppered the air with small scintillas that seemed to sparkle as they drifted through.

"We the people," Jack said, reading the words that were spelled out in red glass under the eagle. He sighed and turned away, taking a seat in one of the pews as Kay leaned back on the edge of one herself.

"So," she said, "you have to admit, it makes a certain amount of sense."

"Maybe," Jack said, glancing back up at the stained glass. "I don't like it though. I don't like it at all. He's still in control of all the *information*." He looked at her. "Doesn't that bug you?"

Kay shrugged, the colored light from the window playing on her face with a soft blue glow.

"What other choice is there? I think..." she shook her head, trying to find the words. "I think this is the best option we have for getting to the bottom of this. Whatever it is."

"Let's get to the bottom of it ourselves, though." Jack found himself crossing his arms again. "By doing this in the palm of his hand we're staying under his control. There's no guarantee the information they give us isn't... I don't know... exactly what they want us to know."

"Where's your sense of adventure Jack?" She smiled at him.

He caught something else in it, in the way she looked at him. Something mischievous. Not for the first time since they'd met, something inexpressible passed between them.

"My sense of adventure is struggling against my sense of wanting to stay alive," he said, returning the smile, feeling an ease in here with Kay that he hadn't felt in a long time. Like no matter what, he had a partner in this. If he was honest with himself, Winspear was right. He shouldn't have made it out of LAX alive, and frankly he hadn't planned to. To be on the other side of it and with a partner no less.

He felt *lucky*.

"Don't be dramatic," Kay chided him, "the simplest explanation is likely the truth. And you have to admit, if someone was going to frame the president this would be a tidy job of it."

"I get what you're saying, but this *isn't* a simple explanation. We've taken a leap from one conspiracy theory to the next." Jack said, unfolding his arms.

"Consider the alternative: Scarly working with McAvoy, seemingly for the advantage of Winspear's companies. Scarly would stand to lose his reputation, and both of them would be risking actual jail time. Why would Scarly ever agree to be part of a cover-up in which he stood to gain nothing?"

"Winspear could have paid him off, made a deal."

"Were you in the room with the same man I was earlier?" She nodded in the direction of the building they'd first been shown to. "Winspear's broken. He knows he's not getting out of this, and it's just a matter of time. No amount of sleuthing will undo years of creating enemies one after the other."

"Your point?"

"That the person who could pilot Duncan McAvoy as an asset, and who could set up Katelyn Patterson and create the NEXT Auto cover-up, whoever they are, they're high functioning. Driven to an end. It strikes me as someone ambitious."

Jack said nothing, meeting her gaze after a moment and raising his eyebrows.

"You have to admit the story is more plausible than the one we'd assumed. And my intuition is on his side, as much as I hate to say it."

Jack sighed. "So you're going to tell Bowers you'll help?"

"I plan to, yes," she said, "but I won't if you disagree."

"You don't need my permission,"

"I know," she said, "but here we are. A team."

"You'd turn over your fund's money to Bowers and them?"

"Well, I'll need to see the details, but I'm open to anything that ends with us pulling the sheet off whatever's going on here."

"And you believe what Bowers said? About McAvoy being out there hunting us?"

She shrugged, "it's possible, and it *would* be a good way for whoever's guiding him to take care of us. It's also a great way to scare us into staying on a short leash."

He lowered his voice. "You really think he's still out there?"

Kay paused a moment, looking down. Realizing she was fiddling with her hands, she stopped. "I hope not. But…"

She didn't have to finish the thought, and in the light from the window Jack could see the pinpricks of goosebumps across her arms.

She came over and sat next to him, taking his hand. They were both thinking about the last time they'd seen Duncan McAvoy, just before he was arrested and later escaped. He'd been holding Jack at gunpoint. Kay's daughter, Suela, had almost been shot. They, along with Kelley Oakley, had all been hostages for a few desperate minutes, and the memory of what McAvoy had almost done was still white-hot.

"Where's Suela?" he asked.

"I've got a friend from work staying with her, my assistant. There's also a security detail. Private contractors."

"Jesus," Jack said.

"I know. But what else can I do?"

He nodded. "Well, at least we know she's safe through all of this. If they come after anyone, it'll be us directly. They want to silence *us*, not hold family members hostage in exchange for information."

He didn't say the thought that came next, that kidnaping Kay's daughter would be the *perfect* way to lure her in.

"How do you think Kelley and Quentin are handling it?"

Kelley Oakley had streamed the altercation with Duncan McAvoy live, and Quentin had helped remotely throughout the investigation into the Shooter Act—when Jack had been holed up inside LAX.

"I don't know. Scared probably."

"We should call them, just give them a warning."

"If you can get ahold of them," Jack said. "They were basically famous after what happened. I saw something on Kelley's profile about how she was changing phones because her number was already out there, and she was getting calls from strangers nonstop."

"Well, we can try to reach out to them anyway," Kay said, "let them know that we're safe, at least."

"You know what they're going to say when we tell them, don't you?"

Kay thought for a moment. "That we're crazy?"

Jack nodded. "Considering everything that's happened… McAvoy almost killed me. You… Winspear had us kidnaped. They could bury us in these woods and nobody would be the wiser. Honestly, why are we not running from this as fast as we can?"

Kay let out a sigh, leaning forward and looking up at the stained glass again.

"I thought that too, at first." She looked over at him. "But something's going on here, Jack. *Some*one's behind this, Winspear or not. We have to figure it out."

"Let somebody else do it." Jack said. "Somebody trained for this. Somebody *ready* for it."

She shook her head. "It's too important. Someone else might get it wrong."

It was his turn to sigh. "So, we're doing it?"

"I think so." She looked at him. "You okay?"

Jack nodded. "One thing's for sure: I'm not just going to take Winspear's word for it all."

"Oh?"

"If Bowers wants you bad enough then he'll probably accept a few demands."

"Well," Kay said, "I think it'll be a long breakfast, but I'm sure we can try to negotiate with him. What are you thinking?"

"First," Jack said, "we should tell them to put a Secret Service detail on Suela—someone more reputable than some military contractor."

"Not a bad idea," Kay said. "And?"

"And if I'm ever going to believe any of this, I want to hear it from Clayton Scarly myself. I'm going with Winspear to the Camplex."

5

One time zone over, Quentin Daniels was finishing up class at the University of Arkansas.

"It's not *that* simple," he said to his students. "There are steps to the impeachment process—it's not instant."

It was the last session before Christmas break, and as all his classes since the incident had, this one was running over by more than half an hour with questions from students.

"Mr. Daniels," he pointed at the student with his hand up, nodding, "what *is* the next step for impeachment? Can they vote him out before Christmas?"

"Oh no," he said. "I doubt they'll even call a vote in the House before breaking, and even then—look, the way an impeachment works is the House of Representatives has to vote as a two-thirds majority to impeach, and *that* just triggers the trial in the Senate."

"A trial?" Another student asked. "Like a trial of Winspear?"

"Sure," Quentin said, shrugging, his leather laptop bag slung over his shoulder as he leaned against the podium at the front of the room. "Why not? The only difference is that for an impeachment trial of the president, there's no jury of your peers. The Senators are judge and jury, and a vote there is what would actually get him out of office."

"You think that'll happen?" another student chimed in.

"I, uh, I didn't expect *any* of this to happen," Quentin said, laughing. "Nothing would surprise me at this point."

Someone was starting to ask another question, but Quentin waved his hand apologetically, checking his phone as he made for the door. "Look," he said, "it's been a great semester guys. Happy holidays."

They groaned as he left, and Daniels smiled to himself, shaking his head as he thumbed through emails. A month ago, only about 20% of the students enrolled in his class—Antitrust Law—had even bothered to come. Now he was at overflow capacity every week, often with other faculty and even *strangers* standing in the back. And with all the questions about Winspear and everything that had happened, he was starting to joke that he should retitle the class to *Constitutional* Law.

He'd had to turn off all his social media, and only now was he coming back online slowly, adjusting to a world in which thousands of people wanted his opinion on what had become a global event. Suddenly, he had people calling him about "managing his platform."

"Platform!?" he'd said to one of them. "What are you talking about?"

That's when the PR firm offering him a few months of free consulting had explained that he, Kelley Oakley, Jack Paulson, and Kay Luo were all characters in a drama that had captured the world's attention. A month ago, for instance, Quentin hadn't logged on to Facebook in a little over year. When he checked last week, there were over a hundred thousand messages, requests, and friend invites.

It was surreal.

He'd gotten a new phone—his old number was blown to bits by all the publicity, totally unusable—and that had been a real bother to set up and move over.

But now he was on the other side of the grunt work. It was looking like this could be his last year teaching. There were book deals, even a note from a bona fide movie company in California that was wondering if he'd consult on a movie script they were fast-tracking.

The phone rang, a number he didn't know, but he'd put a system in place. He pushed it to voicemail, where the message he'd recorded explained that this was Quentin Daniels, that he'd recently had to change his number due to "current events," and that whoever was calling should leave a message only if they'd known him for more than two weeks. Otherwise, they could contact his PR firm.

He walked on, crossing campus from the law building, exiting past the coffee shop that he'd turned into an impromptu research facility during the hectic hours in which Jack Paulson had held LAX up at gunpoint and he—Quentin—had been inexplicably called on to help through a rambling online manifesto. That had easily been the strangest day of his life, and he remembered it vividly, first watching the news, and then *becoming* the news.

He could see his breath as he walked past the student union, turning left toward the engineering building and the parking deck.

His phone chimed, and he saw the voicemail-to-text explaining that the caller was none other than Kay Luo. She was with Jack, and they wanted to talk.

He stopped as he reread the message. Jack Paulson. Kay Luo. His heart skipped a beat. He wondered if something was happening again.

But no, the message seemed normal enough. They hoped he was handling things well. They were safe—a detail Quentin furrowed his brow at—and they wanted to make sure he was safe too. While he was still reading the message, the phone rang again, and given the context he assumed it was Jack and Kay calling back, so he picked up.

"Kay! It's so nice to hear from you guys!"

Nothing from the other end of the line. Then a man's voice. "This isn't Kay."

After a pause Quentin realized his mistake. "Sorry, I thought you were someone else," he said. "Who's this?"

"Is this Quentin Daniels?" The voice on the other end of the line said.

"Yes but—"

"I have information that you need to see. Regarding the president and Clayton Scarly."

Quentin's breath caught in his throat. He turned around, looking for someone behind him, realizing how useless that instinct was as he spoke. "I'm not sure you're contacting the right person. I'm not involved in any investigation or—"

"It has to be you. You're the only person I can trust. Someone on the outside."

"Look, I can listen to what you have to say, but I'm not an authority on what's going on."

"Not over the phone," the voice said. "This is delicate information—deep background. They'd kill me if they knew I had it."

Daniels had to stop himself from guffawing. He couldn't help but assume it was some kind of prank.

But... he'd had his number changed. And after everything that had happened the last few weeks, was it really so crazy to think that a source would reach out to him?

"What do you have in mind?"

"Meet me at the Fulbright Peace Fountain. Tonight."

"No, I can't just—"

"Tomorrow then. It's important."

He didn't say anything back for a few seconds. Then: "Seems a little cloak and dagger, h 'bout a coffee shop or—"

"That's too public," the man said. "You don't understand... I have a family. I can't be seen with you, not with what I've got."

"Well, I'll think about it."

"Peace Fountain, 7 PM."

"I said I'll think about it."

"I'll see you there."

The call cut off, and Quentin stared at the screen for a moment.

He kept walking toward his car, looking over his shoulder a few times as he pulled up Kelley Oakley's contact info. She'd reached out when she swapped phones, right about when Daniels was realizing that would be necessary, and told him how to get in touch if he needed to.

"Hey," he said, "this is Quentin,"

"Hey! How you doing?"

"Weird," he said, and explaining the previous call to her. "It's probably a prank right?"

"It could be," she said, "but it could be real. It could be a source. Will you meet with him?"

He rolled his eyes, feeling ridiculous as he stepped from the role of teacher to spy. "I'm not really sure how any of this works."

"Well, let's talk about it," she said. "Anything that takes us closer to impeachment needs to be out there as soon as possible."

And just like that, Quentin went from teaching about the impeachment to possibly participating in it. He shook his head, wondering if he would ever have another normal day. "Okay," he said finally. "Well I think I have a meeting with him tomorrow."

6

Jack woke with a start, forgetting for an instant where he was and why. As it flooded back to him, he wondered if he might be dreaming. Camp David. The president. And now he could swear that he could smell bacon.

He got up and pulled more clothes on—he'd slept in a thin layer to ward off the chill—then stumbled out of his room.

It was still dark outside, but he could hear talking as he made his way to the kitchen, the smell getting stronger as he went.

Just as he neared the doorway, a black suited figure blocked his way, the hard-lined silhouette of the Secret Service agent framed in the light of the kitchen.

"Sorry Mr. Paulson, we're not ready for—"

"Let him in, dammit," said a voice from within the kitchen. "There's never any spontan*eity* with you people."

The Secret Service agent looked over his shoulder, then turned to Jack and stepped aside.

Jack took a few slow steps into the kitchen, seeing three agents at the dining table with cups of coffee in front of them, and two more standing around the island and its built-in stovetop.

With his back turned to Jack, President Winspear was pulling strips of bacon off of the griddle with metal tongs.

"Jack!" Winspear put down the tongs, wiping his hand off on a hand towel as he turned and took two quick steps over to meet him, hand outstretched.

Jack hesitated, looking down at the hand, and then slowly reached out and took it.

"I hope you like yours crispy," Winspear said, jerking his head back toward the plate of bacon on the island, where the nearest Secret Service agent was taking a piece.

He held Jack's hand for a beat too long, almost seeming to stare at him.

"I'm sorry, about yesterday." he said. "And… for having you kidnaped."

With this, he smiled. It was a big, almost mischievous grin.

Jack opened his mouth to speak, but no words came. He let his hand fall, taken aback by Winspear who seemed like a wholly different person than the one he'd met yesterday.

Winspear turned back to the stovetop, taking the last few pieces off.

"Come on boys," he said. "Get it while it's hot, and make yourself scarce."

"Sir, you shouldn't be left with—"

"Jack," he said, skillet in hand as he headed for the sink, "you're not going to beat me to death, are you?"

"*What!?* No, I—"

"Ok then." Winspear gestured with the skillet toward Jack as he addressed the agent who'd spoken. "See, nothing to worry about."

He turned back to the sink, rinsing the dish off as the agents worked their way out of the room.

Jack stepped toward the counter warily, picking up a mug and filling it from the coffee pot, keeping Winspear, who was putting the skillet down on a drying rack, in the corner of his eye.

"So," Winspear said as soon as they were alone. "Bowers tells me you and Ms. Luo have agreed to help us out."

"Really?" Jack said. "That's interesting. We haven't actually given Bowers our answer yet."

"Ah, well," Winspear said, waving a hand. "Bowers has always been good with these sorts of things. That may be his sixth or even *seventh* sense."

Jack leaned back against the counter, and Winspear did the same next to the sink, his arms crossed. The two of them eyed each other for a moment.

Winspear looked away first, a glance across the kitchen, and then up at the ceiling. His eyes landed on the sink, and as if seeing it had cued him, he washed a dish, rinsed it, and placed it on the drying rack.

"They hate that I cook, you know?"

"Really?"

"Absolutely detest it. The wait staff," Winspear rolled his eyes. "They say my time's too valuable for it, this sort of thing. And they might have somewhat of a point."

Jack sipped at his mug, taking it all in. Winspear seemed jarringly different from yesterday, and the sheer strangeness of him set Jack on edge. He wondered if maybe this was part of the game, as if Winspear was playing a role even now. He thought of the camera near the window in the sitting room and wondered if maybe Bowers owed his info to a microphone somewhere in the chapel.

"Yes, I suppose I've left a lot to be desired on that front," Winspear said, sighing.

"Which front is that?"

Winspear looked at him and smiled, a quick grin.

"Spilt milk at this point. I'm sorry, by the way,"

"For what?"

"Your fiancé."

Jack's fiancé, killed by a campus shooter what felt like a thousand years ago. A different life entirely.

"You... I didn't think you'd know about that."

"Oh yes," he said. "I read up on you. On her, what happened I mean."

After everything, the memory was somehow distant. It had shifted through time. The pain of it had been so papered over and suppressed that even now Jack reflexively didn't feel it—he remembered the shooting that had taken his fiancé from him, but it was like a piece of trivia, the formative event that had started him on a journey that included the drafting of the Shooter Act, and finally into this surrealist sketch of reality, standing in a kitchen with the president of the United States, sharing a plate of bacon.

"I'd probably be making that face if you brought up my dead wife too. Sorry—I guess it's not the best conversation starter."

"No, no," Jack said. "It's okay. I just—"

"You may think I have it out for you, Jack," Winspear said, popping a piece of bacon into his mouth and talking past it, "but maybe you can understand... we're really two containers on the same ship here."

Winspear chewed, watching Jack furrow his brow before moving his hand in a sort of rolling gesture and swallowing as he went on.

"At least from where I'm standing. Two men swept up in the drift of history. Each nursing their own wounds."

Jack didn't know what to say. He had the distinct impression that, despite everything, Winspear was... *opening up* to him. Was he trying to explain himself?

"You..." Jack shook his head slowly as he spoke. "You think that's what this is? That you're a *victim*. That you're *just like me?*"

And then there was a moment, just long enough that Jack saw the glint in Winspear's eye shift. A narrowing of his gaze. Instantly, the crazed look he'd seen the day before was there again. It could have been any of several things. It could have been that Winspear had opened himself up, if only slightly, and on being rebuffed could muster only anger. It also could have been that Winspear was doing what he'd done since day one, lying through his teeth to get what he wanted, and the only response to Jack calling his bluff was to double down, get angry, use emotion to sell the truth of it.

Before either of them spoke again, though, there was another voice from the doorway.

"Sir," Bowers strolled in, and all at once Winspear's attention was on him.

They exchanged pleasantries—Bowers grabbing a mug and piece of bacon, Winspear shifting again—and the moment evaporated like it hadn't happened at all.

Jack was still trying to unpack the interaction with Winspear when Kay appeared next to him.

"Good morning," she said. "Ready to make history?"

"Jesus," he said, "again?"

They traded a smile, and Jack lowered his voice.

"Something's weird," he said. "He's *different* today."

He nodded toward Winspear.

Kay made a look at him, raising her eyebrows as she went for the coffee mugs, and then they joined Bowers and Winspear at the table.

"So!" Bowers said. "What's it gonna be?"

"We'll do it," Kay said, looking at Jack with a smile.

He looked at Winspear, who winked at him.

"But we do have one condition." Kay went on.

"Which is?" Bowers asked.

"Jack will go with you, Mr. President, to see what Scarly has to say about all of this."

"To the Camplex?" Winspear asked, playing dumb.

Jack watched how easily he did it—how he slid into the character he wanted to show.

Kay nodded. "I think that's fair, seeing as we still have our doubts about this whole thing, and the more we know," she shrugged, taking another drink.

"Okay," Bowers said, thinking it over. "Okay, we can do that. He'll have a whole detail of Secret Service agents tagging along; I'm sure one more won't hurt, eh?"

Winspear nodded. "More the merrier."

"How sure are you that he's there?" Jack asked.

"It's the best we've got," Winspear answered. "Someone is still sending out quarterly reports and renewing contracts, the ones that the algorithms don't deal with. With everything else we know, it's the last rock he could be hiding under. Albeit, it's a big damn rock."

"How do you mean?" Jack asked.

Kay, Bowers, and Winspear all looked at him.

"What?"

"You've never seen the Camplex," Bowers said, not a question.

"Well, not in person, no, but I've seen pictures of it and—"

"You've never flown over it?" Kay asked.

"Well no, I… you can see it from thirty thousand feet?"

Winspear laughed.

Bowers just said, "Oh you're in for a treat then. You and Winspear will leave in a few hours by helicopter, on Marine One, so you'll get a good look on arrival. Kay, you and I will review some documents here—that NDA I mentioned—and then we'll head to Washington to get set up with my people in the White House. Sound good?"

"As long as I get the full details of this scheme before any kind of monetary commitment."

"Sure," Bowers said. "NDA, plan, then money. Don't worry."

"On the impeachment," Bowers turned to Winspear, "Vice-President Applegate says we're still good on the vote. We can stall it until they close session at the end of the week, and that should give us time over the holidays to unpack whatever Scarly tells us and sort this all out. Applegate'll be in Washington too, making sure everything goes according to plan. I'll update you as soon as I have time to meet with him."

"Good," Winspear said. "How sure are we that the vote can be stalled until end of session?"

"As sure as we can be. You have more than a firm majority of the representatives on your side still, despite public opinion polls. They need a two-thirds majority to impeach, and they don't have anything near that."

"So, I may live to fight another day," Winspear said. "Brilliant."

"We've gotten in touch with the others where we can," Kay said. "Everyone's being too inundated on their phones and media profiles to get through to directly, but Quentin and Kelley have both apparently read the messages we sent."

"Which said what?" Bowers asked.

"Stay safe. Wait to hear from us. Things might not be as they seem."

"Good. Actually, that's great. We'll need to depose them soon to get all the details of what they did and when. Though, thanks to you, Jack, we have recordings of most of it."

He was speaking of course of Jack's master stroke on the day he took over LAX. His cadre of chosen helpers had broadcast their investigation live across the internet. Remembering it, Jack felt nauseous.

"So," Bowers said, "everyone get another piece of bacon. We've got work to do. Mr. President," he turned to Winspear, "if we could discuss something in the other room?"

They got up, and on his way out Bowers turned to say, "Kay, I'll have someone bring the documents to you in a few minutes."

She nodded a reply, and then it was just her and Jack at the table.

Kay turned to him, saying, "Those guys are running in high gear. What do you think?"

Jack shrugged. "We're in for the ride now."

"Don't look so excited," she said, hooking an arm on his shoulder, leaning a few degrees closer than she absolutely needed to. And not for the first time, Jack noticed. "Don't worry," she said. "We'll be on the other side of this in no time. With any luck, you'll get an explanation from Scarly while Bowers and I chisel out whatever gem of evidence they've found. We could have this sorted out in 48 hours."

"I hope you're right," he said. "I just have a feeling."

She looked at him, smiling. "Yes?"

"I don't know, it's just… it's too easy. It's too clean. We came here convinced Winspear was the bad guy pulling all the strings behind this thing, and in half a day they've sold us the exact opposite." He shook his head. "Something's not right."

"Maybe," Kay admitted, "but we'll have to push through and sort it out if we ever want to know."

He sighed. "I guess so."

"And then," she said, "we'll be on the other side of this. Picture that—a normal Christmas."

"That'd be nice," he said, "I don't know what normal is anymore." He didn't say what he was thinking, that he hadn't known what normal was for the better part of a decade. Not since his world stopped making sense.

"It'll be fine," she said. "We'll get dinner after it's all through and laugh about it." He looked over at her. "I promise."

"Right," he said, trying not to sound too pessimistic. "What could possibly go wrong?"

7

"So, if they trust Winspear, should we?"

It was Quentin Daniels talking, phone at his ear as he looked out the window of his office in the law building.

"Hell no," Kelley Oakley replied from the other end of the call. "And they don't trust him. Kay's text just said they're going to hear him out. Collect some more information."

Quentin slumped back into his chair. This had all been sort of fun yesterday, a burst of adrenaline he hadn't realized he'd been chasing since it all started weeks ago. Terrifying, yes, but exciting.

He should be off already, enjoying the holiday break. The campus was mostly a ghost town.

As if she sensed the turn in his enthusiasm, Kelley said, "You're still in this right? If there's a source that can give us something—"

"We don't know there's a source. It's probably just some student pranking me."

"On your new number? Somebody had the resources to get that."

"And somebody with those resources," Quentin said, trying to not sound annoyed, "would probably have better avenues with which to leak information. To wit, broadcasting it on the net just like Jack did."

"Maybe they're afraid," Kelley said, and Quentin could almost hear her shrugging on the other end of the phone.

"Maybe they mean exactly what they said, that since you are involved and since they know your name, they figure you're as good as anyone. The fact that you're geographically close was also part of it, I'm sure."

Quentin put the phone on speaker, setting it down in front of him and starting to clear piles from his desk. "Tell me more about that deep background thing."

"That's one of the reasons I think it's real," Kelley said. "That's a journalism term."

"So?" Quentin said, tossing a few sheets in the trash.

"So, they know what they're talking about. And that inclines me to at least hear them out."

Quentin sighed, looking at his leather satchel sitting on the chair next to his office door. It was packed and ready to go. Ready to take a vacation that he sorely needed.

He looked at his watch. "Ok, fine." He said, "I'll just…" He shook his head, looking around the office and picking up the phone, "twiddle my thumbs here for a few hours and then meet the guy."

"Good to hear," Kelley said. "You never know; we could find the missing puzzle piece to this thing."

"Can't wait," Quentin said, disconnecting the call and tossing the phone back on his desk.

He looked toward the window and sighed, then stood up and went over to it.

The open area in front of the student union was entirely clear, a well-kept sea of leafless trees and green bistro-style chairs and tables. Normally, even on a cold day there would be students passing through here, the heart of the campus, between the library, the union, and all the other buildings that branched off from them.

He turned back to his desk, to the computer screen where a live news stream was running on mute. It showed the White House and then pulled back to a helicopter landing, and he knew if he unmuted it they'd be saying the same things they had for the last week: Winspear would likely be impeached for all of this, but nobody knew for sure. Quentin had no doubt there was a secret investigation unfolding even now—rumors had started the same day as the incident with Jack at LAX.

And he wondered if maybe Kelley was right. Maybe whatever new information they received from their source would be what it took to stop him.

Sure, there had been some progress in a way. The Shooter Act was at least one way to try to do things differently. And there was something to be said about that. About trying to stop shootings with something more than vague outrage and praying into the wind. But look where it had ended.

It wasn't just the cronyism or the dirty politics that got under Quentin's skin. He knew the system wasn't perfect. In fact, he knew better than most that it was nowhere *near* perfect. The thing about Winspear that really pissed him off— that made him certain even now that he had to go through with this meeting—was the way this so-called president had so grotesquely tarnished the office specifically, and the United States on the world stage in general.

Quentin reached forward and clicked a pop-out link from the video: "Impeachment countdown." He saw it showed the time left for the current House session—two full days, after today.

There was something else on the timer: a ticker with an "impeach/don't impeach" vote. There were more than 10 million responses, with about 71% toward impeach.

Quentin selected "impeach," and when he submitted his vote he said to himself, "Serves you right."

8

Marine One seemed bigger in person. Jack squinted against the thrall of air the Sikorsky VH-3D's rotors slashed around as he headed for the aircraft. Winspear was just ahead, barreling forward into the gale unfazed, his suit coat fluttering behind him like a madman's cape.

Winspear climbed the stairs and disappeared into the craft quickly, Jack still covering his face with one hand as he approached the chopper and took his first step up the fold-out stairs. On the outside, the chopper was painted a dark green up to the top of the cockpit, but past that, the top third was snow white, the visual cue that set it apart from any other Marine helicopter.

Once inside, Jack clumped in close to the Secret Service agents, impressed at just how many people could fit in the helicopter. One of the pilots moved behind him to shut the door. The howl of the rotors muffled by a few degrees.

Toward the cockpit, four plush seats formed a tight rectangle, two on each side facing each other. There was just enough space to walk between the pairs, and each pair had a small table between the seats. Winspear sat at one of these, and two of his Secret Service men took the seats across the aisle from him. Behind the clutch of chairs, two benches lined the sides of the helicopter, and the rest of the group had piled in onto them.

There was one free seat left—the one across from Winspear—and he caught Jack's eye and gestured for him to take it, talking into a thick satellite phone.

Jack overheard him saying, "Fine, yes, I want it to read, 'All will be explained soon. Headed to pay Scarly a visit. Don't believe everything you read.' Okay, yes, send it out."

Jack sat, looking out the window on his right where snow swirled around Camp David as Winspear put the phone down.

There was no broadcast over the PA. After the door was shut, Jack barely had time to fasten his seatbelt before the helicopter lifted. He gripped the armrests, the helicopter rocking as it lifted off the ground.

"Keep watching," Winspear said as the chopper pulled up and started to pick up speed into a turn that pressed Jack in his seat and tilted the whole craft to the right. Camp David sank away below them.

"I love this part," Winspear said, "when you're looking at the ground head on. Spooky."

He watched Jack, who didn't say anything as the helicopter pulled out of the bank.

"Ever been in one of these before?"

Jack relaxed as the craft leveled out. He shook his head.

"No, never."

He felt an uptick in speed and looked over his shoulder, toward where the pilots were.

"Best part about flying is you can always trust the pilot," Winspear said. "They've got skin in the game."

Jack looked back, not responding, expecting a cryptic follow-up.

"That's why I like you, Jack," Winspear said. "You saw a problem, and hey presto"—he whipped his hand out, thumb and index finger forming a gun, pointing it across the small table at Jack—"you went and put yourself on the line to solve it."

He lifted the fake gun up and blew smoke from the imaginary barrel.

"This is the part where you tell me you've got skin in the game still," Jack followed up, "that I can trust you because of that. Right?"

He'd had time to think about the little exchange in the kitchen that morning, and Jack had already decided on a theory: Bowers *had* bugged them somehow, and he'd shared their conversation about Jack meeting Scarly. All that friendliness was him trying to get on Jack's good side. At least that was the only way he could make sense of it.

Winspear laughed at the comment.

"What you'll find, Jack, is that nobody who has as much money as I do truly has skin in any game." He seemed almost annoyed, turning to look out the window. "No, after the presidency, I can do whatever I want. Doesn't matter how bad it goes. *Before* the presidency I could do whatever I wanted." He turned back to Jack, smiling eerily. "Actually, being president is very much a manifestation of my being able to do whatever I want. How's that for you?"

"So, by that logic I can never trust you."

Winspear frowned. "What's this hang-up on trust? Who *do* you trust in your life?"

"Kay, for one." Winspear grunting approvingly. "The people who helped me out, I guess. In the airport."

"You're missing a big one," Winspear said, and Jack thought for a moment.

"I trusted... well, my fiancé obviously."

"Ah," Winspear said, "interesting." He smiled at Jack. "You didn't mention yourself."

"Well that—"

"*Does* it go without saying though?" Winspear leaned in conspiratorially. "I used to trust *my*self," he said. "You know, what I wonder sometimes is, do you ever think that maybe it's other people that allow you to trust yourself? To keep you honest?"

"Maybe," Jack said. "Who was supposed to keep *you* honest?"

"Everybody! Everybody used to love me. They trusted me." He leaned back, looking out the window. "Sierra trusted me."

Sierra Winspear. Jack could just barely remember the details over the dull roar of emotional rollercoaster that the news had been since Winspear started his campaign. His wife, Sierra, had been killed during that campaign. Just before the election—a *month* before the election, if he remembered correctly.

Jack didn't want to let his guard down, though. This seemed like another ploy. A cheap one. That was the second time in two conversations Winspear had steered it to their mutual lost loves. It seemed he thought that was the in with Jack. And it was just the sort of thing he'd expect from a ruthless robber baron like Winspear, dragging out his dead wife's name for sympathy. To try to endear himself.

"I know what you're doing," Jack said, "and it's a cheap trick."

Winspear just looked at him for a moment. He opened his mouth to say something but then stopped.

"Mr. President." One of the Secret Service agents stepped forward from the back of the chopper, his hand on the shoulder of Winspear's chair. "They have a perimeter set up at the facility, but they're having trouble getting the door open."

"Well, right they should," Winspear said, at once back in presidential mode. "We didn't scrimp on security when we built it."

"They said they're going to try breaching charges—" the agent replied, but Winspear cut him off.

"Did anyone do what I said and contact Roy Berry?" Winspear shook his head, turning around to shout at the group of people behind him.

One of them did remember the request, and informed Winspear that though the NSA had blocked it on their end, the CIA was willing to help by passing along what they had access to.

"Glad I still have friends somewhere," he said. "Get a location and pick him up. We're going to need him as soon as possible."

He turned back to Jack, jerking a thumb behind him and making a face, unbuckling and heading for the pilot's door. When he got there, Jack overheard him say something about where they were going to land, but the hum of air outside was just loud enough that he couldn't make it out.

"Hey." It was one of the Secret Service agents sitting across from him, leaning in across the narrow walkway. "Yesterday was her birthday," he said. "Sierra." It took Jack a minute to understand what he meant, and why he was telling him this. "Give him a break," the Agent added, before leaning back in his chair.

Jack looked at him for a minute, then to Winspear's back as he started to withdraw from the pilots. Sierra's birthday. His *dead wife's* birthday. No wonder he was in such low spirits when they'd first come in.

For an instant, as Winspear sat down, two alternate realities played out in Jack's mind. In one, this master trickster was doing everything he could to get the best of Jack. Bowers had bugged them, all his character and affect was a ploy, and the repeated attempts to bring up their dead lovers was a bid for false sympathy.

But in the other version, maybe he was just being paranoid, and maybe Winspear was hurting and isolated.

Despite himself, Jack felt a lump creeping up in his throat. Compassion maybe. For this man who was only trying to reach out. Trying to share his loss and sorrow. For a second, all the conspiracy and intrigue took a back seat, and Jack felt a flash of the raw pain that was still there. A terrible thing to share, but something that—no matter how much Jack didn't want to—he *did* have in common with Winspear.

As Winspear buckled in, Jack shifted in his seat. He felt ashamed for being rude, clearing his throat to try to make conversation.

"Who's Roy Berry?" he asked.

"One of the only people still on the Winspear payroll, in fact the only IT guy who survived the automation push half a decade ago."

"I thought you went to zero workers?"

"Zero workers *in the factory*. You still need people to grind out the nonlinear work. Most of them are remote contractors, chosen from freelance sites by the algorithms. At least that's how it used to be when I was in charge."

"So what does Roy Berry do for you?"

"The question, Jack, is not what he does for me, but what I pay him *not* to do for my competitors."

9

Roy Berry liked to sleep in these days. He didn't have a care in the world. So, it was the light of midday that streamed in the window of his hotel room, stinging his eyes before they were even open.

"Blinds," he mumbled from the bed, already feeling the pounding in his head. "*Blinds!*" he said again, and this time they started to close, drawing the room down into mere dimness.

"Hey," a voice next to him said.

He opened his eyes a little further, smiling at the woman who was propping herself up in the bed beside him, her short blonde hair mussed hardly enough to suggest the night before.

"Suppose you'll want your money now?" Roy said.

She smiled back, reaching up and play-slapping him. Sure, he was paying her to be here, as he had the previous night and the night before that and a long line of nights, in fact, that were coming dangerously close to stretching into what might be considered... something more.

But deep down he knew they'd never talk about it. That one day he'd leave and there wouldn't be any calls, because in the end, this was about the money. She was performing, just like everyone, and damn if wasn't a heartbreaking performance. He really liked her. But Roy knew better than to get attached.

"Breakfast?" she said, starting to make her way out of bed.

He grunted, looking at the shades as he spilled off his side of the bed, swiping for the vaporizer on the nightstand and unscrewing the bottom to see what was left. He nodded approvingly before replacing the cartridge and clicking it on.

"Need to get my head right first," he said, pulling on the stick.

"Right," she said, taking it when offered, exhaling a cloud of weed-scented smoke. She repeated the maneuver as he checked his watch.

"Not breakfast," he said, "lunch."

"What?" She picked up her phone, checking the screen and saying, "Shit. I've got to go."

She tossed the pen down, looking for her clothes.

He tried not to think the thought that came next, but of course that had the effect of bolding and underlining it in his mind. What he didn't say was, "Where to? Another hot date?"

"Sorry," he said, standing. "You know you'd be amazed at what these things can do." He spun his phone in the air, catching it and smiling. "Alarms for instance."

She smiled at him and rolled her eyes, pulling on a shirt that covered just enough to make it to the autocar that was no doubt on its way. They both knew that those amazing things you could do with a bit of tech were just the sort of thing that kept Roy in enough cash to keep paying her so much.

"Same wallet?"

"Sure," she said, turning up the collar on a light jacket that covered some of what the shirt didn't.

Roy watched her go and waited for the door to shut. Then he stood in the silence for a moment before pulling his phone up to tap the universal payment info attached to her contact. Then he tapped the address of the wallet number she'd given him. There was the list of his previous transactions, scrolling down and off the page—a methodic log of trysts.

He hit "repeat" on the last payment, let the phone scan him for confirmation, then closed the app.

"Blinds," he said again, and he stood to face the window as they opened.

"What day is it?" he asked, and the phone answered, "Today is Wednesday, Mr. Berry."

"Okay," he said to himself, feeling the heady rush of wax—his preference over THC oils, which just keep him on the couch. "Let's make some money."

He got ready, showering, putting on some clothes. He put his earbuds in and grabbed the pack of cigarettes and Zippo lighter that were on the nightstand.

He opened his laptop and fished around in the bag next to the hotel table for a USB cord that connected to a square black mat about the size of a coaster.

He opened a program on his computer, plugged in the cord to the mat, which looked like a wireless charging pad and set the Zippo lighter on it.

The two devices started to trade data—the laptop running diagnostics and updating the program on the other computer, the one that was hidden in the Zippo. Everything was looking good.

Roy nodded. "Okay," he said and closed the computer, pocketing the lighter as he stood and headed for the door.

Roy hadn't taken to early retirement well. The monthly pay from Winspear Robotics wasn't small. But he needed something. A project. A *challenge*.

So, it wasn't that he *needed* to steal money from the casinos. It was more like he just did it for fun.

He walked down Fremont Street, taking it slow. Usually he'd be in an autocar, but something about the day, he wanted to get out and breathe the fresh air, if any air around here could be described that way.

He turned into one of many nondescript casinos. It was one of the ones nobody ever hears about, no thousand hotel rooms attached, none of that. These middling ones—where the gambling addicts and retirees congregated—those were the ones that Roy figured were better.

Slowly, he started to case the place.

He walked around, taking a drink, stopping at the dollar slots and playing a few rounds.

"Can I get you a light sir?" a waitress in a tight getup asked him, nodding down to the pack of cigarettes he'd put on the shelf of the machine when he sat.

"No, honey," he said, flashing a toothy smile and pulling the Zippo out of his front shirt pocket, "got my own."

He had a feeling in the back of his neck. Adrenaline. He willed himself not to look up at the camera in the ceiling as he played with the Zippo in one hand, working the slot machine with the other.

This was one of the slot machine models his program worked on, one with cameras built in, which constantly watched the people playing. They scanned for facial recognition and expression tracking, storing a profile that linked up with the casino's rewards program, but they also used all the metadata they could skim—pupil dilation, pigment shifts, frown-vs-smile frequency—to better game every penny they could out of you. And strictly speaking, this was all legal.

Which is why Berry didn't feel bad about what he was doing.

He triggered an input command into the computing unit secreted away in the Zippo lighter: four short clicks and a long open, then snapped shut. It was a simple variation on Morse code, allowing him to select from the presets of programs he had, homing it in to this particular model machine.

Then, carefully, he opened the Zippo just enough that a green laser module in the back of the lid was aimed at the facial recognition camera in the slot machine.

The fundamental premise of any system is that, if there is a way to provide input, there is a way to skew the system.

The laser shone into the slot machine's webcam, giving a small tactile feedback vibration into Roy's hand to let him know it was locked. Then, choosing his moment wisely, Roy took his glasses off, closed his eyes, and grimaced.

The programming of the machine didn't see this expression, or anything like it, often. The standard protocol was to allow the machine learning on the equipment do the heavy lifting, which saved on bandwidth costs, but if there wasn't a big enough dataset, there was nothing to compare it to. So, the machine "phoned home," pinging the manufacturer's servers and querying whether there was any useful parameter to apply changes to, based on this edge-case facial recognition input.

And when the mothership replied, a door was opened. There was a split second where an additional edge case input on the webcam could be sent before the original request was closed, allowing Roy to spillover the code of whatever the webcam was seeing into the machines flash memory. The Zippo vibrated again, and he repeated the expression triggering the hack.

The laser took over, flashing in a prescribed pattern, strobing faster than the human eye could ever detect, overloading the webcam's cheap light-measuring array in a specific pattern, a pattern that would force code that was already spilling over into the flash memory to pile up, to cause problems.

If the spillover was controlled precisely, through the pattern of the laser, then fragments could be pushed and pulled around in the machine's memory. If it was timed just right…

Roy hit the "max bet" button and the slot erupted with a warm, shrieking alarm.

Jackpot.

"Oh my God!" Roy shouted, standing, snapping the Zippo shut and pocketing it.

He knocked the cigarettes in a practiced performance and slapped his hands over his mouth, playing every bit the part of a surprised, dumbfounded idiot.

The machine was still blaring when the waitress and some-one from security, talking into his walkie-talkie, ran over. Roy was smiling, breathing fast and hard.

"What does that mean?" he asked, turning to the security agent and pointing at the machine. "Does that mean I won?"

Other gamblers were huddling around now, oohing and awing as the word spread that the jackpot this guy had just hit on a dollar slot was more than two hundred thousand.

The staff were fawning over him, trying to lead him deep-er into the casino, congratulating him and saying that since he was obviously so hot he should stay.

"Sorry," he said, "but I got somewhere to be. I'll go ahead and cash this out." He was smiling with his betting card in hand.

Roy practically bounced to the cash counter.

"I need this cashed out please, all of it."

"Right away, sir." She'd seen him win the jackpot and had already been radioed that he was coming. "I've got the paper-work started, is there a bank you'd like this transferred to?"

"Oh yes," he said, pulling his phone out.

He tapped away, pulling up the routing and account num-bers, smiling to himself. Every casino in town, or almost all of them. He'd been at this for weeks now, and it really had become too easy. The casinos were all the same, practical-ly speaking. Same carpet, same gilded ceilings, he could al-most convince himself that he recognized the girl at the cash counter—they were all of a certain type, after all.

He slid the phone to the woman, letting her read the info for herself as he turned and leaned on the counter.

Carpet with a busy design, high ceilings, it really was like déjà vu in all these places.

Out of the corner of his eye he saw something big mov-ing toward him. The suited, barrel-chested head of securi-ty. He seemed to be looking right at Roy in a not altogether friendly way.

Déjà vu. Recognition. He looked around the place one more time, and all at once he realized why this casino was so familiar.

He'd been here before.

He'd *run the same scam here* before.

He stood up straight.

"Hey can you speed this up?" he said to the lady behind the cash counter, not hearing her reply as he scooped up his phone and tried to think. They'd have no proof on the machine, but he knew what the cameras would show, the wonky facial expression, the way he'd held his lighter just so before the jackpot. Seeing that once would mean nothing. But seeing it twice in a row... that would mean everything.

"Mr. Berry!" Roy swallowed hard. "You dropped these."

The man held something toward Roy. He looked down, already feeling the sweat on the back of his neck and saw that he was holding out the pack of cigarettes.

Roy took the pack, suddenly aware that there were two security guards standing behind him in addition to the mustachioed muscle in front.

They'd surrounded him.

"Funny thing," the man who'd handed him the cigarettes said, as Roy tried not to eye the others in his periphery. "That's a full pack."

The cigarettes. He meant the pack of cigarettes. He'd already seen the videos—both of them. He'd already put it together.

"We'd like to have a conversation with you in the back, Mr. Berry," the man said, and as the two men behind Berry stepped up and grabbed him by the biceps, the head of security turned to the lady at the cash desk and said, "You can hold off on that transfer, Meg."

And suddenly he was being dragged back toward a set of double doors hidden away in the shadows.

"Wait guys," he said. "Wait just a minute here."

But as soon as they were through the doors the man with the mustache and suit gave him one to the stomach so hard he thought he was about to cough up his ribs.

They turned down a few halls, finally depositing Roy in a room that was something like a holding cell. It had two metal chairs facing each other in the center. The two security guards flanked him, holding him down in one chair, and Roy looked up to see the guy with the mustache sitting down across from him.

"Neat trick," the man said, holding Roy's head up by the chin, "but a little rude, don't you think?"

He punched Roy in the face, the blow coming with a soggy snapping noise. That was his nose breaking.

He groaned as the man felt at his breast pocket for the lighter. He opened it, clicked it shut.

"So!" he said, "you're gonna tell me how it works."

Roy said nothing, breathing hard and tasting blood.

"How's that sound?"

And as if to make his point, he pulled a Taser out of his pocket and made it crackle in the air, the blue lightning between the leads ready to pounce.

"And you can either tell me right now or in a little bit when you want it to stop."

"Okay," Roy said, "I'll talk."

"Good boy!" the man said.

He pulled the lighter back up, setting the Taser on his leg. He flicked it open, rolling the grinding wheel against the flint so that it lit.

"I gotta say, I've never seen anything this fancy." He tilted the lighter, seeing the laser that was mounted on top of the hinge, obvious when you were looking for it. "Tell me how to work it."

"That bit, the top, you pull it out," Roy breathed in and out slowly, trying not to give anything away as he added, "Have do it while it's lit."

It was a poor backup plan, Roy knew, but that's what they were for. He hoped he was far enough away from the gadget.

"Here?" the man asked, pointing to the top of the lighter's housing.

"Yeah," Roy nodded.

He didn't like the next part, but the head of security ought to know better. If he'd watched the videos closer, he'd know that it wasn't lit when Roy was using it.

That's Darwin for you, though, Roy thought.

As soon as the modified housing was pulled free, a spring was released that splashed lighter fluid from the reservoir onto miniscule electrical components hidden in the bottom of the lighter.

As a defense mechanism—Roy had planned for contingencies—it sprayed both ways, down and up. Which meant it wasn't just the illicit computing components that were on fire; so was the mustachioed man's face.

All at once he was screaming, standing up quickly, dropping the lighter, and kicking the metal chair back behind him.

The two security men didn't know what to do, and Roy strained forward against their grip, making it to the floor on his knees, going for the Taser that had clattered off the security officer's leg.

"Hold him!" one of them yelled, and Berry heard the other screaming something into a radio.

He was forced back down into the chair, and he breathed hard for a second, watching the mustachioed—*formerly* mustachioed—security officer try to use his suit coat to put out the fire on his face.

"Better help him," Roy said calmly, but the one shouting into his radio ignored him, and the other just gripped tighter, one hand on Berry's arm and the other bruising the top of his shoulder.

"He's got the Taser!" he heard one of them yell, and the grip on that arm was painfully tight. They had both of his arms, he couldn't reach either of them with it, but he held onto the weapon and tried to pull against them, to jump out of the chair, fund an opening.

The Security man picked his arm up and slammed it down onto the chair arm, trying to get Roy to drop the Taser, but he held it just long enough.

Things were happening very quickly now. They were holding him, looking at their injured colleague. Any second they'd realize it would be easier to knock Roy out and then get the Taser from him, and while they tried to think quick about this, Roy was thinking quicker: he had to act before they could, and there was only the one play left. It was something that was quintessentially Roy—hacking the system through the only input he had available. He held down the button on the Taser and strained, pulling the crackling electric teeth in toward his own leg while the security guards tried to shout directions at each other.

As soon as it touched, the temporary rigor mortis of electrocution set in, and he was along for the ride as the shock traveled through his own body and into the security guards that held him.

He didn't know how long the shock was, but the next lucid thought he had was that he was on the floor under them. The mustachioed man was quietly sobbing into his burnt jacket, and the other two were groaning as they stirred back to awareness.

He didn't wait to see how things turned out, wiggling out from under them and running into the hallway.

Quick as he could, he stumbled down the hallway and back into the casino, looking over his shoulder as he heard shouting from behind.

In front of him, a security guard was rushing up from the right, and he darted past. Forget the jackpot; he just needed to get *out*.

From seemingly nowhere, more security guards started to come from the left and right, but Roy darted for the door.

One of them was close behind, grabbing at him, and he slammed through the doors so hard that the glass in one cracked.

But he was going too fast. He stumbled out, crashing into whomever had the misfortune to be passing by just then and dodging too late, falling.

As he tried to get up, the security guard closest behind fell on top of him, then there was a dogpile of three, then four.

"Hey," someone shouted over the commotion.

Roy heard him from behind, from the road, but he couldn't turn to look.

"Hey!"

"Get off me," Roy strained, and then everything slowed down with the sound of gunfire. The shots were quick, two of them, and from where he was pinned Roy could see the men on top of him looking in the direction of the road.

Slowly, they got off, and Roy could angle himself far enough to see that there were three dark-suited men standing just beyond the curb, their black sedan idling behind them. The man in the middle was putting his gun away.

"Go back inside," he said to the security guards.

As they started to get up, one of them said, "Who the hell are you?"

"Secret Service," the one who'd fired the gun said, holding up a badge. "Don't make me tell you again."

The security staff looked at each other, then retreated to just inside the door, talking to each other and trying to figure out what to do.

"Roy Berry?" the man who'd fired his gun asked, stepping forward and reaching down to help him up.

"I'm not sure," Roy said. "Depends on why you want him."

The agent reached his free hand up to an earpiece. "He's here. We're en route."

"What's going on," Roy asked, but he was already being pulled toward the sedan.

"That'll be clear soon enough," the agent said.

"Listen, I didn't break any laws back there—"

"Save it. You're not under arrest," the agent said.

The door shut, and they were pulling away from the curb.

"Well then you won't mind letting me out at the next light?"

"Can't do that," one of the other agents turned to say. "We have orders to bring you to the airport. Somebody wants to see you."

"Oh shit," Roy said, leaning back hard in his seat, only now reaching up to pinch his nose and stop the bleeding. "Winspear."

10

They were right; Jack was impressed.

Below, the small city of buildings known as the Winspear Camplex sprawled out.

A whole boomtown worth of industry and living space that had been dried out of people, fully automated. But as the helicopter started to lower, Jack saw movement. Streams of traffic to and from the buildings. Flows of drones and automated vehicles.

And the number of objects in motion—not just on the ground and near it, as the small drones and countless vehicles were—but in the sky too. There was a full-scale airport spread out at one side of it all, and an endless stream of convoy drones, some as large as passenger jets, were taking off and landing at odd angles. It looked chaotic to Jack, nothing like the clean lines of a real airport. A *human* airport. Instead, the hodgepodge of planes threaded each other's paths and landed wherever it was most efficient on the spread of tarmac.

As the helicopter got lower, he eyed the biggest jet, which was taxiing toward the warehouse complex. On the side, the ghost of a huge FedEx logo could just barely be made out behind the black and gold Winspear "W" that had replaced it.

Jack had known all this existed, but he'd never understood that it was so alive with activity. As far as he could see in all directions, the Winspear Camplex was whirring away, the heart of Winspear's vast empire. It was one thing to hear about it, but it was quite another to see it all, to feel the expanse of the main warehouse stretching off into the distance.

It was amazing but also eerie. A global-scale bustle of constant motion devoid of the creatures that had created it.

The light was bouncing off the corner of the building just right, off what Jack guessed correctly was a solar farm on top, and he had to squint from the glare. He thought that he could see the far edge of the building in the distance, perpendicular to the airport, but it was impossibly far away.

But then the front of the building blocked his view, and the helicopter rotated as it came down. They were parking out front—avoiding the airport, Jack realized.

When it landed, there was a group of men waiting for Winspear. Jack followed him and saw that there was already a sort of encampment a few hundred yards away, where the entrance to the Winspear Shipping headquarters extended from the face of the building, an art deco gilded maw made of two Atlas figures, each with a world on his shoulders. The two colossuses faced each other, so that the doorway felt guarded. There was the feeling of poised energy, like the entryway might snap shut at any moment.

Jack could see there were structures set up, black SUVs parked in the near distance and men with assault rifles slung over their shoulders running from tent to tent. Where Winspear and the others rushed forward toward the action, Jack took his time.

He tried to take it all in, studying the Atlas figures and then looking up the flat, imposing wall of the building.

There were holes here and there, not windows but ducts, and every so often a drone with a payload exited, drifted several stories higher or lower before reentering. One came out just a few stories above him, close enough that Jack could hear its rotors whining over the chopper's sound before it dove back in. Another came from an even lower duct, not moving up the face of the building but charging across the campus to some unknown destination.

Jack turned, shaking his head a little. It was an interesting feeling, the idea that this hive of a building was fully automated. All this activity was going on with nobody at home to steer the ship.

Well, *almost* nobody.

"Any response from inside? Any sign of him?" Jack heard Winspear asking from inside the nearest tent.

He pushed the blue camo door sheaf aside and saw that the room was kitted out with computers and plenty of men to operate them. Winspear was looking over someone's shoulder at an array of monitors near the front.

"Jack," he said, looking back and waving him forward.

"Still nothing sir," the man at the monitors was saying. "And the vice-president's on the line for you."

"That can't be good," he said. "Bring me a phone."

"Got it."

"Applegate," Jack said. "You said he's handling the impeachment for you?"

Winspear nodded. "You've met him, haven't you? Back when you were in the limelight?"

Jack winced. He wouldn't exactly put it that way.

"If by limelight—"

But Winspear turned away, waving him off, taking the phone that had been handed to him.

Jack bit down hard, grinding his teeth. He remembered working with Applegate well. After the death of Jack's fiancé, he'd become a gun rights activist, making it as far as Washington with his draft bill in hand before meeting a group of people who could make it happen, a handful of senators that included Wilson Applegate.

It was Applegate who had taken control of the bill and helped turn it into the one they passed, known after as the

Shooter Act. Jack winced because, truth be told, he'd never meant for the Act to be what it had finally become: a tool used to erase people from history as an ultimate punishment.

Yes, he'd worked with Applegate, but the memory of it made him sick to his stomach. That's why Jack had to be the one at the airport. With the gun. He helped get the bill passed in the first place, and he was the only one who knew how terrible it was.

Winspear was talking loud enough that Jack could hear his side of the conversation: "Great. Well we'll just have to give them a good reason to get back on our side."

Applegate was a true force, Jack knew. If he was operating now as he had then—when he'd been going around whipping up votes for the Shooter Act even before it got wrapped up in the election as a main plank in Winspear's platform—then Jack had no doubt the president would be spared. For now at least.

"Well," Winspear said to one of the soldiers working at a bank of monitors, "I don't suppose we've got my man on yet?"

"Roy Berry was picked up an hour ago and they're en route here now."

"Good," Winspear said. "Get with him as soon as he's here. He can help you crack the door. We'll need him inside too."

"Yes sir," the soldier said, turning back to his work.

"Don't you own the place?" Jack asked.

"Technically, yes," Winspear said, "but I turned over all authorization and access when I signed over the blind trust. I told you we took it very seriously."

"And Roy, we'll need him because he can hack his way into the place?"

"If anyone can, he can," Winspear said.

"And the manhunt for Duncan McAvoy? I don't suppose Applegate updated you on that?"

"Oh, they're still looking."

"Who is?"

Winspear shrugged. "CIA, FBI, it's a manhunt. All over the news."

"Do they have any leads?"

"Look, Jack, that's really not what I'm most focused on here—"

"You know he tried to kill me, right? That he tried to kill Kay? Her daughter?"

"Listen Jack, I know you're sweet on her—" Jack scoffed, "—and trust me, *trust* me, she's with Bowers right now in the White House. Nobody is coming after either of you. No chance they could even get close."

It was true—he was worried about Kay, but he'd also asked about McAvoy because he realized if they got him, then maybe McAvoy could just tell them where Scarly was. This—searching a huge warehouse—might just be a huge waste of time.

He tried to ignore the bad feeling he was getting, tried to remind himself of what Kay had said, that this would all be over soon.

11

The thing that surprised Kay most about the White House was how old, and frankly *rundown* it was.

She'd barely taken it in when they'd arrived—Bowers wanted to get to work right away—but the white façade was cracked, the paint yellowing at the base of the Roman style columns. You never saw these details from the cameras, the way the windows were dim with a film of dust and how diagonal cracks spider-webbed away from the top of the doorways, telltale signs that the foundation had shifted.

And so it had.

Kay had heard they'd stopped tours years ago. That was before Winspear, but under his administration the country's capital had remained a symbol of something closer to foreboding than pride. If she hadn't sensed this before, then she did now as she looked around the room Bowers' people were working in.

This had once been a banquet hall, she understood. It had probably hosted countless dignitaries and noblemen, the years evaporating as one leader after the next came to power, until this new form of leadership had taken over and spread out across the round tables, analysts in business casual clothes and laminated badges that hung on thick lanyards, the fading light from outside giving way to the harsh blues of the countless screens that had been set up here, their power cords and encrypted data cables threading through the room like umbilicals through which the organism of control processed the nutrients of its kind: information.

Dozens of Bowers Associates personnel were working away here, their high-tech gear contrasting with the hundred-year-old decorations. Analysts moved around the room, some with screens in their hands that flashed like magic against the backdrop of faded wallpaper that had been around before semiconductors were a spark of anyone's imagination.

Bowers returned now, and saw Kay taking it all in, following her gaze to one of the window-panes where the setting sun had caught, glinting, across a spiderwebbed crack. He said, "It's seen better days."

She saw he was offering her one of two steaming mugs, and she took it gladly.

Bowers continued, "Winspear hasn't worked out of here much, and as you know there haven't been many official visits."

She nodded, taking a sip, then said, "The hermit presidency."

After a moment, Bowers nodded.

"It's sad," Kay said, feeling a draft from somewhere in the big room. "So much history here."

"History that has tended to remain just that," Bowers said. "*History.*"

"You don't think it'll change when…" she caught herself, not exactly wanting to say, "when he's impeached." She settled for "when the next president takes over?"

"Tradition has its place," he shrugged, taking a drink. "When it carries experience, it's useful, but things change. The *world* changes, faster and faster. You have to change too, to keep up." He raised his eyebrows at her, taking another sip. "How do you know what's right? Following tradition is easy. Forging a new path, *that's* the hard thing to do."

"You think that's what Winspear was doing?"

"I *know* that's what he was doing. Or what we were going to do, rather."

She looked at him, brow furrowed.

"Very mysterious," she said.

She took a drink from the mug, then tipped it toward the analysts.

"And them? What are *they* doing?"

"Waging a trade war," Bowers said. "That's what it looks like."

"Hm," Kay said, "much neater than the alternative."

"That's right."

Bowers took a drink.

"So," she said, "what sort of new path was Winspear supposedly going to force. Dictatorship?"

Bowers smiled. "Nothing so melodramatic."

He studied Kay for a moment, until she said, "Well?"

"I probably shouldn't say anything about it."

He took another drink. Shrugged.

Added, "I mean, it was all pipe dreams. Big ones, though. That's the only kind of plan Winspear could make, I think. A big one."

"Clearly," Kay said. "He certainly is a force. No matter what we find out, at least *that* much is true."

"No kidding. When we first realized he could actually win the thing—the election I mean—the first thing he did was sit down and come up with a *grand vision*."

"Oh?" Kay raised an eyebrow.

"That's right," Bowers said. "He sent me the file and it was actually named 'Grand Vision,' if you can believe that."

Despite the situation, Kay smiled.

"Somehow, I really do."

She took another drink.

"And what did it say?"

Bowers shook his head slowly.

"He was going to make this country unrecognizable. He had a list of reforms too crazy for any normal politician. How voting works, how the economy works, immigration, we were going to change all of it. That was the plan… before."

"His wife," Kay said, a tingle at the back of her neck, the light out the window sliding further, casting the room in a hollow glow.

Bowers nodded.

"Some things a man—anyone—can come back from. For Winspear—" he shook his head. "I'm still wondering if he can come back."

"Hey," a big white door off the main room opened, and a man with a cigar bobbing in his mouth poked his head out and said, "You guys coming?"

Bowers nodded toward the man and Kay followed him into the room, where a thick oak dining table served as a workspace in the impromptu conference room. Kay instantly recognized the difference between the workers out there in the pit and the ones in here. All these men were *old*. The room had a fog of cigar smoke, and the four suited figures at the table seemed to exchange glances when Kay followed Bowers in and took a seat.

"So this is your ace?" one of them said, nodding to Kay.

"Kay Luo," she said, not waiting for Bowers to introduce her. "And you must be the men who get rich off the work of all those junior-level analysts out there."

"Now wait just a second—"

"Okay, okay," Bowers said, patting the air like he was physically tamping the conflict down. "Kay, as I'm sure you can understand, we do not usually bring in help."

"Oh, I understand fully," she said. "You're the experts. So it's a little silly for *you* to have to call in an expert yourselves, right?"

She smiled at them and sipped at her coffee.

The nearest one put a cigar into his mouth. He looked her over, then gave a brief nod. There was a trace of a smile at the corner of his mouth.

These were not people used to being jabbed at, not by their employees, and certainly not by *women*. But something went unspoken, some crossing of a line. They could all sense that Kay was a force in her own right. That, more than anything else, she wasn't going to take any bullshit.

"Bowers has filled you in then."

Kay nodded.

"She's signed the NDAs," Bowers said, "and I told her the basic situation that—"

"No," Kay said, "I want to hear it from them."

Bowers looked from her to the group.

The man nearest her smiled fully now, swiveling in his plush chair to one of the others. He nodded, and the second man reached forward to trigger a small projector that threw an image onto the far wall.

Bowers went around closing the drapes on the other side of the room.

The man nearest Kay said, "Have a seat then."

On the far wall, the projector showed a chart, a jagged line that stretched from left to right, angling down.

"Here," the man with the cigar huffed, "we have NEXT Auto's share price."

"It's been dropping since the day of the shooting."

He was referring of course to the shooting at LAX the day that NEXT Auto was shown to be modifying its source code to interfere with several accident investigations and frame innocent riders.

"As you might expect."

"As we *all* might expect," the man with the cigar said, "but then there's this."

He gestured, and the chart changed. It was the same jagged line, stretching left to right, angling down, but this new version was zoomed out. On the larger time scale, measuring a few weeks, you could see how the stock price took an initial dive downward, but then stabilized into a more or less flat line.

"Seems normal enough," Kay said.

"We thought so too. Until one of our analysts pointed out the trend with volume."

He raised one finger, and the man with the laptop controlling the screen added another chart at the bottom of the one showing share price. It was a series of bars, growing from the bottom of the screen like a city skyline. From left to right, they started out small—almost like buttons or columns only a few inches high on the projected screen—but toward the right, just as the share price started to level out, they grew comically large, some stretching up the projector screen and overlapping the line chart of share price.

"Daily trading volumes goes nuts," the man with the cigar explained, "and from what we can tell, most of them are from shell companies owned by Winspear Corporations—a lot of them. Dozens. Maybe hundreds."

"Jesus." She looked at Bowers. "The ones you said they were using for the short squeeze? This has to be more than that."

"Oh yes," the man with the cigar nodded, "this is something else. Massive amounts of capital being deployed, buying up shares and stabilizing the stock price. It's not a squeeze, because the price isn't going up. It's basically just a handout—short sellers aren't making money, but they're not being punished either."

"That *is* strange," Kay said. "If it were a squeeze, the price would be going up. Done this way, it's just maintaining. "

"That's right. It's just keeping the price from dropping further as other traders are still selling it off." Bowers added, "It makes no sense. Just a handout to keep the price up."

"So, we found that," the man with the cigar said, again raising a finger to the man with the laptop, "and then we asked ourselves, 'Why this number? Why this stock price?'"

A new line stretched across the screen now, this one red. It traced the black line of share price down at the left side of the screen and then leveled out to a perfectly flat line around the halfway point—just when the share price appeared to stabilize. Then it traversed the rest of the projector screen like a heart rate monitor flatlining.

"We looked at some different indicators. Ran a whole mess of them. It was pretty simple in the end, though, once we tried the right one. That red line is the daily percent loss. I don't have to tell you, Ms. Luo, that just like in nature it is rare to see such a perfect horizontal line in legitimate market data."

"What's happening there?" she asked.

"That's where the stat boys come in. Once they were able to track the volatility back to the little army of shell companies we think are involved, it became clear that there is some kind of relationship here that's automatic. The daily loss of NEXT Auto share price is being managed. It is never allowed to go higher than 8%."

Kay traced her eyes across the line chart, where the flat portion of the red line corresponded to the 8% mark on the axis. That was the point: 8% loss. It never went higher. You'd never catch it if you were watching during a trading day, in real time, but when you viewed the data like this it was obvious.

"How does it work?" she asked, taking a seat at the table.

The man with the cigar cleared his throat. "Let's say the price is falling, it's midday. It hits a loss of 8.0% on the day."

Another of the men around the table picked up the thread. "That number—that loss of value in a single day—automatically triggers the shell companies. They start putting in orders. They buy at market price to prevent the share price from falling further."

"So what, they hold it at an 8% loss?" Kay asked.

"Not exactly. They *keep* buying, until the deadband kicks in."

"'Deadband'?" She shook her head. "I'm not following."

"It's an algorithmic trading term," one of them said. "A range of inputs with zero outputs."

Another of the men simplified, "Something tells the algorithm to start buying—hitting 8% loss on the day—but something also has to tell it to stop. We think the buying is set to start at 8.0%, and it looks like there's another trigger to stop when it has reduced the loss on the trading day to 7.4%. In between—the zone from 7.4% to 8.0%—is the deadband, where no switches are being flipped and the program is just thrumming along working."

Kay looked at him, brow furrowed, and he tried again.

"Okay, so say the stock price is equivalent to water in a bucket. You can add water to the bucket at the top—that's buying—but there's also a hole in the bottom, and the water draining out is people selling. If nobody's buying and people are only selling, the stock price goes down, the bucket is draining. Makes sense, right?"

"Of course," Kay said.

"Okay, so imagine this—there's a hose at the top of the bucket that's set to come on automatically when the bucket is, say, half empty. As it drains," he held his hand out, lowering it slowly—the imaginary water level in the bucket, "the level in the bucket is going down, and then when it hits halfway, the hose turns on and starts filling it up. But what happens if you don't turn the hose off?"

"It overflows," Kay said. "So…" she was nodding her head, "there's another trigger higher up, say three-fourths of the way up the bucket, to follow your metaphor."

"Right," he nodded raising his hand. "The hose is on, the level in the bucket is coming up, but at three quarters of the way up the bucket, it hits the second trigger that turns the hose off. That space—from the halfway point to the three-quarter point, that's the deadband. As the bucket is filling from trigger to trigger, the program controlling the hose isn't doing anything but leaving it on. It's just an on/off switch."

"It's self-perpetuating?" Kay asked. "It will continue to do this in a loop? Or a cycle?"

"Until it runs out of money," the man with the cigar said, chuckling, briefly taking it out of his mouth and raising his eyebrows. "We think so."

"So this is what? Programmatic stock fraud?"

"It's not fraud," one of the other men at the table was quick to correct her. "But it is... disingenuous. It looks more like some kind of internal failsafe. Almost like an immune response to the PR crisis hitting NEXT Auto's share price."

"And the shell companies pouring money in," Kay said, "are under the Winspear umbrella?"

"All the ones we've been able to trace so far," Bowers said. "There was some smoke and mirrors when NEXT Auto was set up, huge investments by some of the largest companies in the world. Winspear said their investments would be protected at a government level. At the time we just assumed it would be part of the legal side of the deal—an actual insurance contract somewhere—but... it looks like this might be the protection mechanism."

"Wouldn't you *know*? I mean wouldn't someone have explained it?" Kay asked him.

One of the men at the table grunted. "Did they explain subprime mortgage lending before 2008?"

"Too true. Unfortunately, no, Kay," Bowers said. "I was on the campaign with him then, but this NEXT Auto deal came out of the blue. It was him, Scarly, and the other CEOs of the companies involved that hashed it out. Everything was happening so fast when they set it up, nobody really stopped to ask what would happen if the company went bankrupt, because they'd sold hundreds of millions in government contracts before the factories were even built." He shrugged.

Kay shook her head.

But if anyone, she thought, *had the resources and sheer guile to have implemented a program like this, it was Winspear.*

"It's some kind of survival mechanism. A life support system to save NEXT Auto in the case of a collapse."

"That's the theory," one of them said.

"And now," Bower said with a sigh, "we'd like to test that theory."

Kay looked at him. "You have a plan?"

Bowers nodded at the screen, saying, "This program—if that's what it is—is set to react to us, but it's still just a program: it's blind. It's listening for triggers to start and stop. And we think we can trick it with the two most important pieces of information we know about it."

"The triggers," Kay said. "8%... and what else?"

"The deadband," one of the other men at the table offered, "the point where the programmatic buying stops."

"Normally," the man with the cigar said, "the shell companies would start dumping money in at 8%, and the deadband trigger on the top tells them to *stop* buying after the share price has recovered enough that the loss is only 7.4%. We want to short it past the trigger, make the shell companies start buying, and then make it *skip* the deadband trigger on the way back up. Keep them buying, maybe until they run out of money entirely."

"Back to our bucket metaphor," the man nearest the laptop spoke, adjusting his glasses. "We'd like to drain the bucket enough that it gets to the half-empty point and triggers the hose, but then dump a whole other bucket of water into it so fast it jumps up *past* the three-quarter mark."

"Do not pass go," one of them said.

"That way we skip the second trigger on the way up," the man with the cigar again. "Fight fire with fire."

"That's right," Bowers added. "If we can short the stock down low enough to start the program, then we can issue a group of coordinated orders so massive it will skew the share price up for the entire market."

"We can make it jump past the deadband trigger, so the program won't get halted at all."

Kay shook her head. "But you're talking about hundreds of thousands of shares, and a liquid market that's constantly fluctuating… you'd need a few hundred million all going into the stock at the same time. Fast enough and big enough that it can skip from 7.5% loss on the day to 7.3% instantly, never actually hitting 7.4%…"

"That's mostly correct, Ms. Luo," one of them said. "From a group of coordinated sources. Hedge funds. Our own army of orders to counter the shell companies'."

"You said 'mostly correct', what am I missing?"

"Well," one of them started, "you're not just going from 7.5% to 7.3%… you have to *start* the trigger first by pushing it past 8%."

"So, what is that?" She calculated in her head. "8% back to 7.3%. You're talking about a volume of trades equivalent to 0.7% of the market cap." None of them replied. "That's not just a few hundred million… it's probably closer to a few *billion*."

"About five and a half," the man with the cigar said, nodding. "Billion, that is. And we'd need it all to go at once, through multiple exchanges. At the same instant. So not only do we need the cash, we need connections at all the major exchanges to get it timed perfectly."

Bowers leaned forward. "Which is where you and Nine Muses Capital come in."

12

It was starting to get dark, and Quentin glanced at his clock. Just then, his phone chimed—Kelley sending another text. Verifying that he was going to remember to set his phone to record before he talked to their source.

He typed a playful message back, only 45 minutes now. He'd watched as much as he could stand of YouTube, and the book he was in the middle of—*Lost Trails, Lost Cities*, by Percy Fawcett—was on the bedside table at home.

He thought about starting another book on his phone, something to drain the next 30 minutes with until he needed to start heading to the fountain. But it was reasonably warm for December. High 40s. Practically walkable.

In fact, with his coat and scarf, it was *very* walkable.

Quentin collected his things. He knew where the Peace Fountain was, but he rarely walked through that section of campus with all its history and character. It seemed nice—the idea of quietly appreciating the place before the Christmas break, time to reflect on what had happened, the unique spot in history that he'd fallen into.

He headed for the door, locking it behind him as he left, and as he headed down the hallway a text from Kelley came through:

"Be careful."

13

In one of the tents outside the Winspear Shipping entrance, Jack watched the news scroll by on one of the monitors.

He'd given himself a brief tour of the camp, and despite all the complicated number crunching and information tracking they were doing, there was somehow still a screen in each tent that seemed to be dedicated to the news. As it flashed by in ever more apocalyptic scenes, Jack realized that all the soldiers here were not just trying to break into the Winspear Camplex, but trying to help manage the massive informational flow as the external conversation was almost inexplicably turning to war.

"China and Russia," the anchor was saying against a backdrop of canned video—Winspear hurrying up the stairs of Marine One, the video stopping just before Jack would have entered the frame—"have each issued grave warnings against the United States's meddling in the global stock market, this coming along with reports from dozens of armchair statisticians that there are certain irregularities in NEXT Auto's share price, as well as suspicious activity on Wall Street by other key Winspear-affiliated corporations."

Jack wondered about Kay, about whether her fund would know anything about that. Or if maybe it was related to what Bowers had recruited her to help with.

"The US stock market," the reporter went on, "was dramatically forced to close early the day of Paulson's shooting"—his heart skipped—"and the so-called circuit breakers controlling trading have forced the market to close early three times since then. Analysts claim that this is business as usual. The circuit breakers are acting as failsafes, put in place to prevent a collapse like the one that led to the Great Depression. However, there is a minority of notable investors, including the heirs of Warren Buffet, who have publicly stated that they are liquidating their positions until the global stock markets stabilize."

"Jesus," Jack said under his breath. He remembered 2008. Was this worse? The S&P 500 index had lost something like 15% of its value in the last week, and it was still going down.

Somewhere above the din of the tent, Jack could hear a helicopter coming in, and a second later Winspear poked his head in.

"Jack, there you are! Come meet our guest."

He followed Winspear and his agents out into the open area where they'd touched down earlier. Now another helicopter was bobbing into place.

It was nearing dusk, and floodlights had been dragged into place, powered by mobile generators. They threw a hard light on the landing spot.

The chopper touched down, the blur of its blades lit from behind by the last dregs of sunlight that silhouetted the skyline of the Winspear Camplex beyond, a jagged, eerie monolith of buildings dark as pitch, having no squares of light—windows—without the humans inside to need them.

The wind from the chopper lashed Jack. He watched as the door to the craft opened and several men jumped out. Two of them were obviously agents, their black suits cutting a sharp contrast to the man who followed them out.

He was gaunt, unshaven, with hair that was tossed in a mad scribble by the still rotating blades. As he stepped closer, into the floodlights, Jack could make out a bloodstain on his shirt. That and a half limp gave Jack the impression he might have recently been thrown out of a moving vehicle.

He came closer, and Jack watched Winspear step forward to greet him.

"You look like shit," the president half-shouted.

They shook hands and smiled, then Winspear shifted, gesturing toward Jack.

"Jack, Roy Berry," Winspear said. "Roy, this is Jack Paulson."

"The gunman," Roy said as he shook Jack's hand.

"Yeah," Jack admitted sheepishly.

"Some balls," Roy said. "You're lucky they didn't disappear *you*, you know?"

"I know," Jack said. "And you? You work for Winspear?"

"Used to," he said, looking over to the president. "I set most of this up."

He nodded up at the warehouse.

"Hey now," Winspear corrected. "You had a team as I recall."

Roy smiled.

"A team of idiots."

"The best and brightest in their fields," Winspear said.

"Like I said," Roy smiled, "idiots."

"Roy here," Winspear turned to Jack, "helped us automate this place."

"And the hundreds of satellite facilities," Roy said. "A well-oiled system, don't you think?"

"You mean all of Winspear Shipping?"

Roy smiled.

"Winspear Shipping, Winspear Robotics, all of it. They work together now."

"Wow," Jack said. "When Winspear said it was all automated, I was still picturing people here and there. But you mean there's *nobody* here at all besides us?"

"That's right," Roy said, "except that snake in the grass Clayton Scarly."

Winspear grunted. "I take it they filled you in."

"Most of it, yeah. So what's the deal? You need me to break in?"

"That's the idea," Winspear said. "We've got to go in and find him."

"Piece 'a cake," Roy said, looking around the tent. "I need one of these worker bee's stations, some coffee, and a phone charger. Does someone have a connection to the front entrance yet? There was a jack behind the palm scanner that—"

"Oh yes," Winspear cut him off. "That's all wired back here. They've been trying to break the encryption for most of the day."

Roy scoffed.

"I designed it to be unbreakable," he said, "but, you know, I left a way for myself back in."

"I'm sure," Winspear said. "And for your trouble, I'm sure we can work out some kind of stock option or otherwise—"

"I'll take 10 million for it, in crypto of my choice, to wallet of my choice."

Jack was surprised at how quickly the conversation had turned, but Winspear didn't flinch.

"Ha! You're still on payroll. You can consider this part of your normal duties, Berry."

"From one perspective, I guess." He shrugged. "From the other, I was just kidnaped, and I suspect breaking you into your own factory would violate that pesky trust they keep talking about in the news. Less than ten is an insult."

"I'd give you five million, Roy, because that would be enough to remote hire half of Bangladesh for the next hour and have *them* crack it."

Roy shook his head.

"It's a lattice encryption. Nobody can break it. *I* can't even break it. My back door is what you're buying, and just because I know how much you like a bargain I'd give it to you for eight million."

"Seven," Winspear said, "and you come with us inside, help us find Scarly, and then remove any evidence we were here."

"Eight," Berry said.

"Seven-point-five, and don't push it. I don't like you *that* much."

"Seven and a half then." He nodded. "And on the other side of this I get a first-class ticket to the destination of my choice, care of Uncle Sam."

"Berry," Winspear said, "we will drop you off at the airport."

They stared for a moment, then Roy reached his hand out and they shook on it.

"Okay," Roy said, "you"—he picked something up off the closest table and tossed it at a soldier typing at the next workstation. He took his headset off, turning to Berry—"get up. I'm using that machine now. Stay close though, I may need some of your logins. Jack,"—he turned to Jack—"you know where these Boy Scouts keep the coffee machine?"

"No but I—"

"Good—I take it black as a raven. And while you're out there, see if someone can find me a phone charger."

As he said this, he pulled his phone out of his pocket and looked down.

"I'm good for a few hours, but my *captors* didn't exactly let me stop by my apartment to get an overnight bag."

"Okay," Jack said, a little annoyed but honestly wanting a cup of coffee himself.

He turned just in time to see Winspear disappear through the tent flap, and sure enough there in the corner a big black insulated cooler was perched with a spigot on the bottom, a stack of Styrofoam cups balanced on top.

He went over to it, filled two cups, and was just reaching out to hand Barry one when the man stood, looking at his phone.

"Where's Winspear," he said.

Jack looked back toward the tent flap.

"He left just before I—"

Jack's phone was ringing. He put the cups down, fumbling for it, seeing that Roy was tapping away at his own rectangle of glass, pulling up a video and turning it sideways.

"A link just went out from his account, on Twitter."

"To what?" Jack asked, pulling his phone up.

But Roy was already turning his toward him, both of them looking down at the dark, grainy video feed. It seemed to be showing some kind of tower, a wide path of brickwork in front of an old building.

"From his account," Jack said, "just now?"

Roy nodded. As they watched, a figure entered the frame, the video showing the man from above.

"A security camera somewhere," Roy said, "maybe a web-cam. Where's Bowers?"

"Washington," Jack answered, "with Kay and—"

"Get him on the phone. Something's happening."

14

Kay had taken a seat in the room with the other Bowers & Associates analysts. With a phone and a borrowed laptop, she'd been able to log into all her main work accounts and get things started.

At this point, the market was closed for the day, but there were alarming rumors all over the news of huge aftermarket moves made by big players. Kay and her people knew the rumors were true, because some of those moves were Nine Muses Capital liquidating positions to generate the massive pile of cash they'd need.

Kay was on a call, the last on her list, when she saw Bowers talking quickly and quietly on his phone. As he spoke, he looked over his shoulder and got up, and Kay saw from the look on his face that something serious was happening.

He made for the back of the room, and Kay hung up her own phone and followed to the conference room. Inside, she saw he was working at the projector, and a voice was coming from the speakerphone. It was a voice she recognized. Jack's.

"—idea who has access to this or who would possibly be able to do it… or *why*."

Bowers said, "We're watching it here too. Do we know anything about the feed? Is Winspear there or—"

"We can't find him, nobody here can find him."

The projector threw up a dark image, a spire of some kind, centered in a circle. A fountain, Kay realized, the angle of the image from somewhere above and to the side. Behind the spire in the center of the fountain, an old stately building filled the background.

"It's a webcam," a voice from the other end of the speakerphone said.

"Jack?" Kay asked.

"Kay?" came his reply. "Are you seeing this?"

"Yes. What am I looking at?"

"This was tweeted from the POTUS account a few minutes ago," Bowers said. "It's a live feed from somewhere."

"The link's been shortened," another voice from Jacks' side of the phone said.

"That's Roy Berry talking," Bowers explained to Kay. "Roy what do you mean about the link?"

"I can trace it back," Berry said, then there was a pause. "It's a live webcam on some university campus somewhere. "

"Where?"

"I've got it, one second. Description of the webcam has it called out as the Fulbright Peace Fountain, University of Kansas."

"Arkansas," Kay corrected.

"Shit, you're right," Berry said, "I misread... but how did you know—"

"Because that's where Quentin Daniels is. Jack, you left him a message earlier?"

"Yeah, but I don't know if he read it."

"This doesn't make any sense," Bowers said. "Why would—"

"You'd better get someone there, now," Roy said, his voice urgent even through the speakerphone. "Someone's about to send a message."

"Jack, can you get him on the phone?" Kay said. "I'll try to call him too."

"Quentin?" Bowers asked, and she nodded, working at her phone, pulling it up to her ear and listening to it ring as she saw the small male figure on the video moving slowly, taking a seat at the rim of rockwork around the fountain.

"*C'mon,*" she said under her breath.

15

Quentin had enjoyed his walk around the far side of campus.

The Peace Fountain was situated between the architecture building and the campus's *original* building, Old Main. He was on the side of Old Main opposite the fountain, looking up at the looming clock tower turrets to either side, taking it all in.

It was mostly dark, with just a hint of twilight peaking over the horizon at his back, and the city was quiet. It always was with the students gone, but especially here in front of Old Main the air seemed too still. Too quiet.

It was a beautiful building, all hard brickwork and stone that marked it as pre-Civil War. He wondered at that—despite all the trivia he picked up from working on campus, Quentin didn't know when exactly it had been built.

As he walked in front of the entrance, Quentin looked down to where the first graduate's names had been enshrined in the sidewalk. That was the tradition at the university. The names of everyone who earned a degree there were cut into the sidewalks so that wherever you walked around campus, the years of achievement literally paved your way. Now, a typical yearly enrollment was something like 25,000, but the first list of names out front of Old Main was only seven long, the graduating class of 1876.

A few years were skipped, the early days of matriculation still finding their rhythm presumably, and the next entry was dated 1880. Also just seven names long. There was a crucial difference here though—a crack that cut through the names. The concrete was split, a violent lightning bolt of black cut through the graduating class of 1880, may they rest in peace. As his eyes fell on this slab in the darkness, Quentin remembered another bit of university trivia: This whole class, as the story went, had been *cursed*.

It was silly, he knew. Probably just a story that started out with a grain of truth somewhere but, over time, was issued the license to become myth. The class of 1880 had all died violent deaths at young ages, shortly after graduating. The crack was often cited as the proof of this local urban legend, and so it had become a kind of in-joke to make a show of avoiding it. Tour guides still directed prospective students and their visiting families to step around that section of the sidewalk, relaying the grim backstory as a charming anecdote, playing up the history of the place.

Quentin was looking down at this, lost in thought, when his phone buzzed in his pocket. He lifted it out, and didn't recognize the number. He silenced it, checking the clock. He had only a few minutes until the meeting.

He stepped squarely on the crack as he tapped at his phone, finding the voice recording app and silencing another call from another unknown number, making his way around the side of the building.

Thinking about the sudden rush of calls, he sighed. He suspected his new number had leaked somehow, and he was going to have to change it again. But he could figure that out later.

He came around the corner, the Peace fountain coming into view, and he saw a dark figure waiting at the base, sitting on the stone wall.

He waved in the figure's direction, and the man waved back. The fountain was quiet behind the man—drained for winter—but the lights illuminating the elegant spire in its center drew the figure at the base in silhouette. Quentin could almost see his face.

"Well, I see you found the place all right," Quentin said in the man's direction, only a couple yards away.

His phone was buzzing again, and he fished it out of his pocket as he closed the distance. This time it was a text, and he stopped short as the phone scanned him, unlocked, and the message unfolded for him to read.

"This is Kay. Get away from campus. Run."

The man closed the distance to Quentin fast. Quentin glanced up, stunned, a deer in the headlights. By the time he'd dropped the phone and turned to run, the man already had an arm around him, pulling him close, pulling him onto the knife.

Quentin tried to speak, but already he could taste blood in his mouth. Then the man who'd stabbed him took a step back, and Quentin recognized him.

It was the same man he'd seen on Kelley Oakley's stream weeks before. The one who'd tried to kill Kay and Jack. The one who'd *escaped*.

The manhunt on the news... Quentin realized in an instant how stupid he'd been to come alone, but it was too late. Duncan McAvoy smiled as he stepped forward and stabbed Quentin again and again, until he fell back, hitting the carved sidewalk hard.

Before Quentin even knew what had happened McAvoy was gone, lost in the shadows like a ghost. In fact, it had been so quick that scarcely anything could be said to have happened at all. The trees swayed, a few dead leaves made a run across the sidewalk in a silent, mad dash from shadow to shadow, and all was quiet save for the sound of thunder somewhere in the distance, a muffled battering at the very edge of hearing. In the scary-real moment of adrenaline surge, that sound played against another for Quentin: a rasping, gurgling noise that, after a moment, he realized was coming from his throat.

He tried to breathe, but he was already dead. He knew that. By God, he wasn't a doctor but he could feel something too wrong to come back from in his chest and in his stomach. Lying there on the sidewalk, Quentin reached toward his mid-section as if daring reality to confirm that this wasn't a night-mare, that the holes he felt were really there. And of course they were. That was it; he let his hand drop, fingertips warm from the blood but instantly cold in the night air.

The thunder kept on in the distance, but here and now the sky was clear, and Quentin stared up at the stars. Steam rose from the puddle of blood that was slowly spreading around him. There were names in the sidewalk here too, and as the blood spread, it seeped into them, filling the names of grad-uates past and tracing through every void and crack along the way. And then, for Quentin, it was over.

Part 2—A Castled King

"After the auction, I went and browbeat the guy who'd been running up the price against me into telling me who was on the other end of the phone. Who the hell else wanted to buy the wasteland that FedEx's Memphis hub had become after the oil crash. It was a classically bad investment, something that only a person as crazy as me would think he could do something with. I had to know who else was on the scent, and why, and that's how I met Clayton Scarly."

—Excerpt from *The First Trillion's the Hardest*,
by J. Woolston Winspear

16

Tarrah Adler clicked the play button again, leaning in close, watching Quentin Daniel's murder on the screen for the dozenth time. She pulled on her cigarette, and finding it was burnt to the hilt she stubbed it out in a stained crystal ashtray, hardly taking her eyes from the screen.

That was Duncan McAvoy all right, and Tarrah had the slightest fear that she might be on his list too. But there were a couple reasons she could push that thought out of her mind. First, she was still working in secret. There was no reason to think she'd be a target yet. Second, if McAvoy had been in Arkansas an hour and a half ago, killing Quentin Daniels, then she had nothing to worry about tucked into the basement of a building that was ten blocks from the White House.

The once white brick building, located on 4th Street across from the National Building Museum, took up the entire block. Now, edging toward the middle of the night, Adler was one of the few people here, and she was the *only* one here who didn't have a badge that said "Federal Bureau of Investigation" on it.

In a borrowed room and working on borrowed time, Adler tried to understand how this new development—the tweet, the murder, the resurgence of Duncan McAvoy—could help her case.

She lit another cigarette, thinking. As she breathed it in, there were two sounds in the quiet: the gentle hiss of the cigarette burning down, and of course the clicking.

Steady as a clock, the tick, tick, tick of her heart went on, smoothed over by the nicotine.

Tarrah had stopped smoking several times, but that was before the debacle of the Winspear administration. The takeover of this, the greatest country in the world, by some robber-baron thug.

The doctor had told her it was bad, obviously, that the smoking would probably kill her eventually, especially considering her condition. That didn't make much sense to Tarrah Adler, though. After all, the Cryolife On-X valve they'd installed into her heart was there because her bum aortic valve couldn't do the job properly. At least not with the damage it'd sustained. She failed to see how smoking would complicate things at this point. The way she saw it, she'd "already died once anyways."

It was a cheeky response, one that had made the doctor sigh as he scribbled something down in his notes. Adler had been mostly joking when she'd made the comment, recovering in a hospital from the surgery, but the doctor gave her a look that said he didn't think it was funny at all.

"Well, listen," she said. "I'll try to quit then. I may even try hard."

Still nothing from the doctor, who was finishing with his clipboard.

"We'd like to keep you one more night," he'd said, finally looking up at her, "for observation. Everything should be fine, but—"

"Listen if I'm meant to be here overnight, you'll have to do something about that clock in the hallway."

"Clock?" The doctor furrowed his brow at her.

"Yeah, the clock ticking away out there. Surely you can hear it."

The doctor smiled.

"That's you, MS. Adler. The valve." She stared at him, her lips parting a little. "Nobody told you. The On-X valve we put

110

in opens and closes with every beat, and if you listen close-ly—"

He came toward her, leaning down, closing his eyes and listening at her chest in a way that, honestly, freaked her the hell out.

"Okay fine," she said. "Jesus. Will it ever quiet down?"

"Oh sure," the doctor said, "but not for a while. It'll be tick, tick, tick, right to the end. *Then* it'll stop. And if you keep *smoking* it'll stop even sooner."

"Ha ha ha," she said sarcastically.

"You'll get used to it," the doctor said, and then he turned to leave.

But she didn't get used to it. She tossed and turned all that first night. And she'd woken up from it every so often since then. The clicking. The faint tick of her heart, always there. It reminded her of that damned Poe poem they'd read in school, where the bird just says over and over and over again, "Nevermore. Nevermore." God knows why—she'd hardly thought of the poem since then—but that clicking valve, the unstoppable nature of it, the unrelentingness of it, something about it unnerved her.

Sometimes it was comforting. She hadn't *gotten used to it*, as the doctor put it, but the sound had grown on her. It had become a kind of companion. "Tick, tick, tick, right to the end." A reminder that she was still alive and wrapped up in that, the memory of almost dying. Of the world closing up into blackness around her and knowing this was the end but waking up in that hospital bed with a doctor that had no sense of humor telling her she couldn't smoke anymore.

The valve clicked away. Tick, tick, tick, as she looked around the small room, which was decorated (if you could use such a word) sparsely: an aging desk, a nearly obsolete laptop, and an ancient TV. Most of the working surfaces were piled with documents. As Tarrah leaned back, cigarette in one hand and the other crossed over her chest, she did a mental tally of the evidence she'd put together so far. Evidence to help make the case for impeachment.

The letter of the law was clear. Article 2 Section 4 of the United States Constitution declared that the grounds for impeachment were "treason, bribery, or other high crimes and misdemeanors," and to Adler that was three boxes checked.

One desk chair in the corner was stacked high with bank statements and signed confessions, proof of bribes accepted so cavalierly, laundered through Scarly and the various Winspear corporations, that it would be laughable to try to defend against them.

Her leather briefcase overflowed with sheaves of paper, her supporting documents for the charge of treason. In this case, emails and handwritten letters from dozens of foreign policy experts weighing in that Winspear's actions—his routine dismissal of foreign countries and casual insults which undermined decades of diplomacy—were not just evidence of bad character and lack of good faith, but something systemic. Even though it was a stretch, at this point they were all willing to say whatever it took to get him out of office, and in this case that meant accusing him of intentionally degrading the name of the United States abroad. Treason.

And as for Article 2 Section 4's third category, high crimes and misdemeanors, Adler had been waiting for the perfect entry here. Sure, what happened with NEXT Auto would count, but she could see the writing on the wall there: They were going to pin that whole thing on Scarly. But this, intimidating your enemies by coordinating the public murder of one of them… it was almost unthinkable.

And in that way, Winspear was actually staying true to form. He'd done the unthinkable for years, something he was happy to boast about in his book, which Adler had read and reread as part of her investigation. She looked at the book, the creased cover staring up at her from next to the ashtray, Winspear's face beaming on the cover.

Using the presidential tweet to intimidate your enemies…

that was enough. This was what she'd been waiting for. If that wasn't abusing the "high office" of the presidency—access to the POTUS Twitter account—then Adler didn't know what was.

She stubbed out the cigarette and got up, heading for the bathroom. Down the concrete hall, through dim light, she could hear the clicking as she stepped inside and splashed water on her face. As she looked in the mirror, the clicking sped up.

She was breathing hard, she realized, with the excitement, the thrill of it coming together. She looked tired, the light of the place not doing anything for the constellation of wrinkles that had started to trace themselves across her face a few years ago. She'd been wearing the same shirt for days. She'd been lost in the work, a state that to Adler was normal. One that her therapist had discouraged her from indulging in too much. *It wasn't healthy*, she'd said, but after a few sessions she'd understood: the work was all Adler had.

She stood up straight, drying her face. As she tucked her hair back into place—she'd worn it in a dark crown braid for as long as she could remember, low maintenance—she saw someone else looking back at her.

It was the familiar shadow of her father, which had shown more and more in her as age did its work. She wished he could be here. Out of habit, she reached down to her hip, feeling the heavy steel of the revolver that he'd handed down to her along with the hope that she'd never have to use it. His service weapon before he'd retired from the FBI.

The same gun, actually, that had belonged to her grandpa. He'd been a Texas Ranger before raising his son at the prison he'd worked at as warden in his twilight years.

It was a line of lawmen that had inexplicably found a law-*woman* at its terminus, the same tool riding on the hip of each of them.

She didn't like guns and never had, but from a young age she remembered the story her father had told, about how when he was being raised at that prison—back then the warden and his family lived on site—Tarrah's grandfather had once sentenced a man to hang. And as the other prisoners worked on building the gallows, Grandpa Adler had sent his son out to help. Tarrah's father had hammered nails into the structure himself and put the planks down that would be part of the trap door. Grandpa Adler had also made Tarrah's father watch when it happened.

"Do you know why Grandpa did that? What he taught me that day?"

This had been just after Tarrah told him that she wanted to join the FBI too. A lifetime ago. Well before the clicking.

"What you have to know is that, to destroy a man is terrible. But sometimes it is necessary."

Tarrah had never used the revolver. Not once. But she always kept it with her, and she was always prepared to use it if she had to. She wouldn't hesitate to destroy a man, if it was necessary.

And now, the clip of Quentin's death playing over in her head again, she knew it was necessary.

When she got back to the office, she picked up her phone and dialed the deputy attorney general.

The *deputy* attorney general, who had asked her to conduct this investigation months ago, doubting that his superior, the attorney general, ever would. The deputy AG had also asked her to do the investigation in secret. They wouldn't announce the appointment of a special prosecutor until the evidence was already gathered and ready. And then they'd present it to the House, right out in the open.

It was a request Adler couldn't have turned down. She'd retired from the Bureau four years ago, but there were some things you came back for. Some jobs too important not to do.

Adler was the perfect choice. She'd made a name for herself ferreting out political corruption. It was on a much smaller scale then, the offenses so trivial compared to the stranger-than-fiction current events that she remembered them with something almost like nostalgia.

Twenty years ago, when Winspear was not yet a household name, Adler had worked with a Texas senator to infiltrate a group of representatives in the House who were recorded taking bribes to change their votes on key bills. Fourteen representatives were impeached and barred from ever holding office again. The trials had been televised, and although she'd preferred to have her name left out of things, once the news stations started referring to the representatives as the *Adler 14,* the moniker stuck. That part—her name—had leaked out from the investigation, but not everything had. There were details of the case, about how what they did almost failed, that never got out. In fact, the only proof of how close it'd been was the constant clicking it had left her with.

It was the middle of the night, but she called anyway, waking the deputy attorney general.

"We're ready," she said to him.

There was no need to explain; like everyone, he'd seen the video of Quentin's murder. All the same, there was a long pause on the end of the phone.

"I'll release a statement tomorrow," the deputy said. "Things will happen very quickly now."

"I know," Adler said.

"Good luck."

She hung up the phone and reached for the laptop, starting the video again. She watched Quentin Daniels stabbed to death, again.

In the dim light of the room, she lit another cigarette and leaned back in her chair. There were two days left in the House's current session. That meant that, no matter what, in 48 hours either the president would be impeached or she would have had failed.

And she liked her odds.

17

Jack hadn't seen Winspear all morning. He looked over his shoulder, afraid that speaking of the devil might have conjured him.

"You still there?" he said into the phone.

"Yeah," Kay said from the other end. "Alone?"

"Alone as I can get without drawing attention around here."

Jack glanced at the military personnel working away in the tent. He'd heard them the night before, coordinating some sort of operation from afar. They'd all seemed on alert and not just because the president's account had tweeted a link to a live murder. Something was going on, but as much as that caught in Jack's mind he didn't have time to worry about it. He and Kay both had much, much bigger problems.

"Did we call this wrong?" she asked.

"I don't know," Jack shook his head, keeping his voice low. "We still don't know anything about Scarly... he's still at the center of this."

"As far as figuring out the truth, you mean?"

"Yeah. I want to ask Winspear about it, but I haven't seen him since last night."

"Even if you had seen him, even if you gave him a chance to explain, what's he going to say? That he didn't know anything about this? That it's more evidence that he's being framed? And we can't disprove that."

"We can if Scarly—"

"We can't if we're *dead*, Jack."

Jack looked over his shoulder at the tent opening again, hoping his nervousness wasn't showing. He hadn't slept most of the night; the video of Quentin being stabbed over and over again playing in his head on a loop.

"It doesn't make sense, Kay. If he was going to kill us—or have us killed—it would have already happened."

"You're sure of it?"

"As sure as I can be."

Kay didn't say anything for a few moments.

"They need me, Jack. I'm wound up in this thing now, with Bowers. At any moment they could decide to, I don't know, have an accident, stage a suicide, anything."

"Well," Jack said, "we have to stay the course. Like you say we're already in too deep. If it's a trap, it's already sprung."

"You should go, get away," Kay said. "If he's going to—"

"No," Jack said, cutting her off. "I have to stay."

"Why? They don't need you to—"

"Because he's going to beat the impeachment, Kay. He's going to get out of this thing unless we do something about it. And then…" He shook his head, thinking though it all. "If we pull out now, we lose. If we stay in this, then there's at least a possibility of success. Of changing something."

"Game theory's easy when you're not the one being stabbed to death," Kay said. "Things are tense here. Something's going on. Something bigger than a murder cover-up. Bigger than NEXT Auto."

"What do you mean?"

"I've signed some NDAs, but have you been watching the news?"

"When I can, yeah—they're saying—" Jack trailed off, as if not saying it out loud might make the looming conflict less real.

"I know what they're saying, and it's true." Kay filled in. "This whole China and Russia thing... it's not just our news raising the volume. It's on Al Jazeera, BBC, Der Spiegel."

Silence from Jack's end of the phone for a moment.

"It can't be a war. Not really. Not like this?"

"Bowers is coming back in," Kay said. "I need to go. Be safe, okay?"

They said goodbye and she hung up first. Jack looked down at his phone. He hadn't known Kay long, but they'd already been through a lot together. And one thing he hadn't seen was her this scared.

Well, he *had* seen her this scared, but only the one time. When Duncan McAvoy had been there with the gun aimed at her daughter.

Whatever she'd seen, whatever she was working on with Bowers, it had her spooked.

He noticed motion in the tent—three soldiers conferring on something at one of their workstations—and wondered if there could be any connection.

This feeling reminded him of that day at LAX, when the information had been coming in too fast for anyone to process. The only thing you could be sure of was that you weren't getting the whole picture and that even the sliver of it you were getting—that was probably wrong too.

"Jack! There you are!"

Winspear stormed into the tent, and Jack hoped he didn't give away his surprise too much as he jumped, almost dropping the phone.

"Ready?"

"For what?"

"We're about to go find Scarly and get you all the answers you want. Are you coming or not?"

Jack nodded, and a few seconds after Winspear turned to leave, he swallowed hard and followed him.

18

"Suppose you'll want to talk about last night," Winspear said, his breath forming a cloud ahead of him that was instantly dashed as he charged toward the front of the warehouse, Jack struggling to keep up.

"I kind of did, yes."

He shouldered past a Secret Service agent who grunted at him.

"I was hacked, Jack. Simple as that."

"Really? You're sure of it? How could someone hack into—"

"Beats me," Winspear said. "Too bad about your friend though."

He looked over at Jack as they walked, closing the distance to the facility fast.

"I mean that, you know. I'm sorry."

"Why would somebody kill him?"

"I don't know, Jack. Nobody does. Well, you know *somebody* does."

"Scarly?"

"Maybe. There's only the one way to find out. Roy, how we comin'?"

The sunken doors of the facility were half cast in the shadow of morning sun. Roy Berry was there, typing away at a laptop that was connected to a panel on the wall through a thick umbilical cable.

"It's done," he said, tearing the cord out from the side of his computer and shrugging his backpack off to stow it.

As the doors opened Jack heard footsteps running up behind them. Up until just then, it had been Winspear, Jack, two Secret Service agents, and Roy. Now, three machine-gun-toting troops ran up.

"Sir," one of them said, and Jack recognized him as one of the men from the tent he'd been in earlier, "we've been ordered to come with you."

Winspear whipped around.

"Ordered? By who?"

"*Whom*," Roy corrected from behind him.

Winspear gave him a look as the troop answered:

"General Mercer."

Jack had heard the name before. National Security Advisor, one that had been spared from the culling when Winspear had taken office. He was widely considered to be the adult in the room when the NSC—the National Security Council—met, and he'd quietly scaled back the numerous global conflicts the United States had been embroiled in for years. This was considered to have been done *despite* the president, not *because of*, the military being one of the last bastions of public trust after decades of the executive branch sliding into routine mediocrity, never missing a chance to meet the public's ever lowering expectations.

"I think the Service will do just fine, boys. You can tell the general that I appreciate his worry, though."

"It's a direct order, sir," the soldier said. "We're not to leave your side."

A moment passed between them as the Secret Service agent nearest Winspear, the soldier addressing him, and finally the president himself held stony stares at one another. Jack had the sense that something was happening. He wondered why Mercer would make such an order, and why it would give

Winspear pause. Extra protection on the president seemed like a good idea, but maybe it was something else.

Winspear seemed to be playing through the same logic in his head.

"So, are you meant to be guarding me? Or taking me into custody?"

"Sir," the soldier started, "General Mercer is concerned for your safety. Nothing more."

"Well, what's got him so spooked?"

"Troop movements, sir, off the coast of Africa."

"Russian?"

The soldier nodded. "And Chinese satellites repositioning in the northern hemisphere."

"Where to?"

"Satellites?" Jack asked, but the troop ignored him.

"Not sure yet. They started seeing propellant bursts yesterday. They're moving them erratically, hiding their final trajectories and calling it a training exercise. When we know where they're headed will give you an update."

"Sir," one of the Secret Service men reached up to his ear, and from the look on his face Jack knew it was more bad news.

Winspear turned to him.

"The attorney general has issued a notice. He's appointed a special prosecutor to investigate you."

"You're mistaken," Winspear said to him. "Tildow would never—"

"Not Tildow, sir," the Secret Service listened at his earpiece for a moment. "Apologies… it appears to have been the *deputy* attorney general, someone called McCauley."

"He can't do that," Winspear said, waving his hand at the idea. "Has Clarence said anything about it? Any statements?"

Jack had heard the first name before. Clarence Tildow. The acting attorney general put in place by Winspear after the election. He had no political experience; in fact, he had no *judicial* experience. He was a Winspear crony, through and through, from back before the oil crash. But for all the names he *did* know, nobody had yet mentioned the one he wanted to know most.

"Wait," Jack cut in, his voice loud enough to not be ignored this time. "Who's the prosecutor?"

"Doesn't matter," Winspear said, turning to enter the facility. "Clarence will shut it down; the deputy AG doesn't have the authority to start an investigation like this."

"Still," Jack said, looking at the Secret Service agent, "who is it?"

"Tarrah Adler."

Winspear stopped in his tracks.

Jack's mouth hung open. *The* Tarrah Adler. He'd read the book years ago, about the Adler 14, the representatives in the House that were purged after an unprecedented sting operation executed by the FBI. In the book, which had come out decades after the event, the story of Adler's work as the inside man—*woman* rather—was made public.

"It *doesn't matter!*" Winspear said, almost snarling at Jack, the anger catching him wholly off guard as Winspear turned and approached him.

Instinctively, Jack backed away, two steps, and then he was against the wall at the entrance of the warehouse.

"Clarence will put this down! Mostly because I want him to, but also because it's *unconstitutional.*"

Winspear pointed a finger at him when he said this, and Jack might have laughed if he wasn't so destabilized by the anger, by the look in Winspear's eye as he went on.

"I know what you think. I know you and Kay and all the others out there judge me. And maybe I should be judged, but ever since I was elected it's been like this. The Shooter Act debacle, your little stunt at LAX, the markets, and now *Russia and China.* Meanwhile I'm being framed for conspiracy to commit murder and God knows what else—*actual* murder, as the events of last night seem to suggest."

Jack hugged the wall, glancing at the Secret Service agents, the soldiers, and Roy—none of them even flinched.

"Do you know what it's like, Paulson? To be the most powerful person in the country and to want to help that country but to be constantly second-guessed, slandered, and have your feeding hand bitten over and over and over again?"

He was trembling with rage, and Jack could see the veins in his eyes.

"I am forever locked in a game of chess against cheaters, spies, and liars, Jack. I'm always in check, with only one move between me and checkmate, so, yes, I play dirty. I hedge my bets. That's what it is to be president… at least in this country. Always in check, always one mistake away from this or that enemy pushing their agenda into your platform. And I've had just about enough of it."

He stopped, almost as suddenly as he'd started, taking a few deep breaths. Composing himself.

He looked around to the others, eyes narrowed, daring any of them to say something else. To light his fuse again.

Jack looked around at them too. Roy met his eyes, then looked away. This was normal to them, calmly and quietly listening as Winspear exploded. They were used to it. This was the Winspear Jack had met at the fireplace two days ago. Unhinged. No Bowers here to calm him down.

"For the record"—he looked at Jack when he said this but looked around at all of them as he continued—"I didn't post that link. I had nothing to do with Daniels's death. Is that clear?"

Nobody said anything for a moment, but Winspear seemed to accept that as a "yes" and turned for the door.

"Come on," he said, and they all fell in step behind him, entering the facility.

Winspear took another deep breath, stilling himself as they walked in.

"This Adler thing is nothing. A fart in the wind."

He shook his head.

"Nothing to worry about at all."

Jack didn't know what he was more afraid of, that Winspear was right or that he was wrong and so hopelessly lost in his delusion that he would never even know it.

19

The news had traveled quickly, but Tarrah Adler was out ahead of it.

Within hours, there were reporters clustered outside her gated home in West Virginia, angling for some kind of statement. But holding the investigation in secret and hiding out in the Capital had been to avoid just such fanfare.

Now, while the press and perhaps Winspear's henchmen tried to track down Adler, she was already in the place they least expected: walking up the clean white steps to the Capitol Building.

The morning light was harsh, the air cold and pulsing with chants of protesters. Adler stopped halfway up the steps to look back at them, hundreds of people crowded around the base of the building, right up to the point where the police had set up metal barricades to block the stairs.

Tarrah thought for a moment. She had dark glasses on and a long dark jacket that she wore with the hood up. She'd been trying to blend into the crowd, but now… well, she was here wasn't she? About to make history.

She went down the steps, toward the protesters, the thrum growing louder as she approached. When she got to the front she lowered her hood.

"Ma'am," one of the policemen said as she approached the barricade.

She waved him off, saying, "It's fine."

She took off the glasses, and the nearest people looked at her, the flash of recognition in their eyes. They stared, a couple of them recognizing her from the pictures that had been flying around all morning since the appointment was announced.

Then they started to point. They turned to each other, and word started to spread through the crowd. The chants fell off into cheering as they realized their champion was here, the woman who was charged with ending Winspear's reign.

Adler smiled wide, waving with a gloved hand, making sure to stay long enough for them to get their pictures and videos.

Pictures and videos, she knew, that would soon be flooding the internet. And that would light a fire under everyone's asses as well as anything would. Not only was the investigation happening, but Adler had already arrived at the House of Representatives to make her case.

It was a tactical move—now the opposition would be scrambling, playing catchup—but it also felt damn good, she had to admit. Nothing like a plan coming together.

After a moment, she turned and climbed up the stairs again. She didn't pause to take in the beautifully tiled floor, moving at once into the cavernous chamber known as the Great Rotunda, over which the domed ceiling arced, skylights casting a glow on the elegant architecture like a living painting.

Adler turned left, heading for the massive doorway off the rotunda that was flanked by two larger-than-life statues.

She was on a mission, the energy rising as she checked her watch again—her aim was to catch the House totally off guard, having prearranged with the minority leader to be introduced at a precise time—but as she neared the doorway she couldn't help but stop and stare at the statues.

George Washington on the right. Thomas Jefferson on the left. Each of them fixed forever in triumphant poses. Legendary symbols of the United States and all it stood for.

Adler was tough, but now, looking up at the statues, the weight of the moment seemed to settle on her. Washington, when he'd had the chance, famously declined to take control of the nation. He could have been king but instead ceded power to the people.

What would he say about Winspear? Adler wondered.

Next to the statue, a group of tourists had shifted their gaze to her. One of them checked their phone, then whispered, "*It's her!*"

Tarrah turned to them, smiled, and nodded.

Then she was off, through the doorway, through Statuary Hall and into the anteroom that opened to the House Reception Room.

"Ma'am, you can't—"

"I think you'll find that the House is expecting me," she told the security guard that had reached a hand out to stop her.

"Name?"

"Tarrah Adler."

The man looked up from his clipboard, eyes wide. After a beat he looked back down to it.

"Right... uh... right this way, Ms. Adler."

She was led to the door that opened to the House chamber, and despite how old-world thick the doors were she could just barely hear what was being said on the other side.

"The House yields to minority leader Burns for five minutes."

That was Speaker of the House Steven Guilfoyle talking, Adler knew. He was solidly in Winspear's pocket, appointed by him and approved by the majority. The *majority* in recent times being short for *pro-Winspear majority*, rather than any specific political party. Guilfoyle would never have yielded the floor to Burns if he'd known what was going to happen next.

"And I," Burns started, "yield my time to the esteemed special prosecutor"—*showtime*, she thought, opening the door wide—"Tarrah Adler."

The room erupted as Adler stormed down the stairs, moving with purpose to the front of the room. The pro-Winspear majority were standing, shouting dissent, and Guilfoyle was already banging his gavel.

"I think you'll find"—Burns was standing on his side of the room, among the pro-impeachment minority members, trying to shout over the din—"I think you'll find that this is well within the rules, Mr. Speaker!"

Adler had made it to the foot of the room, and she looked up at Guilfoyle. They locked eyes, both of them knowing that this was the start, that what happened now would be either the capturing of the country by a warlord or the execution of constitutional checks and balances.

"Order!" Guilfoyle shouted, slamming his gavel.

The room quieted down, though there was a dull background hum of camera shutters and quick, hushed words as the press in the upper wings scrambled to get their shots.

"Mr. Speaker," the pro-Winspear majority leader, Jennings Clearwater, stood on the right side of the room, but Burns cut him off before he could say anything else, yelling:

"The speaker has already yielded the floor, Mr. Clearwater, you are speaking out of turn!"

"Representative Burns," Guilfoyle started, still staring daggers down at Tarrah, "what is the purpose of your ceding the floor to someone who is not acting on the behalf of the American people?"

It was a wordy question, but on purpose. Stalling. None of this surprised Adler.

Burns scoffed.

"I should think that obvious, Mr. Speaker. Though the special prosecutor is not a member of the House, it is my belief that the best representation of the members of my district can be effected by using my time to allow Ms. Adler to make her case."

"Her case for what, exactly?" Guilfoyle asked.

"For the impeachment of President J. Woolston Winspear."

The room erupted again, and Adler couldn't help but think about what this looked like on C-SPAN's stream, half of the US legislative body losing its mind.

"Order!" Guilfoyle shouted again, slamming his gavel and trying to quiet the room.

On his side, majority leader Clearwater was whispering away with several other pro-Winspear members, and suddenly he spoke up again.

"Mr. Chairmen, I ask unanimous consent to speak out of order."

"If the gentleman from California thinks that he will achieve a unanimous vote," Burns said, referring to Jennings but addressing Speaker of the House Guilfoyle, "then he is sorely mistaken."

"You'll want to hear this too," Clearwater said, breaching decorum and shouting this like a taunt at Burns.

"The gentleman from California, Mr. Clearwater, will explain the nature of his request further…"

Burns opened his mouth to protest, but Guilfoyle put a hand up.

"… *with the understanding* that Mr. Burns' time will be re-allotted to him afterward. The gentleman from California has the floor for one minute."

Adler looked over her shoulder as Clearwater conspired in low tones with the handful of men that had clustered around him.

He looked up and said: "Neither I nor anyone in this chamber would protest the presentation by a special prosecutor, but allowing Ms. Adler to speak in this station would be a breach of constitutional order inasmuch as she has not *been named* a special prosecutor."

"Mr. Clearwater!" Burns started, but Guilfoyle slammed his gavel down.

"We have here—" one of the majority members handed Clearwater a piece of paper, and he held it up so everyone could see. The printout had been delivered only seconds before by a runner. "—a notice from Attorney General Tildow that the actions of his deputy were not authorized, hence there is no special prosecutor and no investigation."

The fact that the special prosecutor leading that investigation was in the room, was irrelevant.

"What's more, Mr. Tildow has offered to come and address this body on the matter at once... I yield to the gentleman from Maine," referring to minority leader Burns.

The room mumbled about this, not as passionate as before but still alarmed at the sudden turn of events.

Guilfoyle swung the gavel down.

"Mr. Burns, you will have the floor for the remainder of the time you were granted"—the room held its breath, sensing a *but*—"after a brief recess and an opportunity for Attorney General Tildow to comment on—"

Whatever he said next was lost in the uproar of the hundreds of representatives standing, shouting, and turning for the doors.

Adler, through all of this, had stood quietly at the foot of the room. She'd expected it all. As Guilfoyle sat down, locking eyes with her, he smiled. The first salvo had been fired, but Adler knew she had two days. And she had faith that the minority leader and his party would find a way for her to present the findings from the investigation and ultimately to push a vote on impeachment.

20

Roy Berry nudged Jack and motioned toward his phone, where a live feed of C-SPAN showed Tarrah Adler storming the room.

"Turn that off," Winspear said, passing them, moving toward one of the small chairs in the space and taking a seat.

Winspear had insisted they stop by the building's cafeteria shortly after they entered. It was near the front, and although most of it had been walled off as if for construction, there was a coffee station with all the trappings tucked into one corner. One of the Secret Service agents stepped up to it and went to work, and Jack couldn't help but smile and shake his head a little at the man's unironic sense of civic duty, even for a man such as Winspear.

Not for the first time, he wondered if it was just that—civic duty—or something else that kept these men at Winspear's beck and call despite everything. Was it just the power that left them wiped of personal preference, like a magnet wiping clean a computer's hard disk? Maybe it was blind service?

But Jack had felt something else in the way they deferred. In the way they seemed to be drawn to Winspear, to focus on him, not just his protection, but his atmosphere. His implicit wants and needs, the coffee sputtering out cleanly, the steam from the machine rising into the darkness above like the drawn spirit of the machine itself.

"Sir," the agent said, and Winspear came over to him, taking the cup, giving the man a nod, and something in the way it happened gave Jack the feel that the man—these men—they had the sense of true believers about them. Like the orbited Winspear not out of the gravitational pull of power or duty, but like they were the honor guard of a prophet who was soon to be martyred.

Why? What did they know that Jack didn't?

Now, Winspear said, "Come on; we've got a job to do here," as he sipped from his cup.

They headed back toward the main entryway before turning down a long, wide hallway that housed a strip of dusty workstations.

There were windows here letting in the foggy light, and Jack could see that workstations were situated every eight feet or so, in a line that stretched a few hundred yards. They were standing desks of a sort, with geriatric screens hanging long dormant at eye level. He thought they looked like grocery checkout stations at first, but there were no conveyor belts.

As the group walked toward the empty workstations, Winspear looked over at Jack and saw him taking it in.

"Old pick and pack setups," he said, "where loaders would put items into boxes."

"Really," Jack said, "all day? They'd stand here loading items?"

"Oh yes," Winspear replied, sipping from his drink as they passed into a dimly lit area a few yards behind the stations. "All night too."

"How would they get the packages?" Jack asked, and as if to answer his question a faint whine grew from behind him, peaking just as he turned his head and jumped back.

He felt the air flow of the drone on his face and briefly saw the LED running lights as it dashed forward, disappearing around a corner in the middle distance like some tiny alien spacecraft.

"Robots," Winspear said, "of course."

"They'd bring the packages here?"

"In the early days," Winspear said, nodding, "when shipping was done mostly in cardboard."

"Pickers would load the boxes," Roy said, "and the shelf with the right item would bring it up to the station."

"The whole shelf?" Jack asked. "They *move?*"

"Of course. That's what the lifter bots are for," Winspear said.

"You'll see," Roy said. "The shop is just up ahead, or used to be."

They neared the corner the drone had disappeared around and came to a room that was dark but humming with activity.

In the dim light from the hallway they were coming off of, Jack could make out the hints of rapid, precise motion ahead. Bright pinpricks of LED light moved to and fro, weaving through the space like fireflies in a bottle. A bottle that went on for a very long way, Jack saw, as the dots of LED flowed away from them, eventually growing too faint to see.

Jack was aware, after a second, that the hum of sound had a mechanic nature to it. Dozens—hundreds perhaps—of rotors spinning, mechanical motors whirring, and metal contacting metal.

"Where are the lights?" Winspear asked.

"Dunno," Roy said. "Ought to be smartmotion sensors right—yeah here it is."

Jack saw him reach toward something at the wall.

"Weird," he said. "The sensors ought to 'ave picked us out as human. No big deal, I can—"

He did something and suddenly a swath of the room about fifteen feet on a side was awash in white LED light from above.

Jack's mouth dropped open as the elaborate scramble of machinery was revealed ahead of them.

Huge red-painted pieces of equipment—arm-like with their double joints—swung around in all directions, rotating, elongating, and manipulating.

Drones barrel-rolled and dove in and out of the cacophony, some dodging the arms with elegant precision and swooping down to deliver a part to an articulated gripping attachment. Others perched upside down like bats on a grid work of conduit that laced the ceiling. Still more racing through, purpose unknown.

Below the manipulator arms, in some cases held and spun within their grasp, were round-cornered rectangles of dense equipment painted orange. They were all over the place, Jack saw, in various states of disassembly, roughly three feet on a side and one foot deep and all of them with wheels and pockmarked with dings and scratches that came dangerously close to their optics units. These, Jack understood, were the so-called *lifters* that moved the shelves to and fro.

Umbilical cables whipped around behind tool heads that were being wielded by the manipulator arms. The arms, in turn, were using them to drill, screw, weld, and otherwise manage whatever was caught in their automated clutches. All of it in precise lockstep. All of it only feet away but stretching into the darkness beyond, where the lights hadn't been triggered but the odd drone light or glow from an unknown source danced like fireworks peeking over a distant, shifting treeline.

Jack could see the machines were all packed in far too tightly for the men to make it through without being hit by this or that manipulator arm.

"How are we supposed to get through that," he asked.

"We don't," Winspear said. "We go around."

And he started off against the wall to their left, the lights clicking on just ahead of him as the whole retinue followed in more or less single file. Jack hugged the wall especially close, and Roy explained:

"When we moved to not having people in the shop, it didn't make sense to not make the most of the space anymore and pack the bots in tight. No need to leave room for humans."

Jack was in the middle of the group. As he listened, he craned his neck to look past Winspear to the darkness ahead, where there was no end in sight.

"How big is it?" he asked.

"Don't know," Roy said, "but it's bigger, don't you think?"

He'd asked the question ahead, toward Winspear.

"*Much* bigger," Winspear said, drinking his coffee.

They kept walking, all the while Jack becoming more amazed at the scale of the place. It was two, no, more likely *three* football fields long, never mind how far across.

"What's all this for?" he asked at one point. "What does it all *do*?"

"What do you mean?" Roy asked. "It services the factory. All the lifters, drones, packers—all of it has to be serviced eventually." He shrugged. "They're just keeping up preventative maintenance."

"Who services the manipulating arms?"

Winspear laughed from the head of their troop.

"Who do you think? It sure as hell isn't me or Roy. I don't think Scarly's been down here."

Jack looked at the sea of deliberately moving machinery, realizing the only other alternative.

"The arms… they're packed close enough to reach each other."

"Very good," Roy said. "They service each other. Pretty kinky, right?"

Jack furrowed his brow and kept walking, the Secret Service agents and military personnel keeping largely to themselves, likely subvocalizing their own commentary through earpieces and bone conduction mics.

"And you don't know how big it is?" Jack asked.

"Well, not exactly," Roy said. "I know how big it was when I was here. I can look it up."

"It's the biggest warehouse in the world," Winspear said.

"What do you mean you don't know how big it is?" Jack was getting annoyed, it seemed like they were just dodging the question, but the bots servicing themselves gave him another idea. "Surely it doesn't *build itself?*"

"Bingo!" Winspear said. "Flex capacity. It can grow and shrink. Add shelves, remove them, whatever's needed to meet the demand. This being the headquarters for the whole company and also the central hub, it tends to average out as the largest facility by a few magnitudes."

"Although," Roy cut in, "supplies and resources are constantly being traded by the other facilities."

"Traded?" Jack asked.

"Sure," Roy said. "An internal market, dealt with through a points bidding system. Whichever storage facility needs the space most bids on it. If it needs it remotely, it gets a share here; this facility expands accordingly. If it needs it locally, then the warehouse," he waved to the passing sea of machines, "exports the expansion materials and builder-bots there."

"That's…" Jack started, shaking his head. He didn't know if the next word should be *insane* or *incredible*.

"This is where the sausage is made, Jack," Winspear said as they approached the end of the shop. "This is how Winspear Shipping can get any physical commodity anywhere in the United States in one day."

"And often less than twelve hours," Roy said in a mock-cheerful voice, falling easily back into the company shtick.

"Just in time shipping that guesstimates, automates, and fluctuates its way to having your toothbrush or whatever on the way less than a second after you hit the purchase button."

"And sometimes *before* you hit the purchase button," Roy added, "since a person is really just a shitty program with predictable inputs."

Several of the agents laughed at this, along with Winspear, who said, "You know that's why I hired you, Roy."

"Why's that?"

"Your optimistic view of humanity."

More sniggering from the agents.

"You're so bright and cheery you could be your own sun."

"That's me," he said.

Jack didn't look but he could almost hear Roy's smile at the comment.

"It really is impressive," Jack said.

"Damn straight," Winspear said approvingly. "It ships anywhere in the US in a day, most of the time the same day or if it's in stock, same hour. Shenzhen to New York in 53 hours. All this"—he waved a hand out over the space—"is what net-positive shipping looks like."

Jack had heard the term *net-positive shipping*. That was Winspear's great workhorse of an idea, though Jack had never been interested enough to look up how exactly it all worked. Before he had a chance to ask one of the Secret Service agents piped in:

"Sir, we're losing cell signal."

"Us too," one of the troops added.

"Yup," Roy nodded, "that'll happen. Lots of ways for a signal to get disrupted in this."

He looked out over the bots.

"No people," he said in what was becoming a sort of recurring mantra at this point. "No reason to install cell boosters. All these puppies mesh together, so they don't need it."

They'd reached the edge of the shop, where a narrow metal door stretched up to the ceiling.

"First stage storage is up ahead," Roy said. "Jack, if you think this is cool you're gonna love the next bit."

Winspear pressed through the door, and Roy followed. Then they all spilled out into a space that was almost claustrophobically full.

In all directions, left, right, and ahead, Jack could see nothing but neat lines of shelves eight feet high, three feet on a side. They were packed in tightly for the most part, the occasional gap of a foot or so opening between some of them.

As Jack watched one of these gaps about 15 feet away, he saw it disappearing—closing up as the shelves moved together, the lifters below orchestrating them in a synchronized industrial dance.

Straight ahead, he could see down the narrow gap, a few inches between two of the rows of shelves, and he could see they stretched literally as far as the eye could see.

"Sorry it's so cramped," Roy said. "No—"

"No people," Jack finished. "I get it."

"Where are we?" Winspear asked.

"Beats me," Roy said, shrugging. "This whole place has shifted. The shop was at least three times as big as I remember."

Winspear grunted, "Can we find Scarly in this?"

"Sure," Roy said. "Just have to hope the main office is still where it was a few years ago."

Winspear looked down the column of shelves ahead of them. Just then a drone hurtled out from the gap and swung over their heads and away, ducking through a chute near the ceiling that was sized perfectly for it plus the medium sized plastic container it was toting. Jack watched as the column that the drone had flown down closed up slowly, all of the shelves moving in sync, a whole chunk of them, actually, shifting over to close the gap here and open one somewhere else for some unseen purpose.

"And do we know where the main office is?" asked Winspear.

He looked at Roy.

"More or less," he said, grinning. "Let's, uh, go this way."

And with that, he turned right and started walking.

Winspear and Jack traded a look, and Winspear gestured for Jack to go first. Then it was Roy leading them down the narrow gap against the wall, and then, too quickly for Jack to protest, into one of the open columns between the moving shelves.

"Don't worry," he said. "They won't close up when we're between them."

"How do you know?" Jack asked.

"Well, they can *see* us."

For some reason, that didn't make Jack feel any better.

21

Tarrah Adler had settled in for the performance. She'd left the House chamber along with everyone else during the recess. Gotten a cup of coffee. Seen some of the sights, the statues. She tried not to worry that she was on the wrong end of the most powerful man in the world.

The crowd had grown outside, from hundreds to nearly a thousand and still more piling in all the time. They'd closed off the metal barricade and asked the tourists to leave, so Tarrah had the place more or less to herself.

Now, as she moved through the rotunda, a cluster of representatives looked at her and stopped talking. They gave her a polite nod. She didn't need to hear what they were saying to know what was happening. The lines had already been drawn, pro-Winspear and pro-impeachment, each with their associated leaders and main actors ready to play their parts.

The speaker of the house—Steven Guilfoyle—would do everything he could to stop the vote. A Winspear loyalist through and through, his job depended on it.

Then there was the pro-Winspear majority leader, Jennings Clearwater, who'd back up Guilfoyle no matter the cost. Adler had no doubt the two would work together to exploit any and all arcane rules they could to prevent the impeachment vote.

The entire pro-Winspear side, having shown their hand by supporting Winspear when his public approval rating was solidly down around his ankles, knew they'd be out of office at the next election.

And because their reputations were now a sunk cost, their only option was to double down and keep Winspear in power. Otherwise they'd just ransacked their own future careers for nothing. So, they were playing a game for one year of unlimited power—the rest of Winspear's term—in which they could push through whatever rules made them richest before their certain ejection from politics.

That ejection, moreover, would no doubt come along with Winspear's if a round of follow-up impeachments of representatives (already being planned in grass roots movements) went through. If they didn't stop the vote, they all knew they would be forced to flee politics with whatever they could sweep into their briefcases. It would be either boom or bust, and they weren't people used to busting.

On the other side of all this was the pro-impeachment minority. The underdog heroes, as they were already being cast in the media drama that had blown the entire episode up from dime-store thriller to sea-change revolution of the country and thus the world.

Heading the charge was the minority leader, Jim Burns. A name nobody knew or cared to know 24 hours ago but who now was saddled as the chain breaker, the inside man, the last good politician fighting for the people with his ragtag band of political minutemen.

It was total war, with no option for compromise on either side, and the technology with which it was to be waged was the Constitution, a centuries-old set of rules that could never have foreseen this eventuality.

And Tarrah Adler as special prosecutor was part of the armament with which the war would be fought.

Now, as the chamber came back to order, she watched from the back of the room as a new chess piece moved onto the board. Winspear's attorney general, Clarence Tildow, began to speak.

"As the good gentlemen and ladies of this body are well aware," Tildow read from a script, looking up at the speaker and over to Burns as he explained his position, "special council regulations within CFR 28 clearly state that the appointment of a general council is a matter to be seen to by the attorney general or acting attorney general, and as I have not recused myself, Deputy General McCauley does not have the constitutional *authority* to appoint a special council *at all.*

"Because of that," he went on, the Matryoshka dolls of logic unpacking back to the initial trigger, "the gentleman from Maine, Mr. Burns' request can be fulfilled by this body—yield him his five minutes—but he cannot substitute for his own time that of a special prosecutor since no such prosecutor exists, and even if one did, the regulations prevent any report from being shared publicly."

There were mumbles in the crowd of representatives. Adler's arms were crossed, and she studied Guilfoyle's face.

"Very well," the speaker said. "You are dismissed, Mr. Tildow. Mr. Burns, you have the floor."

Burns stood up.

"My fellow representatives, these are dark days."

A disparate grumbling rose from the pro-Winspear side.

"Since you will not hear the results of the investigation by Tarrah Adler, it is with some trepidation that I must ask you to enter into debate on the topic of Winspear's impeachment without all the facts known."

Formerly entering into debate would allow Burns to force them all to talk about it, with one hour speaking limits that could be used to run down the clock. Adler understood it would be progress of a sort, but not a final solution.

"I motion that the measure of impeachment be brought up for debate."

The minority whip, seated behind Burns, stood quickly and said, "I second the motion."

On the majority side, several representatives leaned in toward Clearwater, whispering. Guilfoyle looked over at them, and Clearwater glanced up, giving a small nod. Guilfoyle communicated that the debate had begun. The House recognized Mr. Burns, to begin.

"First, I would like permission to submit an exhibit for reference into the debate."

That's clever, thought Adler, a grin starting at one corner of her mouth and edging up. A backup plan. Burns must have expected pushback from the AG.

"What is the nature of your exhibit?" Guilfoyle asked down from the speaker's chair.

"I submit the findings of the informal investigation conducted by Tarrah Adler—"

"Object!"

Clearwater was on his feet, the group around him still talking with each other, one of them poring over and highlighting a document that another was pointing at, no doubt planning their next move.

"I object to the entry of this exhibit into debate!" Clearwater yelled out.

"Very well," Guilfoyle said. "On this matter I rule that the exhibit will be denied."

Adler furrowed her brow. *There goes plan B,* she thought. *It was worth a try.*

Burns looked down at a book of notes he'd been reading from, and Adler wondered what rabbit he was trying to pull out of his hat. But just as he was clearing his throat to speak, Clearwater interjected:

"Mr. Chairmen, permission to speak out of order."

"Very well," Guilfoyle said, smiling, "a vote of unanimity is required to speak out of order, Mr. Clearwater."

"Of course. I motion for an electronic vote on the matter."

Clearwater's majority whip was up in a flash:

"I second the motion."

Adler shook her head as representatives began to mill about, many of them standing, a cluster around and including Burns.

She knew enough from her experience with the sting decades ago to guess what was going on now. One of the only ways Clearwater could interrupt Burns' debate was to ask to speak out of turn. If he was allowed, he would have a maximum of two minutes to do so, but that wasn't the point. A unanimous vote was required for him to speak out of turn, something that would have taken seconds if done vocally, but by requiring an electronic vote, it would take up to 15 minutes—the time limit for electronic voting.

The vote would not be unanimous, and Clearwater would not be allowed to speak out of turn, but that wasn't the point. After Clearwater was denied, another majority member would request to speak out of turn on the same terms. And then the next. They were going to run down the clock 15 minutes at a time.

It was unprecedented, to be certain, but if a majority leader and speaker were colluding, Adler guessed they would be able to pull it off. The entire conflict then shifted its weight to this crack in the foundation of the Constitution.

With a sigh, Adler turned to leave. She hoped Burns would be able to figure out something, but she didn't have to stay here for all the greasy bits. She went out of the chamber and then toward the main entrance, but as she moved back through the Great Rotunda she could hear something. A dull roar, like somewhere in the distance a hundred TV sets were blaring at full volume.

Approaching the doorway, she realized it was the crowd outside, and as she came out of the Capitol Building and saw them from the top of the steps, she stopped, gasping at the sight.

What had been a few thousand protesters earlier had grown to a sea of people as far as the eye could see. Easily ten thousand. Likely more. A viral event that was blowing up in every direction. The sound hit her like a wall. Shouting, a rhythmic chant she couldn't quite make out the words to.

She took a few slow steps down the white stairs, looking over the crowd, shaking her head in disbelief, and then her eyes fell on a group of reporters huddled in a semicircle around Clarence Tildow who was just stepping into place to address them from the steps. Tildow looked down at the crowd, and the reporters aimed their cameras up, smartly framing him against the Capitol Building as a background. Adler guessed he was updating them with a summary of his position and the shutdown of the special-prosecutor maneuver.

Adler started to walk down the stairs at a diagonal, realizing she was in the background of the shot and angling away from them, not wanting to get the press's attention if she didn't absolutely have to. But then something else caught her eye.

At the base of the steps, a pocket of the crowd surged forward. The policemen were sporting riot gear, and the nearest helmeted officers struggled to push the crowd back, to contain them behind the metal railing that had been hefted into place but which now sagged inward.

A handful of protesters, maybe three or four, spilled through.

As if in slow motion, Adler watched an officer tackle one of them, but another slipped past, running up the steps.

She was small. Quick. Jerking her arm free from the policeman trying to hold her back, and as she slipped away Adler saw her take the steps two at time up from the crowd, swinging a maroon backpack off her shoulder and reaching into it.

The reporters heard something, or maybe they just sensed it, but either way, several of them turned, as the girl pulled something out of her bag.

A gun.

Adler's breath caught in her throat, but before anyone could do anything the girl was bringing the gun up. A shot rang out, and Tarrah saw the back of Clarence Tildow's head explode across the steps of the Capitol Building behind him, his body falling like a rag doll as two officers tackled the girl and the cluster of reporters broke up, some of then running away yelling and a few of the more hardcore swinging they're cameras around to catch the action.

22

Duncan McAvoy grunted as they replayed the video. After copious warnings that the feed was "of a graphic nature," the news had gone on to replay the numerous views of Tildow's head exploding again and again and again.

But now, as McAvoy took a drag on his vaporizer—his Aerosolized Chemical Delivery Device, as the doctors put it—his handler reached forward and toggled the video off.

"What do you think?" McAvoy asked the man.

"Well," he said, "it's good for us. Tildow was always going to be a problem. I was ready to deal with him."

McAvoy grunted again, taking another pull on the vaporizer. The mixture, a careful balance of fentanyl and antibiotics, cut with an uncareful balance of opiates, kept the pain at bay. That effect was to fight the unceasing pain from a bullet fragment in his spinal cord. His tolerance was huge—a regular dose for him would kill a normal person in seconds—but he'd been under the spell of the drug for years.

The pain-dulling effect would wear off if he didn't continue taking his medicine. But the *side* effects... those were permanent.

The experimental treatment, signed off on with an "X" by McAvoy when he was stuck in a hospital bed begging for them to kill him, to stop the agony, had since been discontinued by the Department of Defense.

The antibiotic in his mixture, perhaps exacerbated by the fentanyl, caused something that they had labeled "chemically induced psychopathy" before shuttering the program that had dreamed it up.

Of course, all of that was a well-kept secret when McAvoy was appointed the enforcer of the Shooter Act. Secret even from him. Nobody had known how bad it was until he'd gone too far: removing Katelyn Patterson and going after Kay Luo, Jack Paulson, and all the rest that day at LAX.

But McAvoy had made it out of that. He'd done exactly as his handler had instructed. When they had him pinned to the ground, the pain too much, he'd remembered his instructions and named Clayton Scarly as his co-conspirator.

Then he'd escaped, and a long chain of events had led him back to Washington—the belly of the beast—after a brief detour in Arkansas to kill Quentin Daniels.

Yes, the plan was finally coming together. The plan to tank Winspear's presidency and eject him from office. The evidence—Scarly's involvement—had been cleanly planted, and everyone had run with it headlong in the direction that McAvoy's handler had planned.

McAvoy and his handler were meeting in a safe house, and they'd just started to discuss the next steps when Tildow had been shot.

"So?" McAvoy asked his handler.

McAvoy was an asset he'd been working for years. One he'd directed on many operations. Murders, several of which had been hidden under the umbrella of Shooter Act enforcement.

"Ironically, we've just been handed everything we need to finish this," McAvoy's handler said. "Tildow was the only thing standing in the way of Tarrah Adler."

McAvoy grunted, pleased.

"That was nice too. Almost too perfect."

"Yes," his handler agreed. "I had my own plan for the vote, but a special prosecutor coming out of the woodworks with a full investigation ready to go—"

He shook his head.

"Couldn't have made that up."

"You think the vote is a done deal?"

"In the Senate," his handler thought for a moment, "definitely. If we get to an impeachment trial, he's out. We just have to make sure it's triggered—a vote in the House. Guilfoyle will try his best to stop it."

"He's next?"

McAvoy's handler nodded.

"He'll be shaken up by Tildow's exit. Go see him."

"His file?"

His handler nodded again.

"Show him the confession tape we got from what's-her-name. Do your magic."

McAvoy smiled. They both knew the plan. Blackmail, simple and efficient as ever. A certain video that Guilfoyle wouldn't want to get out. A certain vote he could shift in the right direction.

"And be sure," his handler said, "he knows we'll send it directly to his wife and children first."

McAvoy said, "Should we celebrate?"

"I suppose there's time for a drink," his handler said, "but we're not out of the woods yet. When the vote's in. There's still cleanup to do."

"Jack Paulson?" McAvoy asked.

His handler nodded.

"Him and Kay Luo. Better to get rid of Bowers too. He's too smart—he may be putting it together already. This needs to be a clean break."

"And Winspear?"

His handler thought about this, sighing.

"I haven't decided yet. He may have his uses. He may even come on board once he understands what's happening."

In their meetings over the years, they'd plotted how best to go after Winspear. Today, tomorrow, these were the final moments of an operation that had been run in secret since before Winspear was elected. And now it was almost to a terminus.

How long had it been since he started planning? Now, so near the end, McAvoy's handler couldn't help but reflect on the moment he knew what needed to be done. And the moment he realized he could do it. The system was broken. Democracy... capitalism... were broken. They had run their course.

When he'd learned that Winspear was running—and more than that, that he had a chance of *winning*—that was too much. Something had to be done. It was time.

And so, an opportunity was created. A weakness found. Winspear's presidency could be controlled, its collapse coordinated, and the ground made fertile for something new to rise from the ashes. A phoenix conjured from the embers that McAvoy's handler knew were there.

The nation was ready for something new. Something firm. Control, by someone who could enforce the punishments and rules required to expand the country once more.

To return to a time of empire.

And now, just a few votes in the House and a few warm bodies stood in the way.

"Kay and Bowers are at the White House," McAvoy's handler said. "I need you to take care of Guilfoyle, and when we have the vote secured, that'll be the time to start tying off loose ends. I'll arrange their delivery to you when the time comes."

"All right," McAvoy said with a note of finality. "The file on Guilfoyle?"

"In a minute," his handler said. "First, we'll have that drink."

The safe house was stocked, and McAvoy's handler retrieved two glasses and a bottle. He poured, and then they raised their glasses.

"To Tildow's exit," McAvoy said.

"And Winspear's," his handler added.

To that, they drank.

23

"Come on, Jack!" Kay said under her breath.

The phone was ringing on the other end, headed toward voicemail for the third time.

Bowers stepped into the small conference room, a phone to his own ear.

"Still nothing?" he asked.

Kay shook her head.

"I just heard from the Service, he's gone inside the Winspear Camplex with them. They think the signal is blocked."

"What do you mean? Somebody's causing it or—"

Bowers shrugged.

"It's a big facility; everyone's off grid for now. There are troops on the president though, along with Service. Everyone's being looked after."

They held each other's eye contact for a second, and then Bowers nodded and ducked out, phone still to his ear.

Kay looked at her own phone. Then at her laptop. There was nothing to do—nothing *she* could do rather. Did Jack even know what had happened to Tildow?

The morning and night had been a whirlwind. She'd hardly slept at all, going over their plan again in her head and trying not to think about Quentin Daniels.

This morning she'd woken up to news of Adler's involvement as special prosecutor, but almost as soon as she'd heard that, there was a competing message, that Adler couldn't be special prosecutor, because Deputy AG McCauley didn't have the authority to appoint her.

By the time Kay had caught up with this, she was watching the live C-SPAN feed of the House floor along with everyone else.

With that playing on one screen, in her hand she was scrolling through a discussion some political junkies were heaving, breaking it all down in a forum, when she heard a faint pop in the distance. She almost hadn't noticed it. But the room she'd secreted herself away in was quiet, and about a mile and a half away out the open window was the Capitol Building.

Bowers had found her and told her what had happened and that she needed to come back to the main room, because they were piling on security and clearing out the protesters. That pop she'd heard, muffled from partway across town, had been Tildow's murder.

"Are we safe?" she'd asked.

"Mostly," Bowers said, then corrected quickly. "Most definitely."

Now, she was tracing the fallout online. She'd downed nearly half a pot of coffee but wasn't sure if she was shaking from that or from what she was really worried about: people were getting killed out there, first Quentin and then the attorney general, and Jack was heading into the lion's den.

A new email grabbed her attention; one of the last wire transfers they'd been waiting for was ready. One left after that. And with a sinking feeling she wondered if they were doing anything close to the right thing.

It had seemed clever two days ago, but that was before. The stakes had seemed high then, but now.... She knew she shouldn't have watched the video. Now when she closed her eyes she saw the spray of blood on the whitewashed steps.

It was horrible.

Kay hadn't felt fear like this before. Anxiousness, bordering on terror. She got up and opened the door, looked out to see that most of the Bowers staff weren't working now. The plans had been laid; it was a waiting game. But they sat and stood in small groups, huddling around screens and talking in low tones.

"Bowers," Kay said, gesturing him over.

"Hey, how we doing?"

"We need to talk."

She waved him in and closed the doors.

"What's up, are you—"

"Look, I don't know about this anymore."

Bowers took this in stride, not skipping a beat before saying, "I know how you feel. It's like a house of cards out there."

"Out there," she said, nodding toward the Capitol Building. "And in Arkansas."

"You think there's a connection?"

"You *don't* think there is?"

Bowers nodded.

He said, "There's just no way to know, okay? That's the only place this logic ends. You saw the news. They have the protester in custody, some poor college girl from a state over who just ruined the rest of her life. This is a tragedy, and I think we'll find that, as with most tragedies, this one was essentially random. There is no connection between J. Woolston Winspear and"—he pointed at her laptop on the table—"that murder. Tildow was one of his men… it simply doesn't make sense."

"Okay," Kay said, feeling herself decompress some. "Okay… I just… it's too much for coincidence at this point."

"You're worried about Jack," he said.

Kay looked at him.

"You're worried about *everything*, I know, but we've all got to keep cool heads. Whatever's going on in the Capitol Building is their problem—we have our own quadrant of this thing to sort out, okay? And if we don't, then we may never find out what's really going on. We need to stay tough. Focused."

They stared at each other, and Bowers asked, "You're not pulling out on me, are you?"

"No," she said, but then she stopped and thought about it for a moment. "But Winspear… how can he come back from this?"

"Kay," his voice was low, and he took a step closer. "He probably can't, okay?"

"You really think that?"

"I don't know how else to read it. Before Daniels, we had a chance. Now… I don't know what's happening in the House but somebody is working for a vote. They want it soon, before the recess tomorrow, and I don't think we're going to get him through it."

"And the vice-president? What does Applegate think?"

Bowers sighed.

"He's delusional, still optimistic that the numbers will be there or that if they're not, we can pull a rabbit out of our hat in the Senate when he hits trial, but that'll never happen."

"I thought Winspear said he was on it? That there were favors you all could call in and—"

"There were," he said, "and we have. Guilfoyle can still probably stop a vote, but only if nobody else gets to him. If Applegate or Guilfoyle can delay the vote until the recess, we'll have the Christmas break to get control of this thing again, but with *this*"—He gestured toward her laptop again—" political assassinations on the Capitol Building steps."—He shook his head—"It's bad."

"And if he's impeached?"

"A trial, then expulsion from office. It could happen the same day they hold the vote; the Senate's ready."

"So… what happens to you?"

"Don't worry about me," he said with a wave. "Back to the private sector. The important thing is that we still have power and access that we won't have on the other side of this. Listen"—He sized her up for a moment—"there's something else. I was coming to update you. They've found something else with the source of funds for the NEXT Auto algorithm."

"The shell companies?"

He nodded.

"I'd told them to keep mapping them. It's not just triple digits."

"Thousands?"

"*Tens* of thousands. And more. There's a sort of surface level—the ones we found earlier—and they all push and pull money all over the *world,* Kay. This touches everyone—Russia, Europe, Asia—it's a huge web of... of *some*thing. This may be the only chance we have to do something like this. To see how far it goes. So please,"—He smiled at her—"don't pull out now."

"Okay," she said, "but I want to see what else they've found. I need to know what we're up against."

"Follow me," he said, and they moved out into main area.

He led her to the first cluster of desks and laptops, and she saw that they were all leaning in toward one.

"Seth, I need you to go through what you showed me earlier with Kay."

Seth was the one at the computer, and as the others peeled away with Bower's approach they saw what everyone had been watching: a live feed from the capital, where Deputy Attorney General McCauley, visibly shaken, was stepping up to a microphone, his face looking almost as white as the paper in his hand.

24

Everyone had been shaken by Tildow's assassination, but to their credit, Tarrah thought, the DC police had handled it about as well as they could. A proper military backup had joined them to shore up the perimeter.

The protesters had all scattered in a mad dash, and the police had closed down the area. Now the only people out front were Adler, other representatives clustering in tight groups, planning, and the few newscasters who were brave (or cold hearted) enough to not be shaken by the murder, still getting B-roll of where a white tarp had been used to cover the blood-stained spot.

When the shot first rang out, Tarrah had seen them tackle the gunman—gun*wom*an, as it turned out—almost at once. Instinctively, she'd turned and fled back up the stairs, angling to the side, toward cover behind one of the huge white columns in front of the door. In case it wasn't just the one shooter.

It had been just one though. In fact, this had turned out to be more of a garden variety shooting, all told. Single target. Not for terror, but political purpose. It was the ex-FBI agent in her that went to this place when thinking through the event, calmly classifying it as she lit another cigarette. If she tried, Tarrah could just barely hear her heart tick-tick-ticking away.

This was the first public shooting since the Shooter Act had been repealed in a special session after the events at LAX, and online, people were already starting to dissect it. The internet mob threw together a psych profile and all the assorted background info of the woman who had taken the shot even before the news had released her name. It was all public: address, usernames, internet history right up to when she'd posted that she was at the protest.

The news did release one tidbit that the internet sleuths couldn't beat them to. They'd learned from the local police that the shooter was wearing a backpack, and in that backpack were printouts of Jack Paulson's blog. The "Paulson Manifesto," which he'd linked to the QR codes pinned to his shirt before taking the gun out in LAX and making them all take pictures of him and post for the world to decode.

That detail, on top of everything else, shook Adler. She'd seen a lot, but this… this was new. Jack Paulson might have believed he was doing the right thing, and he may have been proved right in the court of public opinion—but a certain precedent had been set. A dangerous one. A symptom of what was perhaps a new sickness had just played itself out on the Capitol Building steps.

Tildow may have been part of the problem and even a symbol of the corruption and cronyism that Winspear ushered in, but he had a family. And to them it was a husband, son, and father who'd just been murdered in cold blood.

Adler didn't want to guess who else might be out there planning their own vigilante justice. An ironic overcorrection from the Shooter Act repeal. It proved something that Adler had known all along, that the problem of the gun was just that, a problem with *the gun*. There were certainly overarching issues, mental health, et cetera. The list went on. But the fundamental problem was one of killing power. When the forefathers had drafted the right to bear arms, that wasn't the same as granting anyone the right to have enough killing power to murder a dozen people in quick succession like you could with a semi-automatic rifle.

But it really didn't matter where you stood on the issue, at least not to Adler, because the point was moot. You'd never take the guns away from this country. It was an impossibility. The Shooter Act and Paulson's attempt to fight back against it had showed off the bristly edges of the problem. Not for the first time, she was glad she wasn't in charge of trying to figure out something like that.

She'd been shaking earlier, but now a bit of time—and a few cigarettes—had steadied Adler's hands as she stood at the top of the Capitol Building steps. There would be time later to worry and philosophize about what had just happened… now it was time to get back to the task at hand, and she bent at the knee, stubbing out the cigarette on the steps before fishing a small fabric pouch out of her purse and stowing the cigarette butt in it, with the others.

"That's disrespectful, you know," one of the representatives said, one of the handful returning to the chamber.

He was gesturing down to where she'd left a smear of ash on the white steps.

She started to scoff at the man but caught herself—nothing good would come of that.

Instead, she said, "It'll wash off in the rain, don't you think?"

"Not all of it," the man said back.

"No," Adler said, giving a slight nod of her head, eyeing the white tarp over Tildow's bloodstains as she said, "no, not all of it."

"Here he comes," the man said, looking toward the entrance where Adler saw the deputy attorney general emerging. She hadn't seen him come in—they'd probably used a back entrance as a precaution.

Adler saw him look around the area as he stepped out, saw him look at the representatives who were standing around, all of them far enough away from the tarp for it to not be too morbid, and then in Adler's direction.

Their eyes met, and Adler nodded at him.

McCauley looked at the tarp halfway down the steps and swallowed. The press noticed he was headed down toward them, and so they started up to meet him in a formation eerily similar to the one that had enclosed Tildow hours ago.

Adler shook her head slightly, saying under her breath, "The show must go on."

Slowly, McCauley got closer and closer to the cameras, angling as he walked, aiming for a spot just to the left of where Tildow had stood. He looked at the spot, which was dark under the mostly opaque tarp, and Adler realized that he was doing it on purpose. He wanted to show that, shaken as he was—as they all were—he was here to do what needed to be done.

Even from where she was, Adler could tell he was trembling, but as the cameras spooled their live feeds up to the clouds and to the world, Deputy AG McCauley raised a sheet of paper and began to speak.

"As the acting attorney general," he said, looking up to the cameras and swallowing hard, "I hereby appoint Tarrah Adler as special prosecutor in the investigation of President J. Woolston Winspear. Further, I acknowledge that section 600 point 8, subpart c of the Code of Federal Regulations requires such a report to be presented to the acting attorney general confidentially."

He looked up over the top of the paper for a moment now, and Adler wondered if he was scanning the crowd for someone. For another shooter, perhaps. His eyes fell back down to the speech as he continued:

"It was Justice Louis D. Brandeis who said, 'Sunlight is said to be the best of disinfectants; electric light the most efficient policeman.' In the spirit of Justice Brandeis, I hereby waive the subpart c confidentiality clause, and direct the special prosecutor to deliver her report in the plain light of day, to the members of the House of Representatives."

He looked over his shoulder, up at Adler, who still stood in the shadow of the towering Capitol Building. As the cameras panned up and over, she turned for the doors. Back to work.

25

They had been picking their way through the rows of shelves for a couple hours now.

"Here," Roy said, finally, and Jack looked up to see a wall ahead.

Another wall, one running perpendicular to the one they'd had at their backs when they entered.

"Up to the ninth floor, right?" Roy said, as the small group spilled out from between the shelves, into the narrow corridor—maybe three feet wide, Jack guessed—between the hall and the perimeter of the shelves.

"That's the one, ninth floor executive suite," Winspear said. "I don't exactly see an elevator though."

"I know," Roy said, leading them against the wall a few feet and then gesturing at an opening up ahead on the right. "We got a rampcase up there though."

They were all clustered against the wall now, and Jack craned his head to see into the opening. It was like a doorway, but rather than opening to a hall or staircase, Jack saw the floor sloped up and to the right. It went down on the left side, and Jack realized what he was looking at was the side of a giant corkscrew spiral, one that the shelves could traverse up and down, their lifting bots riding the gentle slope of the ramps. A spiral staircase with no stairs.

"Well," Roy said, "let's go."

He braced himself against the wall on the right and the pillar at the center of the area—which was only about four feet across. Winspear followed, and then Jack.

As they moved up, Jack thought of the shelves, many of which had moved around even as they'd picked their way through the sea earlier.

"Tell me, why this? Why not put in elevators for the shelves to ride or something like that?"

"We *do* have elevators," Winspear said, "but they're bigger, other places. Used for batches of shelves, right, Roy?"

"That's it," he said, "but the rampcases give the programming options. It's fast sometimes. Edge cases, you know. Plus, concrete slopes don't break down or need maintenance."

"What if one comes down while we're in here?" Jack asked.

"Nothing to worry about," Winspear said. "Their programming won't allow it."

He was starting to get winded as they climbed.

Jack pictured an eight-foot-tall shelf, three feet on a side, barreling down the curve loaded with heavy stock and wondered if a few lines of code would help it stop any faster.

They continued to climb in silence, and at each floor the lights clicked on to the same scene: a dense wall of shelves, floor to ceiling, left to right. It reminded Jack of the scene at the end of Raiders of the Lost Ark, when the Ark of the Covenant was wheeled into a massive government storehouse. The difference here was that, if anything, Winspear's warehouse was bigger and much more orderly. Where Raiders of the Lost Ark had ended with the camera panning up across the vast expanse of the space, here there was no airspace wasted, the gap from the top of the shelves to the ceiling on each level being just enough for drones to zip through with their small carrying cases.

He paused as he climbed, at just the right height to look out over the shelves on one level, able from this angle to see them shifting and moving in the distance. Resituating themselves. A drone tracing the scene from right to left, then quickly dipping out of sight.

Another thing Jack was noticing was the variety of items on each shelf. They would pass shelves at the entrance to the rampcase that had been collected seemingly at random—toys, food, bathroom supplies—and then there would be a shelf that was covered in dozens of the same object. He saw one shelf that was stacked with dusty boxes of Honda brake pads, another that was all shoes—but others were a mismatch, with pieces stowed randomly.

"Who decides what's on each shelf?" he asked as they stepped out into the ninth floor, everyone pausing to catch their breaths.

Or rather, everyone who didn't have military training did, which really meant that the Secret Service agents and soldiers waited for Winspear, Roy and Jack to catch *their* breaths.

"The algorithm," Winspear said, "figures it all out, makes it all run efficiently. How to get orders in and out, how to optimize storage for quick-ship items and also clients who use the warehouse as storage space."

Roy nodded, standing with hands on his hips and breathing deep. "Warehouse-as-a-service." He added. "Everything's in the right place at the right time. This stuff closer up is the more regular selling stock. Or maybe just shelves that were called up recently working their ways back as the place shifts," he gestured out over the floor, at the wall of shelves that stretched out from side to side as far as the eye could see, just like the last floor and the one before that and the one before that. "Older stuff is kept in the back, or used to be."

"Kept in the back," Jack said. "So what, drones go back and pick it up from there?"

"Sometimes," Roy said, shrugging, "or else the shelves bring things to the front. The drones leave from all angles—I'm sure you saw their portholes from the outside of the building—so they leave from wherever is the most efficient."

"The way this place works now," Roy looked around, shaking his head, "we had it self-optimizing when I was last here. Those portholes were new. There probably isn't even a front and back anymore, probably the off-peak stuff is stored more toward the center and it migrates outward instead of back to front."

"Migrates?"

"Oh yeah," Roy said. "When we started the self-optimization program, that was one of the first things we noticed. Off-peak items would migrate around the facility like a herd of animals. All the shelves with Halloween costumes, for instance, would cluster and move around cyclically. Valentine's day, Christmas, Easter."

"It's impressive," Jack said, still trying to get a feel for the scope of the place.

"Thanks," Roy said.

"How close are we?" one of the Secret Service agents asked Roy.

"Not far now," he said, "maybe a half hour that way."

"A *half hour?*"

It was one of the soldiers who said this, stepping in.

"We need to regain communication with the outside world. They'll be wondering—"

"All right, all right," Roy said. "The problem is I remember where the office used to be... sort of... but with the shelves moving"—he shook his head, looking both ways before going on—"it's hard to know which path is the right one. We were moving in basically the right direction earlier, but the office wasn't part of the perimeter walls, which I think is where we are now. It was back where the admin area was before this facility was primarily used for storage."

"What can you do to get us there faster?" the soldier asked, and Roy looked around.

"Well," he said, "let's grab one of these drones and I'll send it out on a search for us."

"Seriously?" one of the Secret Service men asked.

"Come on," Roy said, shouldering his backpack off. "Make yourselves useful; fan out and grab me a drone. I can hook up to it and take control."

They looked at each other like maybe he was joking, then the soldiers split up, going in opposite directions at steady clips. The Secret Service agents, maybe out of some quiet competition with the military boys, split and followed in either direction. Roy got out his laptop and opened it, and Jack leaned back against the wall by the rampcase opening.

Winspear reached forward, to one of the shelves, and pulled a box of Reese's Cups off of it. He tore it open, tossing the trash back on the shelf and fishing one of the smaller packages out. He offered one to Jack, saying "Hershey's has used us as a distributor for years. I'm sure they won't mind."

"Thanks," he said, taking it and nodding toward the shelf. "Won't this mess up your algorithms?"

Winspear shrugged, popping one of the chocolate disks into his mouth. Roy was already sitting cross-legged and typing away, preparing whatever program he planned to upload on their confiscated drone.

Jack chewed, savoring the rich flavor, drinking in the utter weirdness of the moment as he looked around to the shelves, the agents climbing one in the distance angling on an incoming drone, and the president of the United States licking chocolate off his fingers. Here he was lost in a warehouse that was basically one big machine, looking for a man who could answer all their questions.

Thinking of Scarly, he said, "What if by the time we get out of here Scarly's already come forward?"

Winspear blew a raspberry, reaching for another pack of Reese's.

"If there's one thing I've learned in three years, it's that things don't wrap themselves up that tidily *ever*, Jack. And things don't get better. Mark my words: It will be worse out there than when we left."

One of the groups of men who'd spread out shouted for Roy, and he took off toward them, a Reese's wrapper dropping to the floor as he collected his laptop and backpack to head over to them.

"Tell me this, Jack," Winspear said, handing Jack another package, which he started to wave off but then shrugged and took. "I hope you won't think this is too personal."

Jack furrowed his brow, half smiling and thinking *here we go again* as he said, "Go ahead."

"Did you ever think about ending it"—Jack stopped unwrapping—"about ending things, I mean? After—"

"Yes," he said, resuming unwrapping the Reese's quickly and popping one into his mouth, nodding as he chewed.

Winspear grunted some kind of acknowledgement.

After the short silence that followed, Jack finally asked, "You?"

"Oh yes," Winspear said quickly, even laughing a bit. "Oh yes, of course."

For some reason, Jack's guard was down. Maybe he was fed up with the absurdity of the situation, or maybe Winspear was working his magic on him. But for a moment, he wasn't obsessing over the angles of conspiracy, the Scarly question, the feeling of lies coming from all directions. For a moment, it was just him and Winspear here. Not a president and a would-be revolutionary, but two men sharing quiet sorrows over stolen chocolate.

"You know I wonder what it would be like if she were here," Winspear said. "It just seems…"—he shook his head—"Everything could have been so different."

"I know what you mean," Jack said. He sighed. "Like nothing else matters anymore. Like time stopped then and there." After a pause, he said, "Like you died right along with her."

Winspear leaned back against one of the shelves, then turned and fiddled with whatever was stored there.

"Except not only does it not matter, but it's all not even real, you know? A shitty movie you just can't stop watching."

Jack didn't say anything for a moment, then he caught Winspear's eye and said, "You know how I dealt with it?"

"How's that?"

Jack started to laugh.

"I lost my mind and took a gun into an airport."

Somehow, against it all, they laughed.

"What was she like," Jack asked, "Sierra?"

Winspear looked at Jack when he said her name, almost as if it surprised him to hear it.

"You know, Jack, I've had a lot of people tell me they were sorry about what happened to her. If I had a million for every *condolence* I was offered"—he waved his hand—"but you know, you're the only person who's ever asked me that."

He closed his eyes.

"She was—"

He thought for a moment, and then shook his head. Jack looked away as he saw something intimate, something private in the way Winspear's face changed when he thought about her.

Winspear let out a sigh, and Jack shifted his weight against the cold metal shelf.

There was a faint whine from Roy's direction, and Jack looked over just in time to see the red running lights of a small drone heading for him and Winspear at an alarming speed.

Jack ducked, but the drone pulled sideways, turned vertical, and missed both of them easily.

"Whoo!" Roy shouted up the hall, jogging back toward them, face lit by the light of his laptop which bounced, precariously balanced in one hand as he steered the drone from his keyboard with his other.

"Okay!" Winspear said, clapping his hands together. "Find us that office, Roy. Let's get Scarly and get the hell out of here."

26

The pro-impeachment block had finally gotten Adler the floor, and live on C-SPAN, she'd made her case for the impeachment. The debate had started, and it had run right up to the end of the session for the day, around 2:45 PM. About then, DC Police had come in and explained there was a bomb threat, and they recommended evacuating the facility until they could get the dogs in and out.

Supposedly, it had been one of Tildow's shooter's friends who'd called it in, though another counter rumor was that pro-Winspear supporters had cooked up the threat in an attempt to run out the clock of the current session.

Either way, Stephen Guilfoyle didn't care. He hadn't been prepared for Adler, but he'd known it was going to be a question of delaying the vote no matter what happened. The fact that the pro-impeachment block considered Adler's testimony a win was not an issue either. They were certainly entitled to their own facts, and if there was one thing that the Winspear presidency had taught Guilfoyle—had taught *all* of them—it was that information, so-called evidence, really didn't matter.

Sure, Winspear had accepted bribes from large companies and Wall Street firms. Tarrah Adler had the emails to prove it. High crimes. Racketeering. Several variations on the theme.

But the people who voted for Winspear knew that. He'd basically done it out in the open, and really it was his Wild West mentality that had drawn in a certain kind of voter in the first place. The rules he broke were unjust, the methods he used were necessary evils to make progress against a bureaucracy worn threadbare by overregulation and calcified by an aversion to hurting people's feelings. It was an easy reality to slip into, easy because you could forget about having to measure anything against an objective code or standard. Anything Winspear did was OK, because *he did it,* end of story.

In fact, the corruption of the existing system—the fact that he took the same bribes as everyone else—was something that earned this kind of voter's attention and respect when he was still "just" the richest man in the world and not a candidate for US president.

Adler could also prove that the tangled web of accounts—the way Scarly managed the blind trust and the way the trust leaned on NEXT Automotive—showed a clear line that ended in Katelyn Patterson's death. For President Winspear, that was conspiracy to commit murder.

And Adler had even made her case for treason. Guilfoyle had to respect her—the sheer balls it took to walk into the Capitol Building, to come to the House floor, and to accuse the president of a bold-faced attempt of dismantling the US government department by department, allowing, in Adler's words, "treasonous negligence of office" to result in the worst recession since 2008. It didn't hurt her argument that even as she'd given her speech, the markets were in a freefall proving her point. They were already calling it the Next Great Depression.

And Guilfoyle knew that, mostly, Adler was right on all her points.

It had always been an inside job, and when Guilfoyle had accepted the position of speaker—a thank you for his generous support during the race and part of a deal that included a 4% ownership share of NEXT Auto if he could get his constituents in what was left of the auto industry on board—he knew that they weren't in this to govern. At least, not exactly.

Before the election, Guilfoyle had been invited to a meeting with Winspear and his party. Winspear explained how, if they won, they could turn the country into the powerhouse it once was. He explained how the democratic system was always destined to end up with a despotic ruler—it was just the thing philosophers of yore had warned about. And Winspear said that if he won, he could prevent that. But he would have to be the despot to prevent it. And he said that if Guilfoyle and a handful of other helpers would make it happen, then when Winspear and his sidekick Bowers rebuilt the country from scratch—America 2.0—they would do it differently.

Their plan—still secret at that point—was moot, since at the time nobody thought Winspear had a snowball's chance in hell in getting elected. Guilfoyle had agreed to help, as had all the rest of them, because the downside was almost as beneficial as the upside. Even if Winspear lost, they'd still have earned the favor of a powerful man, along with all the benefits of almost winning the presidency without all the work of running the country afterword.

But then Sierra had died.

And from Guilfoyle's perspective, Winspear may as well have been in the car with her during the crash. He'd won the election, but that was about where his participation in his own presidency had ended.

The two men never spoke again, save for once at the funeral. Guilfoyle was appointed speaker as planned, and he would have been willing to work with Winspear. In fact, if he were pushed to admit it, Guilfoyle would tell you that he was afraid of Winspear. The richest man in the world. The president of the United States. Guilfoyle was supposed to be installed as the speaker to make sure that any and all laws Winspear and Bowers cooked up got the votes they were supposed to get. It was a remarkable plan—rigging the system on the way in.

And if Winspear and Bowers had gone through with it, something good might have come from the whole thing.

But after the crash, Winspear was largely MIA. He never met with another world leader. He didn't give press conferences. He threw hundreds of years of decorum out the window seemingly because he just didn't feel like going through the motions anymore.

Let them call him the president, Guilfoyle thought, *but you'll never catch him acting like it.*

And this was good for Guilfoyle and the handful of cronies that Winspear had installed before promptly giving up on everything and walking away. With Winspear actively in power, they could have been controlled. But left to their own devices....

It was no wonder the pro-Winspear camp in the House had grown at the last midterms. With Guilfoyle on their side and with a majority to boot, they quickly realized they could pass whatever they wanted. They could *get away* with whatever they wanted. And with no reason not to, they did what you might expect.

Guilfoyle wasn't proud of himself, of the way he'd contributed to the so-called "Hollowing Out"—a period measured in years in which the levels of mismanagement and fragmentation of the US government, through a combination of cost cutting and lack of leadership, had eroded the foundation of not just the bureaucratic system, but of the Union itself.

No, Guilfoyle wasn't proud. But he was sure of one thing: Whatever happened next he was going to set things up so he was rich enough to not have to suffer through it. He was getting out of here, taking his Winspear money and retreating to a tax haven somewhere east.

All that was left was to prevent one measly vote.

Adler had delivered her speech. She'd done her part—as the polls were now showing—and Guilfoyle had to get through only one more session.

Now, in his private quarters, he thought about all this while he drank an amber liquid from a crystal glass, watching the news which was again showing Tildow's skull being blown out.

He thought about what would happen tomorrow. He had a majority. Nothing could go wrong now.

Then, a knock at the door.

He looked at it, said nothing.

His forehead wrinkled as the door began to open.

"Mr. Speaker," came a voice from the darkness just outside.

"Who is that? You're not supposed to—"

Guilfoyle was already reaching for his desk drawer, the one just above where the whiskey had come from, where a loaded gun—

"Uh-uh-uh," the voice said again, the man stepping forward so that his gun, already raised, shown in the dim light.

Guilfoyle slowly brought his hand back up to the top of the desk.

"Who are you?" he asked, heart racing but the whiskey giving the moment a dreamlike quality.

"That's not as important as who she is."

He stepped into the room. Dark gloves, tan jacket, dark hat and in his other hand, a picture.

From his desk, Guilfoyle could see only that much, and he said nothing as the man stepped forward slowly. He kept the gun on Guilfoyle as he laid the picture of the girl on the table and sat in one of the plush chairs in front of the desk.

Guilfoyle leaned forward slowly, taking his eyes off the gun for only a second—long enough to look at the picture.

It was a mugshot, a girl, late twenties but looking worse for wear.

"Who is she?" Guilfoyle asked.

The man tutted, reaching with his free hand into his jacket and slowly pulling out a vaporizer—a narrow black shaft tipped with a blue LED—that he raised to his lips and pulled from.

"Never seen her before," Guilfoyle said, and then as he watched the man pull on his medicine, "You're Duncan McAvoy."

"So, you don't remember her?"

Now Guilfoyle started to worry.

"I don't know what the fuck you're talking about."

McAvoy grunted. "We have a video you know. Her name is Courtney Evans. You might have known her by her professional name, which, she tells us was Kera Night."

Guilfoyle closed his eyes. He didn't remember her, but he remembered many, many nights with many such-named girls. They faded into and out of his mind's eye, largely in proportion to the alcohol or cocaine or methamphetamine he might have been taking during any of his midnight trysts with ladies of DC's nights.

"Once, when you went to see her, she had a pinhole camera in her bag," McAvoy said flatly. "And there's more."

He reached back into his pocket and tossed a USB stick onto the table.

"We caught up with her a few years ago, paid her a few thousand to do a little interview. You might not remember her, but she remembers *you*, Mr. Speaker."

Guilfoyle was sweating now. He was breathing hard, but he left his fists balled up on the armrests. There was nothing he could do.

"What do you want?" he asked.

"The vote," McAvoy said. "It happens tomorrow."

Guilfoyle had been ready for any number of things. He'd been ready for McAvoy to request money. Safety. Drugs. Even some obscure ritualistic murder would have surprised him less than this, the supposed henchman in Winspear's conspiracy blackmailing him into the impeachment vote.

He'd just listened to Adler's investigation and hours of debate that indicated McAvoy, Scarly, and Winspear were all in cahoots on the NEXT Auto coverup, but now this… was Scarly turning on Winspear? Was *McAvoy* turning on them both?

Or was the tyrant king behind it all. Pushing Guilfoyle, testing him, trying to force the vote of his own impeachment in order to pull off some unforeseen stunt. A double bluff. Feints within feints, the whiskey casting an opaque haze over it all.

"I can't—" Guilfoyle said, finally thinking through how a vote might happen and remembering that there was a pro-Winspear majority in the House.

Even if he somehow came forward and told them what the situation was… but no, they'd hang him out to dry.

He looked at the picture. He didn't remember her. He didn't even remember the name McAvoy said she had used, but he didn't have to. He knew what would be on that thumb drive if he checked it.

"You'll find a way," McAvoy said, standing, putting his gun away. "And if you don't, Mrs. Guilfoyle and those little kids of yours will be the first ones to see it. Both videos—the one where you pay Kera to live out your sordid little fantasies *and* the interview we produced of her watching and giving commentary. Just so everyone's sure there's no funny business going on."

Guilfoyle looked up at the man.

"Not my children," he said.

McAvoy shrugged.

"They gotta grow up someday. And besides, if the vote happens you've got nothing to worry about."

McAvoy turned to leave, but as he reached the door Guilfoyle asked, "Why?"

McAvoy looked over his shoulder, taking a pull on the vaporizer.

"Why not, Mr. Speaker? Why *anything?*" he shrugged, turning for the door. "Good luck tomorrow."

He shut the door as he left.

27

"Okay," Roy said, looking up from his laptop, "back up; see if you can spot it."

The soldiers had been annoyed at first, but now they played along. They climbed up on the shelves and watched over them, looking for Roy's drone which was supposed to be blinking its LEDs.

They'd been moving through the floor slowly, using the drone as a sort of directional indicator, which could scout ahead and find open paths in the right direction. But when Roy sent it too far he'd lose it.

"Over here," one of the soldiers said, pointing in the direction he could see the blinking light. Roy glanced up at him, nodded, and turned back to the screen.

"We should be seeing it soon then, or seeing *something*."

"Tell me again what's got you confused about it," Winspear said, "and why you can't just open us up a damn corridor."

"The drone doesn't have those privileges. I can see what it sees, but it's all barcodes and near-field scanning. The weird thing is, just a few rows over, it doesn't see anything anymore."

"But it found the office," Jack double checked.

"Oh yeah, it's right where it always was. Just ahead of the human exclusion zone. This way—"

Roy held his hand up in the direction that the Secret Service man had said he saw the drone.

"—looks like an order's about to be placed that'll trigger the next row over, we should have a corridor opening up any second now, and *that'll* take us to the edge of the shelves here, which we should be able to follow right to the office."

"Human exclusion zone," Jack repeated. "That doesn't exactly sound friendly."

"Just a precaution," Winspear said. "All those shelves we've been walking through, it used to be the admin offices and actual workspace. People used to run up and down these rows of shelves, if you can believe it."

"Once we realized that volumetric space itself was going to be one of our commodities," Roy said, packing his laptop back up and shouldering his backpack, "that was one of the first steps of the automation: prep that area for the building's expansion."

"You mean *your* expansion." Jack said, looking at Roy and then Winspear.

"It's complicated," Roy said. "The computer does all the heavy lifting. That's what I designed it for. We asked it if this space could better be used as storage." He shrugged.

"You asked it?"

Roy just smiled. Behind him, the hallway started to shift.

"He did good work too," Winspear said, clapping Roy on the shoulder as he turned to go down the hall that was opening itself up between the shelves. "Nobody had ever done it before, using a quantum computer to its full advantage. Outcompeting, at some point, is just outcom*puting*."

"Pft," Roy said, as the last shelf ahead of them started to slide away and he walked forward. "Nobody had ever even built one that size before. They don't know how. That's what I—"

"—Look out!" Winspear lunged forward, grabbing Roy by the shoulder and pulling him back, both of them almost falling as Roy flailed out for the nearest shelf.

"What the—" he said, looking at Winspear.

Then Roy looked out ahead, to where he'd been about to step. Jack saw it too: an open chasm beyond a short strip of the concrete floor. Just ahead, the floor simply stopped.

Jack, the soldiers, and the Secret Service agents moved forward slowly, emerging from the shelves and going to the left and right of the opening, all of them hugging the shallow strip of concrete that opened onto an empty expanse ahead.

"Human exclusion zone…" Jack said slowly.

"Unbelievable," Winspear said. "It… hollowed itself out? Roy?"

"The shelves," Roy was shaking his head, looking left to right, then back out into the darkness.

Jack took a step forward. But just a single step—he was afraid of heights after all. He craned his head over the edge of the concrete floor and looked down into the chasm below.

He couldn't see the bottom.

Roy had his laptop back out and commanded the drone back over to them, and suddenly, bright running lights flickered on from the machine, and Jack—all of them—gasped.

Shelves like skyscrapers loomed ahead, some close, some farther away, all of them stretching down into the darkness below, and some of them up, their tops hidden in darkness that buzzed with tiny pinpricks of light.

Drones moved in and out of the cityscape, plucking items here and there, their ghostly LEDs filling the space so that it swarmed with activity.

Roy's drone moved slowly forward, and he rotated it, the light bouncing off towering shelves that clustered ahead, most of them in slow motion, a quiet procession.

Every now and then, a drone would come to a shelf and pause, having to look harder for the item it wanted, and would activate a high powered flashlight to allow it to scan properly on a visual spectrum instead of near field, and these brief sparks of light flashed in and out throughout the space, giving the illusion of a giant, lumbering city moving just ahead.

"They shouldn't be able to do that—the shelves, they—" Winspear was saying.

"The metallurgy changed," Roy said, looking up from his laptop. "It started buying replacement parts in steel after we turned it on."

"I remember," Winspear said, "but this... it removed everything here. It built..."

"It built itself," Jack said, remembering Winspear's words from the day before, understanding them better. Understanding them so well that he had a twinge of something at the back of his neck. A tightening. Maybe a hint of fear, even, a feeling that he shouldn't be here. That none of them should.

"Will somebody please tell me what is going on in here, with all this?" Jack said after another moment of silence.

"What's it look like?" Roy asked. "This is optimized storage. It doesn't need floors."

"*We* needed floors," Winspear said, grunting his approval. "Magnificent."

"*That's* why it upped the drone production a few years back," Roy said, looking over at Winspear. "That was before you left."

"I remember," he said. "All that time... it was planning this."

"You mean to tell me that this—" Jack waved his hand at the open area ahead of them, "was *built by the computer?*"

He raised his voice when he said this, and against the gentle hum of the drones it echoed back from across the expanse: '*the computer?*'

"That's why we win, Jack." Winspear said, smiling. "Roy was my ace in the hole. I discovered net positive shipping, but *this* is why they couldn't copy it."

"You ever wondered how Winspear outcompeted every industry for half a decade?"

"Shipping," Winspear said, raising a finger, counting more off as he continued, "robotics, supply chain management, product development, mergers and acquisitions—"

"All of it—" Jack said.

"That's right," Roy nodded. "Controlled by the computer that I built. 2,500 qubits. Bigger than anything anyone else has done by a magnitude at least. And it can hold a quantum state for *days*."

Jack shook his head. "I don't follow any of that."

"Ha!" Winspear slapped Roy on the shoulder, "me neither. That's why we keep Roy here on retainer. Wouldn't want him building a bigger one for someone else!"

Jack turned back to the cavern next to them, watching some of the vertical shelves—they really were like skyscrapers, he thought—drift past each other slowly.

He shook his head, "This is… unreal."

"Alien," Roy said. "Totally unhuman."

"A triumph," Winspear said.

"Mr. President," one of the agents stepped toward him, "we need to be going."

"Right," he said. "Roy, which way?"

"Follow me," he said, turning to head down the narrow strip of floor.

Jack swallowed hard as he followed, a wall of shelves on his right and the open canyon on the left, with maybe three feet between. As they moved, he leaned over carefully to look down again.

"Looks like more than nine stories," he said.

"It is," Roy answered back. "We had a basement before. If I had to guess, the algos probably wouldn't waste the space. It was another five floors deep. R&D Department. Actually, down there is where we built the computing enclosure. That drop may be something like 150 feet."

"But why—" Jack was still trying to put it all together. "Why stop here? This human exclusion zone? Why not take over the whole building?"

"Well, it can't be coincidence that my old office is right here on the border," Winspear said.

"Correct," Roy answered. "We let it do what it wanted with the admin area, but the machine shop was coded to still be human accessible from time to time in case any maintenance was needed that couldn't be handled internally. And your office would have been coded for permanent positioning."

"Meaning?" Jack asked.

"Meaning it stopped parallel to the office because the cost/benefit of some calculation somewhere told it that, if it couldn't move the office, it didn't make sense to demo further because..." Roy shrugged, thinking, "because it would have had to build some whole new support system for use in reaching the office probably. If it doesn't pay out..." he shrugged again.

"So... it can do that. It can do all of this?"

"Listen," Roy said over his shoulder. "You need to square yourself with the fact that there is a reason Winspear Corp. is the most successful company in generations. Up until about a decade ago, the most sophisticated, cheapest piece of machinery we could source was a *person*. But *my* system broke through that barrier. We don't have to wait on anyone. We don't have to trust people. It's a perfect system: totally automatic, the highest sophistication possible—and it worked with all the bits and pieces we had laying around."

"That's my favorite part," Winspear said. "No new capital other than the computer and a few million IBM sub-millimeter computers."

"You mean all the shelves, the drones, the robotics facility... they were all here first and then—"

"That's right," Roy said. "We plugged them all into my quantum brain. Let it do the thinking. Pretty neat right?"

"Neat?" Jack said, looking for once back at the agents and soldiers following them. "Am I the only one who thinks that's a little scary?"

"Do you think cavemen thought fire was scary?" Winspear asked.

"There it is," Roy said, spotting the office ahead and jogging forward.

Jack saw that he was right. The office was perfectly situated so that the entryway was the same width of the walkway they were on. Everything around it had been rebuilt, and off to the left a chunk of the rectangular space was cantilevered out over the open maw below, held in place by diagonal struts.

"Okay," Roy said, "I'll need a minute here. Gotta break the door somehow, should be a simple backup passcode thing."

"Fine," Winspear said. "How long?"

"I don't know," Roy said, hooking his laptop up to it. "Twenty at the most, have to trigger the backup request without it locking us out"

"Okay," Winspear said. "Jack, are you ready?"

He looked at the door, at Winspear, and out at the cityscape of shelves still moving like great beasts in the middle distance.

"If you'd asked me a few hours ago I would have said yes."

"Oh come on!" Winspear said. "This is it! This is what we came for! Scarly is in there; I can feel it. And he's going to tell us what's going on. Finally, *someone* can clear all of this up."

"I hope so," Jack said, and not realizing it, he took a step closer to the shelves, away from the sheer drop.

28

"Ready?" Bowers looked at Luo, his finger on the button—hovering over the enter key of a computer in the middle of the room.

She nodded, and Bowers looked around at the other analysts who stood nearby. He turned to the older men, the partners near the back of the room. They nodded as well. One gave a thumbs up. The one with the cigar took it out of his mouth and gestured with it to move forward.

At the head of the room, the projector had been set up to show a live feed of the NEXT Auto Share price. It was 10 minutes until the market closed—they'd planned it that close on purpose, so that if whatever they did went wrong at least all trading would stop, allowing them the night to figure out what happened.

Kay almost flinched when she heard him push the button. And then they all watched.

Five seconds passed. Ten.

"The price updates twice a second. We should be seeing something as soon as—" but he didn't finish his sentence.

The NEXT Auto price, until now a jagged line seesawing itself across the screen, fell in an almost straight-line dip. On the screen, it formed a sheer drop just like the one Jack and Winspear were toeing, though there was no way for Kay to know that.

It updated again, and the line went deeper, the rest of the chart squeezing itself toward the top of the screen as the Y axis of the chart resized so that it could show how low the price was going. Kay did the math in her head. Looking at the price it had just dropped to and comparing with where it had started seconds ago, before the drop.

"That's a 10% loss," she said. "We overshot it."

"Doesn't matter," Bowers said. "Look."

He was pointing up at the screen, where the share price was climbing quickly.

"It's coming back up to the 8% loss floor. The algorithms are buying—it's *working*."

There was a sound around the room, not applause, but a sort of concerned mumbling as everyone watched the updates roll in, the line climbing from the deep fissure it had sunk to and regaining ground as the stock price rose from the 10%-loss point.

"It's hovering at the floor," Kay said, watching the new line seesawing across the screen, still jagged but clustering around the 8% loss marker. "It's pumping money in to counter. We need to hit it now."

Bowers motioned to a group of three analysts sitting at their stations.

"Do it," he said, and they flew into activity across their screens.

"Go now," Kay said, "up, up, up!"

The team triggered their purchase orders—the massive trap they'd set. They let loose a torrent of over five billion dollars, all set to buy NEXT Auto's shares.

"Mr. Bowers." It was another analyst, she was turning to them. "Ms. Luo."

"What?" they said, not taking their eyes off the screen, waiting for the jump that signaled their plan had worked.

"We're seeing more funds, more companies… it's incredible."

Kay and Bowers exchanged a look, but the room filled with gasps and real applause this time as the NEXT Auto share price shot up on the screen. It had bounced more than 10% in an instant. Well past the deadband trigger they'd found, higher than when it had started moments ago. And as they watched it kept climbing.

"Holy hell!" Bowers said. "It's really there—look, you can almost feel it."

He was pointing up at the chart, which was still climbing. 11% gain. 12% gain. Rising more as they watched.

"When will it stop?" one of the analysts asked in Bowers direction.

He shrugged, looking form the analyst to Kay.

"When they run out of money," Kay said. "When whoever set this thing up goes bankrupt because of it."

They were all smiling, turning to each other and shaking hands. They'd just done something spectacular, but Kay took a step forward. She watched the price rising, now 15% gain. She shook her head, and Bowers stepped over to her.

"Something's wrong," she said. "We had it down to a 10% loss for a second... that should have triggered the normal stock market circuit breaker."

"10% loss on a single security?"

Kay nodded. "There should have been a circuit breaker built in to halt trading for 5 minutes. But it didn't stop."—She turned the problem over in her head—"Can we get back on the phone with a couple of the exchanges, confirm they've got those circuit breakers active?"

Bowers snapped his fingers at a few nearby analysts and motioned them to their computers. They'd been listening and picked up their phones, making the calls.

"Sir," another of the analysts stepped up with a thin screen in hand, offering it over to Bowers, "the news has it."

He and bowers looked down at the broadcast. The NEXT Auto chart pulsed on the news anchor's screen. The headline was talking about "irregularities" with the share price.

Bowers shrugged, looking back up at the screen which was almost at a 20% gain on the day now.

"We were ready for this, right? We expected it?"

"Yes," Kay said, "to a point."

"And at what point—" Bowers started to say, but one of the analysts making calls to exchanges stood up quickly, covering the speaker of the phone and practically shouting at Bowers.

"Sir—they can't close the BATS."

The Bats Global Market, a stock exchange operating in Lenexa, Kansas.

"What? That's ridiculous," Bowers stepped toward him, and Kay checked her watch. It was one minute past when the markets should have closed for the day.

As if to confirm this, she looked up at the screen showing NEXT Auto's price. It was nearing 21% gain.

She turned to Bowers who had taken the phone from the analyst and was talking into it as he looked back at the chart, "Well, give me your supervisor then; that's ridiculous."

One of the other analysts at the table chimed in, "CHX is still up too—"

The Chicago stock exchange.

"Holy shit," another analyst at the table exclaimed, listening to a phone and turning to Bowers. "They can't close the Nasdaq either."

Bowers' eyes were wide. He looked at the NEXT Auto share price on the screen and swallowed. Turning to Kay, she saw the alarm in his face. They didn't have to say out loud what they were both thinking. It was now three minutes past when the stock markets should have closed automatically, and the coincidence would be too much. Whatever was going on, it was their fault.

And on the screen, the NEXT Auto share price continued to climb.

29

"What are you going to do," Jack asked, "if they impeach you?"

Winspear was sitting at the edge of the narrow walkway, dangling his legs off the side. A Secret Service agent stood very close, ready to grab him if it looked like he was about to fall, but he'd known better than to ask Winspear not to sit there on the edge. At Jack's question, he shrugged.

Jack was sitting cross-legged, leaning against the wall of shelves, and he leaned forward as Winspear turned to answer.

"I don't know. Burn it all down probably."

Jack laughed. "You don't mean that."

"You ever read *Atlas Shrugged*?" Winspear asked.

"Parts of it," Jack said, "a phase in high school, you know how it is."

Winspear's turn to laugh. "I do indeed. You know, in my line of work that book isn't just some angsty phase for people. It's a *bible* to some of them."

"Some of them," Jack said, "but not you?"

"Oh no," he said. "I like to think of myself as more of a Ben Franklin type of opportunist. Ayn Rand—" he shook his head, "—that type of mentality just seems so petulant. So disconnected. Sierra read it too, you know, and she agrees it was all a little bunk, but there was a scene in there. Maybe you'll remember it."

"I think I only made it halfway through," Jack said. "Wasn't it over a thousand pages?"

"Oh yes," Winspear said. "The end of Act 1, I think. One of the main characters—not Rearden, I think it was some kind of oil baron—they decide to nationalize his operation. To *steal* it, if we're going to use the right words here. You know what he does?"

"Burns it all to the ground," Jack said, nodding. "I do remember that."

"And when they find it, he's already gone," Winspear went on, "and all that's left is a sign that says, 'I leave it as I found it.'"

Jack grunted.

"Sierra and I—we loved that scene. Read the book together, you see. That was so... so poignant. Whenever things were going rough," he said, flashing a grin, "whenever I'd been in a mood complaining about this or that, she'd always say that. She'd say 'Well, James, you can always just burn the thing down, leave it as you found it.'"

Jack was behind him, but from the side he could see that Winspear was smiling at the memory.

"Sometimes," he went on after a moment, "I don't think that'd be such a bad idea. I can't help but think that leaving things as I found them, well, it might just be what's best for everyone at this point."

"You're not talking about your companies anymore," Jack said.

Neither of them spoke for a moment.

"You know, I really did want to make things better. For the country. Bowers and I... we had such grand plans."

There was something like a twinkle in his eye as he said this, and for a moment Jack felt something familiar—something like the boyish optimism Winspear had displayed on the campaign trail. A strain of hope.

Jack remembered his platform. The Shooter Act. A new way forward.

"It didn't seem all that revolutionary," he said, "other than the Act and NEXT Auto. It was the same stuff every politician says. *Hope. Change.*"

Winspear looked at Jack, and he shrugged.

"No, no," Winspear said. "We were going to wring some *real* change out of this thing. Revolution, Jack, *that* was the plan."

"Really?" He tried not to sound too sarcastic. "Pardon me if it didn't look so revolutionary from the outside. What exactly were you planning?"

"Change, Jack. Radical change. A new way of life. This went beyond policy upgrades and new laws... it was"—he searched for the word—"something unrecognizable. America 2.0. We were going to upgrade the democratic system, the economy, all of it. Change voting. Change buying and selling. Immigration—we had a plan for immigration that would bring anyone who wanted to come in and work and put them on a share system that would have doubled household income for Americans in a decade... and not just at the highest level, at every individual level. It was complicated... but it would have worked."

"Sounds good on paper," Jack said, "but did you ever think it would be too much too fast?"

"*Life* is too much too fast. We had a list of reforms lined up that would have given us back the efficiency we need to grow at postwar rates again. We would have flushed a hundred years of coalitions and special interest barnacles off the hull of this country."

"Why not? Why not make some of those changes? Where *are* they?"

This was the first Jack had heard of anything like progress from Winspear. Of anything like a change for the better or a change that wasn't just obviously negative.

"It just went downhill so fast, Jack, and the red tape… good *God*, it was hard to even get the people into a room who could help plan it and do it properly. If I could do it again I'd have signed a dozen executive orders on day one. And with Sierra gone…"—he shook his head as he spoke, looking down—"but it's all so much worse than I thought it could be. It's so much dirtier. I was prepared to take it head on. I knew what it was going to take, and I was ready." He shook his head. "But I never expected to have to do it without her."

Jack chose his words carefully. "You know, there may be time to turn this around, or to ease the blow." He shook his head slowly, "maybe."

"I hope so," he turned to Jack. "If they don't impeach me, I'll resign."

"That…" Jack said, "might be what's best."

"Part of me thinks I should fight tooth and nail to stay. That maybe I can turn it around and come back from this… this void that I somehow let myself slip into. But I've already done so much damage, to the country and to the presidency. I want to believe there's a way to make things better, but…"— He shook his head—"things don't get better, Jack. They really don't. Sometimes I think it would've been better if it was me in the car that night."

"What?"

"Sierra's accident," he said. "I was—we had some voting rally thing, I forget the details." He shook his head. "I stayed late, she went back with part of the motorcade, and there was an accident, a hit and run."

"I remember," Jack said.

Winspear sighed. "Tell me this, Jack. Do you think there's a god?"

"I… I don't like to think about it."

Winspear grunted approvingly. "Surprisingly honest. I suspect that's how most people feel about it. Anyone who's had life tear them apart, anyhow."

"What about you? Your voters seem to think you're a believer."

"Ha!"

Winspear leaned back a bit, looking out over the warehouse which stretched stories above, below, and ahead.

"I might have been. Once. Whenever I see them praying, though, I just think of Sierra. All that life, gone in an instant. For nothing. Meaningless. That's when I knew, Jack. There's no one up there. It's chaos... all the way up, and all the way down."

Just then, a loud siren started to blare, coming from several directions at once.

"What the hell is that?" one of the soldiers shouted at Roy, who was still working on the office door about 50 feet from where Winspear and Jack were sitting.

"I don't know," he shouted back. "Door's almost ready."

"What the hell," Winspear said, standing, the Secret Service agent reaching over to help him up.

Suddenly, there was a humming noise from the shelves at their back. Something loud and getting louder. Jack barely had time to yell out in surprise as the sound overtook them in the form of a carpet of drones that suddenly shot out from the narrow gap above the shelves. A swarm thick as locusts poured forward, the air swirling as they careened overhead.

"What's going on?" Winspear shouted over to Roy, who shook his head, barely glancing up from his laptop.

"Mr. President," one of the soldiers said, shouting over the sounds of the ongoing alarm and the drones, "we have to get you out of here! Now!"

"Need you at the door!" Roy shouted.

Through all of this, Jack hadn't managed to scramble up yet. He'd been caught off guard by the drones overhead, and he was still staring up dumbly at the black carpet of tiny flying machines that was spilling out into the cavern of skyscraper shelves in a fit of complicated motion.

That's when he noticed a pressure at his back.

A push.

"What the," he said, turning, seeing that it wasn't something on the shelf that had push against his back. It was the shelf itself, which had moved an inch forward.

As he watched, the shelf next to it moved forward too, and the shelf on the other side crept a little farther still. Looking down the line of them, he could see they were all slipping forward.

"Uh…" he said, scrambling up, "I think we have a problem over here!"

They all saw it now, save for Roy who had his eyes locked on his laptop.

"Door! Now!" one of the agents shouted, grabbing Winspear roughly by the shoulder and jerking him forward. He pulled his gun, seemingly out of instinct.

"Winspear!" Roy yelled over to them.

They were all racing toward him, the shelves creeping, the gap between the wall they formed and the drop off into the darkness below closing from three feet to two and a half.

Jack moved quickly, turning to see that one of the soldiers who'd walked off farther than he and Winspear had was jogging up to them.

"What's happening!" Winspear shouted.

"I don't know," Roy said, standing. "The door—I need a backup passphrase from you."

They were all running toward him, the shelves closing in, and Winspear was close to the door. As Jack joined them, the group formed a rough single file, the shelves still pushing in, pushing them toward the edge and the darkness below. Two feet of walkway now.

"Now!" one of the Secret Service agents said.

"Passphrase," Winspear said, flustered, "I don't—I don't know what backup—"

There was the sound of gunfire, and a scream that raised the hair on the back of Jack's neck. They all turned to see the soldier who'd been bringing up the rear disappear over the edge. As he fell, he pulled the trigger on his gun so that the staccato sound of automatic gunfire was added to the alarm bells.

"Your *backup passphrase!*" Roy shouted back at him.

The shelves were closing in, there was less than a foot and a half of space.

Jack was starting to panic, pressing forward against the Secret Service agent holding Winspear who turned around and barked, "Get back!"

"*Sierra!*" Winspear shouted toward the panel in the wall next to the door. They waited an agonizing second and the red light on the lock turned green.

The door slid open with a loud hissing, and they jumped inside, Jack stumbling against the Secret Service agent ahead as a voice from behind shouted, "Go! Go!"

The office was unlit, the only light coming from behind them, but now the shelves were sliding to block the doorway and cutting off that too. So it was darkness for a moment, all of them breathing hard, stunned. And then the lights clicked on and Jack heard Winspear say, "Oh God."

He followed Winspear's gaze to the other end of the room.

Behind a grand oak desk, the surface covered in a layer of dust that could be made out even from here, sat Clayton Scarly.

And it was clear to all of them that he'd been dead for years.

Part 3—Forward into Darkness

"It was a silly idea—I'd seen the numbers on the new battery tech, and we were all trying to solve the Shenzhen problem. You just couldn't get around it; there was no way to cross the ocean cheaply. The breakthrough was realizing the economy of scale was old news. A tradition. We could build a drone that had solar capacity and battery tech so good it sucked in power twice as fast as it used it. You could fly that over the Pacific in a little over 53 hours, and the battery would deliver charge to the grid on the other end. Charge you could get a premium for if you dumped it at peak demand by timing the routes right. Forget containers—we were going to build a shipping swarm. That's how net-positive shipping was born. And that was my little secret for a dozen years until everyone else caught on. I spent a decade not just shipping products for free, but actually making grid money off the extra battery capacity."

—Excerpt from *The First Trillion's the Hardest*,
by J. Woolston Winspear

30

For a moment, they just stared.

Jack couldn't look away, partly out of morose fascination but also because, if he was honest, he almost expected Scarly—*the body*, rather—to move.

The eyes were open, though hollowed out, the actual eyeballs seeming to have shrunk back in their sockets. His mouth was open too, and in the light Jack could make out the shadow of Scarly's tongue sitting between his bottom row of teeth like a strap of leather.

His face—the skin on it, and the skin on his hands which were placed calmly on the armrests—were also tanned and leathery.

"What the hell happened to him?" Roy asked, finally breaking the silence and stepping forward.

"Wait," the Secret Service agent said, grabbing him at the elbow. "We don't know. No gun. No cups or syringes."

Jack noticed that he was right. There was nothing on the desk save for an obsolete computer and a few sheets of paper, all covered in dust. On top of the papers sat a pen that might have been shiny once, but now had a layer of dust on it.

"It could be a trap," the agent said. "You ever seen a body like that?"

He said this over his shoulder to one of the soldiers, who then took a step forward, shouldering his weapon and aiming the business end of it at Scarly's dead body, an action

Jack couldn't blame him for, considering the level of sheer strangeness at play here.

"No," he answered, and Jack wondered if the faint shake in his voice might be from watching one of his friends fall to his death moments ago. "There's no decay," he said, "or not as much as I'd expect. It's like he's been preserved."

"How long?" Roy asked.

The soldier looked back at him, then at the Secret Service agent, then back to the body.

"No way to tell for sure, but it's obviously been a while."

He took a few steps forward, still aiming the weapon.

"No smell," he said, and Jack noticed too that there was nothing.

No hint of putrid decay. No mustiness.

"It's not right," the other soldier said.

Slowly, he made his way around the desk, getting a look at Scarly from the side.

"Fluid stains on the floor," he said. "It's almost"—he shook his head—"like he just died here and drained out."

"The desk," Winspear said. "Check the papers."

With some trepidation, the soldier leaned over, keeping Scarly's corpse in the corner of his eye as he reached with one hand to grab the sheet of paper.

As he lifted it, the pen rolled off. It surprised him, and he jerked back, his leg hitting the corner of the chair which jolted.

There was a sound like something snapping as the chair moved, and then, quietly, Scarly's jaw fell, detaching from the rest of his face. The soldier jumped back as it tumbled into his lap, and the head lolled forward after it.

"Shit!" the soldier said, just as the head rolled down and onto the floor.

"Oh my God," Winspear said. "What could have—"

He shook his head, taking a step back and reaching up to cover his mouth with one hand.

The soldier had recovered by now, and remembered he still had the piece of paper in his hand.

"There's a date on here," he said, "handwritten. Almost a year and a half ago."

"When's the last time you talked to him?" Roy asked Winspear.

"I—before the inauguration. After the election—when we set up the blind trust."

"So what? three years?" Roy asked.

Winspear swallowed hard and nodded.

Roy turned back toward the body and said, "No weapon. No gun. Poor bastard just, what? Worked himself to death?"

It was an attempt at a joke, Jack realized after a moment, but nobody laughed.

Muffled through the door, the alarm, which had still been blaring, shut off.

The other remaining soldier stepped up to the desk.

Once he was between the rest of them and the body, he turned to speak, "OK. We came here to find Clayton Scarly, and we did. Now it's time to leave."

Jack saw Winspear and Roy exchange a glance. Winspear looked over his shoulder at one of the Secret Service agents.

"I agree," the Secret Service agent said, both to Winspear and the soldier.

"The situation," the soldier went on, "has deteriorated. Someone died out there just few minutes ago, and I think you'll all agree with me that we are under attack."

"Attack!?" Roy said.

"What else would you call that business with the shelves trying to push us off?"

"Some routine rearrangement of—" Roy started to say.

"Quiet," the soldier said. "Let me think a minute."

He looked around the room, pointing his gun past Roy at the door they'd come through.

"That's blocked, right?"

Roy nodded.

"And you can't control the shelves through the drone—whatever trick you did to hack it?"

Roy shook his head. "Their boards just access to the intranet the drone would be querying. I can monitor orders, not make them. Drones don't tell the shelves where and when to move; that's the job of the central computer that—"

"Doesn't matter. If we're blocked that way, then the other side of this wall is more shelves, right?"

He pointed in the direction of the shelves, the direction from which they'd entered the warehouse facility.

Roy nodded.

"Okay. Then unless you know of some kind of escape hatch, we're going to go *this* way."

He pointed to the wall that faced the open chasm.

"What?" Winspear said.

"Mr. President, our primary concern is getting you out of here as fast as possible. I think it's clear that we can't come back the way we came. You," he gestured to Roy, "are there other ways out of the facility? Roof access? Doors on the opposite side of the building?"

"Sure," he said, "I mean, there *were*."

"It's the best we've got."

He turned to the other soldier who was still holding the note from the desk.

"Have the IT guy—"

"My name's *Roy*."

"—scan that and save it. Then leave it and prep breaching charges around that wall."

The soldier nodded, jogging over and handing the note to Roy before slinging his weapon over his shoulder and heading for the wall. As he knelt by it, he pulled a thin coil of something plastic-looking out of a pocket.

"Now," the soldier who'd taken control turned to the group, "everyone move back."

"We need to figure out what happened here," Roy said.

"I agree," Winspear said. "We're not leaving until—"

"Sir, we cannot stay here," the soldier said. "We don't know what killed him, and we don't know what tried to kill us out there just now. For all we know, this is a trap, and we've walked right into it. So I'm getting you out whether you like it or not."

"You're being ridiculous," Roy said. "Look around, there's nothing in here—"

"He's right," the Secret Service agent said, stepping forward, taking the soldier's side, and giving Roy a look that quieted him.

"Ready," the other soldier said from the chasm-side of the room, taking a step back from his breaching charge.

"Do it," the first soldier said to him, and there was a blast that shook the floor.

All at once, they were looking out a door-sized hole in the wall to the sea of shelves beyond.

"Okay," the soldier said, walking to the opening and looking out. "You," he said, pointing at Roy. "How far up are we?"

"Nine stories," he said. "Then the basement levels. Like I said earlier, maybe 150 feet or—"

"And how far back is the other side of this place."

"I—I don't know."

The soldier looked at him, but then calmly replied, "Okay."

He slung his gun onto his back, pointing at the Secret Service agent.

"You first, then me, then the president. And then," he looked over his shoulder at the other soldier, "you follow him, got it?"

The man nodded.

"Everyone else fall in after that."

"What are you talking about?" Winspear asked, taking a step toward him and toward the hole in the wall.

He could see now that one of the skyscraper shelves was within a few feet to the right—a short jump away. Even as he watched, a small flock of drones swooped past.

"We need to go now, before it moves," the soldier said, and when they continued to stare at him, he added, "Unless you have a better idea, we're going to have to climb out of here."

31

Minority leader Jim Burns hit *send* on his phone.

I'm here.

He looked up and down the street again slowly, aware that he was carefully in a dark spot between the streetlights that lit the road and the white stone facades that lined it. Here and there, windows dotting the buildings' sides were bright rectangles against the overcast dark night of Washington.

In the distance, a siren wailed, but other than that it was eerily quiet. Since the bomb threat on the Capitol, they'd put up roadblocks and started checking anyone entering the city. The ghost-town feel of the place spooked Burns almost as much as this cloak-and-dagger stuff with Adler did.

He was outside the FBI building, across the street from the side door where Adler had told him to meet her.

His phone chirped. Adler was on her way up, and he listened as a growl of metal on metal in the distance came closer and an armored troop carrier came around the corner.

Burns wasn't doing anything wrong, but something about the hulking military vehicle on patrol spooked him to the core. He stepped back farther into the shadow as it passed, out of the floodlight-bright lights on the thing scanning the darkness as it moved on down the street.

He watched the vehicle continue, spotlight searching the roadside as it went. He wondered for a moment how much safer they were with the police and military running around with guns drawn. Protection. Occupation. Why was General Mercer moving armored transports into the capital?

Ahead of him, the door opened, a pane of light against the shadows as Burns looked up and down the street, jogging across.

"Congressman Burns," Tarrah said.

"Ms. Adler," he said, stepping in, taking off his scarf.

"Please," she said, "call me Tarrah."

As soon as the door was shut, they both stopped. They looked at each other, and Burns sighed.

The weight of the moment was surreal as they shook hands, and Adler gave him a quick nod, a silent recognition that they were at the cross section of history.

"You think the founding fathers ever thought it would be this bad? That it would come to this?" Burns said.

"Impeachment," Adler replied, turning and heading down the hall with Burns in tow. "Sure. That's why they wrote it in."

"Not just the impeachment," Burns said. "Look at what's happening in the House. They're going to stop us. They'll kill the vote."

"Then they'll get voted out with new representatives, and the *next* batch'll vote to impeach."

"I wish I believed that was the logical outcome," Burns said, "but nothing's logical anymore. You know that better than I do."

Tarrah grunted as they entered the elevator.

"*Electing* him wasn't logical."

"If we don't impeach tomorrow..."—Burns shook his head—"We've got to send a signal to the world that we've got this under control. The market—Russia and China are serious. They've been playing softball up until now. I was watching the news before I came here."

The elevator doors opened on the basement level, and Adler led Burns to the office as he went on.

"You know what they're saying, right? About the markets not closing? The ripples across Europe, the Middle East"— he checked his watch—"Asia."

They were at the small office, and Burns shrugged off his jacket as Adler took a seat and lit a cigarette.

"We've had recessions before," she said, the smoke wafting slowly as she snapped the gold plated lighter shut and tossed it on the table so that it slid toward the ashtray.

"Not like this," Burns said sitting down and waving away the cigarette case Tarrah offered. "Quit years ago, thanks," he said. "I mean, you see how it's going to be played, right?"

Tarrah nodded, taking a puff on the cigarette and letting the smoke out slowly, so that it trickled out between her lips, finally blowing it away as she said, "That we're doing it on purpose. Framing it as an accident."—She shrugged—"Hitting a reset button on the global economy and profiting from the fallout."

"And that doesn't worry you?"

"If we can get it under control," Tarrah said, "they'll do what they do whenever there's a mistake like this: undo it. Scrub the last 24 hours of market activity and call it a glitch. That's why we have a Securities and Exchange Commission."

"That's why we have to—"

Burns shook his head, leaning forward, and said, "You know what, I will take one of those."—He reached for the cigarette case—"The SEC will fix it, sure, if half their staff isn't fired by Winspear just out of spite to muck it all up."— He lit the cigarette, taking a deep breath of it in—"This thing is happening *now*, as in across the globe as other markets are opening and *closing early*, at least in China's case. They're all seeing drops—huge drops—everyone's panicking and pulling money out left and right. Algorithms... don't even get me started on the high-frequency trading shit."

"Triggers tripping everywhere," Tarrah said. "I've been following it too."

Across the world, as the markets fell, automatic high-frequency trading algorithms were panicking just like the humans were, stop-loss orders triggering left and right and adding to the madness.

Burns continued, "And we can't get our *damn exchanges* to close. Do you know how fishy that is? They're saying this was either planned by us or a cyberattack by a foreign agent that is so advanced—"

He leaned back, taking another drag on the cigarette.

"Someone's setting this up," Tarrah said. "That's the only way I can make sense of it. Someone's hacked in and set all our systems up ahead of time to let this happen."

"North Korea," Burns said. "Russia," he rolled his eyes. "It could be anyone—I bet if you went online there'd *still* be someone saying it's the Clinton deep state or something equally ridiculous. False flag crap. Every nut-job theory you can imagine."

"So, what can we do?" Adler asked, stubbing out her cigarette and reaching for another.

"About the vote?"

She nodded.

"Well, if we can get him out, then people will settle down. They'll see the country hasn't lost its mind... that we're willing to work with everyone else to figure out this attack—it *is* an attack by the way, definitely—but *Guilfoyle*."

Tarrah grunted.

"He's in Winspear's pocket. And the majority is too."

"If you trigger the vote," she said.

Burns shook his head.

"I'll get a second to the motion, but he can slap it down. Or worse—he can let it go through and they'll just outvote us. We need a 2/3 majority to impeach, you know."

"I do," Tarrah said, nodding. "But they don't want a vote, do they? They want to be able to cover, to say this time next month that they *would* have voted for impeachment if only the vote had come up."

"Exactly," Burns said. "So they'll try to stop the vote entirely."

"How can they do that?"

"I don't know, but somewhere in Washington they're sitting in a room just like this, planning something, I guarantee you that."

"Well," Tarrah said, "we go in and we try and we see what happens."

Burns looked at her, nodding, leaning back and taking another drag on the cigarette.

"You know, I trust you," he said after a moment, holding her gaze a heartbeat too long. He might have heard a ticking just then, barely, a clock somewhere in the room no doubt.

Adler raised an eyebrow. She'd wondered, when Burns reached out, if this was just a social call. Apparently not.

"Something else?"

"One of my contacts in the CIA."

"Oh boy," she said, "What is it?"

"There was a report generated a few months ago. Pentagon Papers style. *The Effects of the Winspear Presidency.*"

"You're kidding."

"No," Burns said. "And if anyone ever asks, it doesn't exist and I never told you. But they predicted something in that report—that if the US fell into disarray, the other world superpowers—"

"—Russia and China—"

Burns nodded.

"—would have an opportunity to shift the geopolitical center of gravity, that it would be categorically stupid of them to miss. Just by the sheer game theory of things... we're showing them our necks with a dotted line where to cut."

"And we think they're starting to act on that opportunity?"

Burns leaned forward in his chair.

"My contact told me they're picking up troop movements by China into Africa and Russia. *Strategic* movements. And Russia is simultaneously setting up a base in India."

"Strategic, in what way?"

Burns grabbed another cigarette.

"Gold mines."—He lit it, taking a puff—"The largest in the world. And they've both been buying up global supply quietly over the last year or so."

"I don't understand. What's the point?" Tarrah asked.

"Well, they're locking down gold supply worldwide," Burns said. "This is the first step. This is what *shifting the geopolitical balance* looks like."

"But gold… you don't mean—"

Burns nodded.

"They're going to sign an agreement. Swap all of Asia and Russia and whoever will defect from Europe to a new currency, one backed by a gold standard."

"They can't do that."

"Oh yes they can," Burns said, "and they won't even have to twist anyone's arm to do it. The US dollar is the world's reserve currency, and it's starting to crumble from the weight of all this."

"The stock markets?"

"That's just the straw that's breaking the camel's back. Dollar value has been depreciating ever since Winspear came to power."

"But the dollar can't—"

She shook her head, struggling to find the right words. This—global economics—they didn't exactly train you on it in the FBI.

"It won't just be a global recession if we don't get control of this," Bowers said. "If the world starts dumping the dollar as its reserve currency, the devaluing that's already going on will speed up. Say goodbye to your retirement. Your 401(k).

It'll be hyperinflation… and with sentiment across the world so against us and a competitive currency backed by gold *and* two out of three world superpowers."

He shook his head, blowing smoke as punctuation, adding, "The inflation will make the reichsmark look like a goddamn government bond."

"Reichsmark?"

"The Weimar Republic currency—Nazi Germany's dollar—it inflated something like a million percent when Germany decided to go off gold to fund the War. In a period of a few years they went from one mark being worth a few dollars to a few dollars being worth a few *trillion* marks. And if they go through with it… you think *this* administration would be able to negotiate a place in the new future? Or if they'd tolerate it at all?"

"What do you mean tolerate it?"

"I mean these things don't just happen in a vacuum. The current administration—Winspear's supporters, General Mercer…"

He took another quick drag on the cigarette, getting worked up and speaking past the smoke as he explained, "It won't be seen as the natural order of things for us to lose control of the global economy. They'll call it a currency war, economic sabotage by Russia and China, which is true in some sense, but"—he shrugged—"we really are losing control of the dollar, so you can't blame them that much."

"A currency war," Adler echoed. "And let me guess. That has the potential to turn into a shooting war if we don't get our way?"

"Potential…" Burns said. "More like a guarantee. Maybe if we still had a functioning executive branch, cooler heads could prevail."—He shook his head, reaching forward and stubbing the cigarette out—"Mercer's up to something too; you can be sure of that."

"I certainly noticed a... *presence* in the city," Adler said.

"Preparation, maybe. For an attack."—His eyes met Adler's—"For something else."

"Not a *coup*," Adler said, but Burns just shrugged.

Tarrah thought about this, wishing she could see a flaw in the logic. Instead, any hope she'd had now felt like it was being stubbed out in the ashtray too. She'd wondered what Burns had meant about needing to have the vote tomorrow— for Adler, an impeachment now was only fractionally better than one next month, but it was clear there was only a small window of time to change the trajectory. And it was getting smaller by the hour.

Winspear. Mercer. The representatives in the House. Not for the first time, Adler felt like the chaos that swirled around her as all these men jockeyed for position was going to collapse like a house of cards. Like there was a chance to make things right, but only if she could just get a few minutes without someone throwing their own curve ball into the mix.

"Meanwhile," Burns went on, "the *hermit president* is living up to his name. Usually we'd have heard something by now— some backhanded comment about *you* at the very least. But no! Most powerful man in the world is once again MIA. Letting everything fall to shit while he's off—who knows where."

Adler frowned. If Burns was right, if he and his CIA contact both knew what they were talking about, then they really *did* have to get Winspear out tomorrow. They had to send a signal, and quickly, before things escalated past a point of no return.

As she reached for another cigarette, she repeated, "A shooting war."

Burns nodded.

"And if that happens,"—he shook his head—"well, let's just say I'll quit smoking again *after* I'm sure we're not about to be on the receiving end of a few thousand nuclear warheads."

32

They'd climbed for almost an hour before stopping.

The shelves moved around them. Though, thankfully, the one they were on shifted only once. That had taken them away from the wall of shelves outside the office and deeper in, toward the center.

After they reached the top of their shelf, the lead soldier decided that they ought to be moving over as well as up, so they transitioned laterally for a while, clambering across the shelves they could reach, hands and arms starting to go numb. The plan was to make it to the top, to a roof exit if they could find one—Roy said there would be access panels for the solar—but when Winspear almost slipped, the Secret Service agents called for a break.

The soldiers agreed and climbed onto a tall, boxy section of the vertical shelf they were on—one that had about six feet of room top to bottom with upright objects like vacuums, boxed lamps, and cheap flat-pack furniture. They pushed it all off into the abyss, leaving a space of about four feet by four to loiter on. Roy, Winspear, and Jack climbed onto it, as the Secret Service agents and soldiers decided to split up and keep climbing, despite the chance that the shelves would move and mix them up. After all, they could always shout to the others and follow their voices if it came to that.

One of the agents stayed behind, taking up a spot on the tall shelf below Winspear, Jack, and Roy, and they settled in to wait for the others' return.

Close as the forest of other shelves were, there was enough room for drones to fly between everything, which meant there was enough room for Roy to sit facing out, leaning his torso on the steel corner support with his legs hanging off the edge.

Jack sat in one of the corners next to him facing inward, knees up with his arms clasped around them—a close approximation of comfortable.

And Winspear sat cross legged, one hand supporting his chin, the other poking at the drone that Roy had landed on the platform. They'd talked about sending the drone out to do reconnaissance, but it had only so much battery life.

"How long have they been gone?" Jack asked.

He had a watch, but for some reason it felt better to ask.

Roy fished his phone out, checking the time.

"Goin' on four hours now."

Before they'd left, when Roy had asked how long to wait for them before getting worried, the lead soldier explained that if they never came back, then Winspear, Roy, and Jack should stay put.

"Just keep waiting?" Winspear had asked. "What do you want us to do to survive? Forage for food?"

The soldier had said that's exactly what he wanted him to do, if it came to it.

Now, it was the three of them and the agent below, and they all jumped as the shelf started to move.

"Jesus," Roy said with a start, dropping his phone as he grabbed at the bar. The phone hit hard on something as it fell, and he turned to Winspear who shook his head.

"Well," Roy said, "it's not like I had a signal anyway."

"You think soldier boy thought of this?" Winspear said, resigned. "What happens when they come back and can't find us?"

"They'll find us," Jack said.

As the shelf moved slowly underneath them, Jack could feel it swaying slightly.

"You feel that?"

"Yeah," Roy said.

"Mm hm," Winspear grunted.

"One thing I can't figure out," Roy said, "is what happened to Scarly in there."

"Isn't it obvious?" Winspear asked. "He killed himself. Always was a melancholy guy really—I didn't think he was *that* melancholy, but"—he shrugged—"who am I to judge?"

"The picture of his note," Roy said, carefully turning around.

He picked up the drone and carefully reached up to store it on the shelf above, making space for his laptop, which he pulled out now.

"The picture was on my phone but should have synced to my laptop—here it is."

He squinted at the screen, zooming in.

"You know, it's hard to read this thing—the ink's really faded, but—"

Roy looked up at Winspear, surprised.

"It's to *you*."

"What?"

"'Dear James,'" Roy read, then looked up again. Jack's eyes were wide too, and they motioned him on.

"'You won't read this for a long time, I'm sure,'" Roy read, "'but I hope by then you'll understand why I had to do it. I know that this means taking away everything from you—or, while not everything, at least something very, very important—and because of that I have not made the decision lightly.'"

Roy furrowed his brow, pausing long enough to look up at Winspear, who also seemed confused.

"'But,'" he went on, "'I think that if you knew everything that I did, you would consider yourself honor bound to act. I have to end things here because...'"

Roy looked up, shaking his head.

"That's all there is."

"*What?* Give me that."

Winspear took the laptop, seeing for himself.

"I don't know," Roy said, shaking his head and looking at Jack. "It doesn't make sense. It just stops there."

"Not even a signature," Winspear said, and as he motioned the screen away in disgust, Jack took it and looked over the faded lines of script himself.

Scarly's handwriting was neat. Clean. He was one of those people who'd been drafting letters by hand for so long—or maybe he'd just learned it early enough as a habit—that he could justify the line lengths on either side. It was carefully detailed. Thought out.

"How does a guy like this not finish his suicide letter?" Jack asked. "I mean, he seems... *intense.*"

"He *was* intense," Winspear said, "and a pure analytical. This"—he waved his hand at the screen, disgusted—"*all* of this... none of it makes any damned sense at all!"

He looked out over the shelves, shaking his head."

"Occam's razor," Roy said. When they both looked at him, he explained, "The simplest solution is almost always the correct one."

"And what's your simple solution here, Einstein?" Winspear asked.

"Well, think about it. Scarly didn't have his brains and bone fragments covering the ceiling, and he didn't have a knife sticking out of him. He was poisoned—that seems like the suicide method an *analytical* person, as you put it, would use. Except he goofed."—Roy shrugged—"He took his poison too early or else took too much of it and died right in the middle of the closing act."

"Ridiculous," Winspear said. "It doesn't make sense he'd kill himself at all, and it *sure* doesn't make sense that he'd do it as some kind of half-baked revenge plot."

"Revenge?" Jack asked.

"'I know that this means taking away everything from you'? What do you think that means? I *told* you I was being framed, and I *told* you that Scarly being behind it was nuts. Well, what can I say? I wasn't lying to you, but apparently I severely underestimated whatever Clayton Scarly might have had planned for me."

"What'd you do to him?" Roy asked.

"Beats me. I don't do anything to most of the people who come after me," he smiled, adding, "*Jack.*"

"There must have been something," Jack said. "Surely you—"

"Surely I what? Backstabbed him? Played the villain in some vaudeville that'd match the noise level of the news? Sorry, Jack, it was all business with Scarly. He was honored to chair the blind trust. I don't know why he'd use that power to stick me like this, but there it is. Nature red in tooth and claw."

"But why—"

"Why *not*, Jack? You think it's friendly up here? At the top? Scarly did to me what I'd have done to him, probably, if the roles were reversed."

"Winspear," Jack said, shaking his head, "would you *also kill yourself* afterward?"

Winspear looked at him, but said nothing.

Jack said, "Why would he sabotage you and then make sure he wasn't around to take your place? People make more sense than that."

"Do they? Did you make sense when you brought that gun into—"

"You're deflecting."

It was Roy who said it, and Winspear snapped a look at him, realizing that he was not only physically crowded by the two men, but now he was also being ganged up on by them.

"Whatever," Winspear said. "It doesn't matter. They'll impeach me; they'll say it's all true. Whatever Scarly did, it worked, okay? Because without him alive I'll never know—nobody will ever know—and maybe *that's* why he did it, Jack. Did you think of that? Like I told you, it's chaos all the way down."

The shelf had been slowly moving along this whole time, and now it slowed to a halt, causing all of them to reach out and steady themselves.

"What's that thing you said earlier?" Jack asked Roy. "Occam's razor?"

Roy nodded. "The simplest explanation is probably the right one."

"Okay, well here's a simple explanation for you: All of this is *connected* somehow."

"All of what?" Winspear spat.

"This—"

Jack waved his hand out into the sea of shelves, the darkness pocked here and there by a fleeting drone trail, the sound of the shelves creaking as they moved.

"We're trapped in here, in case you hadn't noticed, and someone tried to *kill* us earlier. Scarly, the warehouse"—Jack was ticking things off on his hand—"that show we saw with the drones earlier—the simplest explanation is probably right. And the simplest explanation is that it's all connected somehow."

"So what?" Winspear started. "You think that Scarly set me up, *and* he programmed my own facility to kill me when I came to check in on him?"

"Impossible," Roy said. "Nobody could crack my system."

Jack laughed.

"Somebody sure as hell did! You almost fell off that ledge earlier too—"

"No," Roy cut him off, "it's impossible—quantum computers don't work like that. They can't just *be hacked*. The system would have seen any tampering and quarantined the code, restored from backup. A program this large has an *immune* system. And it's lattice encrypted right up to here."

He held a hand out above his head.

"Well, tell me more about that," Jack said. "We've got time."

"What do you want to know?"

"I want to know how this thing works—how big it really is, because someone used it to try to get rid of us, and they may be using it for something *else*."

Roy thought about this for a moment.

"I—" he started, giving a look at Winspear. "This is stupid."—He shook his head—"I've been trying to figure that out, sort of. What could cause the behavior we saw earlier?"

"And?"

"The drones are package movers," he said, shrugging. "We saw hundreds of them suddenly swooping in, out to the towers. If they were picking up items to ship, then that was people placing orders. But the normal frequency of orders... it doesn't look like that. Usually, there's a bell curve"—he made the shape in the air in front of him—"It follows time zones and peaks at midday Central. There's *never* a volume that would cause that kind of response unless something big changed."

"What kind of something?" Jack asked.

"A huge delay maybe, something that pauses a whole hub for a certain amount of time so that orders build up. Or a new product release, but even then, that wouldn't be distributed across a whole warehouse. Maybe a change in global shipping routes that just got tipped over into profitable or—"

"What about Black Friday?" Jack said, cutting him off.

Roy stared at him.

"It's not Black Friday, Jack."

"I know, but think about it. You've seen the videos—stampedes of people into stores. For the sales."

"You're saying," Roy thought about it, talking slowly, "that maybe there's some kind of price reduction?"

"It makes sense, doesn't it?" Jack shrugged. "I'm not an economist or anything, but I remember supply and demand curves. If there was some kind of huge sale going on, people would be buying more. Earlier, you said the warehouse stock moves around. You used the word migration."

"Yeah," Roy said, "so?"

"So what we saw earlier... what was that? A stampede of drones? Just like a stampede of shoppers on Black Friday?"

"Yeah," Roy said with a little laugh. "Maybe it could have been something like that."

"Is there any way we can access the marketplace? See if something like that's going on? Something big moving across the network?"

"I don't have a signal," Roy said, but suddenly he lit up. "Oh! But the drone—I can access the company intranet through it. Let's just hope there's a little battery left."

He was already hopping up, grabbing the drone from the upper level, and then he sat back down and reached for his laptop.

"Progress," Jack said, meeting Winspear's eyes, but the president looked away.

It was only then that Jack remembered when Winspear had first been talking about Scarly. If all of that was true, then they'd been not just close partners, but friends. And now, Winspear believed that one of his only true friends had literally sacrificed himself just to get the better of him.

Jack didn't want that to be true, but they only had the evidence they had. It was hard to see it any other way.

Despite everything else, he felt for Winspear. His wife

dead. His best friend and longtime business partner a back-stabbing snake in the grass. Quite literally the whole country about to kick him out of his job for doing it so badly, and his name and legacy soiled, never mind how rich he'd still be. Framed. Betrayed. Attacked on all sides.

"Hey," Jack said to him, "it's gonna be okay."

Winspear looked at him and then looked away again, back into the darkness around them.

"Jack, that's the stupidest thing you've said all day."

33

Back in the White House, Kay hovered near the coffee pot. She held a mug in her hand, not drinking, the heat long gone from it, the windows eerily dark as the analysts continued to work.

At least one of them had quit and walked out earlier, grabbing her bag and heading through the big double doors that, since earlier in the day, had been flanked by soldiers who talked into walkies now and then.

Kay couldn't help but look back at them, the soldiers, with their gleaming steel weapons and body armor. The mood in the place had definitely shifted.

Bowers and his high level partners streamed out of the conference room, and Kay saw that several of them were putting their jackets on.

"What's happening?" Kay asked, and Bowers started to say something, but one of the partners cut him off.

"We're leaving," the man next to Bowers in a dark suit said and then he raised his voice, addressing the room, "Hey—excuse me, everybody."

"I really don't think," Bowers starting to say, but the room had turned to the other partner, and now he went on.

"Hey, thanks. Listen, we really appreciate everyone's help, but as of a few minutes ago this is all illegal."

There was a worried stirring around the room. The analysts looked around at each other, their fears confirmed in narrowed gazes.

"Hold on," he said. "Hold on. Everyone's okay."

Near the back, one of the soldiers lifted his radio up and stepped out to talk into it.

"What are you talking about?" Kay interjected, her own voice raised.

"We just got off a conference call with the Securities Exchange Commission and the Nasdaq."

Everyone in the room stared.

"As you know, the Nasdaq is still open. That is *highly* unusual. The Nasdaq is running off battery backups. And somebody has infiltrated their system so thoroughly that the *room to the backups* is inaccessible—something about remote locks—and not only that but the kill switch for the computers allowing the thing to keep working has been disabled."

"Can't they just cut the power?" one of the junior analysts asked.

"They already did," Bowers answered, stepping forward and trying to take the lead. "We are at the point where they have actually cut the power to all of Wall Street at the municipal level, and the SEC is currently working with the local network providers to get it shut down that way."

"What about the brokers?" It was a female analyst who spoke up. "Don't they have automatic shutoffs or—"

"Long story short," the other partner answered, "yes and no. TD Ameritrade has it baked into their algorithms to not let trades be placed outside trading hours on their normal portal, but Capital One, Robinhood, a whole host of others"—he shook his head—"they didn't build it in because they didn't think they'd need it. It turns out, the pipes all point at the exchange and run off its timeline."

"They have advised us," Bowers started in, "to not touch anything—don't delete anything, don't take your computers with you—leave it all as it stands, and go home. Those of you who don't feel safe are more than welcome to stay in one of the White House guest rooms for the night. Capitol police have been notified of the situation and will be on hand to give rides to any of you who—"

"What about the other markets?" one of the analysts asked.

Kay had been wondering too. They'd all been following the news—the ever increasing furor of outrage from the world as the other exchanges came online and experienced the fallout of an American stock market in shambles, still somehow allowing trades to go through that were rippling through the global networks as an obvious tone of panic spread.

"We don't know," Bowers said, shaking his head, "All we know is that the scale of this attack—"

"*Attack?*" Kay asked.

"—yes, that's the word the SEC used. The level of sophistication required to compromise the Nasdaq by this degree is unlike anything they've ever seen. I don't mind saying this since it's already on the news: It is now believed that whatever is going on with the market is being orchestrated by an outside actor, likely another state government—"

At this point someone broke ranks. They stopped listening, deer in the headlights calm, and began gathering up their things. Most of them were pulling their phones up to their faces, heading for the door, never mind the police escorts.

Kay watched it all in stunned silence. She wouldn't be going anywhere; she knew that already.

"Where's Jack?" she said to Bowers, moving past the fleeing analysts. "And the president?"

"We don't know," Bowers said, shaking his head. "They went into the facility early this morning."

"Bowers," Kay said as she got next to him, lowering her voice and pulling him aside, "what's going *on?*"

"I don't know, Kay. I really don't."

"Was this... did we cause this?"

"Maybe," he said, shaking his head, "but I just don't know. This is the safest place on the planet, though. We'll sit tight and wait to hear from Winspear."

As Kay watched the last of the junior analysts leave, she remembered Tildow's brain exploding across the steps of the Capitol Building. The bomb threat that had followed. Before that, Quentin Daniels.

And the news—the most recent communique out of Russia. An intercepted message, supposedly, from the Russian ambassador, which the news had paraphrased as "if the global market is not brought under control soon, we will be forced to take action to stabilize the market for our citizens."

What did that mean, *take action*?

Bowers might have faith enough in the system to think they were safe here, but she didn't feel safe at all.

34

It was nearing in on the middle of the night, and Jack's eyes were starting to droop.

It was cold in here, and one of the soldiers had returned with jackets plucked from a shelf somewhere. They had indeed been able to find their way back, if only after a bit of shouting.

They huddled on their small platform, one of the Secret Service agents and one of the soldiers taking up the shelf below the one that the president was on, the others continuing the search.

Roy was still locked in on his computer screen, the dull glow lighting his face from below like he was about to tell a ghost story around a campfire. And what he'd found had started to sound like a ghost story after a while.

He'd been able to hack into the drone as far as the company intranet, where some basic access allowed him to see the product prices, and that's when he'd nudged Winspear and showed it to him.

"Hell of a sale," Winspear said.

"What's that?" Jack asked.

"Prices," Roy said, "tumbling, all over the site."

"Who's changing—" he started to say, but Roy looked up, "—right, the prices are changing automatically."

Roy looked back down to the screen, saying, "This is incredible. Forty to fifty percent off... everything. This is...

something is very badly wrong. It looks like—I don't know; it's so erroneous it's almost more likely that I'm seeing a fake version of the intranet than reality."

"Statistically, you mean?" Winspear asked, and Roy nodded. "And what are the chances it's real?"

Roy shrugged.

"I'm almost out of battery on this thing," he slid the laptop shut. "We'll know when we get out, anyway."

"What would explain that," Jack asked, "what you're seeing with the prices?"

"I need to think about it," Roy said, "but... nothing comes to mind. A huge glitch. An error so big..."—he shook his head—"But there weren't any errors in the code I put into place."

"Don't bite my head off here," Jack said, "but how do you *know* that?"

"Because I'm *good*, that's why. And because I triple checked."

He looked from Jack to Winspear, who looked unimpressed.

"And... because most of it wasn't written by me anyhow."

"How's that?" Winspear said, looking at Roy like this was news to him.

"Well, after it gets big enough," Roy shrugged again, "I mean it just made sense to let the core program develop most of the background code."

"Whoa... wait a second," Jack said. "You're saying the core program did what? Started coding itself?"

"I mean, within a certain amount of constraining, yes."

They were both looking at Roy.

"Listen, when the computer is smart enough, it's better for you to let it do some of the heavy lifting, right? So I let it fill in a lot of the blanks."

"And that doesn't seem *weird* to you? That this thing that *wrote* itself is now out of control?"

"Well when you say it like that! But the thing is, it's not out of control," Roy said. "It's just not in *our* control."

Winspear blew a raspberry.

"Where's Occam now?" he said.

"That's not—" Roy was getting worked up, "You're not even using that right! And *you*," he pointed at Jack, "you wouldn't know a snippet of code from a *decoder ring*. My program may have had some bugs here and there, but nothing *accidentally* lowers the price site wide by 50%. That's not a bug; that's an *attack*. That's someone who knows what the hell they're doing and why, and if you ask me, the only reason to do something like that is to try and tank the company somehow, or to disrupt the global market somehow, and both of those are things that a human would be interested in. Not a computer."

"You think that's what happened? Somebody hacked in and rigged the system?"

"It makes more sense than Clayton *Scarly* doing it. He was a businessman, not a coder. And coding a quantum machine—there's probably only five or ten people in the world who could integrate that with the rest of the system, let alone understand how somebody else did it. It's better that way—"

"—Security through obscurity," Winspear said, and Roy nodded.

"That was another layer of encryption. I didn't leave any notes or any comments. The code should be totally unintelligible."

"That doesn't seem very sustainable—" Jack began.

"—excuse me," Winspear said. "It might not have been a clean way to run things, but when your main competitors are other world governments, you hide what you can where you can, how*ever* you can. Same reason I didn't file patents in the early days. If we'd written up an SOP on how the thing worked, then the genie would be out of the bottle. That was our secret sauce."

"Well, what happens when you need to update it?" Jack said.

"You still don't get it, Jack. It doesn't *need* updates. It updates itself. It does its own Monte Carlo sims and its own business reports, and it runs a stage-gate analysis a thousand times before taking two steps away from center."

"I don't see how that's different from it being in control—"

"*God* you're thick!" Roy said, barely able to contain himself. "Listen, you're hearing me now, and you're thinking, and you're breathing, and all that shit, right?"

"Yeah," Jack said.

"Well, I did the thinking, OK? The people who developed best business development practices and best coding processes and systems automation and routine maintenance procedures—*they* did all the *thinking*. What the computer here does, the one I built, is to execute on all that thinking. Just like you breathe without having to think about it, it's like this thing is breathing. It's fixing, moving, coordinating a drone fleet that's millions strong"—he waved out over the expanse of shelves as he continued—"and when it calculates that the next step is to update a module of code it can do that too. But what it's *not* doing is thinking and choosing a new path for itself, because there *is* no self. It's ones and zeros. So get that idea out of your head—all that Terminator stuff is just Hollywood-set pieces. Imaginary threats to society because that's all we see in every direction thanks to a million years of evolution."

"What he's saying," Winspear leaned forward, "is that the reason my company is so successful is not because these products are so cheap,"—he waved his hand around at the dimly lit sea of shelves—"because our product is not low prices. Our product is not even the shipping itself. Not anymore."

"*That's* the product," Roy said, pointing down at an angle.

"The computer," Winspear explained, "the warehouse— this whole electronic *organism* is our product. Sure, it used to be all the hardware that made net positive shipping *just work,* but connecting it all with computers the size of a grain of sand and letting *it* do the heavy lifting was the true master stroke, if I do say so myself."

"And that's what a little over 200 billion in R&D buys you," Roy added, "quantum architecture meshed into a bunch of dumb matter, all of it running on lattice encryptions you could never break. Total efficiency, total security. It's unhackable."

"So, it's not an attack—"

"—hell no."

"Okay," Jack continued, "and it's not a bug. So Occam's razor on the thing is—I think I'm using it correctly—is that the only thing left is the computer."

They stared at him.

"Listen, we're all thinking it, I'm just saying it. Is there some way the computer could be doing this? Some reason it would have for this?"

"I already thought of that," Roy said, leaning back against the shelf corner, their life raft in the shelves swaying gently as it began to shift itself again, "but that doesn't work either. It would explain what we're seeing on the price shifts maybe, but... well, this isn't some half-baked sci-fi book... computers don't come alive and *force people to commit suicide*."

"Scarly," Jack said.

Roy nodded and said, "Anything that explains all this has to explain him too."

They were quiet now, all of them thinking. Roy pulled his laptop out again and used the precious remaining battery to obsessively comb through the price changes, hoping to find a pattern. Jack looked at his phone again, not expecting to find a signal but getting some shred of comfort from it, if only for a second. Winspear shifted a bit, trying to stretch out as much as he could, and yawned...

After a while, against the gentle rock of the shelf moving them along, they slept.

35

Kay hadn't expected to sleep at all, so when she was jolted awake and saw light at the windows her first question was, "What time is it?"

"Easy," Bowers said.

He was in the room nearby, his tie loosened and a coffee cup in hand. Kay looked around, startled at first, but then realizing she'd fallen asleep in the conference room. She'd dreamed about the NEXT Auto share price, which they'd watch climb into the wee hours of the morning.

"There's a fresh pot on," he said. "You're going to need it."

He gestured toward the laptop that was on the table in front of him, and Kay's eyes ached as she squinted at it.

"How bad is it?" she asked.

"You'll want coffee first," he said, looking over at her.

"That bad?" he nodded.

She rubbed her eyes as she went and filled her cup, opening the fridge that was tucked away in the corner and grabbing a couple of ice cubes to drop into her coffee.

She came back to the room, taking a sip as Bowers triggered the projector.

She almost spit the lukewarm liquid out. NEXT Auto's share price had continued to climb through the night and was now at an almost 400% gain from the day before.

Bowers looked at her and raised his eyebrows. She didn't say anything. Neither of them did. The whole crazy affair had leapfrogged into the unreal. All she could do was stare in disbelief.

When she'd come to America, she'd started working on her citizenship immediately. It took years, but after a long, long time the gears moved and she got her papers. During that process, there was a phase of becoming immersed in the culture, learning everything you'd need for the exam but, more than that, taking a sort of obsessive deep-dive into all the history, the traditions, the American way of life.

She'd been alone then—that was when she was still pregnant with Suela just after a cabal of Chinese businessmen had ruined her reputation and put her in a bad position with the Chinese government, a cheap trick to swindle control of her father's company, which had been left in her control. That was a long story and one that, when she got to the States, she was all too eager to forget.

So there was a period—months—as she grew larger and larger with Suela growing inside her, where the days bled together as she marathoned through books, TV shows, all the American cultural artifacts that she couldn't get enough of. It was years before she'd start Nine Muses. A period of respite. In hindsight, time between storms.

One of her favorites had been *Alice in Wonderland*, a strange but altogether charming cartoon that she was so intrigued by at the time that she'd started it over again as soon as it ended.

Now, at the table in the conference room, she felt dizzy. She thought of Alice tumbling end over end as she fell back into one of the chairs. Just then, she wouldn't have been surprised to glance up and find that great big Cheshire cat perched on top of the projector screen, grinning down at the absurd share price chart.

"It gets worse," Bowers said. "Some amateur astronomers have spotted Chinese *satellites* moving into position over the Mainland and Hawaii."

"You've got to be kidding."

Bowers shook his head and said, "Whatever rumors they caught in the news yesterday weren't just rumors."

"What are they moving them over us for?"

"Probably to give us all free wireless internet."

He took a drink, catching her eye.

"I see you're already at the black humor stage."

"It's out of our hands now. Over our pay grades. Yours at least."

"Jack? Winspear? Anything?"

"Nope and nope," he said, "though I expect we'll hear from Winspear before too long."

"What makes you say that?"

He reached forward and clicked something on the computer, and the projection changed to a C-SPAN live feed from Capitol Hill. She could see hundreds of suited figures heading in. The camera angle changed, showing the front of the room, where Tarrah Adler was taking a deep breath. Stephen Guilfoyle was taking his seat at the head of the room as the few hundred other representatives shuffled into their seats.

"It's the last day of their session," Bowers said. "They're going to take a vote."

"On impeachment?"

"What else?" Bowers said. "And if they get it, China may recall its satellites."

"And if they don't?"

Bowers looked at her and, after a moment, shrugged. Then they both began to watch as the representatives picked up their electronic recordkeeping devices around the room and started checking in.

36

Or rather, they *tried* to start checking in.

The electronic voting system installed into the House of Representatives as part of the Legislative Reorganization Act of 1970 was very simple. You inserted a card, one issued to you as a member of the House. That card then allowed you to signal your presence in the chamber.

But as soon as everyone started to take their seats and Guilfoyle called the session to order, Tarrah looked around and immediately realized there was a problem.

All over the room, the system was nonresponsive. Representatives were sliding their cards in and out, jabbing at the buttons, turning to their neighbors, and realizing something was wrong.

Adler looked up to Guilfoyle who seemed distracted, then she was aware of hurried footsteps at her side. It was Jim Burns, rushing down the aisle to her.

"Somebody's sabotaged the electronic system," he said, breathless. "We've got to get an official quorum. We've got to—"

He turned, addressing Guilfoyle and raising his voice to rise over the hubbub of the room.

"I motion to begin a verbal quorum call."

From somewhere behind them, in the pro-impeachment section, "I second the motion."

"As the Senate pro-tempore," Jennings Clearwater, majority leader of the pro-Winspear camp said from his side of the chamber, "I'll begin calling the names."

He stood, roll book in hand, and cleared his throat theatrically.

"He was ready for this," Burns said under his breath, looking around the room, signaling at the minority whip and pointing at his watch.

"What is it?" Adler asked.

"The quorum call with the electronic system has a maximum time limit of fifteen minutes."

"And a verbal quorum call?"

Burns sighed, watching as Clearwater called the first name, making a show of saying it wrong, then correcting himself, then pretending for a moment not to find the face in the crowd.

"As long as it takes," he said, and he didn't have to explain the rest to her.

The quorum call of all the representatives in the House was over 400 names long.

"Jesus," she said. "He's going to filibuster the session with a damn roll call."

Clearwater was only now marking off the first name as present, and as he did so he said something about his lead breaking—he was using a pencil—and he put the roll call book down to make a show of sharpening it with a small sharpener he'd pulled from his pocket.

"You can't do this," Burns said in Clearwater's direction.

As if to answer, Guilfoyle slammed his gavel down.

"I'm afraid," Guilfoyle started, and Tarrah looked up to see that Guilfoyle seemed more serious today, maybe even sweating, "that won't do, Mr. Clearwater. Let's keep the roll going at a steady clip. No more than 10 seconds per name."

Burns' jaw dropped. Guilfoyle *could* order such a thing, but to think that he *would*.

"He's different," Adler said under her breath to Burns, nodding up toward Guilfoyle. "Something's changed."

"I'll say!"

Burns looked at Clearwater, who frowned up at Guilfoyle and then in his direction.

"He's stopping Clearwater... he's... on our side?"

He sounded awestruck.

"He wants..." Burns started to say, but he was turning around, rushing back toward the minority whip.

Tarrah watched as Clearwater brought the roll book back up and began calling the names faster, watching Guilfoyle in the corner of his eye, his turn to look worried.

But now another commotion toward the back of the room—representatives were standing, all across the pro-Winspear side of the room they were getting up, turning for the door, starting to file out, and saying nothing to each other.

Burns was at Adler's arm again now, breathing hard from running back and forth.

He explained to her, "We didn't know about this. Guilfoyle's flipped but it wasn't us. He can overrule Clearwater, but—"

Burns nodded toward the back of the room.

Adler followed his gaze and continued the thought, "But you can't have a vote without a quorum. So, what? They're all just going to leave?"

Burns nodded.

"435 members in the House. We need 218 of them here to make the quorum and vote... they've got more than half."

"So this was their backup plan? Flee the scene?" Adler shook her head. "Unbelievable."

Burns nodded, catching his breath.

"They're trying to figure out if we have any options."

He nodded back toward a tight cluster of the pro-impeachment representatives who were consulting with each other, passing an open book back and forth, tracing lines of it with their fingers looking for something. Anything.

"What can we do?"

"I don't know," Burns said, "but we'll have to do it quickly. They'll be in planes, trains, and automobiles out of DC as soon as they can."

"This is ridiculous," Tarrah growled, looking up to see that Guilfoyle was stepping down, going out a back door into his private chambers. "Let me know what you figure out," she said, starting toward the front of the room.

"Where are you going?" Burns asked.

She looked back at him, jerking a thumb up toward the Speaker's chair.

"To see what the hell's going on with Guilfoyle. If he wants a vote too, then we're working with him now."

37

"Wake up."

Jack started, almost jumping up at first but then catching himself, looking down off the side of the shelf, recoiling as he remembered where he was and why.

Winspear was taking up a position on the side of the tower to start climbing. It was one of the soldiers who had jostled Jack.

"Where's Roy?" he asked him, but the soldier shook his head.

"Went to get parts."

The voice came from below, the shelf where the two Secret Service agents were both getting ready to start climbing as well.

"He said he'd figured out something but needed battery for his laptop."

"Okay," the soldier said, nodding and looking around, "we're going to have to leave him."

"*What?*" Winspear said.

"He'll be fine," the soldier cut him off quickly. "There's some kind of prepackaged food on many of these shelves, and he knows the way out. The priority is getting you topside."

"You found a way out?" Jack asked as started to climb out and onto the shelf from the outside.

"Up and over," the soldier explained. "We found the walls but there's nothing there. The shelves don't go high enough to reach, and there's no kind of ladder or stairwell as far as we can see. If we go down, it'll be gridlocked with shelves at the bottom. But in toward the center there's some kind of spire that reaches all the way up."

"You went up?"

"Not me; the other soldier I came in with. He found the hatch to the roof, got a signal out, and came back down to find me. He's on the roof. Now, if you'll all start moving we can be out of here in about 45 minutes."

From the middle distance, a voice came from the darkness, "Wait!"

It was Roy.

They could tell that much even at a distance, and the soldier sighed, shouting over to him, "We're headed in toward the center, then up and out. Follow us."

"No, you've got to stop," Roy's voice came again, now closer, and Jack could start to make out in the darkness a shelf headed their way.

"You found your batteries I guess?" Winspear said.

"That and more," Roy said as the shelf came within low shouting distance, a small drone zipping in between them at an angle.

In the dim light of the place, Jack could just make out Roy in the darkness. He was riding on the outside of the tower with his laptop open on one of the decks above him. He was hanging off the corner like the flesh and bone carving at the bow of a strange alien vessel, now emerging toward them and slowing to a halt.

"Toward the center," Roy said. "Hop on."

The soldier hesitated. "How did you—"

"While you guys were climbing to the top I went toward the bottom looking for a power bank. Found one about nine stories down. Halfway there, though, I remembered something. With the right coords, you can take control of the lifters at the base of the thing."

It was now that Jack eyed his laptop and noticed a bright blue cable that snaked downward.

"Had to do a shitty field splice to get it long enough, not to mention squeeze between a few shelves down there, but it works. So if you want a ride to the middle, hop on. The other towers move out of the way automatically."

The soldier hesitated.

"Okay," he said finally, "everyone move over. Slowly."

Roy turned to his laptop, piloting the shelf tower in closer so that they could all reach.

After they'd climbed aboard he said, "Okay, hold on."

The tower jerked with a start, swaying dangerously, it felt to Jack, but stabilizing as they started to coast into the darkness, other shelves sensing and parting like the Red Sea for them. Off in the distance, Jack saw there was a faint glow from beyond the crop of towers ahead, something backlighting them, throwing their rectangular tops into a wild, shifting cityscape, complete with drones flying to and fro like model airplanes. A whole civilization in miniature.

Winspear turned to the soldier. "You said your man made it to the top. Any news from the outside world?"

Roy cut in, "Let me guess—it's wild out there. Markets are in freefall and the country is on the edge of war?"

Jack thought he was joking. Winspear actually laughed.

But then the soldier said, "How did you know?"

"Wait, what? That's really happening?" Winspear asked.

Instead of answering the implicit question, all the soldier said was, "Sir, we have been briefed that it is of paramount importance that you are returned to the White House at once."

"Jesus," Winspear said under his breath as the shelf moved inward. "Spare me the boilerplate. What's going *on* out there?"

The soldier looked across the shelf where he was holding on opposite Winspear. He looked up to Roy, then craned his neck to look down at the Secret Service agents.

"The market started collapsing yesterday, after a huge run up in NEXT Auto's share price. The Nasdaq was hacked by a third party—some extra-state actor as yet unidentified—and the global economy is currently trying to stem the bleeding of panic sells and withdrawals. It's a coordinated attack."

"An attack," Jack said, "or just a run on the bank?"

"It's a run on all of *capitalism*," Roy echoed him.

Winspear asked, "And what about the impeachment?"

Roy rolled his eyes.

"We don't have details," the soldier said, "but it looks like there will be a vote held today."

"Dammit!" Winspear spat.

"There's more. Apparently, the rest of the world thinks this is something *we* planned. China and Russia have been working on some kind of agreement and have said they're going to release it later today. It is critical we get you topside before whatever they try—"

"Wait a second—just *wait* a damn second," Winspear said.

Jack looked off into the distance and saw the glow at the center of the facility was growing brighter, only a few layers of shelf-scrapers away now.

"Roy, how the hell did *you* know about all that?" he asked.

"Deduction, Watson," he smiled down at the president.

"We don't have time for your shit-eating grin, Berry. Spill it."

"The pricing thing we saw on the intranet—it's not a bug, and it's not a hack, so that just leaves one option: the computer."

"We already said—" Jack started, but Roy cut him off.

"But what we didn't do is try to see the problem from *its* perspective," Roy said.

"Which is?"

"Why would it lower prices and start pushing all the merchandise it has on hand like this? Don't think like a person, think like a factory."

"Think like a factory?" Jack asked.

"That's right, to us these are all things we either want or don't want. For it," Roy shrugged, "they're units to deal with."

"You're saying what? That *Winspear Shipping* is getting rid of all its stock?" Winspear asked. "That it's… getting out of the *shipping* business?"

Roy nodded. "That's the only thing that makes sense. It's liquidating itself on purpose."

"Why?" Jack asked.

"Why else?" Roy said down to them. "It's bankrolling something."

"It's doing this because it *needs the cash*?" Winspear said.

Roy nodded again.

"Remember when we set up the trampolines?"

"Trampolines?" Jack asked. "What are you talking about?"

"Market devices," Roy said.

"Financial instruments," Winspear corrected, "to protect the share price of my companies."

"That sounds illegal," Jack said.

"Ha!" Roy balked. "Tell that to the room full of lawyers who came up with it."

"I may have trusted Scarly with my companies," Winspear explained, "but that doesn't mean I didn't buy myself a little insurance on the way out."

"The trampolines are programs that stabilize the prices of all the Winspear companies," Roy explained. "If the stock ever starts to fall a certain amount, by a certain percent, say, the failsafe mechanisms kick in and start buying it back up to stabilize the price. Through shell companies of course. The price dips, and just like a little brat jumping on a trampoline"—he jerked his thumb up—"the program bounces it right back."

"And those shell companies… they're directed by the quantum computer you built?"

"Exactly."

Jack tried to remember what Bowers had explained to him and Kay at Camp David. They knew about the shell companies, but they didn't seem to know that they were being controlled automatically. That they wouldn't quit. Bowers had said they'd found a "handful" of them.

"How many?" he asked.

"Companies?" Roy shrugged. "Who's to say? They can be bought off the shelf. For all I know the computer has bought more than we'd initially set up."

Jack said, "And this, what we're seeing in here, you think the only way it would be liquidating the facility like this is—"

"That's right, the only thing that would explain this feed-back loop is that it needed the cash for something of a higher priority, and the trampoline mechanisms preserving the stock prices are priority numero uno. It all works like a charm except in some edge cases."

"Edge cases like a financial collapse," Winspear said.

"Here it comes," Roy said, gesturing toward the light that was now only a few shelf-scrapers away.

Jack turned to it, and he saw that even past the nearest tower something taller stretched up to the ceiling of the facility.

The scrapers ahead parted, and the tower they were riding on slowed, pulling to a halt at a perimeter around the center mass of the place, which Jack saw now was a well-lit grid work of ladders, piping, and wires. Thick black cords stretched from the roof downward like huge bean-stalk roots, braiding together, frozen in a writhing formation around the metal support lattice and seeming almost to have grown in place.

There was a geometry to it—it was roughly square, and Jack could see the odd line of a continuous rectangular void off to one side, all the clean lines broken by the snaking cables.

"That," Roy said, pointing at that hollow shaft at the corner of the structure ahead of them, "is an elevator shaft. If we can go down to the core where the carriage is, I think we can all pile into it. And this"—he gestured at the mass of the structure in front of them—"those power cables come from the solar farm on the roof."

"And they go down to what? The core?" Roy nodded.

Jack looked down toward the base of the structure where the grid work of iron and the electrical cables all disappeared into a boxy structure that was well over ten stories below.

"Ok," the soldier said, "let's get out of here, quick. Can you trigger the elevator to come meet us up here and then—"

"Did you hear anything I was saying back there?" Roy barked at him. "We can't leave yet. We have to stop it."

"The solar farm," the soldier said, looking at the tight knit of black cables up and down, "that's the power source—we can head to the top and—"

"That's the *backup* power source," Roy explained. "Primary is geothermal. And there's a third failsafe power supply tucked away somewhere down there too, four cogeneration units that spin up fifty-five hundred-horsepower Rolls-Royce jet engines if somehow the other sources are disconnected. So, cutting the power's out."

"We're getting the president out of—"

"Listen dammit!" Roy cut him off. "Do you want him to go out there and be on the receiving end of a warhead?"

He jabbed his finger down, toward the glowing base of the central spire.

"I don't know what you picked up on out there, but from what I can guess, this thing is swinging the entire world economy around, and if Russia and China think we're doing it on purpose, they're going to swing back. I don't know how many war games you've been part of, but it doesn't take a genius to say that, based on the tech available to all parties now, the side with *billions of people* is going to beat the one with *a few hundred million*." Roy looked from the soldier to Winspear and back, then added, "So we need to go *down*, not *up*—because if I can get in there, I can try to shut it off."

The soldier stared for a moment.

"What do you mean *try?*"

"Nothing," Roy said quickly. "I just mean I can turn it off locally, but I can't do it remotely. We have to climb down there to it."

"Fine. If that's how it is, then you go down. Winspear and the other agents will—"

"No can do, soldier boy. I'll need Winspear's biometric authentication to get in." Roy gave him a minute to think, and then said, "What's General Mercer going to say when he finds out you could have helped stop this thing and decided to literally go the opposite direction and run out of here with your tail between your legs?"

The soldier thought for a minute. "The elevator in the core, we can take it to the top?"

Roy nodded.

"Okay," he looked at his wrist. "Okay, you"—he craned his head over to one of the Secret Service agents—"keep going up, you'll see the access panel up there, and with any luck there'll be a rope thrown down by now. The rest of us," he said, "start down."

38

"Guilfoyle, I know you're in there." Tarrah pounded on the door again.

This time, though, there were sounds on the other side.

Deep within the Capitol Building, Guilfoyle's private study opened and Adler was pushed aside as five of the pro-Winspear constituents thrust out. They were pulling jackets on, and Tarrah recognized Majority Leader Clearwater among them.

"It was a good try," Clearwater said, turning the collar of his jacket up as the others kept walking out, "but this vote was never going to happen. You had to know that."

"So you're running away?" she said to him.

He smiled. "I'm *winning*, Special Councilor."

"This is unconstitutional—"

"Wake up, Tarrah. Honestly! After this is all over, we can look back and tell the truth, that it was rotten from the top down. Bad leadership. Not my fault and not yours."

"And your actions? That justifies your little smash and grab on the way out? You're no better than a looter, you know that?"

"Justification has nothing to do with it—"

"—and you know," Adler cut him off, stepping up close. She was a few inches shorter, and as she looked up to him she said, "Back when Harvey hit, you know what we did to the looters don't you?"

Clearwater had been smug a moment ago, but as she took another step forward he recoiled back, bumping into the wall as she added, "I shot one myself."

Not the whole truth, but Adler could see he believed it as he side-stepped her, trying to get to the open hallway. When he was two steps out he stopped, looking Adler up and down as she stared defiantly.

"The only thing that matters is power, Adler. We might not have it for long, but we have it now." After a pause, "The way things are looking with Russia and China, you might want to start thinking about an exit strategy yourself."

With that he turned to leave.

Tarrah watched him for a moment, then turned to see Guilfoyle's door was still standing open. She stormed in to find the man behind his desk, head in his hands.

"Stephen!" She rushed over to him, sensing that every second, the pro-Winspear camp was continuing their diaspora from the capital, getting as far away as they could, as fast as they could.

"What's happening—who made you push the vote?"

Guilfoyle looked up, face red, eyes bloodshot. Adler could smell liquor but didn't see the bottle anywhere.

"He's got a video of me..."

"Who does?"

"They're going to... they were going to show it to my family. Then—" he didn't have to say the rest.

"Who was it Guilfoyle? Who's behind it?"

"It doesn't matter," he said, slurring a bit. "Nothing matters now."

"What?"

"Blackmailed on both sides," he said, leaning back in his chair and looking past Adler.

She'd seen that look before. They'd broken him, whatever Clearwater and his band of thieves had come in here and said.

Blackmailed on both sides, she thought, and she could see clearly that Guilfoyle's place as the speaker and his ability to halt the vote had been used by both sides. Somebody must have come to him on one side to make it happen—that had been the reason for his sudden change of heart—but now the pro-Winspear camp had volleyed the same ball back.

"Clearwater. What does he have on you?"

After a pause, Guilfoyle said, "Enough. Enough that I'm finished no matter what."

"What can you do—" Tarrah was trying to choose her words carefully.

She needed Guilfoyle to push the vote, but highlighting that he was ruined either way didn't seem like a very productive way of getting him to cooperate.

"I can't—" Guilfoyle said, shaking his head. "It's all over. Everything."

He was crying now, sobbing into his hands, but as Adler stood, backing away, the sound changed. A moment later, Guilfoyle was laughing.

"You know," he said, half-crazed, "they all deserve each other. It's all just a joke."

And as Guilfoyle laughed at this, tears still coming, Tarrah backed through the door and shut it behind her.

She waited, listening for a moment, and then went down the hall. She had no idea what to do. There were no options left. Adler raced back to the House chamber, hoping that Burns had an ace up his sleeve, but the room was mostly empty now.

"Guilfoyle?" Burns said as he saw her enter.

Tarrah shook her head.

"He's gone. Something's wrong with him. Clearwater—and someone else, they've got something on him and—"

"We know," Burns said. "It's all over the net."

"What?"

"It's bad," Burns explained. "He's done."

As if to punctuate this, a yell came from the House chair at the head of the room.

"Order!"

It was Guilfoyle, still red faced, stumbling into the chair, and slurring his speech as he yelled out, "I call this session to order!"

"Oh Christ," Burns said, and Tarrah froze as she saw why.

From the back of the room someone yelled out, "He's got a gun!"

"Shut up!" Guilfoyle spat! Waiving the weapon, knocking his gavel off as he leaned over the speaker's pulpit aiming the gun wildly.

The hundred or so representatives still in the room were rushing toward the doors with renewed vigor now, and Adler dashed behind the chest-high wooden wall that framed the lower area of the room. Just then Guilfoyle fired the weapon into the ceiling.

"You. *You!*" he yelled, bringing the barrel back down and sweeping across the back of the room with it.

"Sir!"

The shout came from one of the doorways. It was a Capitol policeman who'd made his way through the crowd. He had his own weapon out and was aiming it at Guilfoyle.

Adler poked her head up, seeing the officer and understanding that they were now seconds away from something going terribly wrong.

"Put the gun down!"

Another policeman, slowly shuffled up one of the aisles that radiated from the Speaker's chair, his weapon also drawn.

"Stop it. *Stop* right there, dammit!" Guilfoyle said as he aimed his weapon at one of them.

Adler saw the look in the officer's eye. He was about to "respond with deadly force," as the euphemism went.

She jumped out from where she was hiding, holding both hands up, facing the officer, and pulling his attention, very aware that Guilfoyle was behind her with the gun.

"Don't shoot him," she heard herself say, adrenaline casting the moment in razor sharp focus.

She eyed the cops, saw them glance at each other before locking their eyes back on Guilfoyle.

She angled her head, catching Guilfoyle in her periphery and said, "Just put it down, Stephen."

"No!" he spat.

"Representative," one of the policeman said, his voice shaky, "if you keep aiming that gun at me I'll be forced to shoot."

Guilfoyle waved the gun around to the other officer, and Adler turned just in time to see him tense. She spun, facing Guilfoyle and shouting up to him.

"Hey. *Hey!*" she yelled up, waving her hands. "Point it at me. Point it at me, now!"

Guilfoyle looked down at her, as if confused, and Adler nodded, feeling a sheen of sweat on her face, or maybe just going cold. In the moment that passed after, an eerie silence fell on the space.

The cops had frozen, any of the representatives who were going to flee had made it through the doors, and the ones who'd hidden in the chamber behind something held their positions.

So now, as the silence settled on the place and Guilfoyle slowly aimed the gun down at Tarrah, her heart skipped a beat but then the clicking was there. Like a bomb about to go off. Tick, tick, tick.

Tick, tick, tick, right to the end, the doctor's voice played over in her head.

But then she focused on it. The faint sound of the valve, then here breathing... she remembered to take a breath after realizing she was holding it.

One of the officer's radio went off, screeching something Adler didn't catch. She looked over at him, he was taking a step forward, but she caught his eye and shook her head.

She turned back to Guilfoyle.

"Okay," she said, arms still raised. "Okay."

She nodded her head slowly up to Guilfoyle, who seemed to shift back somewhat, catching his breath.

Another sound broke the silence, a tinny jingle from somewhere ahead of Adler.

Guilfoyle fished his phone out of his pocket and held it up, the sound of the ring hollow in the House chamber.

"My wife," he said, and then after a moment he hurled the phone into the chamber like he was skipping a rock. "This is *your* fault!" he said, pointing his free hand at the section of the chamber where a dozen or so representatives cowered, stone still, hiding as best they could. "You pick that phone up and tell her—you explain to her how all this happened."

He seemed to decompress, slouching down, falling back into the chair at the head of the chamber with the gun still in his hand, but thankfully not pointed at anyone.

"I deserve this," he said, "but you all do too."

Adler had just enough time to relax a degree before she realized what Guilfoyle would do now. As she watched, he raised the pistol up, turning it around in his hands. He looked it over, and Tarrah knew what he was thinking. She could see the scales shifting in his head as he weighed the option of ending it here and now versus waiting to watch his life crumble around him.

"You don't have to do this," she said up to him, and he leveled his gaze on her, bringing it up from the gun.

"No, Special Councilor, I think I do."

But then something in his look changed.

The anger was gone now, replaced by something ghostly as he said, "Why don't you come take this gun away from me."

"Are you—" she swallowed. "I'd like that very much," Adler said quickly, moving for the stairs that led up to the speaker's chair.

"But before you do," Guilfoyle said, clearing his throat and standing, putting the gun down, "I motion that the senate sergeant-at-arms find and compel the attendance of absent representatives."

Adler furrowed her brow. The representatives in the room looked at each other, also confused.

There was a clattering as Burns stepped forward, quickly. "*Second!* I second the motion."

For a moment, nothing happened, then Guilfoyle collapsed back into his chair. Adler took the steps two at a time up to him, scooping up the gun and reflexively ejecting the magazine and unchambering the first round before turning and handing them to the Capitol policeman who'd already caught up.

The other policeman was there at Guilfoyle's opposite side, handcuffing him, and Adler looked out to see Burns running for the back of the chamber.

As the police took over with Guilfoyle, she jumped down the stairs and headed for where she'd seen Burns exit and after a moment found him.

"What's going on?" she asked Burns, who was handing a cellphone back to someone with one hand while taking another that the minority whip had been holding out.

He held an index finger up to Tarrah, nodding and talking quickly, and then finally he clicked the phone off with a sigh of relief.

"What just happened?"

"I'll tell you what," Burns said. "The sergeant at arms just issued arrest warrants for every representative not currently in this room."

And then he took Adler's hand and shook it, smiling.

He said, "We're still in this thing!"

39

When the shelf had stopped, they'd all climbed down with Roy leading the pack. He jumped the last tier, landing and coming around the corner of the boxy structure at the base of the facility, the others jogging to keep up.

"Here," he said, coming to a side of the structure with a door embedded in it.

There was a small glass panel in the center of the door, and as the others came up, he cupped his hands around it and tried to see in.

"It's cold in there, frosted over."

"Is that going to be a problem?" The soldier asked.

"Nah," Roy said, slinging his backpack off and kneeling to get his laptop and a few cables out. "Do me a favor and pry that palm scanner off."

He nodded up to the flat plate with a symbol of a hand on it.

The soldier seemed about to protest, but after a moment, slung his gun out of the way and pulled a multi-tool from somewhere and starting working at the scanner.

"So this thing," Jack started, standing by Winspear as they watched the men work, "it controls *all* of this?"

Winspear nodded. "Pretty cool, right?"

"Dangerous is more the word I was thinking."

He leveled a gaze at Winspear, who stopped smiling.

"Well, what do you expect, Jack? Market corrections aren't my fault."

"From what they said, it sounds like this is worse."

"Oh phooey. It's always *worse* when I do it. Everything's been *worse* since I took office, isn't that right? The whole country's *worse*. What do you want me to do, Jack? Take it back?"

"That's not what I mean… it's just—this whole thing."

He waved his hand at the boxy structure ahead of them, which was about ten yards on a side.

"I told you before," Roy said over his shoulder, not taking his eyes off the laptop, "it's not like it's sentient or anything, it's just"—he shrugged—"it's a little carried away with a prime directive, that's all."

"A little carried away?" Jack asked. "It tried to *kill* us earlier, if you'll recall."

"That was something else," Roy said. "That was just, I don't know, normal movements of the shelves. It wasn't trying to kill us, we just happened to be standing there."

"How could you possibly know that?"

"Because *I built it*. I know how it works. And it wouldn't have tried to kill us because *that wouldn't serve any purpose*. Winspear—"

He nodded his head toward the panel that had been pried away, revealing a port that he plugged the laptop into.

"I need your backup audio passcode again."

He stepped up and leaned toward the wall unit.

"Sierra," he said, and there was the sound of a lock giving way.

"Everything it does has a purpose," Roy said, packing up his laptop, slinging the bag over his shoulder.

The soldier politely pushed Winspear aside, entering the room first just in case.

"And what purpose does it run to?" Jack asked as they followed the soldier in. "What is the grand design that this thing is supposedly making all its decisions toward?"

"Isn't it obvious?" Winspear said. "Increasing the net worth of my companies. Ha!"

"Something like that," Roy explained. "It's a complex decision tree, but yes, increasing and retaining future profits have high weights. Retaining profits is the current loop it's stuck in. It's pumping cash into the stock to try and counter everyone selling it."

"So, this thing is causing a market crash out of fiduciary duty?" Jack said, following the others in. "That's ironic, don't you think?"

"Maybe," Roy said, and Jack saw he was distracted, looking around the room they found themselves in.

It was low ceilinged to the point of being cramped, and the outer box shape formed a corridor around another box in the middle, a core within a core.

The walls were lined with computers and monitoring equipment, all of it long abandoned and dusty. The desks were built into the walls, and space-age styled roller chairs lined the workstations here and there, adding to the strange ancient-future feel of the place.

And now Roy stepped forward, cupping his hands against a pane of glass again, this one on the walls of the inner box, which was roughly ten feet on a side.

"This is it?" Jack said, pointing at the central chamber and somehow knowing that the computer was here in front of him.

The door slid shut behind them as the last Secret Service agent came in, and a presence settled on all of them in the quiet.

As Jack approached the center of the place, he couldn't help but feel something. Awe maybe, touched with an edge of fear.

"Okay," Roy said, taking a step back, "what I can do is—"

"First," the soldier cut him off, "the elevator."

He gestured toward the metal chamber in the corner.

"Get it working, and we can send Winspear up."

"Roger that," Roy said, only a hint sarcastically, turning for the chamber in the corner. It was white, about the size of a phone booth, with wire mesh on the inside.

Winspear was showing himself around, looking at the various desks and dusty computers. The Secret Service agents milled about near him.

As he looked around, Jack felt something pulling him toward the box at the center of the room. Almost like a kind of gravity, it sucked him inward, and he took a step toward it.

There was a glass porthole, maybe four inches across, and as he moved closer he saw it was deep—maybe even thicker than it was wide.

He cupped his hands like Roy had and leaned in, feeling the coldness of the chamber within even through the hunk of solid glass.

He didn't know what he was seeing at first. The backdrop was gunmetal gray, and the room was lit from somewhere with bright white LEDs that made it hard to look at compared to the dimness they'd been traveling through for the last few hours.

But then the image started to take shape.

Jack didn't know what he was expecting, but it certainly wasn't this. The computer hung down from the ceiling, a multi-tiered structure that seemed to have grown downward like some technological stalactite.

There were multiple layers to it, and each one appeared to be separated by a golden disk. Wires snaked all over the place, but carefully. There were things that looked like springs and boxy structures mounted here and there that wires disappeared into and emerged from, but all of it had the feel of elegance.

It was beautiful. The confluence of complexity, rarity, and obscurity all coming together as he realized the device he was looking at was the brain of something that could wreck the whole country. It was a computational Faberge egg in which one small, invisible crack was threatening to cause the whole affair to crumple in.

"What do you think?"

It was Roy next to him, and Jack looked over to see the soldier was stepping into the elevator, eyeing how much space it had.

"It's amazing," Jack said. "Too bad you've got to turn it off."

"Yeah," he said, "about that."

Winspear had stepped up to them, and Roy looked at him with a quick sigh.

"I don't really know how to shut it down."

"What!?" Winspear said.

Roy shrugged again.

"I mean, there's an off command, but I can't access it remotely. Maybe one of these computers is jacked into it or—"

"Is there a problem?" The soldier asked, stepping in toward the group.

"No," Roy said reflexively, "no way. Just let me think for a minute."

His brow furrowed, and he reached up and rubbed his temple with one hand.

"For a few minutes, maybe."

40

"Look," Bowers said to Kay as she walked back into the room, "it's getting worse."

On the news, scenes of pandemonium flashed as the newscaster struggled to keep up. There was a shot of a supermarket, shelves bare. An aerial view of a massive pileup on the interstate.

The newscaster explained, "And still, more reports of rogue autocars, leaving their owners and heading for locations unknown, though several citizens have sent in drone footage of—"

The scene changed to a jagged, destabilized image, the camera drone swooping down above what looked like a mix between a junkyard and a foundry, then blinking out in a white-hot flash.

"These videos show autocars being disassembled by the hundreds."

Another drone video now, this one from a different angle and at higher resolution, showing robotic arms-on-wheels moving into position, forming a jagged assembly line around autocars of all shapes and sizes, all of them being disassembled piece by piece, before this footage too, blinked out in a flash. Shot down.

"Nobody knows how or why this is happening," the newscaster said, "and there is panic in the streets"—cut to shots of riots in an unnamed city—"as viral protests throughout the country spill over into violence."

The scene changed to that of a car overturned, burning, a discarded protest sign nearby showing a picture of President Winspear with two red Devil horns.

"We await with bated breath the decision of the House of Representatives, an institution that many have pointed out was never designed to respond to this kind of situation."

"Jesus," Kay said, as the shot changed to an aerial view of the Capitol Building.

"Your daughter?" Bowers asked.

Kay breathed a sigh of relief, putting her phone in her pocket.

"She's safe, not in any of that," Kay gestured up at the screen. "What's going on? This is more than just protests, right?"

"Much more," Bowers said. "The news has mentioned the Chinese satellites, but the internet is taking it dozens of steps farther. They've got conspiracies figured out in all directions, many competing. But one thing they all seem to agree on is this is how World War 3 starts."

He looked over at Kay, eyebrows raised.

"That's ridiculous, isn't it?"

Bowers thought for a moment, looking back at his laptop.

"I wish I could agree with you," he said, "but—" He shook his head. "You know what they're talking about right now?"

He gestured at his laptop.

"I get the president's daily brief, you know. Actually, I read it more often than he does. They're talking about China and Russia dumping the dollar as their major reserve currency."

"You're kidding. For what? There's no other currency that—"

"For something *new.*"

The word hung in the air for a moment as Kay thought through this.

"They can't possibly issue something that could compete... that other countries would swap out the bulk of their reserves to."

"Maybe," Bowers said, "maybe not. But we have it on good authority they're moving forward with it. Supposedly it'll be gold backed. Issued by both countries in tandem."

"That's absurd." Kay said. "One of the features of a reserve currency is that the issuer is *trustworthy*. Nobody will invest a billion of their reserves in a currency controlled by *Russia*. Backed by gold they *promise* they have."

Bowers looked at her and sighed. "That's why they'll store the gold in Switzerland. They'll be neutral. Nobody can argue with that if they don't even have direct control of the lion's share of the bullion used to back it."

Kay shook her head. "Dammit, that would work. But trying to dump the dollar just like that... it's crazy. They're just flipping the card table over, reworking the whole system."

"Can you blame them?" Bowers sighed. "We used to be a standard bearer—the country I mean. Now... now we're too unstable to even try and talk them down. And if they really pull the trigger on this thing—try to form a whole parallel global economy and ruin our currency in the process, well, that *is* war."

"Can we stop it? Is there *any* way to stop it?"

"Oh sure," Bowers said. "Just figure out who hacked us, get the market under control, and impeach the president." He checked his watch, looking up to say, "and all of that in about six hours, before whatever trade deal China and Russia are cooking up goes live. Because once they announce it, that's a bell you won't be able to unring. And, oh yeah. Those satellites? There's no way to know for sure, but the CIA has pretty much confirmed they're military."

"You think they're already preparing for an attack?"

"Well they're prepping for something," he said. "Could be nukes. Could be some other kind of advanced weapon as yet undreamed and undefended against. Either way, they're getting ready for a first strike. They know their trade deal could trigger a war, so they're hoping that if it comes to that, they'll be able to cut the head off the snake before… before it has a chance to do the same. Obviously, we don't want to push them into that."

"So what? We'll agree with them, go along with the deal?"

"Really? *This* administration?"

He reached forward, changing the projector feed to the live C-SPAN coverage of the House floor where representatives were being brought in in handcuffs by Capitol police.

"We have one shot, Kay," he said, nodding at the screen. "If they can impeach him and send a signal to China and Russia that we know there's a problem, that we're ready to start talking about fixing it, maybe—*maybe* they make a deal."

Both of them stared at the screen. Tarrah Adler was near the corner of the shot watching handcuffed representatives cast gloomy looks at her, at least one of them with a bloody nose.

As they watched, Bowers said, "What a circus."

41

The same live feed of C-SPAN was being viewed all over the world. People were awake in China, watching. People in Africa watched on their phones. US Space Station personnel, on high alert due to the Chinese station's burn, which had brought it into a closer orbit, were streaming it from the bridge of a satellite group attack cluster. From as far away as low Earth orbit, then, to as close as right down the street, the world was tuning in to a historic moment.

This included Duncan McAvoy and his handler, who watched the screen with pessimistic intrigue.

"They can't make this work," McAvoy said, "can they?"

On the screen, yet another Winspear loyalist was being hauled in—literally carried by four Capitol policemen, his hands handcuffed in front of him. Clumsily, they set him into a chair, and a number on the screen keeping track of House members present ticked up.

"They can," his handler said, "but I don't think they'll see how."

McAvoy gave him a look, brow furrowed.

"Clearwater knows how to break this. Burns needs a quorum, but if they bring in too *many* of the pro-Winspear camp, then they'll be able to break the one-third vote. Impeaching requires two-thirds."

"Clearwater knows that," McAvoy said.

"He does," his handler sighed. "And now he controls the vote. He controls when he closes the doors and they open the session."

"So he'll just call to start the session when they have enough votes to win," McAvoy said.

"He will," his handler said, "and that's our opening. But Burns—" McAvoy's handler shook his head, "he knows how to play dirty, but only in theory. Really, he—*we*—have only one option to still make this vote happen."

He stood, shouldering on his overcoat.

"I'm going to have to go down there and tell them how to pull it off."

"Now?" McAvoy said, standing with him.

His handler nodded.

"Now or never. We've got only a few hours left. At the rate the Capitol police are bringing representatives back, Clearwater will have the one-third of the quorum he needs to block the vote soon."

"Then... it's happening?"

His handler nodded.

"I'll send a group with you to the White House—to collect Kay Luo and Winspear's sidekick."

McAvoy smiled. "Time to clean up."

"That's right. Bring them along later and we'll figure out what to do with them. We'll need them just in case Winspear wants to try anything. Hostages."

"Got it," McAvoy said, following his handler out of the room.

They separated, and McAvoy took another drag on his medicine, his spine tingling not from the pain that was constantly just at bay, but from the thrill of a plan welding itself into reality.

42

"Count it again," Burns said to the one with the clipboard. There was a small group of them at the back of the room, clustered around Adler and Burns, turning through rulebooks and scrolling across slates, trying to find something—*anything*—that would let them take control from Clearwater, who was at the head of the room.

Adler looked at Burns as the one with the clipboard read the numbers off again.

"Damn," he said. "They're close, five or six more people and they'll have the numbers to break the vote."

"So," she paused, thinking through the numbers that the pro-impeachment camp would need. "68, 69?"

She raced through the numbers again in her head. When the pro-Winspear majority had started to leave, they were well over 2/3 of the group. Of the 435 representatives in the House, Winspear's side made up 287, give or take a couple.

But they'd done a good job fleeing the city. The police had been able to bring back only 68 so far, and Clearwater, making 69, had come back as soon as he realized what was going on and that he could control it.

"And there's nothing we can do about Clearwater?" Tarrah said under her breath.

She glanced up at the man who was sitting where Guilfoyle had earlier, eyeing his own list of numbers with a crony at his arm double checking.

He nodded at her, and Adler didn't like how confident he seemed.

"I'm afraid not," Burns answered. "As the speaker pro-tempore he controls the House when the speaker is un-available, and since the *previous* speaker has been removed from office, Clearwater is in control."

He didn't have to say the part they'd already discussed, that Clearwater was simply going to wait until he had the numbers to beat an impeachment vote and begin the session then.

"148," Tarrah said, "we've got 148 members in the room who are pro-impeachment. Plus Clearwater and his, that's 217 warm bodies. A quorum is 218."

The minimum number of representatives that must be present to vote—the quorum—had almost been met.

"So, they just need—"

"Oh no," Burns said, looking at the back of the room.

A group of pro-Winspear representative—Adler counted 7—was being rushed in by Capitol police.

Adler looked up just in time to see Clearwater stand.

"He's been counting too," Adler growled.

At the head of the room, Clearwater shouted, "I call the session to order, please close the doors and begin the quorum call."

He indicated to one of his men, who was ready with his list, clearing his throat.

"Don't pause more than a heartbeat between names," Clearwater called down to him. "Let's get this over with."

He looked down at Adler as the man started calling out names.

"There's got to be something," she said, but Burns shook his head.

After a moment, as the roll call ran, Burns leaned back against the low wood wall and shook his head slowly, sighing.

"We were so close," he said.

"No," Tarrah said to him. "Don't give up. There has to be *something!*"

She watched and listened as the roll was called. 224 names. 148 pro-impeachment, and just over 1/3—76—against. Which meant the vote would fail.

"*No,*" she said.

"A quorum is present," Clearwater announced, "and I call this session to order."

Just then, the door at the back of the chamber opened.

"I'm sorry," Clearwater said, "but we are currently in session—there will be no more—"

But he stopped short when he saw who it was.

McAvoy's handler stepped into the room, his small retinue of Secret Service agents flanking him on either side.

"Mr. Vice-President," Clearwater said, "to what do we owe this honor?"

43

Vice-President Applegate smiled, looking around the room, letting it sink in for a moment.

"I was hoping for a word with Mr. Burns," he said. "In private."

Tarrah watched Burns look up at Clearwater and then to the vice-president. He shrugged.

"I—of course," he said as he walked slowly, then with a little more energy toward the back of the room.

The vice-president ducked back through the door, and Burns poked his head out, apparently listening as Applegate told him something out of earshot.

Clearwater looked down at Adler. She might have noticed he looked nervous at this new variable, but she was too busy turning the situation over in her head as well.

Applegate. The vice-president. Here, talking to Burns.

It could only mean one thing: Applegate was helping him. Which meant Applegate wanted the vote to go through.

He was betraying Winspear.

The reality of this hit Adler like a brick wall. She reached down, gripping the wood, steadying herself, the clicking in her chest speeding up. She'd spent so much time focused on the crimes of the president, but Applegate....

She started up the stairs—she had to talk to him, to ask him to his face—but as she got to the backdoor Burns was coming back in and pushing past her. He was distracted, running back toward the House floor. But she turned to see this only long enough to understand something very strange was going on. Turning for the door, she pushed through after Applegate.

He was already walking away, Secret Service in tow, but Tarrah shouted, "Hey—*Hey!*"

Applegate stopped short.

"Special Counselor," he said, reaching out to shake Tarrah's hand as she quickly closed the gap. "I suppose I should be thanking you."

She didn't take his hand.

"Mr. Vice-President," she chose her words wisely, not sure how to express what she was thinking other than to come right out with it, "The president... Winspear... if you did anything to *accelerate* this process—"

"Oh Tarrah, we both know Winspear did that all by himself. It's been a sad run, but"—he shrugged, finally letting his hand fall—"this is what's best for the country." He leveled his gaze at her, adding, "I hope you'll agree."

Tarrah looked at him. At his eyes. At the way he smiled.

Something was wrong.

"Go on," Applegate said, pushing her a little too hard toward the door of the House chamber. "You don't want to miss your spot in history."

"*What?*"

Applegate laughed as he turned to leave, and, stunned, Adler slowly turned for the House chamber.

44

"**M**r. Speaker," Tarrah was still reeling as Burns' voice filled the room. "I motion for a vote."

"I don't think that's a surprise to anyone at this point," Clearwater said down to him, "but as you surely know, you don't have the numbers for impeachment—"

"Not for impeachment," Burns said. "I motion to elect a new speaker of the House of Representatives."

Clearwater's face had just enough time to twist in alarm as another pro-impeachment member shouted, "I second the motion!"

"You can't—only on the first day of the session—" Clearwater said, but Burns cut him off.

"*Or* in the event of the resignation of an incumbent speaker."

"I—" Clearwater stammered, looking over at his men, one of whom shrugged. "This doesn't change anything Burns—you still don't have the numbers! You don't even have a *candidate!*"

"Oh yes I do!" Burns said.

Adler had been in the back of the room this whole time, watching, and now she was aware that one of the pro-impeachment members was running from the front of the room, up the aisle toward the back door. He had something thick in one hand. A Bible. As he approached, she moved over to let him through, but he didn't go through the door. He stopped.

He stopped right next to *her.*

Then Burns's voice from the front, "I nominate Tarrah Adler."

The dean of the House, the man in charge of swearing in new members and a pro-impeacher, was the one who'd stopped next to her, breathing hard, trying to catch his breath as Adler looked from him, to Burns, to Clearwater.

"Second the motion!" another of the pro-impeachment members shouted up, and the Winspear loyalists began to realize what was happening.

"We'll have the yeas and nays!" Burns shouted over the growing voices, and the pro-impeachment side of the room thundered their answer.

"The Yeas have it!" Burns shouted up.

Clearwater was leaning forward now, stabbing out with his index finger as he snarled, "This is ridiculous! She can't be the speaker—she's not even a member of the *House*—"

"And she doesn't have to be," Burns thundered back. "Article 1, Section 2—we can elect whoever we like. It just so *happens* that all previous speakers have been members."

Clearwater said nothing, looking at his men, hoping for one of them to offer some counter to this. None of them did.

"And something else interesting about the process of choosing a new speaker," Burns went on. "It requires only 50% of an established quorum. So the yeas *do* have it, and"— Burns turned to the back of the room, where the Deputy was already hefting the Bible up on one hand, next to Adler—"Mr. Deputy, if you will."

"Tarrah Adler," the deputy said without pause.

She turned to him, to the Bible next to her, trying to keep up with what was happening. The vice-president's words echoed in her head, "You don't want to miss your spot in history." This had all been his idea.

"Tarrah Adler, please raise your right hand and place your left on the Bible."

Slowly, as if in a dream, she reached out and placed her left hand on the outstretched Bible. The right, she raised, and then it began.

"Do you solemnly swear that you will defend the Constitution of the United States against all enemies, foreign and domestic—"

Adler looked around, at Burns who was smiling up at her and at the cameras in the overhead seats.

"—that you will bear true faith and allegiance the same—"

She swallowed hard, turning to the deputy who was reading from a script, none of it seeming at all real.

"—that you take this obligation freely without any mental reservation or purpose of evasion—"

She tried to think through the logic of it… they still didn't have the numbers to win on impeachment.

"—and that you will well and faithfully discharge the duties of the office on which you are about to enter, so help you God."

"I—" she looked to Burns, who nodded. "I do."

The pro-impeachment side of the room cheered, and Clearwater swung the thick gavel down for quiet.

"Burns, this won't stand! None of this is—"

"Sorry," Burns shouted up at him, "but you're sitting in her chair!"

He pointed back to Adler as he said this, and the pro-impeachment camp cheered again.

"And now," Burns said, "I motion that the House bring forward Articles of Impeachment on President J. Woolston Winspear."

"I second the motion!" came from somewhere behind him.

"Speaker *pro tempore*," Burns said, emphasizing the title as he spoke to Clearwater, "I think we both have our headcounts here, and as you know, we are one shy of the two-thirds majority required. As you may also know, the acting speaker of the house is permitted a tie breaking vote not just when the votes are split fifty-fifty, but—and I'm quoting here—'*whenever that casting vote would shift the outcome on a given motion.*'"

They'd done it. They'd created an extra vote out of thin air.

Her vote.

Burns turned to the back of the room. Adler watched as *all* of them turned to the back of the room, where she was still standing, rooted to the spot just inside the Chamber doors.

"Ms. Speaker?" Burns said, and only after a moment did Adler realize he was addressing her.

She faltered, her mouth moved and nothing came out. She looked around at them, at the expectant stares, and listened at the held breath, the only other sounds in the place the distant shutters from the media in the upper level and of course the backdrop click of her heart, racing, ticking away.

Finally, she said, "I vote to impeach."

45

Bowers jumped up.

"Did that really just happen?"

Kay's eyes were wide. She was on her feet too, both of them staring at the C-SPAN feed.

"Incredible..."

"Yes!" Bowers said, bending over and working away at his computer. "The Senate's a lock, they'll vote as soon as they can get Winspear in the room for the trial—a formality, but they'll want to wait for it."

"Where is he?" Kay asked. "And Jack?"

"They've made contact at the Camplex, both of them will be extracted soon. We need to get Winspear on the phone with the Chinese before—"

There was a knock at the door.

"Who is it?" Bowers shouted, but the door opened, and two camouflage-covered soldiers with assault rifles in hand came in.

Behind them, two dark-suited agents of the Secret Service.

"What—" Kay started to say, but then her voice caught in her throat as she saw the man who entered the room behind them.

His hat threw a shadow over his face, but she could still recognize him just fine.

Duncan McAvoy.

She acted on instinct, sweeping the coffee cup next to her off the table and throwing it in his direction, moving forward in the confusion to throw a punch, but one of the soldiers caught her hand in midair.

"Ms. Luo," he said, "we have instructions to bring you to Air Force One."

Kay looked from him to Bowers, his hands raised, and then to McAvoy, who was wiping lukewarm coffee off his chest with a look of disgust.

He stepped toward her and looked from under his hat.

"You got away once," he said.

After a pause, he smiled.

"Please," Kay said, addressing the agent who still had her by the arm, gun in his other hand. "You know who he is... you can't—"

"We have orders from the vice-president, ma'am," the other agent said, advancing toward Bowers and tossing a chunky zip tie on the table. "Mr. Bowers, please fasten this around Ms. Luo's hands, behind her back."

"Where's Applegate? He's behind this, isn't he?"

McAvoy didn't say anything, and Bowers added, "I want to talk to him before we go anywhere."

"Can't do," McAvoy said. "He caught Marine One about 20 minutes ago, on his way to intercept the soon-to-be ex-president." He looked at Kay as he added, "And your friend Jack."

Bowers looked over at Kay, and they both knew what this meant. They were hostages now.

"And you two," Bowers said as he looked from one of the soldiers to the other. "Mercer's helping him."

Bowers shook his head. There was no response from the soldiers, who watched on like statues.

"Clock's ticking," McAvoy said.

Slowly, Bowers picked up the zip tie and moved over to Kay. She looked at him, then at the agent, who let her jerk her arm away.

"They know the *truth*," McAvoy said, addressing Kay and Bowers and waving his hand to the agents. "They know you helped frame Winspear and Katelyn, and that it was Applegate and *me* who were trying to shut it down this whole time."

"You bastards," Kay spat. "Nobody will ever believe that."

"They will, Kay. Or some version of it. They'll believe what we need them to. Mr. Bowers, please don't make this hard—my clothes are already stained."—He glanced down at the broken coffee mug—"I'd hate to get blood on them too."

Bowers looked at Kay, and their eyes met. He knew they were on the wrong end of this. There was nothing they could do, not now. Kay gave him a small nod, permission to follow through with the demand to zip tie her.

When he was done, one of the agents did the same to Bowers, and in silence, they were marched out of the White House and put into the back of a dark SUV, on their way to meet the new president.

46

Deep within the Camplex, Roy rushed from one computer to the next.

"It's fighting me," he said. "There's too many backups. I can't cut power. I can't crash it."

"You said this was going to be straightforward," the lead soldier stepped toward him, a bead of sweat on the side of his face.

He wanted the president out an hour ago.

"Just shut it down," Winspear said, exasperated.

"I'm *trying* to shut it down, but it's," Roy shook his head, looking down at the computer, then at the box in the center of the room where the quantum brain was chilled to deep-space temperatures. "Something's not right. It's accepting the shutdown commands, but it's throwing errors—different errors each time. It keeps logging me off and back on. It's... messing with me on purpose I think. Like it's stalling or..."

He slumped into one of the chairs, out of breath.

"We'll do it manually then," the soldier said, slinging his weapon up, stepping toward the inner core, "and then get the hell out of here." He raised his barrel to the porthole and said, "Move around the back."

"No!" Roy said, jumping up, still winded, slumping against the inner core as he said, "It's less than a Kelvin in there. Blow that seal and we'll all freeze to death in a few seconds."

Winspear, Jack, and even the soldier all looked at him wide-eyed.

"Fine," the soldier said, lowering his weapon. "But we're leaving. President Winspear, elevator, *now.*"

"Wait," Winspear said. "This is *my* computer, okay? *My* system. Roy, talk me through what you're seeing. We can figure this out if we just—"

"No!" the soldier said, starting toward Winspear. "It's time to leave."

He put a hand on the president's shoulder, but Winspear jerked away, wheeling around with a finger in the man's face, and the three of them formed a loose huddle that one of the Secret Service agents moved toward, reaching in to separate them.

As they shouted at each other, Jack stepped away from it, toward the elevator, past the porthole.

He was trying to think. He had the feeling they were missing something. Something big. Because something about all of this was badly wrong. Not just a computer that wouldn't respond or a warehouse that controlled itself or a dead man lost in a corner office for years.

Jack had thought Winspear was behind Katelyn Patterson's murder, Duncan McAvoy's killing spree, and the bastardization of the Shooter Act.

And then McAvoy had named Scarly at the last second.

Scarly, the dead man in the heart of the machine. The man who was supposed to be able to clear Winspear's name. The one who backstabbed him... who addressed his actual *suicide* note to Winspear despite everything Winspear would have thought. He'd apparently framed the president, but for what? He had no motive... not to frame him, and certainly not to kill himself, but the suicide note... the suicide note that said—

"Wait," Jack said, eyes widening. "*Wait!*"

He stumbled back over to the group, tripping, feeling light-headed with all the exertion and climbing around the last 18 hours, he guessed.

They were still in the midst of a shouting match, but they turned as Jack yelled.

"Will you three *shut up*!"

They turned to him, and Jack saw that Winspear was breathing hard. The soldier was too. Their eyes were blood-shot as they looked at him. Roy was leaning against the inner core again, haggard.

"Roy," Jack said, "pull up the picture of the suicide note."

Roy stared at him for a minute, but then pushed himself off the inner core wall and did as he was told. He leaned on the desk where the laptop was, using one arm to support himself as he navigated the screen, pulling up the picture of the note before handing the laptop across to Jack.

It felt strangely heavy in his hands, and the words seemed fuzzy, hard to focus on, like the screen was fuzzy, but Jack could read it well enough. He muttered the words under his breath:

"Dear James, you won't read this for a long time, I'm sure, but I hope by then you'll understand why I had to do it. I know that this means taking away everything from you—or, while not everything, at least something very, very import-ant—and because of that I have not made the decision lightly. But I think that if you knew everything that I did, you would consider yourself honor bound to act. I have to end things here because…"

As Jack finished reading through it, Winspear fell back into one of the roller chairs, still trying to catch his breath. Roy was massaging his head, squinting against a throbbing headache.

Winspear said, "What does Scarly's suicide note have to do with any of this?"

"Everything," Jack said, noticing his own piercing head-ache, "because"—he looked up at them—"it's not a suicide note."

The screen was getting fuzzier, and all at once Jack's legs were weak.

"What—" Roy started to say, stumbling forward toward Jack, but stopping as he had to brace himself on the desk to keep from falling. He shook his head hard.

"Something's... happening. Jack—"

With his free hand he pointed at the laptop.

"He's right," the soldier said, voice husky with heavy breathing as he spread his legs slightly, bracing himself on the wall of the inner core. He shook his head from side to side, blinking quickly. "Something's happening to us."

"The only thing that fits—" Jack said. "This letter... he's talking about... shutting down *the computer*."

Roy read through the lines, looking up and reading aloud, "'I have to end things here—'"

"He was going to *turn it off*," Jack said slowly, "and this wasn't a suicide note, because... because he wasn't talking about killing himself."

"Then how'd he die?" Roy asked. "And why."

He was still breathing hard too, looking over his shoulder at the elevator.

"Why," Jack said, "the computer... it saw him writing this—maybe through the webcam on his computer or... or however else. But it couldn't let itself be shut down."

"That's nuts," Winspear said.

"No," Jack shook his head.

He started to turn the laptop so Winspear could see it, but instead it fell off the table. He reached for it, stumbled, and found himself on all fours breathing hard.

"I can't—" he said, trailing off as his muscles started to strain hard against gravity, started to fail.

"Jack—" Winspear said, reaching down to him, but his body was starting to fail too.

The weakness came in a wave. One of the Secret Service men got Winspear under the arm and pulled him up.

"Come on," the soldier said, "quick. We have to get out of here."

"Elevator," the other soldier said to them. "*Now.*"

"This thing you built," Jack said, head lolling over his shoulder toward where he thought Roy still was, as the soldier hoisted him up.

The programmer's eyes were shut as he leaned back on the console.

"I just need a minute. To think. There's got to be a way to explain this."

"The smartest computer in the world," Jack said. "So smart it's stupid."

"What—" Roy said, an edge of anger in his voice, but just an edge as the last soldier started to pull him forward.

"If Scarly was going to shut it down," Roy said, "then it would have seen him as an obstacle to be removed. But how could it kill him?"

The soldier carrying him forward said, "The same way it's trying to kill us right now."

47

"There was no bullet wound on Scarly," Jack went on, taking a deep breath as he found himself tucked into the back corner of the elevator's steel cage. "No wound at all."

"Poison," Roy said, falling in next to him.

"No," Jack shook his head, "this system—supercooled right?"

Roy nodded.

"Liquid nitrogen?"

Roy nodded again, "For the early stages, then vacuum to get lower."

"Liquid nitrogen that it could route into the air control system?"

"Damn." Roy nodded. "Scarly wasn't poisoned, he died of *asphyxiation*."

There was a brief pause as they all tried to sense the air.

"So it *was* stalling," Roy said. "Keeping us here while it swapped out the air in the room."—Roy smiled to himself—"Exactly what I would have done."

"Sorry sir," one of the Secret Service agents said as he practically stuffed Winspear into the small chamber, already overfull.

As they hauled the door shut, Roy laughed. "It's really doing it. It's really trying to kill us."

"Whatever control it has," Jack said, "it must work slowly. It's pumping nitrogen in here but the oxygen concentration is still high enough"—he stopped, rubbing his head, the headache making it hard to think—"it's high enough… we're still alive."

"We'll pass out soon," Roy said.

"*Get it set!*" the soldier nearer the back said, addressing his counterpart who was kneeling at the base of the inner core, just under the viewing port.

"What are you doing?" Roy said.

And the soldier answered, "shutting this thing down."

He unspooled the length of plastic explosive breaching charges and started molding it into place, pressing it up against the wall of the inner chamber.

"No!" Roy said. "You can't—"

He was trying to get out of the elevator, but one of the Secret Service agents pushed him back against the cage.

"If we can shut it down… I can… there are backups, I can fix it."

"We're past that," the soldier said.

Jack watched him press the explosives into place. He saw him connect some sort of control unit, and his vision was going gray as the soldier poked away at it, setting a timer.

"I can—" Roy said, and then he collapsed against Jack.

"Come on," the soldier said, jerking the door to the elevator shut as soon as his man was inside.

Jack was going too, the sounds becoming distant as he heard the soldiers cursing, trying to close the door but somehow unable to.

"Move him," the soldier said.

Winspear grunted as the other soldier and one of the Secret Service agents manhandled him out of the way, pulling his leg out of the gap and finally closing the gate.

The seven bodies took up every inch of space in the elevator cage, pressing back on Jack, and now he was vaguely aware that someone was saying his name.

"Listen to me, Jack. The panel is next to you. You have to—"

The rest of the words were lost. Jack's ears started to ring as he shifted his weight, trying to see the panel on the wall at his side.

He stared at it for a moment, then put his hand against it.

"*Access denied*," a computerized voice said.

"What the hell," the soldier said, and Jack could hear the fatigue in his voice.

He was fading too, and everything was turning to a blur of shapes. He had a moment, giggling, as he realized they were all going to die here, and this elevator would open on the next floor with seven bodies spilling out like some presidential clown car.

Someone was shaking Roy.

He mumbled, "Backup... biometric auth—"

His words trailed off as his head lolled to the side, and one of the soldiers counted to three, at which point he and the service agents shoved Winspear up and toward the back of the space.

"His hand," the soldier said. "Get his hand, Jack."

He was still lost in his own space, laughing at Winspear's limp hand that flopped wildly into frame. Jack took it and stared, squinting, confused, but after a moment he was able to press Winspear's palm against the reader at an odd angle. He was seeing black now, but he held the hand there even as the world started to spin. He heard the soldier say something about the bomb, about how long until it would go off.

Finally, the panel chimed, and the elevator jerked into motion against the weight of too many passengers. Slowly, it carried them up and out of the chamber.

48

The next thing Jack knew, he was spilling out into a rush of cold air. He collapsed forward out of the elevator, the light so bright that he couldn't see anything for a moment.

Wind whipped past them, and he heard someone—the soldier—shouting orders.

They were on the roof, he realized, and even though his pupils were catching up, his brain was still several steps behind as he tried to process what he was seeing.

It looked like a field of mirrors spreading out from them in all directions, coming up to shoulder height. Silver and chrome hedging that seemed overgrown with threaded steel vines and rectangular leaflets of solar panels.

From one dreamscape to another.

"What the—" he said, and Roy—already stumbling to his feet—looked from Jack to the field of panels.

"It's an emergent design," Roy said. "Something calculated by the computer to ratchet the most energy out of a given area of panel by using the same trick mother nature did with trees, a diminishing spiral set in a Fibonacci sequence."

"Why am I not surprised?" Jack said back to him, on his feet as well.

Winspear was near them, shaking off the Secret Service agent, and the head soldier jogged out from the field of panels and into view just ahead of them, another of the troops in tow.

"Damn you!" Roy said, running forward and shoving the soldier who'd placed the charge on the inner chamber.

He absorbed the blow, spinning Roy around and pushing him toward the other troop who pushed him forward, in the direction of the solar fields and away from the elevator.

"Two minutes," he said to the Secret Service agent next to Winspear. "We need to get away from the center. The blast shouldn't be big enough to bring down the building, but the elevator shaft—"

They all understood well enough to be in motion instantly. They followed the two soldiers as they turned, ducking into the field of panels.

"This way," one of them yelled, and they quickened to a jog away from the elevator.

"One minute," the soldier said.

"I could have stopped it," Roy said. "I could have reprogrammed it. *Years* of fine-tuning—"

"Save it," the soldier said.

Jack tried to keep up as they headed for the edge of the building. There was the sound of a chopper in the distance.

"Okay," the soldier said, stopping, "get down, hold on."

They listened, waiting for a tense moment until there was a deep rocking noise from the direction of the core below. It grew as they looked around at one another, the rocking changing by degrees into a screeching metal sound.

"The shaft," Roy said.

"What's going on?" Winspear asked as the sound of the explosion faded and he noticed another sound—the helicopter—growing in the near distance toward the edge of the building.

"We're headed for Air Force One," one of the Secret Service agents explained as they stood and started jogging toward the edge.

"The vote?" Winspear asked, breathless as they moved along.

"It's done," one of the soldiers answered. "They voted to impeach."

"So you're taking me to the Capitol?"

He nodded, not making eye contact with Winspear as he said, "We've been ordered to bring you to the Senate Chambers for the hearing."

"For my trial, you mean."

As they moved, Winspear looked back over his shoulder at the trail of smoke coming up from the center of the building.

"What was that explosion?" the soldier who'd been on the roof asked.

"Long story," the other answered. "Keep moving."

"Look," Roy said, pointing out over the horizon, where a flock of black drones could be seen making an escape.

Beyond them and above, the larger drones were still going about their business, some as big as small passenger jets, others looking like military drones with their oddly thin bodies and bulbous, sensor-packed tips. They seemed to swirl around, careening dangerously.

"They're rerouting, going into hold patterns because the warehouse—"

"So it's still functioning?" the soldier asked.

"I think so," Roy said. "The inner chamber is blast shielded. The explosion probably severed the solar array, but it'll just swap to geothermal."

"You've got to be kidding me," the soldier said.

They were all still moving toward the edge of the building. The sound of the helicopter was so loud he had to half shout over it.

"How did they get the vote?" Winspear asked.

"It was close," the agent started. "Tarrah Adler broke the tie—"

"Adler? How—"

"It's been nuts down there," the agent said. "Guilfoyle stepped down and they elected her speaker."

"*What!?*"

"With all due respect," the soldier said, "we've got bigger problems, sir. You're still the president, and they've already prepped the situation room on Air Force One for you to attempt communication with the Chinese."

"They didn't back down?" Winspear asked.

"Not an inch, sir, and they've refused to remove their satellites from over the US."

Winspear growled, "Assault on all sides."

As they closed the distance to the edge of the building, Jack was working on his own puzzle.

"There's something else," he said, "Scarly—"

"He didn't frame me," Winspear said.

They were emerging from the solar forest, heading toward a clearing big enough for the huge helicopter—Marine One—that was coming in to land eerily fast.

"But if he didn't—" Jack said, yelling over the sound of the rotors as the helicopter dropped into position, rocking to a halt. "McAvoy—somebody was working with him. The tweet."

Jack shook his head.

"Somebody used him," Winspear shouted over the roar. "They *told* him to name Scarly… they sent you—sent *us*—on a wild goose chase."

"A diversion," Jack echoed the thought. "But if it wasn't Scarly—"

Two agents jumped out of the helicopter, looking both ways, guns drawn. They turned and shouted something, but it was lost in the noise, and then two more agents descended trailing another man.

He wore a suit, and as he walked up to them, the wind whipped his tie and overcoat around him. As soon as Jack recognized Vice-President Applegate, he knew what had happened.

McAvoy. Katelyn Patterson. All of it threaded through the needle of the Shooter Act. The bill that years ago Applegate had helped Jack and Winspear get passed. The bill that had led to all of this, in one way or another. McAvoy named Scarly as his partner in crime—a clue that, in hindsight, was left on purpose. A feint. Smoke and mirrors.

Applegate had used the bill to his own ends. To frame the president. To finally get what he'd been maneuvering for this whole time, the presidency itself.

"You," Winspear said as Applegate came closer. "I should've known."

"Yes," Applegate said, nodding, "you should have."

Part 4—Winspear's Revenge

"I'll leave you this before you read—to answer the question of why I should be president, let me ask you: Do you want the same thing, again? The same administration your parents complained about? And that you and your friends have found appalling year after year? It was just a few turns of the century ago that the Wild West was ending. The age of outlaws was drawing closed, and the modern world was forged in blood and sweat. With change like that—with progress like that so near in our, the greatest country's history—how is it that you and your parents' generation and their parents' generation have become so ossified and stuck in their ways? Let me ask the question in a different way: Don't you want to try something different? Something new? Are you ready to get going again? Because if you are, then vote for me, America. You won't regret it."

— From the Forward of the republished edition of
The First Trillion's the Hardest, by J. Woolston Winspear

49

"Now, Mr. President, if you'll step aboard," Applegate said, "we have an impeachment trial to get to."

Nobody moved. The chopper's blades thrummed away as Marine One waited.

"Don't."

It was Jack who said it, stepping forward, grabbing Winspear's arm even as Applegate's agents countered forward, guns still drawn. Applegate held a hand up to stop them.

"You won't get away with this," Jack said while he and Winspear glared at the man.

"If you go," Jack said to Winspear, "you'll be making it okay. All of it. If he wins—"

"He's *already* won," Winspear said.

"Please hurt Mr. Paulson if he speaks out of turn again," Applegate said to the Secret Service agent on his left, and the man watched Jack closely from behind his sunglasses. "And"—Applegate checked his watch—"we really do need to be going. The Senate's waiting."

"Fine," Winspear said, and he shook Jack's arm off as he took a step forward.

"No, you can't—" Jack said, but the Secret Service agent by Applegate took a single step forward and punched him in the chest.

It wasn't too hard—certainly not as hard is the man could have hit him—but it was enough that Jack staggered backward with a gasp, almost falling.

Winspear looked back at him, shaking his head.

"Trust me on this, Jack; it's not about what's right and wrong now. It's *survival* now."

"I was hoping you'd see it that way," Applegate said. "You always were a survivor, Winspear. That's one of the things I like most about you. It's admirable."

Winspear grunted as Applegate turned toward Marine One, the rest of them falling in. One of the agents came for Jack and Roy and jerked them toward the chopper. Jack rubbed his chest as they walked, looking back to see the soldiers were talking into their radios as they watched the group walk away. Jack wondered why they were letting this happen but remembered the exchange with Winspear when they'd joined the party. It was starting to seem like Winspear's paranoia was warranted. Mercer's soldiers were clearly on Applegate's side.

It was hopeless.

On board Marine One, the Secret Service agent who'd punched Jack earlier now pushed him down onto one of the benches at the back as the chopper lifted off.

Nobody said anything for a few minutes as the helicopter gained height and started to pull around the facility in a wide circle.

"There's something you need to know," Roy said to Applegate, jerking his shoulder away from the Secret Service agent who'd rested his hand there as an implied threat.

"Thanks, but I think I know about all there is of the situation," Applegate said, smiling, his gaunt cheekbones rising almost to points. "I'm about to be the president of the United States," Applegate said. "And who the hell are *you?*"

"He's right," Winspear said. "You don't know—"

"Listen, *you're a moron*," Roy said, and he ducked as the agent reached out for him.

Before anything could come to blows, Applegate said, "You're making a powerful enemy."

Winspear broke in, "Just *listen* to him, ok? This business with the market—China and Russia—"

"Ah!" Applegate said. "This is the part where you try to convince me you're the only one who can talk them down, right? That my trying to deal with them will be World War 3?"

"Give me a little more credit than that, Applegate," Winspear said. "I'm aware that I'm part of the problem here."—Applegate raised his eyebrows—"Believe me, I know. But what *you* may not be aware of is that the only way to stop what's going on with the market is to *shut down that facility!*"

He pointed down through the floor of Marine One, toward the warehouse.

Applegate thought about this for a moment.

"Fine," he said. "We'll cut power to—"

"Oh no you won't," Roy said. "It's got backups on its backups. And forget blowing it to hell—one of Mercer's men tried that on our way out. As you can see,"—Roy nodded toward the window where drones could still be seen flying to and fro outside—"the system is still functioning just fine."

Applegate stared at him and Winspear for a moment.

"Ridiculous," he said. "A poor last attempt at a bargaining chip, Winspear. You're out of this, do you understand?"

"I get it," Winspear said, hands raised plaintively. "And believe me, I've seen the devil enough to know it's better to be in his right hand."

Applegate smiled at this.

"You *bastard*," Jack said, and when Winspear and Applegate were both looking at him he looked from one to the other and added, "both of you. I *trusted* you, Applegate. And *you*—" he looked at Winspear and shook his head.

"That was a mistake, Jack," Applegate said back.

"The Shooter Act," Winspear said, and Applegate nodded. "I always wondered at the time, why you suddenly took an interest. When it started gaining ground in the press...

that's when you came to me as a running mate. The bill bought you enough support to—"

Winspear trailed off, shaking his head, trying to piece it together.

"Bought *us* enough support. Almost enough to turn your ridiculous campaign around," Applegate said.

Winspear stared daggers at him.

"Listen," he said. "I'll play ball with this trial, and I can keep quiet about the truth of what happened here, so long as I'm taken care of," he said, "but Roy's serious about the facility. We've got to shut it down."

"Well, we can get Mercer on the phone," he gestured to one of his agents, who started working away at a slate. "I'm sure he can compel the thing to shut down with the proper armaments."

Roy scoffed, and Applegate shot him a look.

"Ah, there she is," Applegate said, gesturing out the window. "My new ride."

Winspear followed his gaze out the window and grunted. Jack looked out and saw that Air Force One was dropping toward the runway. They watched it touch down, and the helicopter changed direction, slowly lowering itself toward the end of the Camplex's airstrip where Air Force One would come to a stop.

Nobody said anything as they descended, and a few minutes later the helicopter was touching down almost in the shadow of the great beast of a plane.

"All right. Changing planes. Don't try anything funny." Applegate said, and they worked their way out of Marine One and onto the tarmac of the Winspear drone-strip.

In the distance, white carrier drones were in neat rows, and at the other parallel strip, a larger shipping plane was taking off, the sky above continuing to buzz with activity.

"Whatever is going on here," Applegate said, "I'll deal with it later. As the first act of my presidency, how's that?"

He said this over his shoulder as they closed the gap to the impressively looming Air Force One, a monstrous Boeing VC-25. As they approached, Jack looked up at the fuselage where it said "UNITED STATES OF AMERICA" in letters the size of buildings.

They were at the stairs, Applegate starting up with his agents, but Jack stopped.

"No," he said, "I won't do it. I won't go with you."

"Jack," Winspear started to say, but he was cut off as Jack turned on him.

"How can you do this? After everything... after all the trouble you've already caused? You've got to take a stand somewhere. To *stand up* for something. *Anything.*"

Winspear looked from Jack up to Applegate.

"Please, Jack," he said. "You were lucky to live though that stunt at LAX. We've got no choice."

"There's *always* a choice," Jack said. "Just... don't go with him. Don't let him sanctify this—this *coup*—by actually going to the Senate. Hold on for—"

"For what?" Applegate spat down. "For the next session? The House has already made their move. *I* own the Senate."

He jerked his hand up, pointing at himself.

"Face it; you were both outmaneuvered. Don't be sore losers. Better yet, don't be *dead* losers."

"Jack—" Winspear said again, and they looked at each other, Jack shaking his head as Winspear sighed, shrugging.

"It's nothing to you," Jack said to Winspear in disbelief. "It's just so easy for you to... to turn your back on everything. Everyone."

In the back of his mind, he could hear Winspear's words from in the warehouse echoing: *chaos all the way down.*

Winspear sighed, the fire in his eyes gone.

He said, "I'm just so tired of it all."

Jack looked at him. He searched Winspear's face for a moment, but it was already done. The man was defeated. Jack looked up at Applegate. At Air Force One. At the drones filling the sky overhead.

"Well, I won't."

Jack shook his head as he took a step back.

"I won't go," he said. "If you're going to kill me, you'll have to do it right here."

"Jack—" Winspear was starting to say, but Applegate cut him off.

"All right then, Jack. You know I never was one for trust. Call me old fashioned, but I like to have an insurance policy. Maybe you misunderstood when I said you were outmaneuvered. Let me be more clear. Kay Luo is on board the plane already."

Jack stared at him.

"She's with Duncan McAvoy. So let me assure you that the *choice* you think you have is a figment of your imagination. If you cause any problems—"

He didn't finish the thought, shrugging.

"You piece of *shit*!" Jack said, storming up the stairs toward Applegate, Winspear grabbing him even as one of the Secret Service agents moved to intercept.

"Whoa! There's that fighting spirit!" Applegate said. "The last time I saw you this passionate was when you were shopping that bill around telling anyone who'd listen about your dead fiancé."

"That's not necessary Applegate—" Winspear said up to him, climbing the stairs himself.

"And *you*," Applegate cut him off. "Just so we're clear, all of us: I have Kay Luo on board, *and* Ronald Bowers, and"— he gestured toward Roy, and as he did so one of the agents grabbed him by the forearm—"we have whoever *this* is, so just in case you were feeling any kind of change of heart coming on—"

He didn't have to finish the thought, waiting for an answer from Winspear that came in the form of a grunt as he moved up the stairs.

"Good," Applegate said, and as they reached the top of the stairs he added, "Not a word of this—any of it—to any of your staff on board, or they might have an unfortunate accident. I'm sure you understand."

50

As soon as they entered, the president and vice-president went one way while McAvoy led Jack and Roy another. As they walked, the plane started to taxi. After a moment the Secret Service agent flanking them opened a door, and McAvoy shoved Jack and Roy through.

"Jack!"

It was Kay, rushing over and throwing her arms around him.

"I was so worried," she said.

"Me too," he said. "Me too."

He pulled away, looking at her for a second before hugging her again.

"Get a room," Roy said. "Oh wait"—he tried the door, found it locked—"I guess we've *all* got a room. Mr. Bowers," he said with a nod.

"Berry," Bowers nodded back.

"You two know each other?" Jack asked, pulling out of the hug but keeping hold of Kay's hand for a second longer.

Roy and Bowers explained that they'd bumped into each other while working for Winspear, and then Jack gave a quick rundown to both Bowers and Kay of what they'd seen in the facility

"Jesus," Bowers said. "So it wasn't all us?"

"We thought—" Kay started, explaining what they'd done and their perspective on what was going on in the markets.

"That's ridiculous," Roy said. "That's… it's so simple. It's just liquidating product to generate enough cash to keep funneling into the stock."

"You mean this is *all* the computer?" Kay asked.

"Sure," Roy said. "It has a prime directive. Nothing else matters. It needs the cash, so it can't allow the markets to close. It's taking control of firms all over the world and liquidating them to free up cash. It's a runaway train."

Jack looked at him. "A computer so smart, it's dumb," he said again.

"I'll say," Bowers offered.

At this point they all started to sway slightly, as the acceleration of the plane down the runway of the Camplex shifted them.

"Whatever started here, though, it's not done. If they can't blow the thing up, how can they stop it?"

"Beats me," Roy said. "Drop a nuke on it I guess, or otherwise destroy the facility. Bunker buster might do it."

"There's not enough time," Bowers said, looking out the window as the plane was building up speed, the backside of the warehouse in view past a field of variously sized drones taxiing in all directions.

"What the hell," Roy said, looking out another window.

Jack got low, following Roy's line of sight. From another window off the room they were in, Bowers shifted his gaze up and Kay came to see too, joining just in time to see a matte black fighter jet slash across the sky, a thin trail of munitions ending up in an explosion a bit ahead of it. They were high up, easy enough to see but the sound of the burst of machine gunfire and explosion reached them only after a handful of seconds, and even then it was muffled by the sound of Air Force One rushing forward.

"They're clearing the airspace," Bowers said. "That's the only thing I can think of."

"Maybe," Roy said, "or maybe they're getting rid of any drones that could be turned against... ones big enough to retrofit a bomb onto."

"What? Why?" Kay asked.

"They think this market thing is a hack by the Chinese," Roy said. "Or the Russians, whoever. They don't want anything flying that could be hacked and turned into a weapon."

"Jesus," Jack said. "This just keeps getting better."

The plane was taking off, canting up at a sharp angle so that they all had to reach out and hold themselves steady on the few seats and corner table that lined the space.

"Relax," Roy said. "The warehouse doesn't have any reason to come after us with drones. In fact, it should already be pushing normal traffic back, rerouting to other facilities. Some stuff is probably in a holding pattern waiting for us to get out of the way."

"So, it's that bad then?" Jack turned to Bowers and Kay. "They're so convinced we're under attack that they're shooting down drones that *might* be able to be turned against us?"

Kay and Bowers exchanged a look, then Bowers said, "There was a video going around late yesterday—two brokers jumping off the 50th story of Freedom Tower. Markets are falling. Grocery stores are running out of water." He shook his head. "People are panicking."

"People really think we're going to war," Kay added, "and the Chinese and Russian leaders are playing it all up, threatening to open their own trade network based on a gold standard."

"The only problem is they're not just stoking fears," Bowers said. "They mean business. The Chinese have had satellites hovering over key spots of the States since yesterday morning and are refusing to even *acknowledge* them, much less clear our space. It's brinkmanship, that or preparation to come out on top. Probably both."

"Damn," Jack said under his breath, "and Winspear... behind *all* of this is that spineless—"

He shook his head.

"It was Applegate who framed him," Bowers said, sighing, "but that was the window Winspear left open. His biggest weakness."

"We shouldn't have a president," Jack said quickly. "*Nobody* should have that much power to misuse."

"At least he's out now," Roy said.

"And you think Applegate will be any better? Applegate will be Winspear with *purpose*. He'll dismantle the government even further. He'll fill the vacuum with something worse. He—"

Jack thought about Katelyn Patterson. Duncan McAvoy.

He said, "He's not just a crook. He's a murderer."

They looked around at each other.

"We have to stop him," Kay said.

"I agree," Roy said. "Except, oh, wait, we're locked in a little room headed for thirty thousand feet, with no weapons and no way to even talk to the outside world."

Kay and Jack looked at him.

"Oh come on," he said. "Wake up. There's no winning this thing. You hate Winspear because you say he's weak—that his weakness led to all this—well you heard what Applegate said out there: He's a *survivor*. I don't know about you, but I'd be pretty happy to survive this incident, if that's even still a possibility, and we're not going to do that if Applegate thinks for even a *second* that you're cracking some harebrained scheme."

"He can't get rid of us just like that," Kay said.

"Do the math. We're all witnesses. And you two"—Roy nodded toward Jack and Kay—"you've already proved you're willing to take up arms for your ideals, meaning you can't be bought off. And you"—he looked at Bowers—"you better just hope that Winspear can vouch for you keeping your mouth shut."

"What about *you*," Kay asked. "Of all of us, you seem to be just as expendable."

"Maybe, except I'm like Winspear. I'd rather let the devil know I'm safely in his right hand. *Alive*." He shrugged. "Somebody's going to have to rebuild the computer after this."

"Well good luck on version two!" Jack said to him, glaring. "I hope *that* one isn't as sloppy as the *one that tried to kill us!*"

"That couldn't have been predicted!" Roy shouted back.

They advanced on each other, but Bowers stepped in.

"Hey, *hey!* Shut up, both of you. We've got to stick *together* here, all right?"

The plane was still climbing, and as the background hum of the engines tapered off a bit, Roy and Jack stared at each other but stayed where they were.

"Now," Bowers went on after the moment had passed, "we need to figure out what we're going to do when we get to Capitol Hill. If we can—"

Just then, the door to their room opened, and Duncan McAvoy stepped in.

"Well, well," he said, looking Jack up and down. "Recovering nicely I see."

Jack reached to the scar at his stomach, and for an instant he remembered how the bullet McAvoy fired had felt punching through him, back to front.

"Thanks to your terrible aim," he said back to McAvoy, who grimaced.

"You'll get yours soon enough," he said. "*You*"—he turned to Kay—"come with me."

She hesitated.

"Don't look so scared," he said, baring his teeth. "We need an interpreter, the one we brought is ill."

"Meaning he's refused to work with Applegate." Jack said. "You know he has no claim to the presidency, right? That framing Winspear is treason?"

"Aren't you a smart little—" McAvoy said, stepping toward him.

Key stepped in between them quickly.

"I'll help," she said. "Just tell me who we're talking to."

McAvoy didn't say anything for a moment, looking past her to Jack, holding his eye.

"Is it the Chinese president?" Bowers said. "Because if that's the case—you know as Winspear's aid I was somewhat of an expert on foreign relations and—"

"Fine, you come too."

"We'll need Roy and Jack with us," Bowers said quickly, and McAvoy looked at him with his brow furrowed. "Applegate and Winspear are probably talking about how to shut down the warehouse, right?"

It was a gamble, but a good one.

McAvoy didn't respond for a moment but then said, "Fine."

With that he grabbed Kay by the arm and nodded toward Roy and Bowers.

"You two first," he said to them, and as they stepped toward the door he nodded Jack over. "You after them. Anyone tries anything and, well, it's easy to snap a thin neck like this one."

He moved his hand up from Kay's arm to the back of her neck as they trailed the rest into the hallway.

They moved through the plane, and Jack noticed it was eerily empty—there were no staff or Secret Service agents running around. In fact, it seemed like a ghost ship, and Jack swallowed hard as he turned around, seeing the look on Kay's face.

Finally, about halfway along the plane, they reached a wide spot in the corridor. In the open area just about where the wings of the aircraft were, the hallway narrowed in either direction, and a door off the corner of a large room was just up ahead.

"Knock," McAvoy said, gesturing to it.

Bowers knocked, and the door opened to reveal a conference room with a long wooden table that terminated in a clump of videoconferencing equipment.

Winspear was already there, along with a handful of Secret Service agents and Applegate. The screen was dark in the background.

"Where is everyone?" Bowers asked, referring to the normal retinue of department representatives and advisors that would be present for something like this, a call with a foreign president during what might be wartime.

"Back of the plane," Applegate explained. "Easier that way. You know, in case there are any *special counselors* looking into this eventually. Fewer people to interview. Ms. Luo, are you ready to help?"

McAvoy threw her forward so that she had to catch herself on the wood table.

Jack started to reach for her, but McAvoy grabbed him by the arm, stopping him, his iron grip surely leaving bruises.

Kay looked back at Jack, then at Applegate, who said, "You're going to make me say it, aren't you?" He rolled his eyes. "If you *don't* help me, your daughter—we'll find a way."

"No!" She said quickly. "I—I'll do it. I'll help you."

"There we go!" Applegate said, reaching forward and taking the conference equipment off mute. "Okay, go ahead put him through."

The screen at the head of the room flickered to life.

51

They all stared as the Chinese president appeared in front of them.

He spoke, delivering a quick sentence before narrowing his gaze at the video feed from his end. Applegate turned to Kay and said, "Well?"

"I—he, he says thanks for giving him an audience."

The Chinese president said something else, practically spitting the words.

"Better... better late than never," Kay said.

Applegate grunted.

"Ask him if he's aware that I am now in command."

Kay spoke, and the Chinese president replied.

"He—uh—he says that he's been told you aren't sworn in yet. He'll only deal with Winspear."

"Mr. President," Applegate said, addressing the monitor and pausing for Kay to translate as he spoke, "as I'm sure you are aware, President Winspear"—he gestured toward Winspear, who gave an awkward wave from the sidelines—"has been impeached and will shortly be removed from office. I will be the new president."

Kay finished relaying this, and the Chinese president responded quickly.

"He says he'll deal only with whoever has the power to make decisions *now*," Kay said, "and... and if he's not allowed to talk to Winspear then they'll be forced to take action."

Applegate smiled, saying, "What a pissant—*don't* translate that. Winspear"—he turned to him—"get over here. Tell him that if he doesn't stand down now, we'll reserve the right to execute a preemptive strike on his satellites."

"That's not a good idea," Bowers chimed in, and McAvoy moved toward him.

"Hold it," Winspear said toward the back of the room. "Touch him and I'm not helping."

McAvoy growled, Applegate rolled his eyes, and the Chinese president shook his head, muttering something which Kay interpreted.

"He says if we can't give him some assurance that the markets will be shut down soon, he and Russia will begin the process of moving their trade spheres to a gold standard."

"This is okay," Bowers said as Winspear moved forward. "We were expecting this."

"What do you want me to tell him?" Winspear asked Bowers.

"The only thing we have left," Bowers said, and as Winspear, Applegate, and Kay all turned to him, he shrugged as he added, "the *truth*."

Winspear took a deep breath, then looked at Kay and back to the screen.

"We—uh—have a problem on our end," he started. "There's an issue—a computer algorithm that's out of whack. We can't control it. Or rather, we've *lost* control of it."

Kay relayed this message, and the president appeared to think about it for a moment. He reached forward, toward the video feed and then spoke to someone off screen, the mic muted. He came back after a moment, looking angry as he spat a string of words Kay struggled to keep up with.

"He says that's ridiculous, that if you really expect him to believe this is some accident and not an attack then—"

"Hey—" Roy was coming up the side of the room, waving his arms up at the screen. "Hey—you need to listen to us, ok?"

Kay hesitated a moment, looking from the screen to Roy before translating.

Roy didn't wait for a response, and Kay relayed everything as he continued.

"Our system—*that* system"—pointing down through the bottom of the plane—"the warehouse is out of control. It used the market system to buy up hundreds of shell companies to pull this thing off, and now it's using *you* just like it's using *us*. It's liquidating global markets as fast as it can to keep a number on a spreadsheet in the right range. I know it sounds ridiculous, but it's real, and if you don't stop it, it'll just keep going."

Kay finished, and the Chinese president seemed to lean back in his chair and think for a moment.

He replied, and Kay turned to Roy, relaying, "If this is a financial program, how do you explain the exchanges? He says we're enabling it on our end."

"No," Roy shook his head, "it's locked us out of the exchanges. It hacked its way in and won't let the exchanges close from the software side. They all have electric backup, so we can't shut them down on our end, short of blowing them sky high."

The Chinese president muted himself again, talking to someone off screen before coming back.

"The level of complexity..." Kay interpreted. "If what you're saying is true, it must be one of the most advanced systems ever created."

Roy smiled. "Yes."

The Chinese president paused for a moment and shook his head.

He replied in monosyllable, and Kay turned to Roy and translated, "How?"

"It's a damn good computer, that's how," Roy said. "The only 2500-bit quantum computer in the world. Programmed by yours truly."

Kay passed this along, stumbling over the technical terms so that the word "quantum" was in English among the rest of the Chinese words, standing out as much as Roy did.

Immediately, there was conversation from the Chinese president's side of the screen as unseen people talked quickly about this. The Chinese president listened for a moment, then raised a hand to stop the chatter off camera, and then he spoke.

"He says he'll help," Kay passed along. "They're offering their assistance. They're saying... they can have one of their satellites in place in—"

"No," Roy said. "You can't just blow it up. We've tried that. It's too deep to—"

In the flurry of speech, Kay had to lean in to listen to what the Chinese president was saying, and she turned to the rest of them and relayed his message.

"The satellites aren't carrying conventional munitions."

"What then?" Winspear asked.

"He called it a high powered electro-magnetic pulse weapon."

Winspear reached forward and hit a mute button on the conferencing equipment. Then he turned to Bowers, saying, "You don't think this is—"

Bowers sighed. "I do."

"Out with it," Applegate said, and Bowers turned to him.

"We had a report a year and a half ago—an agent we had in deep cover told us about a Chinese program that was developing directed electronic counter devices."

"CHAMP," Winspear said, "Counter-electronics high-powered microwave advanced missile project."

"My God," Applegate said.

"It's real," Bowers said. "They've taken it a step past mounting it on aircraft for delivery, though, which is what we thought they were doing. Kay, ask him what sort of outage their satellites can drop."

Winspear reached forward and took them off mute. Kay asked, and her eyes widened as the Chinese president answered.

"He says they can deliver an EMP drone with a hundred and fifty kilometer area of effect radius anywhere in the US... in nine minutes."

"My God," Bowers said. "That's one hell of an upgrade over what Mercer thinks they're capable of."

"Okay," Winspear said, thinking. "Okay. Roy?"

He turned to him.

"That'll do it," he said. "If it can get over the building, a pulse that strong will go straight through the blast shields. They won't get the backups of normal code, but it'll destroy the entanglement of the unit. Everything that's gone into achieving a stable quantum state"—he shrugged—"It's all local. It'll all be wiped out."

Winspear turned to Kay and then the screen again.

"Mr. President, I'd like you to drop one of those drones on my manufacturing facility as soon as you can."

Kay relayed this, and the Chinese president nodded.

"He says they'll help but—but they require something in return."

"Let's hear it," Winspear said.

"They want the technology, how we built the computer."

"Depends on how much they're paying," Roy said.

"No," Winspear said, quickly holding a hand up to Kay.

He nodded his head at the Chinese president.

"Kay, tell him we'll do it, but they have to call off the currency shift until we have a chance to negotiate after all this."

"You think I'm helping them?" Roy said.

"You'll be well reimbursed for your time."

"How much?"

"Think of the highest number you can and double it," Winspear said. Kay cleared her throat and relayed the message.

"He says the drone's away. We've got seven minutes and… and they'll be in touch afterward about the technology they need."

With that, the Chinese president reached forward, and the video feed cut off, and all that was left now was a timer, counting down from seven minutes.

52

"Okay," Bowers said, "maybe I'm missing something, but we're still pretty close to the warehouse. Kay, what did he say the radius on that thing is? A hundred and fifty kilometers?"

Roy said, "In English that's like what? 60 or 70 miles?"

"Try a hundred," Bowers said.

"So we're going to get hit by it?" Kay asked.

"Relax," Roy said. "We're far away from there. Besides, this is Air Force One; it's shielded six ways from Sunday—"

"Shut up—all of you shut up," Applegate said. He turned to them, pointing at Winspear and saying, "You just can't help but make things worse can you?"

"What did I do?" Winspear said.

"Your little quantum dream-boy promise there. If you think we're surrendering any kind of advanced technology to the Chinese, then you're—" He shook his head. "I can't even believe I'm having this conversation."

"Watch it Applegate," Winspear said. "I'll give up the presidency quietly, but all of this doesn't just go away after."

"Oh, yes it does," Applegate said, "because I can burn you whenever I want, and you know it. The last three years… we may have kicked the impeachment into motion, but we didn't make up the fact that you're the worst thing that ever happened to this country. All the more reason to start from scratch."

"What do you mean 'start from scratch?'" Bowers asked.

"I don't know if you've been paying attention, but we're about to kick off World War 3 out there," Applegate said. "You think we're giving the Chinese that technology? You think we'll ever sit down with them *again* now that they've proved how ready they are to cut us out of geopolitics altogether with their little gold standard ploy? No—there's no taking back that threat. It's on the table. Between that and the satellites, we'll have to escalate. We'll crush them with sanctions and tariffs and after that with aircraft carriers and submarines. This is going to be a new era for the US. We're going to *stop* all this… this softness and ignorance and—"

As he spoke, he'd been gaining steam, and he caught himself, a bead of sweat running down his forehead as he took a deep breath. "But first, the trial."

Winspear looked him over as the clock on the screen ticked down.

"How long Applegate? How long have you been planning this?"

Applegate smiled.

"Before the election?" Winspear asked.

"Oh yes," Applegate said, nodding. "There was no way I would have ever gotten the nomination from either party—getting on your ticket was the way in. You had just enough of the sympathy vote that, with a proper politician as VP, the Electoral College went like that."

He reached up and snapped his fingers as he said this.

"And once you were in," Bowers went on, "what was the plan then?"

"To tell you the truth I didn't have a plan for him winning." Applegate shrugged. "It was clear from day one, though, that he'd eventually stumble into a scandal big enough to make stick in the Senate. A waiting game. And just when I was getting tired of waiting…"

Applegate waved his hand over to Jack, who looked confused for a moment.

"The Shooter Act," he said. "Katelyn Patterson."

"That's right," Applegate said. "A scandal bigger than anything I could have planted on him, and luckily *you* were there to blow the conspiracy theory right into the stratosphere."

"No…" Jack said, "no, I didn't…"

"Read 'em and weep, Paulson," Applegate said. "But don't shed too many tears. What's coming next will be best for the country. I guarantee it. We're going to take this nation back to its former glory—"

"Hold on just one *goddamn* second!" Winspear said, slamming his fists on the table as he stood, taking a step toward Applegate that made him recoil toward the nearest Secret Service agent as Winspear went on. "It doesn't surprise me that you wanted my job"—he jerked a thumb up at his chest—"but how the hell does Clayton Scarly fit into all this? If you had anything to do with his—"

"Just a bit of smoke and mirror," Applegate said, "prearranged with Duncan. He knew if he got in trouble, that's the hint he was supposed to give. The fact that Scarly was missing and apparently dead was just a happy accident. Luck. Either way, it worked—everyone was off McAvoy's trail and onto yours, because it was just oh-so-believable."

Winspear grunted.

"That's what I'd have done too," he said. "And after this? Are you planning to have me tarred and feathered?"

"Maybe," Applegate said. "And this goes for all of you." He looked around the room. "You know just enough that I have to deal with you—so here's the deal: Play along and you get to walk away and fall right off the record with the rest of this."

"And if we don't?" Jack said, taking a step.

Applegate smirked.

"You disappear into a CIA black site, maybe. Or suddenly a bunch of kiddy porn is discovered on your laptop." He shrugged. "Take your pick. Either way, I'm the president, and I can pull more strings than you can. Remember that while you're weighing your options."

The clock was ticking down behind Applegate, showing just over three minutes left.

"Well," Winspear said, looking around the room before his eyes landed back on Applegate. "You can put me down for the pardon."

"Good," Applegate said. "I look forward to working with you."

He reached out and Winspear didn't hesitate, taking his hand and shaking it.

Jack's eyes were wide at Winspear.

"I can't believe this... you *bastard!*" His hands were balled into fists. "All of this has happened because of you—because you left yourself... you left *the country* open to be manipulated"—he grimaced, turning to Applegate—"by *him* and others just like him."

"What do you want me to say, Jack?" Winspear yelled back at him. "That life isn't complicated? There are 350 million people in this country, and if 51% of them go to bed safe and sound tonight, then my job's done! Okay? You, and *her*"—he nodded toward Kay—"and all your supporters and complainers out there picketing for me to be out of office... isn't this what all of you want? Me out of the job?"

"It's not about that. Your *job* was to protect us from people like him," Jack said, pointing at Applegate as one of the Secret Service men stepped in from one side and McAvoy from the other, both headed toward him. "Your job was to protect us and the *Constitution*," Jack yelled as they grabbed him, pulling him back.

"The Constitution," Winspear shook his head. "Jack... what Boy Scout's wet dream are you living in? The world has changed. Since you've been alive, the presidency has been about one thing and one thing only: power. Look around, look at all this." He gestured to the plane, the conference room. "Does this look like the plane of a servant? Of a representative of the people? Get real. America, the one you've built up in your mind with all its myths and legends, is a bald-faced lie. It's what we tell ourselves when the glimpses of power become too much to stand. The truth is that life is pain, Jack. It's suffering. It's chaos, with life and fairness and the ones we love crushed always under the iron heel of power."

He was shaking as he finished, and Jack was too. Jack's knuckles had gone white, and he could feel his nails biting into his palms.

"Well said," Applegate offered after a moment, stepping closer to Winspear. "And the choice you have is whether you'll be the one under that heel being crushed"—he looked Jack in the eye—"or the one wearing the boot."

Jack said nothing. None of them did.

Applegate gave a curt nod to McAvoy and said, "Very well. Lock them back in the press room."

McAvoy was moving now, reaching for Kay and grabbing her by the arm, headed for the door as a Secret Service agent opened it. Bowers and Roy followed, and with a push from behind Jack went out the door too.

As he left, though, he made eye contact with Winspear for another moment, just long enough to make sure he was listening as he said, "What would Sierra think about what you've done? About what you're doing?" An agent was pulling Jack out, but he added, "About what you've *become*."

Then the door slammed shut, leaving Winspear alone with Applegate and his thoughts, the screen behind him counting down the half-minute to the EMP.

They moved down the hallway a few steps, the line of them headed by two Secret Service agents as they moved through the neat columns of swivel-chairs.

As they headed down the hallway, Roy said, "Oh *shit*… there it is."

They looked toward the window, where the sky blue was glowing, brightening to a flash. As soon as it was there, it was gone, and they had all stopped, watching at the row of rectangular windows and waiting for something to happen. Nothing did, though. There was just the sound of the air rushing past outside, the dull roar of the General Electric engines galloping on, all of it eerily unchanged.

"See," Roy said, "nothing could—"

But they didn't hear what he said next. It was lost to a roar of shearing metal and F5 wind speed as a section of the plane's fuselage ripped away.

53

Twenty seconds earlier, Air Force One had been flying away from the Winspear Camplex. They'd just hit cruising altitude and engaged the autopilot, course set to Washington.

Roy was right—the plane was shielded in several ways from an EMP. That was standard military grade design ever since the Cold War, when the threat of a nuclear blast and its accompanying electro-magnetic pulse became well understood.

But Winspear's drone fleet... that was another story. Say what you will about net positive shipping. It worked like a charm, but it had also caused the commoditization of each and every part of a delivery drone, the evolutionary vice of weight reduction guiding design down to the cheapest, lightest, thinnest materials that could be tolerated.

And when that was what you were designing, you sure as hell didn't have room to install EMP shielding on the motherboards.

It was a small drone cruising at super high altitude, gliding in a holding pattern in the lower stratosphere where it could balance airspeed, drag, and solar feed to stay up indefinitely. It was coming from one of hundreds of storage facilities, the algorithms having sent it marching orders to relocate an item to the Camplex. Before it could reach its destination, though—when it was a little less than a hundred miles out—it had received an updated instruction to go into the hold pattern. After the explosion at the core, seismic sensors halted most of the incoming traffic, but the drone didn't mind. It would glide the winds of the stratosphere until its instructions were updated.

After the EMP burst flashed across the wafer of silicone that controlled the drone, the perfectly angled gliding fins all shifted at once, and then the drone's only guide was gravity. Suddenly it was just 45 pounds of carbon fiber, batteries, and fried electronics with a pair of vintage Air Jordans in the cargo bay.

Air Force One weighed about 20,000 times as much as the drone, and if it had hit the fuselage of the Boeing VC-25, even at terminal velocity it would still be like a flea jumping on a housecat. Inside, they probably wouldn't even have heard it. But the drone wasn't heading for the Boeing. It was on a collision course with something else.

From the cockpit of one of Air Force One's escorts, a fighter pilot—call sign Grey Dog—replied to his accompanying escort, the one he could see out his window flying above and to the left of Air Force One.

"Copy. Just saw a bright blue flash, we're still sitting pretty."

"Grey Dog, Roger," the other pilot, call sign Force 12, replied. Then he said, "Check radar on our 12 o'clock. Looks like planes crashing into the warehouse."

"Yeah, copy that."

Grey Dog glanced at his radar, reaching to toggle it so that he could scan back and down, where the warehouse was, but something else caught his eye.

"Hold up, Force 12. You have something inbound on your vertical. Do you have radar contact?"

"No, I don't—"

"Force 12, I'm reading… holy shit! Whatever it is, it's accelerating. 500 FPS. There's multiple inbound. 600 FPS, tally-ho, tally-ho!"

The drone was falling at a few hundred miles per hour.

"Force 12—do you copy!"

Grey Dog looked out the window just in time to see something smash into and through the wing of Force 12's PCA fighter jet.

The damaged fighter jet lost control. It tipped down, the nose dipping first, pulled toward its damaged wing. The drag and airspeed did the rest. If it had been a speed boat skipping along a lake, the nose tipping down and hitting that wall of water would have flipped it end over end, battering it to smithereens. The fighter jet tipped nose down and under the wave of wind speed just the same now, but instead of toppling end over end it corkscrewed in the direction of the broken wing.

No matter how good the pilot was, he'd never be able to pull out of that spin. The jet would twist in the corkscrew pattern all the way down, drilling toward the ground from thousands of feet up at fantastic speed, vaporizing most of its components and leaving a crater the size of a small building when it finally hit. But Force 12's fighter wouldn't be going straight down to the ground. It had a pit stop to make. You might even call it a brief layover.

The Boeing VC-25 was a militarized version of the Boeing 747 commercial airliner, and it *was* shielded from EMPs in several ways, and even blast-hardened and armored for limited air combat. But what the military wonks who'd designed the flying fortress for the president could never—not in their wildest dreams—have planned for was what happened next.

The jet tipped down into its death spiral and then collided midair into Air Force One.

The planes crumpled against each other, the fighter jet tumbling in several pieces as the Boeing bucked skyward. A section of Air Force One's fuselage the size of a school bus was torn away, taking the "UNI" from "UNITED STATES OF AMERICA" printed on the side with it.

The pieces of both planes fell until a half-second later, when they were all lost in a cloud of fire and smoke, the fuel of the jet having found a light somewhere in the confusion. The explosion tipped Air Force One forward from the tail end, the shockwave playing havoc with the pilots' attempts to respond to the initial collision.

In the cockpit, the Air Force colonel in charge of the flight was repeating orders to his copilots, three of them, one on his right and two behind. He wasn't shouting, but his voice was raised.

He saw the loss of cabin pressure, felt the plane's responses through the stick, the drag pulling at the craft. His eyes flitted over the instruments, the copilot shouting out several alarm codes, and all at once he understood.

"There's a hole in the plane," he said. "Port side."

He was instinctively reaching for his oxygen mask, and sliding it into place as he added, "Ahead of the wing, I think, but not the wing."

Thank God not the wing, he thought.

He checked his engine readouts, one by one, the fuel gages—

"Sir—" the copilot said, just as the colonel was bringing his eyes back to the fuel readout.

"I know. Something clipped the center tank."

He was talking about their main fuel tank. The Boeing had 3 of them, one in the center and two in each wing, and now they were losing fuel fast from the center tank. Something had clipped them deeply, and they were dumping an amazing amount of fuel. In the time the colonel had been thinking through all this, more 10% of the tank had drained out.

"We've got to dump it," he said, and they all knew it. If the trail of fuel they were spewing found a spark, that would be it. It was a liability.

"Starting the purge," the copilot said.

"Okay," the colonel said.

The plane was shifting wildly, but the training kept his voice even, though his knuckles strained white on the stick.

"Okay... we're still in this."

Inside the cabin, things got very loud and very cold faster than Jack thought possible. The decompression at more than 30,000 feet sucked at everything with a violence that was in-human, like the very skin on his hands might be lashed away. He might have screamed, but there was nothing that could be heard over the howl of the air, and he could barely breath as it was.

They'd been on their way from the front of the plane back toward the wing when it happened, and in the hallway in between there was nothing to grab onto except for the chairs that lined the aisle. Jack held on for dear life, squinting past the rush of air and looking down the aisle, seeing Roy and then Bowers ahead of him, and past them he saw something else: Down the hallway they'd been heading for, there was a bright light.

Sky.

Just down the hall, the plane's wall was gone. And he could even see the front of the wing—what the colonel would call the "leading edge"—at the bottom of the opening in the fu-selage, which had taken some of the floor away with it as well.

Then he saw Kay. She'd been at the front of their group as they moved down the hall, and so now she was only 20 feet or so away from the opening in the hallway, holding on to one of the chairs on the left side of the aisle.

Jack wasn't afraid. There was no time for fear. He under-stood something in a way that was diamond-clear: Ahead of them, toward the back of the plane, was the hole and the sky, and behind them was the conference room they'd come from, and one of those directions was one they could possibly sur-vive in. Careful to not lose his grip and be sucked toward the hole he started to move not back, to safety, but forward. To where he could see Kay holding on.

Just ahead was Roy, and they made quick eye contact. Jack pointed back toward the conference room. Roy nodded, and started to grab his way back, chair by chair, one hold after another, then both of them froze for a moment as the plane bucked wildly, the angle changing down toward the conference room so that Roy was almost falling forward toward it and Jack, as he turned, felt like he was starting to climb up the side of a mountain in a hurricane as he took another step in Kay's direction.

In the cockpit, the colonel was balancing several needs as best he could. In the pressureless cabin, the president of the United States might be slowly asphyxiating.

Priority one was to get the plane under control, and that was more or less done since they weren't falling out of the sky. And since the main fuel tank and its leak had been dealt with, the next priority was getting to a breathable altitude. He needed to get the plane lower, and fast. He brought the thrust levers back to idle and started a descent at max speed. That is, the max speed he'd dare, considering the hole.

They were losing altitude just fine now, but the nature of flight meant that they were trading that altitude for speed, and that was quickly going to be another problem. They couldn't stay up, not like this, and so at some point in the not-too-distant future they were going to have to attempt landing or something like it. He'd need to drop a lot of speed between now and then, so he deployed the air brakes, but something was wrong. Something about the hole in their fuselage, or maybe something *had* clipped their wing and wedged a few pieces of metal somewhere. Either way, he could feel the breaking was uneven, as the plane began to wobble and shake violently.

Jack felt the vibration start in the floor, but within seconds he could feel it through the chair he was holding onto as the whole cabin started to shake. He'd never been in an earthquake, but he felt like this was damn close. He started to take another step forward, toward Bowers who was holding on to a chair on the right side of the aisle.

He reached him, crossing the aisle with a quick jump and catching himself ahead of Bowers before the wind could suck him toward the hole. It wasn't pulling as hard now, but if he fell forward it would take him. There was no question of that.

He made eye contact with Bowers, and they held it for what felt like minutes but what was probably only a few short seconds as Jack pointed toward the conference room. Bowers looked back and shook his head.

"*You have to go,*" Jack shouted, though neither of them could hear it.

They did hear something now, though. The vibrations crested and peaked for a moment, and above the thrashing wind there was a scream of tearing metal.

Jack looked over his shoulder and up the aisle. What he saw in that instant would stick with him.

Another chunk of the plane had fallen away—the hole had grown closer to them, to Kay, creeping in from the hallway and taking more of the plane's wall and flooring with it. Now Jack could see more of the wing and even some of the great engine that clung to it.

At the end of the aisle, at the frontmost chair on the right side, he'd seen a Secret Service agent holding on earlier. Now, that man was still holding on, but he was upside down. He was holding on to the chair with both hands, his mouth open in a scream that was lost in the howl of wind, his feet pulled toward the hole as if a giant was tugging him, hoisting him up and out, and then, in an instant, he was gone.

Jack looked back at Bowers, who had craned his head to see this as well. Bowers nodded, eyes still wide, and turned to start making his way back toward the conference room.

In the cockpit, the colonel was starting to level the plane. The vibrations were still bad—very bad—but there were bad decisions on one side and death on the other. Speaking of which, his copilots were weighing in on the plan for survival.

One of the copilots in the rear was calling out an airport about 150 miles ahead they could just make it to, and the co-pilot next to the colonel was repeating the heading, reaching forward to change the plane's route accordingly.

The colonel said, "Stop. Starboard tank, what was it 60 seconds ago?"

The copilot pulled up a graph, called out the volume, and drew the same conclusion the colonel had with a glance at the gauges.

"Christ," he said. "It's leaking too. Into the main tank."

"That doesn't make sense," one of the pilots behind the colonel said, bracing himself against the cockpit wall. "We were hit on the other side."

"The valve system," the colonel said. "The tank wasn't hit but we've got no balance controls."

He didn't dare take his hand of the stick, the plane still bucking wildly, but he nodded up at one of the sea of blinking lights above the window. All of them looked at the one labeled FBS.

The fuel balance system, the subsystem that managed the weight in the wings by moving fuel to and from the three tanks as needed. Now, the control was blinking red. Failure.

The fact that they hadn't been hit on the starboard side, then, was irrelevant. Something supporting that system had failed. The power supply to the valves, maybe. The wiring to the fuel gauge sensors. It could be anything, and it didn't matter what it was in the end, because that fuel was leaking out no matter what.

"A valve's stuck," the colonel said. "Or something. It's leaking internally from the starboard side to the center tank."

And then out the plane, he thought.

He watched the gauge a second longer.

"It's moving too fast. We're going to lose balance in the wings."

"We can purge the port side," one of the copilots offered.

Dump fuel out of the port side of the plane to balance what was leaking out of the other.

"No," the colonel said, "we can't. We don't have enough time."

The variables raced in his mind. The fuel. The hole. The loss of altitude. The distance to the other airport.

"We have to go back. We can't make it anywhere else," the colonel finally said.

Behind him, the copilots looked at each other. This was a new problem. The Camplex airport was closer, but it was *behind* them.

"Can we make it with a bank?"

The colonel thought he knew the answer when he asked it, but he wanted confirmation. The copilots shouted out numbers, one of them running a simulation on a back panel and another scribbling large numbers on a notepad, the jagged scrawl agreeing with the final values he saw on the screen.

He answered the colonel, "Affirmative. If you start in about the next 35 seconds."

"How hard?"

The copilot shook his head as he delivered the answer.

"All the way."

The colonel was cool under pressure. One of the best—that's how you get this job—but at this, he looked over his shoulder at the copilot behind him, his eyes stopping on the copilot to his right as he came back around. Several things were going unsaid. Understood... *terribly* understood... but unsaid.

The colonel sighed, then asked, "Can she take it?"

"We don't know the damage," the copilot to his right said. "The Structure... it could be bad."

"Worst case?" the colonel said.

"Worst case?" the copilot repeated, staring ahead out the window, one hand on the throttle to his left and with the other reaching up to silence one of the many alarms. He answered, "Worst case she breaks apart."

The colonel nodded, his eyes moving across the various panels of information.

"Okay," he said, thinking. "Okay."

Jack reached Kay at the front of the aisle, trying to not look out the gaping hole that was within throwing distance. He glanced outside and saw the violent black blur in the center of a white housing, the engine, thundering, massive, just outside. As he stopped behind where Kay was, the airspeed pulling him forward, one of the swivel chairs on the right broke loose with a chunk of floor and toppled out of the hole with tremendous speed, bouncing off the top of the wing before disappearing.

Jack moved forward, and then he saw why Kay hadn't made a move for the conference room yet. At the front of the aisle on the left side there were two seats, and as he came around he could see that, while Kay was holding on to the bottom half of one, Duncan McAvoy held on to the other behind her. His right hand was wrapped in the seatbelt strap of the chair and his left held fast to Kay's arm. He was facing her, and now that he could see Jack, he smiled madly at them both.

Kay looked over at Jack as he came into her vision. The plane had levelled off and slowed just enough that he could hear her shout his name. He looked from her to McAvoy, then down to McAvoy's hand. Jack held on to the chair with one hand as he reached across Kay to try to pry McAvoy's hand off her with the other.

He tried to claw his fingers up, and Kay tried to jerk away from him, and they were making as much progress as could be expected without either of them daring to free their other hands, which were holding on to the chair. Jack looked at McAvoy, his face an insane, silent laugh that was lost in the noise, and then all at once McAvoy let Kay go. She'd been pulling, and she crashed toward Jack who kept his grip on the chair.

McAvoy was angling himself, kicking, hitting Kay once, twice, and Jack understood that if she let go they'd both be sucked out.

He reached forward and slammed his free hand down hard on McAvoy, as hard as he could, losing track of where he was hitting him as he punched again and again. Then he saw McAvoy bringing his hand back around, his gun in it, and he had just enough time to see this to reach up and catch him by the wrist.

McAvoy was trying to bring the gun around to aim it at them. Kay was recoiling away from him, but she was still trapped by Jack who was now holding on to the chair with his left hand and McAvoy's wrist—and gun—with the other. The gun went off, the sound a tight crack among everything else, but Jack felt the shock of it through McAvoy's arm.

Jack didn't know what to do now. They were stuck. He was holding McAvoy and couldn't let go with the other arm. Kay couldn't get past. If he dropped McAvoy's arm and they made a run for it, he'd gun them down. If he tried to get the gun away, he'd have to let his other hand go. The wind wasn't as bad now, and he might be able to hold on and not be sucked out of the plane. But what if—

Too late. Duncan dove forward, past Kay, head-butting Jack savagely. Jack saw stars as he fell back. He tried to hold on, but his grip on the chair was lost.

He focused on the gun. He still held McAvoy's wrist, and now someone was grabbing at him. It was Kay, pulling him toward her, holding him against the pull of the wind. They were a tangle now, McAvoy trying to push Kay out of the way to get at Jack, Jack holding his wrist and Kay throwing elbows back even as she tried to tug Jack closer, to keep him from sliding toward the hole and the engine that churned away just outside. McAvoy's gun went off again, and though Jack was still holding his wrist, McAvoy had brought the gun down lower and Jack felt the bullet go past his head.

"Go!" he shouted to Kay.

If she went now, she could make it. Back down the aisle. Back to the conference room. He could hold McAvoy here, keep the gun pointed… somewhere else. *Anywhere* else.

Kay might have gone then if they'd had a moment longer. She might have run.

But then something changed.

Jack felt the shift first from McAvoy's gun arm, as he started to put more weight on it. A look of surprise crossed McAvoy's face as he seemed to lean in toward Jack. But he wasn't leaning. Slowly, he was *falling*. Then Jack could feel it too, first in his legs… his legs which were shifting on the floor, shifting out from under him.

A second earlier, back in the cockpit, the copilot's words echoed in the colonel's head: *worst case she breaks apart.*

"Sir," the copilot behind him said. "We've got to start now if we're going to make the runway."

"Hold on," he said, working the stick to start the maneuver.

The plane started to shift on its axis, to twist left slightly, then not so slightly.

"It's been an honor serving with you," the colonel said to his copilots.

As he continued to turn the plane, he said his wife's name, and his children's.

The three copilots reached out to brace themselves as the colonel left a final message on the plane's black-box flight recorder. One by one, eerily calm, they did the same as the plane twisted farther and farther.

Soon the plane would not just be banking, but rolling on its side, one wingtip pointing straight down and the other reaching up to space. They all knew that when the plane was mid-roll—that's when the strain would be the worst.

As his copilots delivered their final messages, the colonel's lips moved silently, praying.

Jack flailed out at the seat behind Kay, grabbing for something, *anything*, as his legs started to slide out from under him faster. He found one of the seatbelt straps and held on to it now, somehow keeping hold of McAvoy's arm as they all started to slip down the floor and now off it entirely.

The plane had calmed somewhat in the last few seconds or minutes or *however* long it had been, but now the vibrations were back. As the angle shifted, the plane rolling onto its side so the pilots could make the turn fast enough, the torque of the plane tested the structure and the hole grew behind them. Until now it had just barely crept in from the hallway, but it doubled in size as another chunk of the fuselage tore away, taking chairs and floor with it, along with the rest of the word "UNITED."

To make things worse, this hole was now not behind Jack's shoulder as it had been moments ago, but *below* him as the plane tilted. And as weight shifted, Kay fell forward onto him, holding on for dear life, her eyes wide as she looked down at ground below, Jack and Mcavoy and, by extension, her, dangling, holding on by the two strips of seatbelt straps.

In his other hand, Jack felt McAvoy flailing. He was trying to tear his hand away, to free his gun and use it, and Jack felt his other hand slipping. He had to make a call and quickly. As his fingers began to go numb and give way he had no choice but to let go of McAvoy and grab the strap with both hands.

Kay held on to him, one arm around his neck. With the other she took up the fight against McAvoy. She tried to wave the gun off as he attempted to aim it at them. She pushed him, and they swung against each other on the straps as McAvoy fired once, twice, both of the bullets lost, thankfully, into the fuselage.

Jack closed his eyes, holding on as tight as he could, feeling the nothingness below, the sure death waiting to swallow them up.

He heard the gun go off again and then a scream, this one heard above the howl, and he looked to see that Kay was scratching McAvoy, cutting at his face, now lacing it with deep nail wounds as he tried to bring the gun back around and she again batted it away, sending him twisting on his seatbelt strap, the blood dripping off him and swallowed up by the wind.

Gravity was shifting again. They were coming out of the roll, the floor shifting back into place, and all at once Jack could feel the solid floor below him again. Kay shouted at him to move.

But at first, he wouldn't let go of the seatbelt, looking past Kay to the open sky beyond. She reached up, pulling at his fingers, glancing over at McAvoy who was thrashing his way up now too, and then Jack caught up and realized they needed to move. *Now.*

He let go, his fingers flashing with pain from holding tight so long, and then Kay was pulling him down the aisle, away from the hole, away from McAvoy. They stumbled as quickly as they could toward the conference room, seeing that Roy and Bowers were beckoning them in.

They spilled through the doorway, and Jack had just enough time to look back and see McAvoy moving toward them. His face was bloody, and his gun was in his hand. Over his shoulder, the plane's wing and gigantic engine were now in full view, and the wind whipped at McAvoy. For a glorious second Jack thought it might just take him and end it once and for all.

But then McAvoy took a step forward and raised the gun. Bowers slammed the door and dove across it, tackling Roy, both of them hitting the floor before three clean bullet holes punched through.

"Where is he?" Jack said, breathless, looking to Winspear who was in the back corner of the room bracing himself against the fuselage as the plane bucked underneath them. "Where's Applegate—"

"He—" Winspear started to say, half shouting over the noise of the plane, but then from the opposite end of the room Applegate emerged from the doorway.

"Call off your dog," Jack shouted over to him, and Applegate smiled as he stepped in the room.

Jack saw he was carrying something in his hand. A gun. And in the other, a blocky backpack, olive green, dangling by a strap. There were two straps of the same color on either of his shoulders, and all at once Jack understood.

Two parachutes. One for him and one for—

The door slammed open next to Jack and Kay, and on the other side Bowers and Roy spilled back as McAvoy stepped through, blood dripping from his face as he took a slow step in, aiming his gun, lining it up with Jack who said nothing, only raising his arm reflexively.

"No," Applegate said, and over the uneven motion of the plane he began to step toward McAvoy, his own gun raised at them. "No Duncan. There's a better way."

54

Applegate eyed them, his gun half raised as he slowly made his way around the table and handed the parachute to McAvoy, who smiled.

McAvoy put his gun down on the table and shouldered the pack, the motion of the plane starting to send the gun sliding off the edge until he caught it and turned to Jack, giving a toothy grin and saying, "You lose."

"We had a deal," Winspear said.

"Sure," Applegate said, covering them all with the gun as McAvoy reached up with one hand and tightened the parachute straps. "But that was then."

He smiled at Winspear. He smiled at all of them, the light glinting off the metal handle positioned just over his heart—the parachute's ripcord—as he looked around at all of them.

Winspear was backed into the corner. Roy and Bowers had fallen to the ground and stayed there, and Jack and Kay were in a similar state on the opposite side of the door.

Applegate surveyed them all, pointing the gun.

"Now," Applegate said, "you two"—he pointed the gun at Bowers and Roy—"move around the table."

He gestured toward the back, toward Winspear, and after a pause they started to move.

"That's right, all the way around. You too," he said, gesturing with the gun at Winspear, who moved along with them.

Jack and Kay had gotten up slowly, and they were clumped together on one side of the room.

His gun still trained on them, Applegate worked his way over to the doorway, where the sky roared past, filling the cabin with noise and a constant whirlwind. He looked over his shoulder at it, then shook his head.

"What are the chances?" he said, smiling as he looked back at them. "Another happy accident!"

"You can't kill us," Winspear shouted to him over the dull roar of wind past the plane, past the hole.

"I don't have to!" Applegate said. "You think there'll be any bodies left in a crash like this?"

McAvoy smiled and said, "Ashes to ashes."

"Duncan," Applegate gestured toward the front of the plane with his gun. "Why don't you go make sure the pilots play along."

McAvoy didn't bother wiping the blood off his face, and drops rained off his nose and chin and onto the floor as he ejected his gun's magazine and pulled another from somewhere. He slid it in, pulling back on the gun's slide and chambering a round.

"No problem," he said, starting down the hallway toward the cockpit.

"You're insane!" Jack shouted.

"Give it a rest!" Applegate shouted back. "You want your last words to be the same old dead horse? You're pissing into the wind, Jack."

He had the gun pointed at them, the wind whipping papers from the conference room's floor out of the cabin, headed for the great beyond, as Applegate took a step forward.

"Don't blame me; blame *him*."

He pointed the gun at Winspear.

"It's Winspear's fault you're all mixed up in this. *He's* killed you, not me. Isn't that right?"

He turned to Winspear.

He continued, "It was you who killed them, when you weren't in the car that night."

"What are you talking about?" Winspear spat back at him.

Applegate said nothing for a moment, but then he laughed.

"You really haven't figured it out yet?"

Jack watched him as the pieces fell into place.

Applegate, who'd needed him to get on *any* ticket, not just a winning one, blocked by both parties and left with only one option.

"You said..." Jack was trying to remember. "You said him winning wasn't part of the plan. Winspear was never supposed to make it to the election."

"That's right, Jack. We had the votes. We had all the momentum. The campaign would've survived losing *him* at that point. They would have been forced to accept me as the primary on the ticket, and with all the steam we'd built up, all the favors I'd already called in to get the campaign where it was"—he shook his head—"it would've been me"—he grimaced, turning to Winspear—"but instead"—he shook his head—"one month out from the election, and you decide to stay late at the Raleigh get-out-the-vote rally."

Jack hadn't understood the true meaning of all this, the true depths that Applegate had gone to to try to seize power, but now—

"Sierra," Jack said. "It was you. The hit-and-run."

There was a pause as Applegate smiled.

Finally, he said, "McAvoy was driving the truck."

Jack shook his head, unbelieving.

"And so," Applegate went on, talking to Winspear, "this is all *your* fault. You should've been in the car that night."

He took another step forward, moving even closer to them. The gun shook slightly in his hand, Jack saw, and despite everything else he was newly frightened by it, because he could see the shaking wasn't from Applegate being cold or weak. No, he could tell by the look in his eye he was shaking with *excitement*.

"This way's better though," he said. "I'll get the rest of your term plus two more, that's *nine years*, and by then I'm sure we'll figure out something with the term limits."

Applegate smiled at them again.

"I can run this country like it *should* be run! We'll have the war if we must, and we'll conquer the world if they make us. You had a chance for power, Winspear, and you couldn't handle it. But I can. I *will*."

"You—" Winspear said.

Jack turned to Winspear. The president was shaking his head, looking down at his hands and burying his face in them.

"That's right," Applegate said. "That's *right*! I beat you, Winspear! I put you right where I wanted, and you know what? It was easy!"

Winspear looked up finally, and there was something in his eyes... something past the glassy emotion, and in that moment Jack remembered what Winspear had said about none of it mattering. About the fact that he was under attack, always. He'd known that much—he'd understood it—but this, knowing Sierra's death was part of the byzantine machinations of his own pursuit for power...

Jack felt it just before it happened. He had just enough time to flail both hands across the others, practically falling back and taking Kay and Bowers and Roy out of the way as Winspear burst forward past them.

Applegate had been starting to say something else, but it was drowned out in an animal roar that came from Winspear as he dove forward.

Jack saw the gun go off, Winspear's body jerking violently with the impact but not stopping his charge. Roy shouted and fell even as Winspear flailed against Applegate.

Jack looked over at Roy, who'd crumpled, holding his arm, blood flowing from somewhere. The bullet must have gone through Winspear and hit him, but now Jack's attention was drawn back as the gun went off again. And now again, and Jack and Kay were ducking, trying to move away as Applegate and Winspear crashed against the end of the conference room table, the gun trapped somewhere between them as they struggled.

"You can't beat me!" Jack saw Applegate shout, and then he was pulling himself away from Winspear.

He brought the gun up and fired again and again. Winspear fell back against the table, bleeding, but just as Applegate raised the gun to deliver another bullet, Winspear summoned a final burst and elbowed himself up off the table.

He jumped against Applegate, the holes in his back wet with blood as he collapsed forward onto him. The gun was trapped between them again, and Applegate struggled to escape, to pull the gun out for a final shot. Winspear threw one arm around his neck in an awful embrace, and with his other hand he pawed at Applegate's chest, grabbing for something, his fingers finally finding and closing on it—a metal handle.

The ripcord.

By now Jack was moving forward. He was reaching for them to… to do *something*… but halfway there he saw Winspear's arm jerk back, and then the parachute was bursting out of Applegate's pack.

His back was to the doorway, and the whirlwind caught the chute and took it like an angry god claiming a burnt offering. It jerked Applegate back in an instant, and Winspear, his arm still around Applegate's neck, right along with him.

With impossible speed, they all saw it happen. The parachute and the two men were sucked right out of the plane, out the massive hole and into the thundering engine just beyond, which made a sound like a train crashing as it flamed out and exploded.

55

The explosion threw them all back, and the plane jerked wildly. Jack lost track of the others as they were thrown by the plane's bucking. He hit his head hard, and then he fell onto what he realized after a moment was the conference table.

His ears were ringing as he looked around, slowly rolling off the table as the plane roller-coastered beneath them, and he saw Kay scrambling up from the floor, yelling something he didn't hear. Then Bowers was there, and he and Kay were moving along the wall, bracing themselves on it and trying not to fall down as they moved quickly toward the front of the plane.

Jack's hearing was coming back now, and he could make out what Roy was shouting to him.

"—the *pilots*."

Roy headed down the hallway after Kay and Bowers, and now Jack scrambled up to follow.

He chased them down the corridor, the lights flickering on and off and the sound of wind screaming past the opening chorusing with an alarm that wailed from all directions.

And up ahead, gunshots.

He spilled out of the corridor into the small space behind the cockpit and saw McAvoy, Bowers, and Kay in a melee on the floor. The door to the cockpit was open, and there was a body on the floor at the threshold, a white uniformed shirt stained with blood. Another of the copilots was taking cover just inside and shouting something as he moved around to try to take a shot at McAvoy, following the tussle on the floor with his gun.

The pilot took a shot and Jack saw that it hit Bowers, who screamed out, and Jack realized that the pilots thought the president was somewhere in the back of the plane still and probably didn't care who these people were. He'd shoot all of them to secure the plane if he had to.

Jack raced forward, stumbling over the body on the floor as he jumped into the cockpit, knocking down the man with the gun. The gun bounced away somewhere, and before the copilot could find it Jack was backing up as fast he could. He joined in as Kay and Bowers continued to pummel McAvoy.

McAvoy whipped his gun around, and Kay punched him as Jack seized his wrist with both hands to keep him from pointing the gun at anyone.

The gun went off again and again, and somehow McAvoy began to twist it inward—his strength was surprising, almost unreal.

McAvoy might have said something. He might have been yelling something as they fought, but Jack didn't hear any of it as the gun went off next to him and his ears started ringing again.

And then, out of the corner of his eye, Jack saw something huge and heavy swing down on McAvoy.

The arm Jack was struggling against went limp, and the gun fell out of it.

Jack loosened his grip, rolling back from McAvoy, breathing hard, seeing that it had been Roy who'd slammed the fire extinguisher down onto McAvoy's head.

Kay hauled herself back up, breathing hard as Roy staggered back, one of his arms still bleeding. Bowers was still on the floor, clutching at the bullet hole in his leg, and for a brief moment they all waited for McAvoy to move, but he didn't.

Roy kicked Duncan's foot, and as the fire extinguisher rolled slowly with the motion of the plane, he said, "What an asshole."

The two remaining copilots stormed into the area just outside the cockpit, guns out and yelling, "Hands up, don't move!"

They complied, staying where they were as the two pilots looked the scene over, then exchanged a glance with each other.

56

One of the copilots stayed on them, covering the whole group as the other disappeared back into the cockpit. From inside, Jack could hear the alarms whining madly.

"Where is the president?" the pilot asked, aiming the gun at them, but before they could answer there were shouts from inside the cockpit.

The one who held the gun on them looked over, frustrated, panicking, and finally let his gun drop.

"Go buckle in somewhere!" he said, leaning down to drag the dead copilot's body inside the cockpit far enough to clear the doorway.

As he started to shut the door, Kay shouted, "Can you land the plane?"

"We're about to find out," he said as he hauled the cockpit door shut, a loud *thunk* following as he locked it.

"Hurry," Kay said, pulling Jack up off the floor, and then both of them turned to lift Bowers.

He threw his arm over Jack's shoulder, and Kay had him on the other side. Roy limped forward ahead of them. He'd hit his leg on something during the whole affair. And the four of them struggled back up the plane, to the first outcropping of tan leather seats they could find.

Roy slumped into the first one, leaving a dark smear of blood on the metal seatbelt as he worked it into place.

"We need to stop the bleeding," Jack said, lowering Bowers into a seat.

Roy pulled off his belt onehanded, fishing it out from under the airplane seatbelt and handing it over.

Kay was in the seat next to Bowers, and they could hear the change in the sound of the plane as it got lower and lower. Jack tied the belt off at Bower's left thigh, hoping that would be good enough. Kay grabbed him, pulling him toward the free chair next to her.

"Come on," she said. "Quick."

"What's going to happen now?" Bowers said, breathless, as Jack reached across Kay to jerk at the belt, making sure it was pulled tight on Bower's leg.

"I don't know," Kay said to him. "They'll land the plane and... and..."

"No," Bowers said. "With *the country*."

Then the whole world started to quake beneath them.

The lights went out.

One of them screamed.

There was the sound of metal tearing away somewhere— great industrial groans.

It was over in seconds, but time stretched like eternity as the plane hit the ground, sliding, G-forces pushing them forward, then to the side. Then all at once it was only the seatbelts holding them in place against gravity that threatened to drop them onto the floor as the reinforced steel tube of the plane turned and rolled.

And suddenly it stopped.

Quiet settled on Jack, and in the darkness, he thought for sure it was the deep dark of forever. It was death, come for him at last through all this, and then...

... and then there was a light from somewhere

And they were alive. All of them.

Jack's head throbbed. He was seeing stars, and something was cutting into his midsection. Kay reached for his seatbelt, unlatching it, and he fell to the side and out of the chair at an odd angle.

The plane had come to rest so that they were all somewhat above the floor, and one by one they spilled down onto it. Kay and Jack quickly took Bowers up again and worked their way through a hallway that was eerily skewed. Everything was at funhouse angles as they moved through, balancing themselves with hands on the floors and feet on the walls at some points, and after a few strangely quiet moments they'd made their way back to the gaping wound in the side of the airliner.

They jumped out, ducking under a newly busted section of fuselage, the air filling with smoke as they moved away from the looming wreckage of the craft.

They were on tarmac, and looking up, Jack realized they'd ended up back on the Camplex's runway. The pilots had twisted the plane around to ditch it here.

They moved farther away, none of them talking or looking back. They were in shock, and they kept walking away like zombies until Kay stumbled and fell. Bowers went down too of course, and Jack with him, slowing the fall. Roy stopped and looked at the smoking wreck for a moment. Then he sat down with them on the runway, legs crossed.

They looked back now, not just at the smoking wrecked behemoth that was Air Force One with its other survivors moving out and away, but at the other myriad spots of fire and fury across the horizon, the countless drones of all sizes that had crashed as soon as the EMP had gone off. And at the Camplex in the distance back behind it all, from which pillars of smoke rose in all directions, the accumulation of hundreds of exploded lithium ion battery backs and fallout from the larger drones that had crashed.

Jack saw someone coming toward them from the wreckage, his white shirt stained with blood.

As he got closer Jack could tell it was the copilot they'd seen before. That was just a few minutes ago, he realized, though it felt like another lifetime.

The man's head was bleeding. There was a gash two inches long over his eyebrow, and he held a mess of rags against it. In his other hand, Jack saw there was a thick black walkie talkie.

"The president," he said, limping as he approached them. "You were the last to see him. Do you know if—"

"He's dead," Jack said. "Both of them."

The pilot stared at him.

"Both," Roy echoed. "Good riddance."

Dumbfounded, the copilot turned back to the ruined plane. He lifted his radio and spoke into it, and when he was asked to repeat himself, he did.

57

At the House of Representatives, nobody knew what had happened at the Camplex. Not yet anyhow. Only now, across the screen mounted in the corner of the gift shop in the Capitol Building, were the first video feeds of the explosions coming in.

The television was behind her, so Tarrah Adler wandered through the shop blissfully unaware.

Whoever had been manning the register had fled temporarily, and there weren't any tourists to be seen. She found what she was looking for—one of the sets of shelves with novelty candy on it—and selected a chocolate bar with the Constitution printed on the outside.

She was famished and opened it on the way to the counter, pausing to take a bite while she looked around awkwardly.

There was nobody.

She put the chocolate bar down, reaching in her purse and extracting a few dollars. Then she scrawled on a piece of paper, "T Adler, 1 chocolate bar," and put the note with the bills. Then she took her candy bar and turned again to the shop's interior.

It was strange. So much history locked into these trinkets. Shirts. Keychains with your name on them, a gilded outline of the Capitol at the bottom.

As she walked around the place, savoring the chocolate, it was quiet save for her own slow footfalls and of course, the clicking.

Her heart. Ticking away.

It had been a good day, she thought. She'd come and done her job, and they'd succeeded as much as could be hoped for. Shortly, she knew, Winspear would return, would stand trial in the Senate, and could be cleanly removed from office.

Honestly she was relieved. Even if he did somehow make it through the trial, at least she'd tried. At least she'd done her best.

She was coming around one of the stalls, meeting row after row of postcards, the last bit of the chocolate in her hand and on its way to her mouth when she stopped.

The TV. They were showing the explosion again. The sound was off, but the shape of what they were showing on the ground.

It was Air Force One.

At the same time, she heard yelling down the hall. Footsteps. Many of them.

The TV volume was off, but from here she could read the closed captioning scrolling across: "—President and vice-president unaccounted for after Air Force One—"

Now a group of dark-suited agents tore around the corner, one with his gun out.

He was black, tall, and breathing hard as he pulled back his jacket to replace the gun and say over his shoulder to the rest, "She's over here!"

As he stepped forward, Adler stepped back. Her free hand came up to her mouth, and just above the sound of her heart clicking at double-time she heard her own shaky whisper.

"No!"

"Ma'am," the Secret Service agent said, still trying to catch his breath as he stepped over to her, the handful of them behind him speaking into unseen microphones and looking over their shoulders warily.

"We need to get you somewhere secure, ma'am."

"No," she said again, tears in her eyes. "It's not right. I was speaker only for—"

"That doesn't matter," he said, "ma'am. The president and vice-president have been involved in an accident, and at this time are missing and we think"—he sighed—"we think they're both dead. The line of succession—"

He didn't finish. He'd almost caught his breath now, and all he did was shake his head slowly as the other agents stepped in closer.

She realized they were watching her. Waiting.

Tick, tick, tick.

Some of the agents looked at each other. They wore dark glasses, all of them save for the one right in front of her. He had brown eyes, edged with a bit of green.

She wasn't sure why she was so fixed on them, why she noticed, but as she held the man's gaze he smiled.

After a second, he looked down. The last bite of candy was on the floor. Adler hadn't realized she dropped it, and he bent down to pick it up.

"This is a mistake" she said, reaching up with one hand and wiping away a tear.

"With all due respect, ma'am, I'm not so sure it is."

And there it was. Shifting like an avalanche within her.

Something unstoppable.

She took a deep breath and fumbled at her purse. She got a cigarette out and tried her lighter once, twice, then three times before it caught.

Her hand shook as she lit it, and then there was the small sound of crumpling ash as she pulled on it. That, and the ticking.

As she let the smoke out, she looked around the room, the gift shop.

Then she took one more drag on the cigarette and said, "Okay. Let's go."

58

Jack checked his watch, looking up from the bar. It was too surreal to relax as he waited, sipping at his beer, glancing over to see someone paying for a drink with a crisp fifty-dollar bill.

The inflation had started, and seeing the cash change hands, the wad of hundreds in Jack's pocket felt suddenly lighter.

Layers of strangeness compounded as he looked up at the television screen, where a ticker along the bottom of the screen showed the current value of USD measured against a symbol that had become familiar in the last week. A capital 'Z' overlaid with two vertical lines.

The symbol of Russia and China's new gold backed currency: the zoble.

He took another drink and then heard a familiar voice.

"Well"—it was Bowers, coming up and leaning his crutches against the bar carefully—"we survived."

He slid into the seat next to Jack, who turned to shake his hand.

"For now," Jack replied, looking down at Bower's leg.

It was in a brace from the knee down. He nodded down to it.

"How's that doing?"

"Nothing that won't grow back with a few stem cell injections," he said. "Hurts like a sonofabitch, though."

"I'll bet."

The bartender came up and nodded as Bowers asked for a whiskey and coke.

The place was crowded, and as they greeted each other, onlookers mumbled in hushed tones about who'd just entered. Bowers and Jack weren't exactly famous faces, but it was hard to tow around a couple of Secret Service agents each without people realizing someone of note was around.

Their agents distributed themselves as best they could, not wanting to crowd the place.

"Where were you?" Bowers asked, nodding up toward the TV screen where, above the USD-to-zoble ticker, they were replaying video clips of the funeral procession that had gone through Washington, D.C., a few hours earlier.

"4th St. and Constitution," Jack said. "Where they flew the planes over."

"Ah," Bowers said, "a good spot, or as good as it gets considering the circumstances."

"I'll drink to that," Jack said, and their glasses clinked together as the news cycled through more shots of the hearse that had carried Winspear through town.

The bar thrummed around them, the somber tone of the day finally giving way to a sense of relief. It had been a long time since things felt normal, and as charged as the air was with the uncertainty of Adler's presidency and the turmoil in the global economy, something about putting Winspear to rest gave a note of finality to the day. A quietness.

Maybe even a hint of what it used to be like when someone could go a whole day without having to think about politics…

"Oh," Jack said, looking down at his phone, "this is Kay; hold on."

He talked into the handset for a moment.

"She's almost here."

"Roy should be joining us too," Bowers said, glancing up at the door. "Speak of the devil."

"'Sup, fellas," Roy said, stomping in, not taking off his dark glasses as he slid up to the bar next to Bowers, his own retinue of agents definitely tipping the place into crowded.

As Roy ordered his drink—a lavender gimlet—Bowers laughed and nudged Jack, nodding toward the agents who were awkwardly greeting each other and trying to keep a low profile.

As the bartender mixed the drink and set it on the bar, they saw Roy flash his phone forward, the bartender staring for a moment before glancing up at the screen, shrugging, and pulling his own phone out to accept the payment in digital transfer. He scanned a QR code on Roy's screen before turning to the next customer.

Roy pocketed the phone, turning to Jack and Bowers, who'd watched the exchange.

"What was that?" Bowers asked.

"Crypto-zoble," Roy said.

"A little unpatriotic, don't you think?" Bowers said, a hint of mocking in his voice but light on offense.

In the first few days, there had been outrage at early adopters trading their savings over from USD to zoble. Then people started to check their bank accounts, and the outrage had given way to practicality.

Roy laughed, turning to them fully with his drink in hand, speaking past the thin straw he held between his teeth as he said, "Well, here we are boys. We made it."

"Did you, uh—" Bowers asked him, gesturing up toward the TV.

"Hell no," he said, shaking his head. "Funerals bum me the hell out. I mean, what's the point? What'd they put in the casket?"

Jack laughed. Bowers smiled too, but he looked over his shoulder as he did so.

The public knew Winspear was dead, obviously, but the full story of it... they certainly didn't have reason to believe there wasn't a body in there.

"You know, you *seemed* the conspiracy type when I first met you," Bowers said.

"Baby," Roy said, taking a full drink, skipping the straw, "I *am* a conspiracy theory at this point."

They all laughed, and Kay stepped in just then, her eyes instantly catching Jack's from the doorway.

She was taking a red scarf off, telling her own agents to *wait the hell outside* after seeing the state of the place. A few of the other agents seemed to take the same hint and make some silent arrangement to split their groups, some heading out the front and the room opening up as Kay closed the distance, and they all greeted each other.

"So," Roy said after Kay received her drink, a Moscow mule, "should we find a booth?"

They made their way across the place, sliding into a cozy spot in the corner with a view outside, where edges of light were peeking out from behind gray clouds.

"President Adler," Jack said as they settled in. "Who'd have guessed it would all end that way."

"And just in time," Bowers answered. "Couldn't have planned that better if you'd done it on purpose."

"No," Roy said, "and seeing as somebody *did* plan it on purpose, I'm surprised any of us made it out at all."

"Bastard," Kay said, and they all knew she was talking about Applegate.

"There's just one thing I haven't been able to trace back through all this," Roy said. "Maybe you two can help me out. Applegate wanted Winspear out from the beginning"—his voice was low—"and he thought that if Winspear bought it before the vote he could just, what, *slip in* as the candidate?"

"It makes sense," Bowers said, shrugging and taking a sip of his whiskey and coke. "There was a huge block of third-party voters ready for anything different—unions, Green party, *centrist-independents* whatever the hell that means." He shook his head. "All of them were ready to go against the two-party system. A viable candidate was all they needed as a tipping point, that and a few hundred million ad dollars pointed in the right direction. His plan probably would've worked too, but he didn't bargain for fate stepping in."

"Sierra," Kay said. "She was the only one in the car, so instead of killing Winspear and taking the election himself, Applegate caused an outpouring of sympathy for the man he was trying to beat."

"Damn shame," Roy said, knocking back the rest of his drink and signaling for another. "Winspear was a good guy. One of the less stupid people I've ever worked with, if I do say so myself."

"High praise," Jack said, "but, I know what you mean. He just…"

Jack shook his head, but Bowers picked up the thread.

"The problem with Winspear was that, deep down, I don't think he really *wanted* to be president. He wanted the *idea* of being the president… and I think if Sierra had been there pushing him he'd've made a great one despite that."

"Behind every great man is a woman," Kay said flatly.

"Exactly," Bowers said. "And more than that he was just crushed. Those were dark times… I wish he was still here with us, but there's also part of me that thinks—not that he's in a better place—but that at least he's not *suffering* anymore."

Jack sighed, "I think you're right."

Kay put her hand on his, and they were all quiet for a moment.

"And Adler?" Kay said finally, looking at Bowers. "I heard a rumor that she's asked you to stay on and help untangle things."

Roy looked over to him, narrowing his eyes.

"You sly dog you. I thought I was the only one who was going to turn this into an appointment."

"You?" Jack said, trying to not sound too surprised.

"Hell yeah," Roy said, working on the next drink with some vigor. "As soon as China demanded Uncle Sam turn me over with whatever computing tech they wanted, I became a hot commodity. Adler's got some balls on her, I'll tell you that."

"What do you mean?"

"Well," Roy explained, "maybe Bowers here can confirm, but the way I heard it through the grapevine, they'd negotiated a stop to the zoble plan. But when she told the China'a president he wasn't getting even a smell of our quantum tech, he threatened to move forward with it, and she said, 'Fine, do it.'"

"That's a *little* bit of an oversimplification," Bowers said, shifting as he said, "but the core of the story there is true."

"You mean she had a chance to stop the zoble launch after all?" Kay said. "I figured Russia and China went ahead with it just because they could."

"As with anything, it's complicated"—Bowers took a drink—"but, yes, words were had. They threatened to move forward with the zoble unless their demands were met." He shrugged, taking another drink and smiling before adding, "And she told them to do it and hung up on them."

Jack and Kay laughed, amazed, and Roy slapped his hand on the table, saying, "They were already prepping me an office at the NSA."

"Really?" Kay said, impressed. "*Were?*"

Bowers was smiling, shaking his head at this.

Roy wore what Winspear would have described as a "shit-eating grin" as he pointed up at the screen. Kay and Jack turned to see Roy up on it, frazzled, barking something to an unseen reporter in the White House Press Briefing Room.

"You've got to be kidding me," Jack said as he looked from the screen to Roy and back. "Is that—what's going on with your tie?"

"What *indeed*," Bowers said.

"It's called a trinity knot," Roy said.

"A little *goofy*, if you ask me," Kay said, looking at the multiple folds of the tie that, along with Roy's shabby suitcoat and half-shaven features, gave him somewhat of a ruddy royalty look.

"Oh yeah?" Roy said, leaning in with his arms crossed. "Well, it's working then."

"How do you mean?" Jack asked.

"You're all talking about the tie"—he gestured up toward the screen with his drink in hand—"none of you are *listening*."

Bowers laughed at this, signaling for another drink.

"Can't argue with that."

"Press secretary? Really?" Kay asked him.

"Who the hell knows?" Roy said. "The truth is I was there, they were there"—he shrugged—"seemed like a good opportunity to add to the confusion."

"You mean Adler didn't ask you to—"

"Ha!" Bowers laughed. "What they're not showing is the Secret Service hauling him off stage a few minutes later!"

"Doesn't matter," Roy said, unphased. "I could have it if I want it."

"Well," Kay said, "you're probably right. I hear it's a madhouse trying to staff up."

"It—uh, it sure is." Bowers said. "In fact—"

He looked over to Kay, who furrowed her brow. She watched Bowers shift in his chair, looking from him to Jack, who was also intrigued, and back again.

"This probably isn't the right place or time, but... " he continued, "but that hasn't stopped any of the rest of this from happening. I know it's been quiet since Adler took office."

He was referring to the media silence since Adler had been sworn in. There had been a short video clip of that shared on social media and the government website, but since then there had been no speeches. The president was presumably locked in emergency negotiations with half the world as the problems in the global market were quarantined and corrected. The only inkling of information from the White House had been that a speech was planned after Winspear's funeral, Adler's first address to the nation.

"She—the president I mean—asked me to plant a seed with you."

"A seed," Kay echoed.

"Have you ever heard of FinCEN?" He pronounced the acronym, "*fin-sin.*"

Kay shook her head, and Bowers glanced at the other two, who also shrugged. Then he went on.

"It's a treasury department started up during HW's administration, early '90s if I remember right. The *Financial Crimes Enforcement Network.*" He let the words hang there for a moment. "As you might imagine, it's been gutted during the last few administrations."

"No shit," Roy said.

Bowers nodded gravely.

"That's right. And the president wanted me to ask…"

He looked down at his drink, suddenly a little sheepish.

"Go on then," Roy said. "Ask her to work for it."

"It's not just a staff job," Bowers said, making eye contact with her. "She wants you as the director."

Kay didn't say anything for a moment, thinking.

She started to open her mouth, to say, "I can't—"

But Bowers raised his hand up, stopping her.

"Just think about it," he said. "No pressure. She'll understand. But"—he lowered his voice—"she's going to go after some people. Some big ones. It's going to be messy. We need people we can trust."

None of them spoke for a few sips, the news blaring away under the current of music, a few glasses clinking with ice-cubes.

Finally, Roy finished his drink and slammed it down a little hard, making all of them jump a bit, but just a bit.

He broke the spell by adding, "Well, well, well! All four of us back in the good graces of the United States government! God help us!"

"It's funny," Jack said. "I wonder why she didn't wait to ask you herself?"

"Oh yeah, you all have a date?" Roy asked.

"As a matter of fact we do. She's asked us to have dinner with her later tonight," Jack explained.

"What time?" Roy asked.

"Actually," Kay said, checking her watch, "pretty soon. At some restaurant called 1789."

"Oh wow!" Bowers said. "That's a great place. I've only been once."

"Pretty sure all the presidents eat there," Roy said.

"Well, it should be an interesting experience," Jack said. "I guess we need to be on our way."

They said their goodbyes and outside entered their respective motorcades—special order by the Secret Service until the entirety of what had happened was sorted out.

As they parted ways, Bowers passed a final message along, nodding at Jack and Kay and saying, "Don't miss her speech tonight."

Jack and Kay nodded back and then politely ignored the Secret Service agents' requests to reenter the cars they'd come in, instead opting to get into one together.

On the way to the restaurant they exchanged a few words, but both of them were mostly lost in their thoughts. Bowers words floated through their minds. *Going after some big people.* That's what he'd said. *Watch the speech tonight.*

At some point they found each other's hands, and to Jack it felt especially warm against the frigid cold of Washington.

59

"We're—uh—here to meet President Adler."

Jack looked at Kay, raising his eyebrows. How often would you be able to tell a hostess something like *that*?

"I don't think I'm dressed up enough for this place," she half whispered to him as the hotel manager came over.

"I know," Jack said, taking his jacket off and looking around the place.

It was like an 18ᵗʰ century manor house frozen in time. High ceilings and elegant wooden tables were set with multiple courses' worth of silverware, all of it candlelit.

"Quite a *romantic* dinner we'll be having with the most powerful person in the world," Kay joked as the hostess led them toward their table.

Jack noticed as they approached there was no sign of Adler yet.

The hostess seated them, and explained, "The president left a message for you."

She gestured toward a card on the table.

Jack held it so he and Kay could both read it, the gilded lettering starting at the top of the page.

From the desk of the President of the United States of America:

Jack, Kay,

I hope you'll excuse my absence tonight and the slight deception of setting up this dinner at all. I never intended to come, though I assure you we'll all three sit down for a meal sometime in the coming months.

It seemed strange to me that I had never heard either of your names before a few weeks ago, and stranger still that the country now owes you so much. I thought that, considering all you've been through, a small token of my appreciation might be this gift to you, a chance to have a normal night, free of conspiracy and subterfuge.

An opportunity to feel normal again. A luxury I don't suspect we'll have again anytime soon.

Sincerely

Theresa Adler, POTUS

"Wow," Jack said, reading the note again.

"What's that mean at the end there: '*don't suspect we'll have that luxury again anytime soon?*'"

"Something about her speech maybe?"

They were only an hour out from the first scheduled address to the nation by Adler as president.

"Who knows?" Jack said with a half sigh. "Sounds like she knows more than we do about whatever's happening next, though."

"I don't mind," Kay said. "Not now. Not for tonight at least."

"She's right though," Jack said, reaching over and taking Kay's hand. "This is long overdue."

"Hmm," she said and stared at him for a moment. "There's just one thing—"

She slid out of her chair.

"What—"

He had just enough time to say the one word before she was kissing him, somehow pulling it off and retreating back to her seat with catlike grace, smoothing her napkin on her lap and smiling over at him.

"*Long* overdue," she added, picking up her menu and looking at it.

Jack was blushing, and he pawed his menu up too.

He looked at it for a moment, but he couldn't focus.

Finally, he glanced over the top of the menu at her and saw that she was doing the same, and when they caught each other's eyes they really did feel like things were normal again.

For a few seconds, they forgot it all, and for the first time in a very, very long while, they laughed so hard that by the time the waitress came back they were wiping away tears.

60

Epilogue

As the sunlight faded over the wreckage of the Camplex, floodlights flickered on around the perimeter.

The company that had been hired to come in and start the cleanup and recycling efforts had put the lights in place, and now that dusk was approaching, the lights would stand in for sun as the night shift rolled in to continue the work.

It would probably be weeks of round-the-clock labor as the various intelligence agencies and the recycling company picked through it all, carefully excavating down to the quantum computer that had supposedly caused all of this.

Some of them were interested in what they might find at the bottom, but to most this was just another job. A giant one—one they'd brag to their friends about being on: the *Camplex cleanup job.*

One of those workers stepped out from a row of portable toilets that had been set up near the airport-side of the jobsite. The floodlights here played on the wreck of a medium-sized carrier drone that was caution-taped off, a few sparks still lazily sprouting from where one of the wings had been torn away.

The worker fastened his belt, pulled the zipper back into place, and looked the wreck over.

He had a few minutes, and he pulled a pack of cigarettes from his pocket and lit one, looking at the downed drone and the countless others dotting the runway, shaking his head.

The sun was almost gone now, disappearing over the horizon, and as he worked his way through the cigarette and looked up past the airstrip, he could see movement on the horizon.

Backlit by the orange-blue shimmer of sundown, a black mass undulated in the distance, writhing over the treetops, the dense pack of birds dancing against a backdrop of clouds that were—for a few seconds—cast in lavender tousles of light.

He watched the birds moving in their alien yet familiar way and pulled at his cigarette.

But as he squinted hard into the distance, the birds—they were too far away to tell for sure, but he thought… for a moment he thought they looked different. Like maybe they weren't birds at all, but small drones, all of them moving in sync.

But no, that was crazy. A trick of the light, that's all.

As the sun ducked below the horizon, he tossed the cigarette butt down and stomped it out, turning back to the jobsite. It was a big one, huge, but they'd tackle it the same way they always did, one piece of rubble at a time. And when they were done, he knew, someone would build it again and hope that next time it would be different.

As he went back to his work, the undulating mass in the distance began to retreat. And who could say, from this distance, whether it was a flock of birds headed for the horizon or a pack of surviving drones keeping the waning sun on its myriad panels?

Maybe it was a last bastion of the computer's program, seeking whatever something like that would seek now that the warehouse was gone.

And maybe, when they rebuilt the place, they'd do it all the same, but it really *would* be different.

Maybe President Adler would change things, and one day, they'd look back from a future in which this past had been the worst of things, and somehow, through sheer hope and optimism, convince themselves that they understood just what went wrong and why.

Or maybe it was just a trick of the light.

Author's Note

Thanks for reading. I appreciate your time, which more and more is at a premium, thanks to the constant battle for our eyeballs these days. That's why I try to do something a little more in the Shooter Act series and my other books. To give you a real double whammy: a badass story with some very interesting and very *real* meat on the bones.

Many of my readers have told me that one of the things they like in my books is that level of realism. Obviously, this is fiction, but there's not very much "making it up" in there when it comes to details on what is happening and why. That may be surprising, so, if you have just a little longer, here's a rundown of some of the seeds that helped grow this thing, and a little bit on just how real they are.

For instance, all the vote counts, details about how Impeachment works, and how it might be thwarted in the House of Representatives are accurate. I'll admit that some of the real parliamentary procedure—how conversations actually happen within the House—were sacrificed in the effort of making something that doesn't read like a court recording. The elements of what happens in the legislature and why— the maneuverings around the Special Counselor, the AG and Deputy AG, specifics about CFR 28 section 600, those are all real. The various hijinx employed to dodge a vote on one side and force it on the other are real things that could happen, and some of them really *have* happened. In 1942, Democratic Majority Leader Alben Barkley really did direct the Sergeant at Arms to arrest absent southern senators to achieve the quorum required to continue the fight for Civil Rights. Someone who isn't a member of the House *can* be voted speaker by a simple 50% vote, and then be 3rd in line for the presidency.

The threat of another world superpower tanking the Dollar and resetting the financial chessboard of the world overnight using good old fashioned gold, that's something economists really worry about. In "Currency Wars: The Next Global Crisis", James Rickards does a fantastic job of detailing the hows and whys of this strategy. Rickards even served as a facilitator of the first ever financial war games conducted by the Pentagon, and in the book he gives a firsthand account of how one of the teams at the games used this strategy to try and bring more awareness to this fundamental geopolitical weakness. During the wargames, that team was ruled to have "violated the rules of the wargames" and so this wasn't really considered a problem by the powers that be. That sure helps me sleep at night. After all, enemies always "follow the rules" right?

Winspear's factory. Amazon already uses hundreds of thousands of bots to move shelves around their warehouses. These are what I refer to as "lifters" in this story. Amazon makes no secret about wanting to swap out human laborers with robots, and the company's founder and, at time of writing the richest man in the world—Jeff Bezos—hosts an annual conference called the 'MARS' conference, concerned with 'machine learning, automation, robotics, and space exploration.' About the conference, why they hold it, Bezos has this to say: "If you could hold a conference about the beginning of a golden age, why wouldn't you? [...] And I really do believe that we are on the leading edge of an incredible renaissance." My story takes the 'MAR' of this conference to their logical extremes, and actually doesn't even touch on how a company like Amazon may implement plans they have for the 'S'. In that way, I'm likely underestimating the impact that can be made here.

Winspear's net-positive shipping scheme. That might be able to work if currently theoretical battery technologies are able to be commercialized. But this is real pie-in-the-sky. I'll have to admit this part is more guess than forecast, but hey, even a broken clock is right twice a day. The quantum computer, it's physical description, how it might operate to calmly and (literally) coolly calculate that someone shutting it down should be gassed to death with nitrogen is about as simple as: "If X, then Y."

To be very clear, the description of quantum computing software and its use here—parallel coordination of a massive shipping company—that's mostly made up, though the theory is solid. However, the way this quantum computer fails, ending up in a loop that happens to be wagging the entire world's economy, there's plenty of precedent for that. Google the Flash Crash of 2010, and consider reading Michael Lewis' *Flashboys,* Sheelah Holhatkar's *Black Edge,* and the Panama Papers to connect how the intersection of high frequency trading, shell companies, and massive hidden wealth might all come together in a scenario much like the one I describe in this book.

What else? The situation on Air Force One as it scrambles to land, that is all very much real, a hybrid of several real crashes that I studied to put this scenario together before having it vetted by a bona fide pilot. Air Force One may have some tricks up its sleeve for surviving this scenario, but I'd need a lot higher security clearance to know about them. They don't come right out and say it, but it's almost certainly EMP shielded.

And since we're talking about EMPs, the CHAMP weapon I have the Chinese using, that's real too. The Counter-electronics High Power Microwave Advanced Missile Project, though, is luckily a development of the US Air Force, not the Chinese. It would be foolish to think they don't have an equivalent program, and, not to be alarmist or anything, but a single missile equipped with this technology—just one—could take out every electronic device in the United States if it was detonated at just the right spot. In a 2018 report generated by the United States Air Force Air University titled *ELECTRO-MAGNETIC DEFENSE TASK FORCE,* it is casually noted that "the grid will likely remain in a failed state from weeks to months" after such an attack. The consequences of this (lack of communication, working vehicles, vital medications, and *food*) are explored in William Forstchen's novel *One Second After.*

But listen, it's easy to read all that, and my story, and think that the takeaway is that there's no hope. That things are bad and getting worse, and mine is one of many equally likely competing futures ready to gobble us all up. It's not. It's just a light shown on one small grid that makes up the map of the future. A little investigation of what one possible future might look like. It's not meant to be a hand-wringing parable, but more of an iceberg, dead-ahead. Something that, now that we see it, we can steer around. The question to me comes down to this: are most people good or bad? A quick tally may let you know where I stand on that. For every McAvoy, I think there's a Kay. For every Winspear, I think there's a Jack. But which side wins? Good or bad? Where does Roy fall? Bowers? And which way will Tarrah Adler tip the scale, finally, armed with such sudden and ultimate power…?

Until next time,
- Turner Tomlinson, May 1, 2019

Acknowledgements

For helping me mold this at the outline stage, thank you to my wife, Lauren Rosso, and the guy who keeps hanging around to listen to all this junk, Will Chesser. You believed in me, and this story, even the second and third times I had to write it. For the small army of beta readers who read this in early, and sometimes not so early stages, thank you again Lauren, Caleb Steiner, and Margaret Jazinski. For beta reading *and* doing a healthy amount of editing, thanks to Debbie Graff, Bill Kennamer, and Karen Rosso. You were all right, about everything. And one last quick shoutout: Pierce Cable, pilot extraordinaire, thank you for weighing in on the climax.

The generosity of ya'lls time is one thing, but the honesty and integrity of telling me the things I needed to hear were quite another, and the authenticity that comes across to readers is the result of our group project here, not "mine." Thank you.